A descent into terror.

Legends tell of a hollow earth, a world beneath our own. A world filled with wonders... and danger. But what if the legends are true?

Delve into dark worlds in HELLHOLE, where death lurks around every corner, and come face to face with creatures from your worst nightmares in this collection of dark thrillers. New York Times bestselling author Jonathan Maberry and Bram Stoker Award winner Rena Mason headline a cast of bestselling and award-winning authors.

Praise for Hellhole!

"Deliciously gory and enough monsters and mayhem in the depths to satisfy even the most jaded spelunker!" William Meikle, author of *The Valley*

"A thrilling collection of underground terror from a cross-section of the best horror writers working today. It'll shine a light on your deepest, darkest fears." Alan Baxter, author of *Devouring Dark*

"A collection of claustrophobic horror that drags readers into the darkness!" Paul Elard Cooley, author of *The Derelict Saga*

HELLHOLE

AN ANTHOLOGY OF SUBTERRANEAN TERROR
EDITED BY LEE MURRAY

HELLHOLE: An Anthology of Subterranean Terror

Published 2018 by Adrenaline Press
www.adrenaline.press

Adrenaline Press is an imprint of Gryphonwood Press
www.gryphonwoodpress.com

Acquisitions editor: Lee Murray
Cover designer: Christian Bentulan
Copy editor: Melissa Bowersock

ISBN-13: 978-1-940095-94-3
ISBN-10: 1-940095-94-8

CONTENTS

ONE HELL OF A WHOLE

James A. Moore

I love anthologies. I can't stress that enough. I used to hate short stories and the very notion of an anthology was wasted breath, but I got over that around the same time I actually read an anthology of shared world stories – the shared world was the *Thieves' World* as edited by Robert Lynn Aspirin – and realized that short stories could be as refreshing and exciting as a novel. The rub had been, apparently, that I hadn't read any good short stories, or very few in any event. I thrilled over my pulp favorites, like Fritz Leiber, H.P. Lovecraft, and Robert E. Howard, but otherwise I found few tales were worth the telling as far as I was concerned.

I wanted the depth, you see. I wanted characters that had life to them and had back stories and emotions and a history, with other characters that went beyond a sentence explaining that Bill and Bob did not get along very well and never had. To be fair, those stories probably existed, but I was addicted to comic books at a young age and was used to getting backstory by the bucket load. All I had to do was look over my previous issues to see all that had happened between the Fantastic Four and Doctor Doom. Short stories? Pfeh! Why bother?

You live. You learn. Sometimes, what passes for wisdom takes a while.

I don't know if it was my impatience as a young reader or if it was simply that I ran across a lot of mediocre (in my mind) stories, but at any rate I didn't used to like them very much.

Happily, that changed as time went on, first, because I was convinced to give a few writers a chance and I listened to the suggestion that I just might like their short stories, even if I didn't much care for their novel-length works. Honestly, if I'm telling the truth, there are several writers who, for me, cannot understand the form and function of a novel-length work, but who have mastered shorter fiction. No, I will not mention names, but meet me some time in person and maybe I can be convinced to discuss the matter.

The second reason is that there really are some incredible stories out there. You just have to look for them, or find a good editor or editorial team. In the case of the book in your hands, it's one editor and Lee Murray managed to knock this collection out of the proverbial park.

I'm working under the assumption that you read what the anthology is about, so no surprises here when it comes to the concept, but it's still a notion that fits perfectly in my wheelhouse, I heard about the anthology and was already excited. I read the list of contributors and was excited all over again. S.D. Perry has never disappointed me with a story. That's a rare and precious treat. *Guard Duty* keeps the record of winners running at one hundred percent. Jessica McHugh was an unknown quantity and her story, *Ghosts of Hyperia*, blew me out of the water. I do so love reading new talents and being surprised by the writing. I had the pleasure of being on a panel with J.H. Moncrieff at the last Horror Writers Association annual meeting. She was delightful. That said, I was even more delighted by *The Offspring*. The lady is charming, lovely, and properly twisted.

Remember how I said I love reading new authors and not being disappointed? You can add Aaron Sterns to the list with his novella *Black Lung*. I may well never look at criminal pursuits the same way again. Michal McBride's works are well known to me and finding a new story is like finding twenty dollars in your coat when you haven't worn it in months. *A Plague of Locusts* is more like finding a fifty, actually. A damned fine read by a damned fine author. Sean Ellis manages to keep the levels of what-the-hell-was-that high and fine. It's always best to end an anthology with a strong story and I didn't have to worry about Ms. Murray not understanding that notion. *He Who Fights* is a mighty fine way to wrap things up.

On the opposite end of that spectrum, you had best start an anthology with a hard hitter and few people know how to deliver a punch as well as Joe Ledger or his creator, Jonathan Maberry. *The Devils Are Here* is Maberry at his best, and his best is a very, very hard act to follow. Rena Mason carries it off, though. That's not a surprise, really. If you've ever read the lady, you know she's well beyond competent. She's incredible. *The Devil's Throat* lives up to the high standards I expect from Ms. Mason. Sometimes an author just throws a title out there that should be impossible to do justice to. I find the title *Ginormous Hell Snake*, is one of those titles for me. How the hell do you live up to the expectations that come with a title like that? Jake Bible, that's who. The story was warped and fun and absolutely a pleasure to read.

The biggest problem I usually have with reading a new author is being disappointed. Sometimes the biggest problem comes from wanting to read every last thing the author has ever written, which can get damned expensive if you're not careful. Paul Mannering's *Where The Sun Does Not Shine* has made a fan of me. Either the story is a fluke (doubtful) or my first glimpse at a serious talent. Looks like I'll be ordering a few books from Amazon to find out which. Proving that she doesn't like to be outdone Kirsten Cross added *Pit of Ghosts* to the blend. Again, a writer I have not read before and now one I must examine more carefully. There's a lot of that going on here. I'm delighted by the notion.

The only surprise I found in *Hellhole* is that not a single story slowed me down. I can bank on at least a few tales failing to catch my attention properly on an average day, but Lee Murray picked carefully, either when she chose the authors, or when she chose the stories. Either way, I am delighted to be included in this book. Best of all, I get to be included without actually having to write a story. I get to ride on the coattails of excellence and look like I did any of the hard work. Really, I can't call this effort. I had far too much fun reading the stories.

James A. Moore, 2018

ALL THE DEVILS ARE HERE
A Joe Ledger/Lizzie Corbett Adventure
Jonathan Maberry

1

Darvaza Gas Crater, Karakum Desert, Turkmenistan

"Look at the spiders," said the guide.

The American diplomat, James Mercer, did not look up. He stood staring out over the rim of the fiery pit.

"It's been burning for over forty years," Mercer murmured, but the guide did not react. Both men were caught up in their own thoughts, as if they were in different movies playing at the same time.

The guide, a thin young man named Çariýar, stood on a piece of rock and kept turning in a slow circle, looking down. "Look at them, sir," he said in a mixture of fear and fascination. "There are so many spiders..."

"Everyone thinks this was an accident," said Mercer. "A mistake made by employees of a drilling company." He smiled. His eyes were completely unfocused as if he wasn't really seeing the tongues of flame licking at the sky.

The hole had a diameter of seventy meters and plunged to a depth of twenty meters. Big, deep, ablaze. The stink of methane filled the air and soft columns of gray coiled upward like snakes coupling in an eternal and erotic dance. It fascinated the diplomat, riveting him to the spot.

There was no one else at the site. Tourists did visit the pit, drawn by the lurid news stories or YouTube videos of the place known as the Gate of Hell or the Door to Hell. Turkmenistan did not see a lot of tourist dollars, and so encouraged the visitors. Today was an off day, though. Cold and cloudy, with a biting wind out of the northeast. The young guide shivered in his anorak, and the diplomat—a senior assistant to the American ambassador—wore a heavy coat, hat and gloves. He, however, was sweating. Not from the heat, which was considerable but from blood pressure that had risen steadily since coming here.

A third man, the embassy driver, sat in the car with the heat on and the radio tuned to a station featuring dutar and anbur music. The late and very great musician, Abdurahim Hamidov, was currently working his way through a classic tune and the driver was lost in the melodies. He was not paying attention at all. He did not see the spiders and could not have cared less about a big pit of fire that was the result of a bunch of stupid decisions made by natural gas miners years before he was born.

The wind blew past the car and past the two men near the pit, on into the deeper desert.

The diplomat had a bulky briefcase with him. More of a small suitcase, really. Heavy with the burden of what was inside. It took real effort for Mercer to turn away from the flames. They were so beautiful and they spoke such lovely things to him, the smoky wind whispering in a language that Çariýar could never hope to understand. But Mercer managed to wrest his attention from the flames and down to the briefcase, which stood a few feet away. He felt a catch in his throat when he thought about what he was here to do. The honor of it was nearly too much to accept. To be chosen for this—for this—was incredible. It was the kind of thing the people in his group dreamed of, prayed for, ached for with every fiber of their being. There were older members, more important members, people of staggering importance, and yet this task had fallen to him. This undertaking. This gift.

He lowered himself to his knees and carefully placed the case on its side. His fingers trembled so badly that it took five tries to spin the dials of the locks. The click was so soft that he knew only he heard it. He took a breath and then opened the case to reveal the book.

The book.

Good god, how beautiful. He mouthed the words but did not say anything aloud. It was bound with heavy wood covers wrapped in skin. There was no writing on the cover, no title or author given. Instead it was engraved with spiders of every kind, including some Mercer had only seen in dreams. Vast, ponderous monsters with three legs instead of eight. Most, though, were kinds he knew well; like the kind that held the guide in such horrified awe. Jumping spiders and orb weavers and cellar spiders and wolf spiders. Beautiful animals. Perfect in their clever cruelty and wise in endless patience.

Mercer bent and kissed the book, making sure first that Çariýar and the driver were not looking. The kiss lingered and to him it was like kissing the thigh of a beautiful woman. Warm and yielding, as if the skin was alive. He felt himself grow hard. Ending that kiss was so difficult. It hurt him, but this was not his to linger over and he knew it. After all, they were watching. They were waiting.

He took off his gloves and then removed a small sheathed knife from his coat pocket. It was not much larger than a steak knife, and the silver metal with its razor edge had been properly blessed and seasoned, tasting only the blood of infants before now. He murmured a prayer in a language not spoken in this place in thousands of years. Then he gripped the handle in his left hand and drew the blade across his right palm, making three long cuts that formed a bloody star. Then he switched the knife to his right and repeated the action on his left hand. He placed the knife carefully in the open lid of the case and pressed both hands to the front cover of the book. He winced as the book drank his blood.

It took a lot but not too much because he had so much work still to do.

Mercer opened the book to a page marked with a lock of hair he had cut that morning from his little daughter's scalp. She would not need the hair any longer. A small part of his mind idly wondered if they had found the bodies yet. Daughter and wife, maid and cook. They were there to be found. He didn't care when or by whom.

Then he shook the thought from his mind and concentrated on his sacred task. The page was written in a dead language, but it wasn't dead to him. It was so completely and thoroughly alive. Each word burned in his mind, flooding him with love and hope and purpose. Tears ran down his cheeks and his mouth curled upward in a smile of the purest joy.

The next action took the greatest effort and actually caused him pain despite being absolutely necessary. It felt like sacrilege as he took the corner of the exposed page and tore it from the book. The page did not cry out, but Mercer did. A guttural gasp of agony as real as if he had cut off his own hand.

"Bless me," he said. "Forgive me."

The torn edge of the page glowed as if somehow fire burned in its fibers. The page was not consumed, though, and he rose with it in his hand. He did not forget to take the knife, too.

Çariýar was still staring in fascination at the dozens of spiders that wandered out of the desert and crawled along the edge of the pit. Some scuttled over the edge and fell; others attached webs and lowered themselves into the hellish heat.

"I don't understand," said the young guide for maybe the tenth time. "Mr. Mercer, you should really see this."

"I can see it," said Mercer. Çariýar jumped and turned, surprised that the diplomat was there, and that he'd come up so silently. It took the young man a moment longer to register all of the things about Mercer that were wrong.

The spiders that climbed up the older man's clothes, and inside trouser cuffs and beneath his coat. One crawled across Mercer's smiling face. That smile was wrong, too. The guide frowned at the torn book page and the small knife, unable to process all of these strange things at once. Worse still was the blood that was so bright it seemed to scream. Mercer's hands were soaked with it, and there were spatters on the man's brown topcoat and shoes.

"Mr. Mercer, sir," gasped Çariýar, "have you cut yourself?"

"Yes," said Mercer. "I have. Here. Take this."

He reached out quickly, slapping the page against Çariýar's chest and, before the guide could properly react, pinned it there by driving the knife to the hilt in the young man's chest. The angle of thrust was something Mercer had practiced for years and despite his trembling hands, he did it exactly right. The blade punched between ribs and muscle and into Çariýar's heart.

"I love you for this," said Mercer as the guide coughed once and dropped to his knees. Çariýar looked at him with a confusion that was profound, and then his eyes rolled up and he fell sideways, one arm flopping over the edge of the pit. Several spiders immediately crawled over him and raced to the ends of his fingers, stood for a moment, and then dropped off into the fires below.

Mercer let out a ragged sigh that was nearly orgasmic. Then he turned and walked quickly over to the car, approaching from what he determined was the blind side, and circled around to the driver's side, effectively positioning the car between him and the corpse, drawing attention his way. He reached beneath his coat for the second weapon he'd brought with him. It was a small automatic, a Glock 42, with six rounds single-stacked into the magazine. As soon as the driver began rolling down the window, Mercer emptied the magazine into the man's face. It was very loud and very messy, and the body flopped back with very little of the head left intact.

"I love you for this," Mercer told him. He dropped the pistol, went over to the briefcase and removed the book, giving it a loving kiss and a covetous lick before walking over to the pit.

No one was left to see him step over the edge and drop into the mouth of hell.

2

Over Turkish Airspace

I am not a very nice guy. That's not my job. They don't call me when they want to make people happy.

Same goes for the two guys sharing the ride with me—First Sergeant Bradley "Top" Sims and Master Sergeant Harvey "Bunny" Rabbit. Like me, they were ex-US military. Like me they didn't work for anyone in the US of A anymore. Like me they weren't all that nice.

We're good guys, but "nice" isn't a job requirement. For what we do. All three of us were big men, though Bunny abused that privilege and towered over us at six and a half feet. Top was an even six and I was six-two. Bunny could bench press both of us and have some room for one or both of the Dakotas. Big moose of a kid from Orange County. Sandy blond hair, blue eyes, a surfer's lazy smile and a good heart, unless you got between him and his mission objective.

Top was the old man of the team, clocking in somewhere north of forty and lying about it. He wasn't slowing down much that I could see, and the only evidence of all those hard years was the network of scar tissue—old and new—patterned across his dark brown skin.

My girlfriend likes to tell people I look like the guy who played Captain America in the Marvel movies. I don't. He looks like a pretty nice guy and I seriously doubt he's ever drawn blood with bullets, blades or hands. I have. Sure, I'm a blond-haired, blue-eyed all-American boy from Baltimore, but when people look me in the eye their gaze tends to shift away. The ones who don't are either bad guys making poor life choices, or fellow soldiers who have walked through the valley of the shadow.

We were on my private jet crossing Turkish airspace on the way to Turkmenistan. I've been all over the world—all three of us have, separately and together—but none of us had been there. And we didn't know why we were going there.

There was a soft bing-bong and the pilot's voice said, "Captain Ledger, the big man is on line."

Bunny reached over to the high-def screen mounted on the wall. The cabin was sound-proofed and we all had cold beers.

A face filled the screen. Church is a big, blocky man with dark hair going gray. He wears tinted glasses because he prefers not to have people read him—and eyes are a common "tell." His suits are more expensive than my car and he wears black silk gloves to hide severe frostbite damage from a previous case.

Once upon a time Church was some kind of high-level field operator. A shooter and a spy. I don't know all the details, but from what I've been able to piece together he was a true and legendary badass. He scares the people who scare me. So, even guys like us sit like school boys and pay attention.

"Gentlemen," Church said, "are you familiar with this?"

The screen split so that a new image appeared, showing a large, round hole clearly blazing with fire.

"Yeah," I said, "that's a bathroom selfie of me after Rudy made that chili with ghost peppers."

A beat. Church said nothing. The weight of his disapproval was crushing. Bunny stifled a grin and Top gave me a slow, sad shake of his head. I am nominally the boss, but Top's usually the adult in any given room.

"No," I said contritely, "I don't know what it is. Other than a burning hole, what is it?"

"It's called the Gates of Hell."

"Sounds right," said Bunny.

"It's also known as the 'Door to Hell'," said Church. "The official name is the Darvaza gas crater. It's located near the village of Derweze in the Karakum Desert of Turkmenistan, roughly two hundred and sixty kilometers north of the capital city of Ashgabat. This pit is what's left of a natural gas field that collapsed into an underground cavern. The collapse released clouds of methane. The team of geologists apparently believed that the methane could easily be burned off, and so they ignited it in hopes of reclaiming the natural gas deposit. That was one of a number of strikingly ill-considered decisions and the pit has been burning continuously since 1971. It shows no sign of burning out anytime soon."

"Well now, that's a level of stupid all its own, isn't it?" said Top sourly.

"It creates a challenge to sympathy," admitted Church.

"All that said, why am I looking at...this? What do you want me to do with a giant fire pit? Shoot it? Try and piss in it to put it out?"

Church reached out of shot and returned with a cookie. He always had a tray of cookies, mostly vanilla wafers. Once in a while he'll add some Oreos or, if he's in a particularly jocular mood, animal crackers. He bit a piece of the wafer, chewed it, studied me. Then he picked up his narrative without actually answering my question. "The site draws a fair number of tourists each year and has become something of a bucket-list item for world travelers."

"It's not on my bucket list," Bunny said.

I nodded. "And you still haven't told me why we're going there."

"Three days ago, a key American diplomat, James Mercer, went missing at the site," said Church. "He is ostensibly the senior aide to the ambassador but is actually with the Agency. His brief is to track illegal shipments of technology and other items passing though that region."

Top held up a hand. "Don't mean to be contrary, but are we working missing persons cases now? Can't the CIA mind its own missing sheep?"

"The situation is much more complicated than that, First Sergeant," said Church. "Two bodies were discovered yesterday at the rim of the crater." He explained about the murders of a local guide and the diplomat's driver. "The embassy's security team was able to take ownership of the scene thanks to a little Agency bullying. They did a quick forensics workup on the knife used to stab the guide and the handgun used on the driver. Both had clear fingerprints, and both sets match those of James Mercer. And Mercer's blood was all over the handles of each weapon, so it's clear he was injured as well. There is no sign of a struggle in either case. Just clean kills."

"Um..." began Bunny, then shook his head. "Nope, got nothing."

"Have local police been involved in a search?" asked Top.

"Yes. And the military police—theirs and ours. Bug and his computer team have done deep searches on Mercer. None of his credit cards have been used and facial recognition hasn't picked him up on airport cameras. There are no traffic cams in Turkmenistan, and very few CCTV cams, so Bug is limited there. It seems clear, though, that Mercer has either gone to ground somewhere or—"

"Or maybe jumped into the fire pit?" Bunny suggested, and Church nodded.

"If he's toast," I said, "they don't need us there. So, you're thinking he's in a bolt hole or safe house somewhere?"

"We have to accept that as a possibility."

"Does the Agency think their man's been turned?" I asked.

"Unknown. I've pulled some strings to have the case taken away from them."

"Why?"

"Because of this." A new image flashed onto the screen. It was of a large page that had been torn from a book. There was one ragged edge and a slit in the middle. Blood mostly obscured the page, thickest near the slit. Church explained that the page had been pinned to the dead guide's chest with the knife.

We all leaned forward to study the page. I'm really good with languages, but it looked like chicken scratches.

"What language is that?" asked Bunny. "It's all Greek to me."

"It's not Greek, Farm Boy," said Top.

"I know that. It's just an expression."

"The language is part of the reason I asked for this case," said

Church quietly. "It is an extremely rare subdialect of Sumerian. An attempt by later writers to modify cuneiform."

"Really," said Bunny again, "I got nothing."

"The page is believed to have come from this book," said Church, and another image filled the screen. A very large book lay in a niche in a stone wall, its covers secured with heavy chains and ancient padlocks that looked to have been welded permanently shut. "The book was part of a private collection overseen by Islamic and Eastern Orthodox clerics. A very special kind of shared conservancy, and it's a stewardship that dates back centuries."

I felt my heart go cold and sink to a lower and darker place in my chest. Top and Bunny came to point like hunting dogs, but not happy ones.

I said, "You're going to tell me that this is one of those books, aren't you?"

Church did not smile. He didn't actually move.

"The Unlearnable Truths," whispered Top in a hollow voice. "Fuck me..."

We logged a lot of silent miles before any of us spoke. The Unlearnable Truths was like a hex to us. They were books belonging to a very specific list of works that have been deemed "dangerous." There was a larger list, the *Index Librorum Prohibitorum*, also known as the Pauline Index, named for Pope Paul IV back in 1559. Most of the titles on the Index were merely heretical or viewed as contrary to the politics and agenda of the Catholic Church. However, there was a second, shorter list that was never shared with the public. Word leaked out, of course, but secrets are like that. This second list became known as the Unlearnable Truths. Many of the titles on that list were individually known to the public, but once leaked there was a pretty effective campaign by church spin doctors to make people think they were entirely fictional. Books like the Necronomicon, which is widely believed to have been created by the pulp fiction writer H.P. Lovecraft, and is part of 20th century horror fiction history. Except it wasn't. That book, and many others, are real.

Now, whether these books are literally dangerous was an open question for a while. They're supposed to be books of magic. Yup, actual black magic. Couple of years ago I'd have laughed at anyone who said that magic was a real thing. Not so much anymore, though I don't believe much in the supernatural. What's changed is that I've come to believe that a lot of what people called magic is actually some aspects of a science we haven't really begun to understand. My lover, Junie, calls it the 'larger world.' I call it Freaksville.

When we went up against a group using the Unlearnable Truths, very bad things happened. People I cared about died. And some stuff happened that hurt all of us. Top, Bunny, and me. Hurt us bad.

Nearly destroyed us, leaving scars on body and soul and mind.

"I've called in an expert to advise," said Church, bringing me back to the moment. "Dr. Elizabeth Corbett, formerly of the Beinecke Rare Book and Manuscript Library at Yale."

"Corbett? I've heard that name," I said. "Wasn't she the one that found the Templar treasure a couple of years ago?"

"A large part of the treasure, yes," said Church. "She's a rare book scholar of some note and an expert on ancient languages. She was in Syria working with a team to acquire and preserve artifacts targeted by ISIL. She'll meet you at the airport."

"Does she know about the Unlearnable Truths?" asked Top.

Church sliced off a thin sliver of a smile. "Yes," he said, and disconnected the call.

3

Ashgabat International Airport, Near Ashgabat, Turkmenistan

She was standing there at the bottom of the stair-car as we deplaned. Thirty-something, bookish, medium height, with lots of frizzy ash-blond hair that framed a pretty face. Big glasses, bright blue eyes and firm chin. If you didn't look closely, and if you were the kind of lout prone to sexist and belittling assumptions, you might call her a nerd girl. And she probably was nerdish, but so what? So was Junie. So, in fact, was I at times. But as she stepped forward to offer her hand, I saw past the scholarly disguise of ubiquitous khakis, button shirt and many-pocketed vest, Hogwarts wristwatch, and New Age jewelry, and saw deep intellect in those eyes. It radiated like heat. Not just knowledge but the promise of wit and insight.

And Church trusted her, so that spoke volumes.

"Captain Ledg—" she began but cut herself off and flushed. In a whisper she asked, "Sorry, should I use some kind of code name?"

I grinned and shook her hand, which was thin and strong. "I don't think this is a combat callsign kind of gig. Joe Ledger, pleased to meet you."

"Lizzie Corbett," she said, giving me a final pump before letting go.

I introduced Top and Bunny, and she gave Top a longer and more lingering appraisal than she did Bunny. He has that effect on some people. He's no Idris Elba, but he's not a cave troll, either. The women who take particular notice of him tend to be more educated and more complex than the surfer gals who drool over Bunny. I noticed that Top dialed up the wattage on his smile. Not a lot, but it was there.

"I have a car," she said. "We can go directly to the site." She glanced past me to where the flight crew were unloading several metal cases. "Luggage?"

"Toys," I said.

Ten minutes later, we were driving toward the Door to Hell.

Lizzie drove fast but not well. While the miles rolled past, she talked.

"Mr. Church said that you guys know about the Unlearnable Truths," she said, "so we don't have to cover that ground. I have to ask, though...do you believe in what they are?"

Bunny said, "We've seen some shit. Far as I'm concerned, I'm keeping an open mind."

"And a loaded gun," added Top.

"Hooah," Bunny agreed.

Lizzie studied them for a moment in the rearview mirror.

"You have a problem with that?" asked Top.

"Not as much as you'd think," said Lizzie. "I've seen some stuff, too."

I smiled. "You were going to say 'shit,' weren't you?"

She gave me a small grin. "I won't ask what you've seen because I assume it's classified."

"That's complicated," I said. "It was classified while we were working for Uncle Sam. We don't do that anymore. We're building a new outfit. Unaffiliated and international."

"So I heard. Very hush hush. Very Mission: Impossible but without the politics."

"Close enough."

Cars whizzed by. Apparently fast and reckless driving was the standard here in Turkmenistan. Fun. Wish I had a bottle of Jack Daniels and a sippy straw.

"The book," I prodded.

"The book," she said, nodding. "The book itself has no actual title, though it's informally known to certain scholars as the Book of Uttu, named for the Sumerian goddess of weaving, who is often depicted as a spider. The text on that page matches some on file."

"Wait," said Bunny, leaning forward between the front seats, "I thought it was, like...bad...to even open those books. Isn't that why those monks kept them locked up? The picture Mr. Church showed us was of that book chained up, and it didn't look like anyone's opened it since the tenth century."

"Close," said Lizzie, jerking the wheel to avoid a goat standing in the middle of the road playing chicken with high-speed traffic. "That photo was taken four years ago, when the book was rescued from a temple overrun by ISIL. The monks were killed and many of the artifacts destroyed or sold to the black market. A Turkish black marketer named Ohan has a deal with some ISIL leaders to discreetly obtain and sell certain items, with the profits going back to fund ISIL's activities."

"Ohan's not doing that shit no more," said Top.

She turned to glance back at him. "How can you be sure?"

He grinned, showing a lot of teeth. "Reliable sources."

Lizzie thought about that, shrugged. "No great loss to humanity. He was a slimeball. Anyway, he sold the book before—whatever happened to him happened—and it went through several other hands. The photo of the book chained and sealed was taken by Ohan and used during his sales process. One of the people who had the book briefly, an Iranian, removed the chains and opened the book. He was a scholar of Sumerian and Babylonian history and had very noble intentions. He scanned the pages and put them on a scholarly site, with access only to select experts. His plan was to form an international team of language experts to decrypt and translate the text." She paused and chewed her lip for a moment. "That's where I came into this. One of my...friends...contacted me after translating a partial chapter. He knew that I was more comfortable with a variation of Sumerian used by Mesopotamian priests. My friend could read their entries, which were written in the margins as warnings to anyone who attempted to translate the original text."

"I do not like where this is going," said Bunny.

"No," she agreed. "Reading the warnings in straight translation is moderately easy for an expert, but they are heavily couched in metaphor and symbology specific to their sect of the priest class. You have to get into their heads and know a lot about their culture and practices to understand the importance of the warning, which means it was written only for others of their sect to ever read."

"You're taking the long way around the point, doc," I said.

"No," she said, "I'm not. It's important to know this, because there have been historical references to a lineage of those priests. I once saw a record that covered most of eighteen hundred years, and there's one in London that lists an unbroken lineage going back to the Akkadian Empire, which was founded in 2350 BCE, and that list referenced an even older one that goes back to the founding of the Sumerian culture. If all of that is true—and I have reason to believe it is—then the priests tasked with guarding that book have been at it for nearly forty-four hundred years and, if I'm correct, possibly as far back as the Sumerian proto-literate period. We're talking six thousand years ago. Who knows how much farther back it went before the development of cuneiform?"

"And what does all that mean?" asked Bunny.

"It means that people have dedicated their lives to keep the information in that book secret and have kept it sealed since the dawn of civilization," said Lizzie. "And Mr. Church had someone named Bug—who I assume is your computer guy?"

"Yeah," I said, grinning.

"Bug did a deep background on James Mercer. He is not European but actually Iranian. Not a spy or anything, just in terms of heritage. The Iranian branch surname is Mehregan, and variations of that name go way back, to versions established well before the rise of Islam. Thousands of years before, actually. So, Mercer's family is very, very old. His branch has been in America for only three generations, but there is an ancestor of James Mercer mentioned in the Epic of Gilgamesh, which is the first known major piece of writing."

"So...what's Mercer's connection to the book?" asked Top.

"The last known sale of the Book of Uttu was by a third party working on behalf of James Mercer. Mind you, this is stuff I've found out with help from some of my own contacts, but Bug was able to verify it. James Mercer purchased the book, but what I don't know is whether he opened it out of curiosity or opened it because he was following some other agenda."

"What agenda?" I asked.

Lizzie drove for almost a mile before she answered. The clouds were thick and gray over the desert, but it didn't feel like rain. Just dreary and sad. Maybe ominous, too, but I wasn't trying to spook myself out. Lizzie was doing a pretty good job of that.

"If there is a group trying to protect something," she said, "it kind of suggests that they are trying to protect it from something else."

"Yeah," said Bunny, "but the stuff on that Pauline Index is mostly supposed to be naughty shit. Stuff the Church doesn't want people to know. Like the fact that they've edited most women out of old biblical stories, and that maybe we should all stop feeling guilty and enjoy getting laid."

Lizzie grinned. "Well phrased. Some of it is that, actually...and I may quote you on my next paper. But that doesn't account for the Unlearnable Truths. Those books are flat out dangerous. They aren't banned because they promote free and independent thinking, sexual equality and general tolerance. They're books of very dark magic." She paused. "If you believe in that sort of thing."

"Keeping an open mind," Top reminded her.

"Me too," she said, though she did not elaborate. "ISIL killed the clerics guarding the book. Ohan sold it, a scholar bought it and began scanning it, and then James Mercer bought it. Not sure how he found out about it, though I suspect he had informants in the right places throughout various church groups and all through academia. He bought it, and I think he brought it to the Door to Hell. He killed two people and used a sacred knife to pin a key page to the body of someone he forced into the role of a sacrificial victim."

"To what end?" I asked.

We passed a sign that said: Darvaza Gas Crater in Turkmen. Beneath, in spray paint, was Door to Hell. A small weathered-stained sign was hung in front of the words, partly obscuring them. CLOSED.

"Remember I said that the title of the book was incorrect? It's called the Book of Uttu, but that was a guess because the cover is decorated with stylized spiders. However, the book is not about Uttu. Not really. Uttu, though a Sumerian goddess, was a benign figure. The goddess of weaving and of dry goods. In the translated pages, there is only a passing reference to her and instead another name is used. And that's what troubles me so deeply. The name mentioned over and over again is Atlach-Nacha."

"Who?" we all asked at the same time.

"Atlach-Nacha is a gigantic spider god with a humanlike face. In the stories, it comes from another planet and has become trapped here on Earth, forced to live in caves beneath a fictional mountain range in an equally fictional Arctic kingdom. Neither place is real."

"You lost me on that," said Top.

She held up a hand. "Getting there. Bear with me. In the story, Atlach-Nacha is trying to reconnect with her home. Not through physical space but via a spiritual pathway. Call it an interdimensional gateway for convenience's sake. She is trying to spin a web of some kind that will connect Earth with her world. And—just to make this all even less sane—that connection will exist in a dream world, and once formed will allow her armies to come out of dreams and into our waking world."

"So..." said Bunny slowly, "whoever cooked that up was smoking serious crack."

"This is sounding familiar to me," I said. "Dream worlds. Do you mean the Dreamlands? As in the fictional place from the Lovecraft stories?"

"Yes," she said, as she pulled off the main road onto a side lane that curved around toward the massive firepit. "Though in the case of Atlach-Nacha, the story was written by August Derleth, one of Lovecraft's friends. Lovecraft allowed and even encouraged his friends to write stories using the gods, monsters and locations he came up with. He encouraged them to create their own and expand it. After a while it was like people were filing field reports from other worlds. They call it Lovecraftian fiction or Cthulhu Mythos. And thousands of writers contribute to it all the time. Even Stephen King has done Lovecraft stories."

"Yeah," I said softly.

"When I spoke with Mr. Church," continued Lizzie, "he told me about a theory that you all played with, that the pulp fiction movement of the twenties and thirties, as well as the surrealist movement of the same era, might have had less to do with imagination and more to do with people having visions of other worlds."

"Other dimensions," I suggested. "And yeah. That was a theory, and it explained some elements of our case. It explained how things like the Necronomicon and other Unlearnable Truths wound up in *Weird Tales* magazines. It explained some of the images from Salvador Dali and others."

"If so," she said, pulling to a stop one hundred feet from the edge of the pit, "then that's something that may have been happening for hundreds, maybe thousands of years. People having genuine visions of other worlds, other dimensions, and writing them down as stories or religious visions."

We started to get out, but she stopped us.

"There's another way to look at it, too," she said. "If there are creatures from other worlds trapped here, and if they have somehow managed to invade the minds of certain people and fill their dreams with visions, surely it suggests a purpose. An agenda."

We looked at her.

"Mr. Church told me that one of your cases dealt with a young man, a genius really, who found some kind of mathematical code in the Unlearnable Truths and used it to build and program a machine to take him to one of those worlds. That he was from there, or at least a descendant of people or beings from there. Church said that other people you've met may share the same connection to other worlds."

Top cleared his throat, and Bunny looked away.

"It's possible," I said.

"So, if that young man used information to open a doorway to go home," said Lizzie slowly, "is it really so far outside the realm of possibility that someone else might want to open a door to let someone or something come into our world?"

Bunny closed his eyes. "Well...holy shit."

We got out of the car. The first of our equipment we unpacked was the guns.

4

Darvaza Gas Crater, Karakum Desert, Turkmenistan

There were six US marines standing watch over the site. They eyed us warily and a sergeant came over to meet us, giving my team a thorough up-and-down appraisal. We were not wearing uniforms or insignia of any kind.

"This is a restricted area," he said. He was a lantern-jawed guy who could have come from Central Casting. His parents might as well have enrolled him in the Corps as soon as he was born.

"Your boss told you we were coming," said Top.

The sergeant's eyes narrowed, and I knew he wanted to ask for identification but had no doubt been told not to.

"I'm Mr. Red," I said, then nodded to Top. "He's Mr. White. The big guy is Mr. Blue. The lady is Dr. Corbett." I read the sergeant's name tag. "And you're Brock."

No one shook hands.

I looked past Sergeant Brock to where the car sat inside a circle of traffic cones. Guess they didn't use crime scene tape here. More cones were set in a couple of places closer to the edge of the pit.

"Walk us through the scene," I suggested.

Brock nodded and did so.

"The forensics team has been all over everything," he said. "They left the car and other stuff in place for you but transported the bodies. Oh, and they took the murder weapons. So there's not actually a lot to see."

I made no comment.

The car was pretty much what I expected. Blood and broken safety glass on the seats, bullet holes from where Mercer's rounds went through the driver. Small flags pinned to spots where rounds had been removed for ballistics.

"Window's rolled down," observed Bunny. "He didn't know what was going to happen."

"He had a Glock 26 in a shoulder rig," said Brock, "but there was no indication he'd attempted to draw it."

"Driver was American?" asked Top.

"Of Turkmeni extraction," agreed Brock. "Guess that's why he got the gig. Spoke the language."

We stepped away from the car and he led us over to a heavy-duty briefcase that lay open on the ground.

"He'd have brought the book in that," said Lizzie.

There was a blood smear inside and spatter all around. Before I was a special operator, I was a detective in Baltimore and had worked enough murder cases to be able to read a scene pretty well, but before I could explain what I was seeing, Lizzie spoke up.

"Mercer probably used a ritual knife to cut himself," she said. Brock shot her a look, but I held up a hand to encourage her to continue. "It would be appropriate to the kind of ritual he was attempting. Historically accurate. It's a sign of humility and commitment. Blood of the faithful. That smear inside the case is probably where he set the knife down afterward, while he opened the book and selected the page to tear out."

"Pardon me, miss," began Brock, "but how do you know all that?"

Top, who squatted down beside Lizzie, swiveled his head around and gave the sergeant a long, silent stare. The sergeant looked briefly contrite and straightened, clamping his mouth shut.

Lizzie gave him a brief, almost apologetic smile, then scowled down at the case. "Once Mercer tore out the page he would have needed to make his sacrifice. He took the page and the knife and would need a good spot to..." She looked over her shoulder for a likely spot. Brock cleared his throat and pointed to a small cluster of traffic cones near the edge. Lizzie added, "That's where he sacrificed the guide."

I saw Brock's lips silently repeat that word. Sacrificed. He was going to have a lot of unanswered questions. As an NCO, he was probably used to some level of that.

"Hey," said Bunny, who was scanning the area, "look at that."

We all turned to follow where he was pointing. A line of spiders was running toward the edge of the pit.

"Yeah," said Brock, "that happens. Spiders are always coming here. No one knows why. Maybe it's the methane smell or something."

"Or something," Lizzie said quietly.

She met my eyes. I nodded, though a chill rippled up my spine, like someone walked over my grave.

Spiders. Shit.

We straightened and followed the spiders to the edge of the pit and looked into the mouth of hell.

It was twenty meters deep—not a single mass of flame but rather patches of it, as if fire was burning through the skin of the Earth to expose burning wounds. It looked like cancer and it stank of shit.

"Door to Hell don't really cover it," said Top quietly.

Bunny came up beside him. "More like the ass of Hell."

Sergeant Brock cleared his throat again. "A lot of people have been all over this site, but I was one of the first Americans to arrive after we got the call. There's something maybe you should see."

We followed him a dozen yards along the curving lip of the

crater and then stopped as he squatted down and pointed. At first all I saw was a cluster of spiders a bit heavier than elsewhere on the rim; and at least a dozen different kinds. But that wasn't what he was pointing at.

Although partly obscured by scuff marks from what I presumed were police and forensics people, there was a line of footprints that led from the pit to this spot. I got up and backtracked, then walked the scene quickly to verify what Brock found.

"Those are Mercer's prints," I said. "Same prints go over to the car and back, go to where the guide was killed and back, and then from the briefcase to the edge."

"Yeah," said Bunny, "but I don't see any prints coming back from the edge."

"That's 'cause he didn't come back, Farm Boy," said Top. He got down nearly into a push-up position and peered at the print closest to the edge. "See here? This one's a little deeper, right at the sole. Like he pushed off right there."

"Pushed off?" echoed Lizzie. "But that would mean…"

The last print was right at the edge. There was only one direction to go in, and that was down.

Top got up and dusted his hands off. He cut me a look. "Probe, Cap'n?"

"Do it," I said.

Bunny went over to one of our equipment boxes, opened it, and came back with what looked like a pigeon made from plastic. In his other hand, he held a small controller.

"Surveillance drone," Bunny explained when Lizzie and Brock looked expectantly at him. "Specially made for scouting combat environments. Durable, covered in flame-retardant and heat-resistant polymers. You can send one into a burning building and get good video feeds from up to a mile."

Bunny pressed a button on the pigeon, then handed it to Top, who held it ready over the edge. Then Bunny powered on the controller and gave a nod. Top hurled the pigeon high into the air and it immediately deployed its wings, flapped around until its internal gyroscopes and guidance were synched, and then dove into the smoke.

"Nice," said Brock. "Haven't seen that model."

"And you're not seeing it now," I told him. He nodded.

"If Mr. Mercer jumped down there," said Lizzie, "what do you expect to find except charred bones?"

"Don't know," I said. "If we find bones, then this investigation shifts lanes and goes looking for answers elsewhere. If not, then we reassess what we know of Mercer."

She nodded, accepting that.

While the drone flew, Bunny frowned at the small video display on the control unit. "Lot of smoke. Shifting through the spectrum to see what I can see."

A few seconds later...

"Wait, I think I see something."

Then...

"Holy fucking shit," cried Bunny. "Guys!"

We ran back to him. Bunny held the control device up and we crowded around to see the image. Top, Lizzie and Me. Brock stood to one side, unsure if he was invited but also clearly alarmed at Bunny's tone.

On the screen the picture was hazy because of the smoke, but we could still make out what it was. It's just that it made no sense.

It's just that it was impossible.

It's just that it sent a thrill though me that was not revulsion at seeing a burned body, or any other normal emotion. What I felt was an absolutely ice-cold knife of real terror stab its way straight through my heart. Lizzie grabbed my wrist in a hand gone icy; her grip was vise-hard. Top made a sound that was part gasp and part cry of strict denial.

James Mercer was down there. He was at the bottom of the burning pit. His clothes had all burned away. His flesh was cracked and splotched with brick red and charcoal black. His hair was gone.

But he was alive.

He knelt, naked and cooked alive, holding the big book out in front of him, reading from it even though blood and pus leaked steaming from his eyes. His cock was erect, and the skin bubbled with blisters that swelled and popped.

Spiders—tens of thousands of them—crawled all over his body, and swarmed around him, and scaled the side of the pit. And before Mercer, as if opened like a wound in the world, was a cleft. A kind of doorway. Light poured through it, brighter than the fires that flickered around him.

Through the speaker on the monitor we could hear the rustling of the spiders, the crackle of flames, the hiss of smoke and steam, and the constant, droning, inexorable mumble of James Mercer reading his prayers from the ancient book. The light from the cleft bathed Mercer in a hellish glow, and it showed us what all those spiders were doing down there.

They were eating the dirt—clawing at the living rock, dragging tiny bits of it away on either side of that obscene cleft. I stared at it on the screen and felt as if the whole world was tilting under my feet. Mercer, driven to madness, kept alive through some means that could not make sense in any way, not in the wildest, warped reinterpretation of reality as I knew it. And the spiders. Milling with constant energy. Tiny creatures trying to tear open a wall of solid rock. For those small monsters it was a labor assigned in the deepest pit of insanity, and the spiders worked with tireless diligence to widen the crack.

No.

They worked—as Mercer worked with the prayers his cracked lips recited—to open a door.

But...to where?

5

The Pit of Hell, Karakum Desert, Turkmenistan

"**What's the plan,** Boss?" asked Bunny. His voice was full of cracks. "'Cause if you don't have one I have a suggestion."

"Does it involve dropping a big fucking bomb right over there?" asked Top, pointing. "Because I'm all over that idea."

"No!" cried Lizzie. "You can't."

"Why the hell not?" I demanded. "Right now it seems both poetic justice and good common sense to hit this whole area with a whole bunch of Hellfire missiles. I'm pretty sure—foreign soil or not— I can arrange that in under fifteen minutes. One, maybe two phone calls and it's done."

"No," she insisted, her face going from flushed to deathly pale, "if you do that you'll kill us all."

"We'd actually drive away first," said Top, forcing a smile onto his face despite the fear in his eyes.

"You don't understand," she said, "if you blow up the pit, if you destroy that book, then you let it out."

"Let what out?" asked Bunny. "No, don't tell me because I probably don't want to know."

She pointed to the pit. "Mercer tore off one page of the book and look what happened. That page, that small bit of damage to the book, did something down there. It opened a door. You can see it on the monitor clear as day." She looked from Top to Bunny to me, her eyes wild. "Why do you think this book was guarded for all these centuries? For millennia? These books aren't bullshit church politics or contrary doctrinal points of view. These are books of power. Real power. The darkest power you can imagine."

We said nothing.

"If you've dealt with the Unlearnable Truths before, then you have to know how dangerous they are. How dangerous this book could be?"

"Wait...could be?" I bellowed. "You don't even know if we can safely destroy it or not? Is that what you're telling me?"

Brock and his marines, drawn by our raised voices, began hurrying over, but Top stepped to intercept them, arms wide, shaking his head. Brock slowed and gave us all an uncertain look. He retreated with great reluctance.

I leaned close to Lizzie and lowered my voice. "You don't know?"

"No, Captain, I don't," she snapped, moving so close I could smell the fear in her sweat. "And because I don't know, I can't let you go off half-cocked and just bomb the hell out of the pit. We need to recover that book. We need to seal that—rift, or doorway, or whatever it is. We need to stop whatever Mercer is doing. Maybe then I can figure out how to seal the book again. Or, maybe I'll find out that we can destroy it. But I'm telling you right now that your plan has a lot more ways to go wrong than mine."

"You don't actually have a plan," I snarled.

Again, she pointed to the pit. "Sure I do. You need to go down there and get the book."

Bunny said, "Fuck me."

I closed my eyes.

"Jesus H. Christ," I said.

6

Bunny brought the pigeon drone up and landed it on the rim, where it squatted, steam rising from it. We all ran for the car.

The equipment Church recommended we bring included Dragon fire-suits. The company makes a line of body armor for combat in virtually every possible circumstance, from deep Antarctic winter to cities on fire. The fire-suits were ultra-high-tech, costing over a million dollars per set. Lizzie and Brock watched as we stripped to our underwear and began pulling them on.

The fire-suits are similar to the Hammer suits we wore when going into biological hot zones. They were flexible and durable, perfect for agile movement and physical combat. The skin of the suits was made from a blend of synthetic carbon fibers mixed with spider silk. That irony was not lost on me, by the way. But, fuck it. The suits could stop an ordinary bullet shy of armor-piercing rounds, and the network of air distribution tubes allowed us to regulate temperature.

"Will those things be enough?" asked Lizzie, clearly skeptical of suits that fit like gloves instead of the bulkier garments worn by firefighters or volcanologists.

"That's what it says in the catalog," said Top as he buddy-checked Bunny's seals. The answer did little to reassure Lizzie.

Brock said, "If you have another one of those, I'd be happy to—"

"Thanks," I said, "but no. We brought enough for us. But, thanks."

He nodded and then lowered his voice. "Look, Mr. Red...I couldn't help but overhear a lot of this stuff and I know it's above my paygrade and all, but if something happens and you need some muscle or an extra shooter, then I'm here. I didn't get an embassy posting because I don't know which end of a gun goes bang. Three tours in Afghanistan, one in Iraq. Been to a lot of loud parties. I don't want to just sit up here and play with my dick the whole time."

I smiled at him. "I appreciate that, Sergeant, but we really do have only these three rigs. If you want to help, though, watch over Dr. Corbett. She's important and I need her safe. If things go south, get her the hell out of here and call the number she'll provide. Talk to my boss. His name is Church. Whatever he says to do, you do it. Can you do that?"

"Yes, sir, I can," he said.

I started to lift my helmet to put it on, then paused. "Tell you what, Sergeant," I said, nodding to the pit. "We have two cases of weapons and loaded magazines. Lots of fun toys. If you see anything come over the edge of that fucking hole that isn't one of us, kill it."

His eyes turned cold and he gave me a nod. "Yes, sir...I can do that, too."

He turned and walked over to his men. I saw them immediately begin checking their weapons. Bunny, who was a former Marine Recon, nodding approval.

"Semper fi," he said quietly and then put his helmet on. He opened a canvas gear bag and began taking out long guns. His weapon of choice is a drum-fed combat shotgun that he lovingly calls "Honey Boom-Boom."

Top had another of our cases open and was removing rappelling gear.

Lizzie touched my arm. "Joe," she said, "is there any way that drone of yours could get close enough for me to see the book?"

"Maybe. Why, though?"

"If I could see what he's reading then maybe I can understand what he's trying to accomplish."

"Does that matter?"

"Yes. The page he took out first was a kind of spell," she said. "It's intended to both summon Atlach-Nacha and also begin something described as a 'ritual of opening.' I think we've seen what that looks like. But he went down there, and he's clearly in some kind of trance. And he's done something that is preventing him from being consumed completely by the heat. Call it magic or weird science or whatever you want, but he's been down there for days now. Whatever spell or ritual he's performing must be very complex. If I know what it is, then maybe I can figure out the best way to stop it."

"How about I put three rounds into the back of his head?" I suggested. "Wouldn't that stop it?"

"I actually don't know if that would work anymore."

I stared at her, waiting for the punch line, but she wasn't joking.

Beside me, Top said, "Well fuck me blind and move the furniture."

To Lizzie I said, "Have you ever worked a drone?"

"Sure. My group works in areas where ISIL could be hiding anywhere, so I use them all the time to assess a site." She named a few commercial and professional models she'd used.

I picked up the controller for the pigeon drone. "This is a lot like those."

She was quick and was able to launch and manipulate the drone with ease.

"If that one burns out," said Bunny, "there's two more in the case."

I said, "Lizzie, we're all wearing earbuds. There's a microphone on the controller. See? Right there. Leave it turned on. The speaker's good, so you'll be able to hear us, too. If you can get eyes on that book and read what Mercer is reading, let us know." I raised my forearm to show small flexible-panel computer screens. "You can send the video feeds to us on these. But we won't be watching those feeds unless it's something important. We're probably going to be busy. So, pick your moment."

"I understand," said Lizzie. "I promise not to distract you."

"You're not a distraction," said Top, and she actually blushed. Bunny rolled his eyes so hard I'm surprised he didn't bruise his brain. Then, in a more serious tone, Top said, "Let us know when we can end that evil motherfucker down there, feel me?"

Lizzie nodded. "God...be careful. Please."

Top gave her a grin. "It's all good. Just another day on the job."

We put our helmets on, grabbed our guns, and walked over to the edge of the pit. Brock and two of his men helped anchor us for the rappelling maneuver. I adjusted my suit's environmental controls one more time, cut looks at Top and Bunny, then nodded to Lizzie.

"Good luck," she told us, and again her eyes lingered on Top's.

Bunny turned to Top. "'Just another day on the job?' Seriously? That's the worst pickup line in like...ever."

"Oh, shut up."

"I can actually hear you," said Lizzie.

Bunny blew a kiss at Top, who shot him the finger.

And then we were over the edge.

7

No mission ever goes off without a hitch. Not in my experience.

You try to make it otherwise. You gather as much intel as possible, you plan, you train, you theorize to predict variables, you allow for things to change as the mission unfolds. You even stay mentally flexible in case of mission creep—which is when an operation changes substantially in nature while you're in situ.

But things always go a little wrong.

Sometimes the situation twists in your favor. Or, so I've heard. My luck doesn't tend that way.

Sometimes thing change and you can easily roll with it. You call in back up, or throw some extra ordnance downrange, or otherwise deal with shit.

And sometimes nothing is what it seems.

Case in point...

8

We went down into the pit.

Twenty meters is nothing when rappelling. You drop down on a rope, kicking off from the wall every few meters to slow the rate of fall and keep yourself from gathering enough momentum to slam into anything. The walls of the pit were sloped, so we also had to shove off to keep dropping. Fires burned all around us. Even with the cooling system in the suits, I could feel the heat.

How the hell could Mercer still be alive down here?

My mind rebelled at the thought of actual magic. This had to be some kind of science. But...what kind?

Over the last few years, I'd run into all kinds of things. Genetically-engineered assassins designed to approximate vampires. Lycanthropic super soldiers. Transgenic soldiers amped up with ape DNA. The God Machines built with science that came to its designer from dreams of other worlds. Doorways into other dimensions opened using mathematics from the Unlearnable Truths. So, yeah, I've had to expand my mind or go crazy. Maybe it's fair to say that because I've been forced to expand my mind I've gone crazier. A case can be made for that. And yet in each case there was science behind it. Every single time. Weird science, to be sure. Radical, possibly alien, certainly beyond my understanding, but science nonetheless. If there was something that fit the literal definition of supernatural, then I haven't hit it so far.

But how could science explain how a man with no protective garments survived for days in an actual inferno? How could anything make sense of that?

We dropped and dropped.

I looked down at the floor of the pit and saw something else that made no fucking sense at all.

The floor of the pit seemed to be...receding?

"Boss?" called Bunny, his voice crystal clear through the high-tech earbuds we all wore. "Are you seeing this?"

We paused, toes touching the slope.

"Cap'n," growled Top, "either I'm losing my shit or that floor is dropping."

We watched, looking for signs of structural collapse, for cracks in the ground, for sudden releases of trapped gas, for the tumble of boulders and debris. All of that should have been happening if the pit floor was falling inward.

That's not what we saw.

It's just the floor was farther away, as if the pit itself had been somehow stretched.

"I can't be seeing what I'm seeing," said Bunny.

"Keep your shit wired tight, Farm Boy," snapped Top. "If that's what's there, then that's what's there. So nut up and deal with it."

Bold words. Probably as much for himself as for Bunny. Meant for me, too.

I checked the line, making quick calculations. "We're going to have to hit the slope twenty feet above the bottom and walk down."

"What if it keeps...um...getting deeper?" asked Bunny.

"Then we figure it out on the fly," I said.

"Hooah," said Top, and after a moment Bunny said it, too. "Hooah" was the Ranger catch-all phrase for anything from "yes, sir" to "fuck you," and right now both seemed applicable.

We kept dropping.

The floor receded more and more.

"Fuck this," I bellowed and hit hard on the slope, unclipped and ran into the pull of gravity. I heard thumps and curses behind me as the others did too. The slope was steep, and gravity wanted to kill us, but we ran into its pull, angling our bodies for balance and to slough off the acceleration. For a wild moment I thought we would keep running and running until we reached Hell itself. The actual hell. The devil and his demons and all of that biblical bullshit.

This was close enough.

Goddamn, it was close enough.

And then the floor was there. Hard and rocky and real. It was stable, too. I don't know how the bottom got deeper, but whatever it was seemed to have stopped. It was ordinary ground under my feet. I wanted to kiss it.

Bunny and Top came running down to where I was, and then stopped, trembling, panting—more from fear than the exertion.

Top unslung his weapon, a Heckler & Koch MP7 with a forty-round magazine, and he had a Milkor MGL 40mm six-shot grenade launcher slung over his shoulder. He had not come to screw around. Bunny had his shotgun in his big hands and was sweeping the barrel around the perimeter.

He froze, looking behind me, and I whirled, drawing my Sig Sauer fast and bringing it up in a two-handed grip. Top turned, too, and we realized that the pit floor wasn't the only thing that had gone off its rails.

"What the?" was all Bunny could manage.

The drone descended and hovered about his shoulder.

"Lizzie," I said hoarsely, "are you seeing this, too?"

Her answer was an inarticulate croak.

We were all seeing it.

I don't know where we were, but it wasn't the same pit we dropped into. It couldn't be. Even with the ropes still dangling above us and the drone having followed us here.

We stood on a flat space of ground that was much wider than the opening of the pit above. No idea how that was possible, but it wasn't the weirdest or worst thing about this moment. James Mercer, naked and burned but alive, knelt a dozen paces away, the Book of Uttu in his hands, his blind eyes clicking back and forth across the pages as his lips read words aloud in a dead language. Beyond him was the wall we'd seen in the drone's camera, with the obscene vertical slit from which poured an unnatural and lurid red light. There were the legions of spiders gnawing at the opening.

All of that was what we expected to find. Kind of.

But not the rest.

Not the dozens of people down there. Thirty or forty of them, dressed in robes of white and red and gray. Robes set with jewels and metals I could not identify. Men with muscular, bare arms and long plaited beards, like priests from some old temple carvings. Except they were very real and they held tools—axes and sledgehammers. All of them had swords and knives in leather scabbards at their hips.

They all stood in attitudes of surprise, frozen in their act of attacking the wall.

Even that wasn't the worst.

Far from it. Give me enough whiskey and I could work out some logic to them being down here. That, at least, was close enough to sanity for me to postulate something I could force myself to accept.

But the spiders? No. Not them.

And I'm not talking about the thousands of small ones that had survived the hellish heat to climb down here from above.

There were other spiders here.

Big ones.

Strange ones.

Some the size of rats. Some the size of dogs. A few as big as wild boars. Massive, bloated monsters that quivered on hairy legs.

And the others.

Ponderous and improbable abominations with speckled red and black bodies that stood not on eight legs, but on three. Tripodal spiders with too many eyes and mandibles that snapped and clacked and dripped with steaming drool.

I knew for sure—without the slightest doubt, without needing to lie to myself—that nothing like them had ever before walked on this green Earth. I had no idea where they were from, or how Mercer had conjured them into this place, but they didn't belong in this world.

I heard a sound, a high-pitched whimper, and prayed that it wasn't coming from my own throat. Though it probably was.

In my ear, I heard Lizzie's hushed and horrified voice. "Joe...is this real? Am I seeing it?"

"You tell me," I said quickly. "You're the expert."

"Not...god, not in this," she gasped. But a moment later she said, "Those men, they're dressed like Sumerians. It's like they stepped right out of a bas-relief carving from one of the ancient temples."

"Those fucking spiders, Doc," asked Bunny nervously, "you got anything on them? What are they?"

"I don't...I don't know."

The spiders and the armed men stared at us, surprised for a heartbeat—and that was all it was—by our presence. Of aliens in their sacred place.

Then, with a ululating howl that tore the air, they all swarmed toward us.

9

I generally like to know who the hell I'm fighting. I'm a long damn way from the concept of "kill 'em all and let God sort it out."

Most of the time.

This wasn't one of those times.

10

The priest—and I had to accept that it was what he was—closest to me raised an adze and swung it at my head. I shot him in the face. Twice. Because I really meant it.

The back of his head exploded and showered the priests behind him with red-blue and gray brains.

Top shouted, "They can bleed."

Bunny yelled back. "Fuck 'em."

The priests swarmed toward us, and as they did so they ran to put themselves between us and Mercer. Two of them swung their weapons in the air, and through the pall of smoke I saw that they were aiming at the drone, but Lizzie steered it sharply away.

Bunny and Top fell back a few steps to give the attackers a long run. It wasn't because the priests were particularly hard to kill—they had no armor, no advanced weapons—but because there were so damn many of them. If we were all in the belly of a Black Hawk helicopter, hunkered down behind a minigun, then maybe this would be a quick fight. This was a different kind of fight. We had the best weapons and we had enough ammunition, but there was no guarantee at all that we had enough time to kill our way to Mercer and that damn book. Now the sheer number of people we needed to kill exceeded the time it would take to do that.

Which was bad enough. And then the spiders stopped chewing at the wall and attacked. The little ones moved like a black carpet across the ashy floor, swarming through and around the feet of the priests, climbing over the bodies that fell as Bunny fired blast after blast of his shotgun and Top burned through one magazine after another with his rifle.

I pivoted and fired over the carpet at the first of the big spiders, hitting it with three clean shots. Pieces of its carapace blew off and green muck vomited from the wounds, but the three heavy legs propelled it forward. It screeched, though; the sound was eerily like that of a child in pain. As it barreled toward me, I lowered my gun and aimed at the cluster of blazing eyes and fired again. Once, twice, three times, blowing those eyes apart but not stopping it. Not even slowing it. It was the fourth shot that hit something vital. The creature suddenly canted forward and collapsed, its momentum and weight sending it into a clumsy, broken tumble.

I tried to replay that last shot to identify exactly what I'd hit because two more of the brutes came at me. I backpedaled and fired until the slide locked back. The last bullet killed another and it fell clumsily as the third tripped over it. By the time the beast clambered back up, I had a new magazine swapped in and shot it from three feet away. Two bullets and it fell. Maybe the first killed it. I'll never know.

More of them were coming and the pit was filled with the thunder of gunfire and the horrific cry of the monsters. I holstered my sidearm and swung the MP7 from my back, switched the selector switch to semi auto and began firing in short, controlled bursts. Top was still hosing the priests, but I needed more precision to kill the spiders. Four of them were circling the priests to try and get behind my guys. I whirled and fired.

The creatures died. The priests died.

And we kept losing ground because we were trying to use buckets to stop a tsunami.

"Cap'n," huffed Top as he fired, pivoted, fired, "I can get Mercer from here. I have the grenade launcher. I can blow that asshole all the way into orbit."

"No," cried Lizzie. "Not while he's holding the book. Not until I can see what he's reading."

I shot a spider in the head and needed two bursts to knock it down. "Lizzie," I yelled, "how do we end this?"

The drone flew over my head and over the heads of the throng of priests. They swatted at it, but she kept it moving, dipping and swooping and dodging.

"Shit," she hissed. "I can't get a clear image."

"Listen to me," shouted Bunny. "There's a green button on the lower left. It's a Steadicam feature. Hit that and then hold the blue button to take high-speed high-def pics. Oh...shit..."

I saw him turned and kick a priest in the groin and then chop him across the face with the stock of his shotgun, then wheel right and fire three times at the men behind him. The shotgun was loaded with double-ought buckshot that tore ragged red holes and set priests screaming away as they clutched stumps of arms or tried to plug gaping wounds in their stomachs or chests. It was a dreadful thing, though, to see that most of them somehow managed to fight past the immediate reaction of pain and fear, and stagger forward again. Christ. Even knowing they were dying they kept attacking. I heard Top and Bunny both make sick sounds because it was immediately clear to all of us that wounding our enemies was not going to be enough. We had to kill them all. They were either fanatics or they were insane. Or both.

And killing requires a lot more precision—and often more ammunition—than wounding. It takes a fragment of each second to aim with precision, and we didn't have that time to waste.

Nevertheless, Top roared, "Center mass, god damn it."

"I am shooting center mass, Old Man," complained Bunny. Then he saved the rest of his breath for fighting.

11

Lizzie Corbett knelt in the ash at the edge of the pit, holding the drone controls in both hands. She followed Bunny's instructions and fired the high-def camera over and over, playing with both optical and digital zoom functions. Images popped onto the screen and she froze one, discarded it because it was still too blurry; repeated the process. Again and again.

And then, on the tenth try, the image of the page popped up as clear and readable as if she held the book in her own hands.

She bent over it, eyes inches from the screen, lips moving as she worked. When doing translations, it helped her to mouth the words as she read them. It somehow made them more real.

The process of interpretation and translation was something that would normally take days or weeks, even for someone who knew the language and understood quite a bit about the culture. What confused the process was that the writing on the page was not all in a single language. There were blocks of text that were in Sumerian, but the style of the translation suggested that the translator was Akkadian. Other sections were in Latin and some short phrases, scribbled in the margins, were written in Arabic, Amharic, Tigrinya, and Hebrew. She fumbled her way through it, digging deep for the right words and meanings.

She stumbled through it, feeling the terrible burden of seconds burning off as Joe Ledger and his men fought for their lives down in the pit. The sounds of their battle rose with the smoke, though it was oddly distorted, as if their battle was a mile or more away.

Sergeant Brock leaned over the rim, coughing and using his hand to fan away the noxious fumes. He held a pistol in his other hand, and the other marines stood nearby, all of them looking as helpless and impotent as Lizzie felt.

"I can't see a fucking thing," complained Brock. "I mean... I should be able to, but I can't."

Lizzie hit a section of the text that suddenly jumped out at her. She yelled into the microphone. "Joe, Top...they're trying to open a gate down there."

"No shit," growled Bunny's voice. "It's already half open."

"Can you see what's inside?"

"Red light," said Top. "Can't see more than that."

"Listen to me," she said urgently, "I thought that this was an attempt to invoke an ancient goddess, Uttu or Atlach-Nacha. But it's not. Everything on that page is about numbers. It's not a spell...it's a series of mathematical formulae."

"The fuck...?" said Bunny.

"I think I know what this might be, but I need to know what's on the other side of the gateway. If it's a cavern with glowing moss, then we have to handle it one way. If that's all it is, then I think I know how to destroy the book. If it's somewhere else, then we need to get the book and bring it up here. But I have to know one way or the other. We need to know. Can you get closer to the opening?"

"Not a chance," said Ledger. "We're falling back..."

"No! You have to tell me what you can see through the gateway."

There was a heavy rattle of gunfire, screams, shouts and curses. Through it all, Ledger managed to spit out some words. "Use the...fucking...drone..."

Lizzie wanted to smack herself upside the head. Of course!

She took the controls again and went to work.

12

I **saw the** drone go sweeping overhead, moving in a straight line toward the cleft, which seemed to be swelling as more of the intense red light pushed through from the other side.

And I realized what I was seeing. This wasn't just the priests and spiders trying to break through from the pit—something over there, on the other side of the wall, was fighting to get out. To break free.

To come here.

I shifted to my left to get a better view, but had to shoot my way there, killing a priest and three more of the tripodal spiders. Smaller spiders were climbing all over me, and I could hear them scratching at the fabric of my Dragon suit. The material would stop a bullet, but, like most fabric body armor, it wouldn't necessarily stop a blade. Or a claw.

I paused to slap at the little bastards, squashing several and brushing dozens to the ground, but they immediately swarmed back up my legs. Top and Bunny were likewise covered with the little monsters.

A big one—much bigger than the others, nearly as large as a baby elephant—came scuttling toward me, with two priests flanking it. I switched to full auto and burned through the rest of my magazine to cut them down. As I swapped in a new one I crabbed sideways to try and get a better look at the cleft. The light was blinding, making it difficult to see anything clearly, but I thought I saw shadows. Small and large. There were more of the tripodal spiders, but also larger shapes. And stranger ones, but none that I could identify. They crowded the entrance and I knew that if they broke through, we were lost. Me and my guys. Maybe more than that.

Maybe the world.

Every fiber of who I was, and all of my instincts told me that was not an exaggeration.

Top and Bunny had backed all the way to where we'd first come down the slope. There was nowhere else to go. I was separated from them by a running sea of spiders. No matter how many of the little freaks I killed, there were always more. Were they somehow squeezing through the cleft? Or had Mercer conjured them from some nightmare reality? I didn't know and wasn't sure I wanted that answer.

The priests tried to swat the drone out of the air. They jumped up and swung their weapons at it, but Lizzie was sharp. Damn, she was sharp. The pigeon wings flapped, and the little machine tilted and dipped and swooped and even though the axes and mauls and waving arms came close, they could not not tear it down.

The opening was still narrow, though. A few inches, though the spill of light created the illusion of it being larger.

"The drone won't fit," I warned.

"I know," she snapped. "I'm going to try something."

The drone accelerated, the wings becoming blurs as it shot forward toward the wall. A priest climbed onto the shoulders of two others and leapt at it, trying to grab it and pull the machine down.

He missed, but only just.

The drone smashed into the wall.

No. It smashed into the cleft. The head buried itself into the narrow opening and lodged there. The wings snapped and the body sagged down.

"Shit," cried Bunny, but I understood what Lizzie was trying to do. She needed to see what was on the other side. The cameras were in the drone's small head.

I heard a sound, though. From Lizzie.

She cried out as if in physical pain.

At the same time, Bunny glanced up, probably to judge how far above them the ends of our rappelling ropes were, and I saw him stagger. Actually stagger, as if someone had hit him. His knees began to buckle and he had to visibly fight to keep standing.

"Jesus Fucking Christ on the cross," he breathed.

I looked up, too.

I wanted to scream.

No, I wanted to lay down my weapons and sit down and cry. And let the monsters get me, because there was no reason to keep fighting. The world was broken. Everything was broken.

Above us should have been the slopes of the pit. Above us should have been the ropes and the smoke rising into the air over the Turkmenistan desert. Above us should have been the world.

That's not what Bunny saw. It's not what I saw.

Above us there was darkness.

Above us there were stars.

It was like looking up from the surface of the moon.

The sky was gone. And the world was gone and where in Heaven or Hell were we?

"Joe," came Lizzie's voice. "Look at your computer screen."

"Not now," I said, firing and firing.

"Joe...you have to see this."

I backpedaled and took a grenade from my belt. "Frag out!" I bellowed and rolled it like a bocce ball beneath the closest of the giant spiders; then I spun, crouched and covered my head with my arms. The blast, even muffled, was like thunder, and I was splashed with green ichor. I cut a look to see that everything in the blast radius was dead and it gave me a few seconds to check the screen.

If I thought it was going to be as bad as seeing the stars above us on a clear afternoon, I was wrong.

It was worse.

So much worse.

The computer screens we wore were small, but they were ultra-high-definition and the colors were accurate to an incredible degree. I gaped down at the image fed to me from Lizzie. The image of what the drone was seeing through the cleft.

There were thousands upon thousands of figures on the other side of that wall. But it was not a cave or cavern over there. It was not anything on Earth at all.

Through the proxy of the drone's video camera eyes, I looked onto the landscape of another world. I saw vast stretches of sandy, rocky ground and towering mountains. It was all painted a lurid red. Sand and rocks and blowing grit. All red.

Filling much of that landscape was an army.

It was the only way to describe it. An army. An invasion force. Countless thousands of them. I saw hundreds of the three-legged spiders, some of them as small as the ones I'd been killing, but most many times bigger. Bigger than full grown bison. And people. If they were people. Bipedal, with round, erect heads and large eyes in dark sockets; their bodies fitted out with armor like exoskeletons, as if their limbs were unable to support themselves. They marched forward like slaves being forced into battle.

Behind them were other creatures and it was instantly clear that they were the masters of these combat slaves. They rode in devices like a kind of chariot, with flat bases and lots of devices whose nature I could not begin to guess. These chariots moved nimbly on mechanical legs. Three legs.

Worse still were the things that towered above them.

Monsters made of glittering metal that stood a hundred feet tall and walked on three titanic legs, many flexible metal tentacles whipping with furious agitation in the air. Behind each, bolted to its body, was a massive steel net, and with each step jets of green gas erupted from its joints. Each tripod had a clear dome and inside I could see the masters of this ungodly army. They were hideous, with octopoidal bodies, and massive heads with bulging eyes and v-shaped beaks. Smaller tentacles framed their mouths, twitching and obscene.

My mind felt like it was cracking, breaking apart, and taking the last of my sanity with it. I knew these things. These metal monsters. I'd read about them as a kid, saw them in movies. They weren't real. They were the creations of a British science fiction writer from more than a century ago. They were fiction.

Except that they weren't.

And I immediately understood why this was real. How it could be real.

Just like H.P. Lovecraft and August Derleth writing about Elder Gods, the Great Old Ones and other cosmic horrors, HG Wells had not created the Martians in his novel, *War of the Worlds*, from whole cloth, but had seen these horrors in dreams or visions. He had glimpsed the terrors of another world and knew, on some conscious or subconscious level, that these creatures coveted our blue world and had, in literal point of fact, drawn their plans against us.

Here was proof.

Right here, in this pit. Monsters from that world had already slipped through. These spiders. And in a flash of terrible insight, I realized that perhaps the spider goddess Atlach-Nacha was very real. Maybe she was one of those monsters who had come through a similar crack thousands of years ago and had become trapped here. She, and the mad priests who worshipped her, had labored all these millennia to help her open the door, so that her masters could come through with their armies and their fighting machines to make war on humanity. To conquer and own this world and leave their own dying world.

I had no proof of that, but I believed it. I knew it.

And I had to stop it.

Somehow.

Jesus Christ.

Somehow.

13

Lizzie Corbett had seen some very strange things in her life. Most of them over the last few years, since discovering a vast portion of the lost treasure of the Knights Templar and then being recruited into the Library of the Ten Gurus. That group, run by Sikhs, fought a bizarre war on two fronts. The public face of their group worked with the United Nations and UNESCO to preserve artifacts, religious items, and books that were targeted for destruction by extremist groups like ISIL.

The other arm, which was smaller and much less passive in important ways, worked to reclaim books like the Unlearnable Truths. To take them away from whomever had them and make sure they were protected and properly locked away. She had not shared this part of her life with Joe, Top and Bunny. Only Mr. Church knew about it, and he had provided funding and material support for the Library's work.

It had been Church who brought her into this matter, and who had warned her that the Book of Uttu might not be what it seemed. She did not know how Church acquired this information, but her Sikh friends knew of him and said that he could be trusted. Church had told her she could trust Joe Ledger and his team, and she did.

Church had warned her that this matter could be dangerous, but even he did not seem to know how dangerous. How could he? That awful book had held its secrets for so long. The priests and imams who had protected it had kept the world safe from its potential.

And now it was all falling apart.

The Sikhs were too far away. Church was too far away. Joe and his men were at the bottom of an impossible pit. Maybe not even truly on this Earth, or in this dimension. She couldn't even start to understand it all. How could she? How could anyone?

All Lizzie had to work with was her knowledge of books like this—and with what was written on the two pages she had photographed with the drone. There was so much there, written in a dozen different hands, in half a dozen languages. And the text itself was conflicted, confusing. It was a mathematical formula written as a conjuring spell. It must have been meaningless to the priests who recorded it. Though maybe not. The Sumerians were known for an exceptional mathematical brilliance, for having developed high math skills with no recognizable backtrail of development. As if the knowledge sprang suddenly into being within a generation or two. Scholars and historians had puzzled over it for years, but now Lizzie thought she understood. It was Atlach-Nacha. Somehow that creature was no mere spider, not even a monstrous alien spider. She—it—was sentient and intelligent and somehow able to communicate to those ancient Sumerians. She had taught them advanced math, and engineering and other skills. But then something happened to break that process. Atlach-Nacha had become lost, trapped in the earth. Possibly some natural disaster, or the actions of another culture. Perhaps sanity prevailed within the group of priests and there was a rebellion in order to save their world. Lizzie did not know how that happened, or why. Probably no one would ever know because there was no record of it at all. The Sumerians went into decline and the planned invasion was forestalled. The knowledge had been recorded in a book, and that book hidden away and guarded fiercely for thousands of years.

Until now. Until ISIL and Ohan and Mercer.

Until an act of murder cracked open the world and the invading army mustered, ready to complete an invasion eight thousand years in the making.

The gunfire and explosions from below were continuous. There was no sign of the battle slacking, but Lizzie knew there was only one way for it to end. Joe, Top and Bunny would run out of ammunition, and then they would be overwhelmed. Then Mercer and the priests would finish their ritual to open this world to the horrors of another.

Lizzie read over the page again and again looking for some clue, some hint. Some hope.

Then, suddenly, she turned to Sergeant Brock.

"How much rope do you have?"

"What?"

"Rope. How much? Can you reach them?"

He looked at the three lines that went down into the nothing below.

"They're too short."

Lizzie shook her head. "Pull them up."

Brock gaped. "What?"

"Pull them up, Sergeant. Do it now."

14

I got caught in a deadly pinch when I reached for another magazine and found that there were none left. Three priests rushed at me, two swinging pick-axes and one with a sledgehammer.

There was no time to draw the Sig Sauer. None.

I faded left, ducking in and under one pick-axe, and chopped upward with my forearm. Even insane ancient Sumerian priests have balls, and I hit his real damn hard. He let loose with a whistling shriek that hit the ultrasonic. I straightened fast and took the pick-axe from his hands, shouldered him into the sledgehammer guy and swung the axe at the third priest. The spike of the big tool punched a big wet hole in his solar plexus. I let go as he fell, taking his pick-axe away, following it with a ballet pirouette and slammed the spike into the crotch of the sledgehammer priest. He sat down and fell back, screaming something in a language I didn't know. Maybe calling on his god. Maybe calling for his mother. I didn't give much of a fuck.

I moved to the priest I'd clubbed in the nuts and he looked up as I came at him. He had no time at all to block the kick to his throat.

I drew my pistol and fired at two more of them, killing one with a single shot through the face and knocking another down with a sucking chest wound.

In my ear, Lizzie was yelling at me. "Get the book, Joe. We need it."

"Get it and do fucking what with it?"

The answer hit me across the shoulders and I slapped it away, thinking it was a snake. It wasn't. It was one of the rappelling lines. I looked up and saw that far above me it was knotted to a second line. And, I presume, the third far above that. Smart lady, that Lizzie Corbett.

A moment later something thumped down hard behind me and I spun. It was a big canvas equipment bag. My equipment bag. I fired six shots at some spiders and then rushed to it, tore it open and nearly wept.

Fifteen magazines for the MP7s. Grenades. More magazines for sidearms.

I don't know if that was Lizzie's idea or Brock's, but one of those two was going to get a big wet kiss.

"Echo Team," I bellowed. "Ammunition. On me."

Bunny and Top shot looks at me, saw the bag and the dangling rope. They understood. They began sliding along the wall, firing with renewed frenzy. Top's MP7 was slung, probably empty and he was using the grenade launcher. There were dead bodies everywhere. Dozens of them. It was a slaughterhouse. It was what we call a target-rich environment, except that usually doesn't mean that the shooters were likely to lose.

But now we had a chance. I laid down covering fire with my MP7 and lobbed a few grenades as party favors. They ran. We all reloaded and stuffed the magazines into our pouches.

The priests and the spiders kept coming.

There were still so many of them.

I picked up the empty bag and pointed to Mercer. "We need to secure the book and send it up on the rope. All other considerations secondary, hooah?"

"Hooah," they said.

"Grenades," I said. "Blow these fuckers up. Buy me time."

Bunny and Top stood their ground and as Top fired, Bunny hurled one fragmentation grenade after the other. They set a pattern, tossing the grenades just over the front rank so that the priests and spiders in front shielded them from the shrapnel. It was a rinse and repeat method, but we knew it couldn't last. It just had to last long enough.

I threw a pair of grenades underhand at the killers and monsters between me and Mercer, making sure not to over-throw. Lizzie didn't say that I could kill Mercer. Which sucked, because I really, really wanted to.

The pit was filled with lightning and thunder as the grenades detonated. Cracks appeared in the walls. Even worse, the cleft was widening—either from the concussions, or the spell, or the diligence of the spiders in this world and the aliens in the next. It was madness down there. Total madness.

I don't know how long it took me to kill my way to where Mercer knelt. Ten seconds? Ten years?

Time was meaningless. Hope was a nail hammered into the center of my chest. Hate filled my head with thorns. I was deafened and screaming at the top of my lungs.

As the spiders and priests died, I saw Mercer again. With all of the violence and madness around him, he had not moved. Never even looked up, as if he existed in a space apart from this hell hole.

I switched from grenades to knife, not wanting to risk accidentally shooting the prick. There were four priests between me and Mercer, and they tried to form a protective wall.

They tried.

They had big weapons. My knife is a Wilson Rapid Response folding knife with a three and a half inch blade. They should have won, at least in the way they would have calculated the odds. But the math works best for who wants it more. They were fanatics, but I'm actually crazy.

Batshit, monster-in-the-dark crazy.

They tried to keep me from saving my world. They tried hard.

I cut them to pieces.

As the last one fell away, his hands clamped to what was left of his throat, I stepped up to Mercer. He knelt there, his skin steaming with heat like a roasting pig. His dick was still fully erect as if in the throes of the most intense and existential of sexual encounters. I was very tempted to use my knife on him, because this son of a bitch deserved it. But not yet.

Instead, I put my knife in my belt pouch and reached for the book.

Yes. I thought it would be that easy.

Fuck.

15

Touching the book was like touching a live electrical power cord. Not a little one, but a big one. The shock was so intense that my hands clamped onto the covers and I suddenly felt as if I was on fire. My body went totally rigid except for my hair, which stood straight as needles from arms and scalp. The pain was off the scale. There's pain, and then there's agony, and then there's a level that is so big, so comprehensive that you can almost stand back from it and watch. Like seeing your house burn down and take everything you own with it. You're aware of the pain, but it seems somehow unreal.

That kind of pain.

I don't think I screamed. Pretty sure I couldn't at that point. Nor could I move. All that was left for me was to experience it. And to feel myself die.

They say your life flashes before your eyes. That's not true. I've been out on the very edge too many times, so I know.

What happened—at least to me—was that I saw the things I haven't done, the life I had yet to live and would not get to live. I saw my lover, Junie Flynn, running through a dying world as monstrous fighting machines burned the city around her with heat weapons. I saw my brother, Sean, and his family, tangled in the big baskets on the back of one of those tripods, caught like trout and devalued to nothing more than food. I saw my friends and allies, and my fellow soldiers, fighting a losing war against an unbeatable army. Wave after wave of jets and helicopters going after the legions of fighting machines, and then falling like spent fireworks from the sky. I saw the green earth become choked by red weeds, in which the last free people suffered and starved and died.

I saw that.

It was all going to come to pass because of me. Because I'd failed in this task. To take a book away from a man who was not even able to resist.

Because I was not strong enough to do even that.

I wanted to scream. To beg for mercy from everyone who I'd failed. To cry out to Junie and my brother, and all of them.

The heat burned me, and I knew I was dying.

Except...

Maybe it was the Dragon suit that saved me.

Maybe it was that I saw a smile form on Mercer's face, blossoming like a flower of hate in a blighted field. Maybe it was that. A last insult. The sting of mockery, the gloat of triumph.

I don't know what it was. I'll probably never know.

But my hands became mine again. Mine to use, mine to choose.

Mine to move.

My thumbs lifted first. And then each finger in a slow—bitterly slow—choreography of obedience.

And then I was falling. Free of the book. Not free of the pain, though. That came with me as I collapsed. I dropped to my knees. The world was full of thunder and I could feel something warm leaking from my nose and ears. Blood, probably. I coughed and could taste it in my mouth as well.

Mercer turned his head slowly, focusing his blind eyes on me. "Your world will fall."

"F—fuck you," I gasped. I coughed again and spat more of blood into the hood of the Dragon suit. It painted the visor with viscous red, partly obscuring him. All I could see was that smile.

"Joe?"

The voice was in my ear and for a moment I could not tell if it was Junie or my dead mother or...

"Lizzie?" I whispered.

"Joe," she said, "listen to me."

"I..." But really, that was all I could manage.

"Joe," said Lizzie as if from a million miles away, "all we need is the book. Do you understand?"

I mumbled something. Not even sure if they were actual words.

"We just need the book, Joe. Can you hear me?"

"B-b-book..." My vision was dimming. The world was turning red as the edges of the cleft began to crumble. Mercer's smile became a laugh.

"Joe," yelled Lizzie, "we don't need Mercer."

She shouted those words. Over and over again. Trying to reach me. Forcing me to understand.

I spat again. The visor was totally blocked now.

My hands, swollen and burned and nearly useless, rose as if from their own accord. Finding my hood. Finding the seals. Fumbling their way through. Tearing the hood off.

The air was so hot. Like an oven. Like hell.

But I could see.

And I could see James Mercer's fucking smile. That smug, superior, malicious, evil goddamn smile. I wanted to wipe it off his face.

One hand dropped to my lap.

The other dropped to my waist. To the pouch. I could feel the hardness of the folded knife there.

I think maybe I smiled, too.

Mercer stopped smiling when I cut his lips from his face.

16

They pulled me away from him.

Top and Bunny.

What was left of Mercer—what I had left of him—slumped down in red ruin. And as he fell it was as if time caught up with him all at once. His skin immediately caught fire and burned, the fats and oils sizzling and popping and steaming away as he withered to a blackened husk.

I shook free of the hands of my friends and saw that Top had the canvas bag the ammunition had come in. I tore it from his hands and pushed him away from the book, which had fallen to the ground.

"Don't touch it," I wheezed. "Don't."

I wasn't able to do the job, though, so Bunny took the bag from me and used it like oven mitts to nudge the book inside. Then he zipped it up.

When I looked around I saw that the priests were dead. All of them. While I'd fought with the power of the book and with the evil of James Mercer, they had been doing awful work in the cavern. How many dead were there? I don't know. Fifty? A hundred?

The last of the big spiders had retreated and were tearing at the cleft, which was now twice as wide as before.

"We need to get this to Lizzie," I said, trying to stand. They caught me, and we staggered together to the dangling rope. Top took the bag and tied the handles to the rope and shouted for Lizzie to take it up.

The rope shivered and trembled, and then the slack went taut and the Book of Uttu began to rise. We three turned and faced the cleft. With palsied hands, we reloaded and stumbled across the death pit, firing at the spiders. Firing through the cleft. Waging war against the invaders for as long as we could. The pit got hotter and hotter, making it hard for me to breathe without my hood.

Then I heard Lizzie yelling.

"I have it. Get out of there. Joe, Top, Bunny...get out."

"How?" asked Bunny bleakly, but then he turned and looked behind us. "Guys...guys. Look!"

We turned.

The rope was back. But instead of one, there were three. And fires burned more fiercely all around us. Fires that had not been there before. The mounds of priests were already starting to burn.

The wall of the pit had changed, and when I looked up there were no longer stars above us. Instead, through the gas and smoke, I saw the cloudy afternoon sky of Turkmenistan. The walls were no longer impossibly high. Up there, twenty meters above us, I could see

Lizzie and Brock and a bunch of US Marines. And above them two Black Hawk helicopters.

I looked at Top and Bunny. We all glanced at the cleft and then at the ropes.

"Fuck this," I said, and we ran for the ropes.

17

As it turned out, sealing the book was a process. A bastard of one, but Lizzie said she could do it. We lay sprawled at the edge of the pit. Burned, sweaty, half deaf, scared, watching her work. Not understanding a single damn thing of what she did. Trusting that she knew what she was doing.

Then she looked up, flushed and sweaty, with blue eyes as bright as a summer sky. She glanced at the helicopters and down at me.

"Do they have some kind of missiles or rockets or something?"

The Black Hawks had ESSS systems, which are stubby wings loaded with things that go boom. I grinned. "Yeah. They have all of that. Sixteen Hellfire missiles each. How many do you need?"

She chewed her lip for a second. "All of it?" she asked.

I made a call and then we started running away from the pit.

In the brief pause between my order and the execution, Lizzie said, "Hellfire?"

"Yeah," said Top.

"Seems weirdly poetic."

"Yeah," he said.

And hellfire it was.

18

The helos hit the pit with all thirty-two missiles.

Then four choppers from the Turkmeni army came and threw in their own party favors. Four hours later—when we were all at a safe distance—a CIA black ops bird flew over and dropped a fuel-air bomb. Nothing survives that. The pressure wave kills anything organic and the fire cleans it all up. It's the most powerful non-nuclear weapon in existence.

They've since done ground-penetrating radar. There's nothing down there. Nothing moving. Nothing alive.

We survived our wounds. Time will tell if we would survive the memories, and the knowledge that there is an army waiting for us somewhere. Is it actually Mars? I don't know. Certainly not the Mars we know. But I've learned that there are many worlds, and many versions of each world.

That army is out there somewhere. Now we know it.

And...now we're ready.

I hope we're ready.

ISIL is still out there destroying sanctuaries and churches and sacred places where things like the Unlearnable Truths have been stored and protected. We got lucky with this, but Lizzie said that there are many more of those books out there. A lot of them are in lands torn by war. In Iraq and Iran, in Syria. Elsewhere. Even in America. The Library of the Ten Gurus is searching. So are we. So are select friends.

We need to find those other books first.

We need to.

We need to.

The End

THE DEVIL'S THROAT

Rena Mason

Dr. John Blake's gloved hands floated between striated rock walls as he swam through the ancient lava tube toward Shelf 5. The color footage went gray before white horizontal bands rolled down the video screen.

Cyan leaned toward the glass and tapped the monitor. "What the—"

Static blasted from the speakers. "Bloody hell!" she said, jumping back.

"Dr. Blake?" Kau said, his timid voice unexpected from his broad, Māori physique.

Cyan slid the microphone from Kau's hold. "John, what's happening?"

"Wellington, we have a problem." Fear skirted John's voice.

She hated his Kiwi versions of Yankee phrases. They'd met in Corpus Christi, Texas during a Fossil Fuels Drilling and the Environment Conference, and bonded through marine biology, genetics, and ocean science. A perfect match since research consumed ninety-five percent of their lives.

A hazy image froze on every screen in the control room, and then all systems went down.

"Kau, get him back online!" Cyan rushed to the power box and flicked switches.

Kauri Tāmihana, the communications specialist, pounded the dash with his massive fist. Tribal tattoos rippled up his arm as a metallic clang resounded off the aluminum walls. Cyan glared at him from the other side of the room.

"Oops. Sorry."

As it quieted, they tuned their ears into the silence. Panel lights flickered then steadied. Some blinked red.

Mackenzie Brown's voice came over the loud speakers. "Sorry 'bout that, Cy. Generator's fucked."

"Mack, get your ass to comms." Cyan hunched over Kau's shoulder and watched him reboot. "Can you pull up—"

The last bit of feed from John's camera blinked onto his computer, cloudy and fixed.

"Thanks," she said. "But can you clear it up and get it in color?"

"That is color."

Cyan scrutinized the picture. "Are those knots?"

"Black ones?"

"Video cables?" she said. "Did he get tied up in old equipment?"

"What's going on?" Kauri's wife Maia, the station's cook, stood in the doorway.

"Dr. Blake's A/V stopped working," Kau said.

"I'm sure it's something you did." Maia dried her hands with her apron. "Can I help?"

A towering shadow shifted behind her. Mack moved Maia aside and walked in.

"You can go," Kau said to his wife.

"What's wrong with the generator?" Cyan looked up at Mack.

"Couldn't find anything specific," Mack said. "Seems to be happening more. I'll check the cooling systems. Might have to call mainland engineering in to have a look."

"Anything yet?" Cyan rested her hand on Kau's shoulder.

Kau shook his head.

"Dammit. I'm suiting up." She headed out.

Cyan shaded her eyes as she stood on the curved dive entry deck of the partially submerged Rori Underwater Research Facility, built for the scientific study and genetic manipulation of rori—Māori for sea cucumber—for their water filtering abilities. From the air, RURF had the shape of a puzzle piece: two circular areas at bow and stern and the entire deck constructed of long teak planks. The center housed solar panels arranged like flower petals above the generator, pumps, cooling systems, and everything mechanical to do with running RURF. Comms, the lab, kitchen, and their quarters, edged the perimeter. Ballast tanks lined the underside, ocean water pumped in and out to stabilize the platform on the sandy bottom, cooling the equipment and providing air conditioning. Every year scientists and engineers from all over the world visited RURF, a foolproof engineering marvel until now.

Twenty-two meters out, a dark blue circle of calm water separated Cyan from her husband, Dr. John Blake.

Whooping helicopter blades blew golden strands of blonde into her face. "This can't be good." She pulled her hair into a ponytail and hurried to get her gear on.

The chopper landed on the pad, deposited four men in uniform, then took off again. Cyan hadn't even zipped her wetsuit when one of them approached.

"Dr. Blake!" he said.

She ignored him and tugged on the cord behind her, using the helicopter noise as a good excuse to pretend she didn't hear him.

His footsteps rattled the boards under her bare soles. "Dr. Blake. I'm Captain Richards."

Cyan huffed and turned around. "Captain, I don't have time...

What are you doing here? Never mind. Talk to Mack, he's in charge of whatever's going on with the generator. I'm going in."

"No, you're not. Ensign Smith is. I have orders to—"

Kau's curly black hair came up the stairwell, followed by the rest of him. "What's going on?"

Cyan checked her tank, put her vest over the top of it, then latched it into place. "Kau did you call these guys? Maybe Mack did?"

"He's still working on the generator."

Richards stepped in front of her. "Dr. Blake, at zero, eight, thirty-seven hundred hours your husband set off a sensor at Shelf 9. We were deployed immediately as that's a violation of—"

She stopped fidgeting with the regulator and gauge hoses. "What are you talking about? Besides being physically impossible, we never go past the third shelf," she lied.

Within the last few weeks, they'd noticed more productive filtration coming from the sea cucumbers the deeper they went. They'd needed more specimens to study the anomaly. That's why John had gone down to Shelf 5, a restricted area only because of its sixty-meter depth.

Underwater caves and lava tubes branched off the main vent of a dead volcano and then ascended onto dry land shelves further inside. The shelves contained breathable air, making it optimal for human exploration.

Richards' team carried and rolled big black cases and trunks to the dive entry deck. They set them down near her gear and prepped equipment onto a frame she'd always wondered the purpose of. It appeared these men had more familiarity with RURF than she did.

One of them, Ensign Smith she presumed, already had on an NZDF issue black wetsuit. "Oy, why's your gear strapped to nitrox if you ain't going past thirty meters?" he said.

Cyan pointed at Kau and lied some more. "He brought me the wrong tank. See, we're all in a bit of a rush to get to John."

The other two Defence Force members pulled a large helmet from a box and attached it to Smith's odd, hybrid atmospheric suit. It sealed with a click and a hiss. Before she could ask, Ensign Smith stepped into the water carrying a large pack, blasting up plumes of creamy sand and silt.

Asshole.

"Where's your operations room?" Richards said. "My men need to link the A/V."

"Captain, I don't care who you are, we're not switching John's feed to yours."

Richards reached for his sidearm. "I have orders to—"

"John's is still down," Kau said. "I think it'll be okay if they use it."

"Thanks a lot, Kau." She'd said it sarcastically, but he likely just saved her ass.

"Sorry." Kau shrugged and lowered his head.

"Show these men to comms. I'll be there soon." Cyan glanced at the sword and writing on their uniform patches.

The men followed Kau below. She peered over the deck and watched Ensign Smith approach the blue hole, leaving a milky ocean behind him.

"Come back, John," she said. His diving skills ranked in the pro level, and they'd stored plenty of nitrox tanks on the shelves for deeper dives, but she worried anyway. Cyan stepped away when dark water caught her eye. The sunlight and waves distorted everything under the surface, so she squinted and lay prone with her head over the deck.

Ensign Smith's landing had shifted the cover of hundreds, maybe thousands of black sea cucumbers, *Holothuria leucospilota*. Cyan had never seen such a dense population before and wondered how far they spread around RURF's platform. Long white strands, their innards, or Cuvierian tubules, undulated below. Like her, they saw Smith as a threat and went guts out, a self-defense mechanism. She'd see the ensign eviscerated before doing that to herself. Dozens stuck to his boots and legs. No wonder he made such massive silt clouds. Cyan headed for the engineering room. She needed to calm and think straight, not that she'd get that from Mack.

The Aussie was up to his neck in a panel box when she arrived.

"Is that a good idea?" she said.

His head banged gray aluminum as he backed out. "Ouch." He rubbed his skull in quick circles. "You told me to look into it, and that's what I'm doin'."

"So, what's the story with the pumps?" Cyan leaned against a post.

"I can't figure. Says they're functional. Pressure's right. We're still running on stored battery power though, and the cells won't last more than a day or two. We'll have to shut down energy suckers like the lab. And pray clouds don't roll in."

"You call someone out?"

"Thought I heard a choppy topside. No way it's those engineering dills. So, who's here?"

"Military. But not like I've seen before. There's a long sword on their insignia. *Innovative and Agile* or something it reads at the bottom. You were Anzac. Know it?"

Mack scratched the stubble on his chin with the wrench in his hand. "Hmm... Special Ops Forces. What those diggers want with RURF?"

"It's something in the blue hole they're after. They've already sent a man down."

"I'm sure they're just here to rescue John."

"Captain Richards said they came because John triggered an alarm on Shelf 9. Why would they have alarms down there?"

"They've had control since its discovery. RURF's crew's the first non-military they let go near it," Mack said. "How far down you think their secret project goes?"

"I don't know. Deeper than we can venture with our gear." Cyan took in a breath then exhaled. "Honest, I don't give two fucks what's down there, Mack. I just want John back."

"And you trust these diggers'r gonna do that?"

"Come up with me. There's something I need to show you. I have a bad feeling about John, and we can't leave Kau alone with those soldiers for too long or he'll give away all my lies."

"Bloody natives." Mack smiled but kept the wrench in his hand as they headed out.

Cyan didn't question his weapon of choice. Topside, she showed him the dark water, now spread beneath RURF. Off the bow, exposed rori cut a black road to the blue hole.

"Fuck all. What're they doin'?" Mack stared down. "Looks like they're headin' out on holiday to feed the *rēwera o korokoro*."

"Don't call it that! John's down there." Cyan lowered her eyes and waited for them to focus. "Dear god. Their motility..."

"So much for inching along the bottom with their little feet."

"They can't be advancing that fast!"

Fixated, Cyan and Mack followed the movements of the rori horde, raising their heads to the blue hole, or as the Māori call it, the devil's throat.

In comms, Richards gave orders to his men, as well as Kau.

"What's all this?" Mack said.

Laptops from more of their black cases sat atop of the control dashboards, linked by wires and cables.

"Oh, hey," Kau said. "These guys have some cool equipment, you should see—"

"That's classified," Richards said. "A need-to-know only basis, and they don't need to know. We're square on that, right Tāmihana?"

"Okay. Yeah. Sorry." Kau went back to typing on one of the military keyboards.

All the screens blinked on with rock wall shaded in blue hues. Cyan walked over to a laptop monitor that displayed Smith's vital signs. "I see what you mean by cool, Kau."

"I'm coming up on Shelf 3, sir." Ensign Smith's voice came

through cleaner than she'd ever heard. "Permission to head in?"

"Wait," Cyan said.

"Is there something you want to tell me Dr. Blake?" Richards smirked.

"John was going to Shelf 5. We needed specimens from that depth to—"

"Negative, Ensign. Head to Shelf 5." The captain turned back to the screen.

Smug bastard.

The live feed had unbelievable clarity. As he descended, floating white streamers ruffled all around him.

"His suit is impenetrable, right?" she said. "Their excretions can be harmful."

"Yes, ma'am," one of the soldiers said.

"Thank you, Simms," Richards said.

"I've reached Shelf 5, Captain. Permission to enter."

"Go ahead, Ensign."

Cyan sat down in front of a monitor. Mack stood behind her. Ensign Smith hovered in front of the opening.

"Thrusters on," the other soldier said.

"Affirmative." Richards watched Smith propel into the cave.

Lights came on, illuminating dark rocky walls.

"Simms?" Richards said.

"All systems functional, Captain."

Lighter bits of marine life, their excrement or what remained of them, floated in the water like dust motes drifting in air. Cyan synced her breathing to Smith's.

"Do you see any sign of John?" Cyan knew it was a reach, but maybe he'd dragged the cords from the last image his camera froze on with him.

Smith lowered his head, giving them better visuals of the cave bottom.

"Thank you," she said.

Sand and silt covered most of the floor. Occasional dark rocks jutted, but no cables, wires, not even a single fish came into view.

"Have you seen anything swimming around down there?" she said.

"Just me," Smith said. "And this white shite."

"That's unusual. Can he? Can you, get a closer look at those rocks?" Cyan hoped they might be rays, skates, or nurse sharks.

Petty Officer Taylor typed on one of the black keyboards. Then Ensign Smith smacked head first against the bottom of the cave. "Dammit, Taylor!" Smith said.

"It's hard to adjust buoyancy in small spaces. Hang on, or you'll hit the ceiling."

Cream swirled past onscreen. White streamers shot up from the sand.

"What the fuck?" Smith said.

"Ensign, report." Richards leaned toward a monitor.

"Worms. Giant black slugs, crawling on my helmet. Taylor, get me up!" Smith's heartbeat pounded from the laptop, and his breathing became rapid and shallow.

"Calm down," Cyan said. "They're harmless."

The image went out of focus as Smith's suit lifted off the cave floor.

"We can't see them," Taylor said.

"Switch to the suit cam," Richards said.

"Yes, sir. Interior camera on," Simms said.

Black tentacles from the sea cucumbers' open mouths searched the glass for purchase. Their tubule innards stuck to it in a wrestle, like oriental noodles crammed into a package.

"Fuck, that's gross," Simms said.

"Can't you get them off?" Ensign Smith shouted.

"With what?" Taylor said. "The grabbers won't reach. Find something after you molt. Just keep your eyes closed. We'll steer the ADS in."

"That's one helluva suit. Clever bastards," Mack said.

"They're not aggressive." At least Cyan hadn't seen them behave that way before today.

"You sure?" Mack put his face next to hers and stared at the screen. "These look like they'd eat his face if they could get in."

"Something's not right," she whispered.

"Switch back to exterior camera," Richards said.

Overhead lights flickered, the room vibrated then shook. Cyan steadied a laptop as it slid across the dash. Comms panels rattled around her.

"What's happening?" Richards said.

"Mack?" Cyan said.

"I'm on it." He headed out with his wrench.

"Captain, Ensign Smith's reached the surface of Shelf 5," Taylor said.

"Atmosphere? Systems?" The captain stepped to the laptop displaying the exosuit's digital readouts.

"Sustainable, sir. All systems functional," Simms said.

"Proceed with ADS removal."

"Smith, keep moving your legs. It'll feel like you're walking up a ramp."

"Do the thrusters work when he's on land?" Kau said.

"No," Taylor said. "A specialized hydraulics system takes over. That's Simms's specialty."

"That's enough, Taylor," Richards said. "Simms, let's see what you got."

"Has the ground leveled off, Ensign?" Simms tapped the laptop keys in front of him.

"Yeah," Smith said.

"Then sit down where you are and follow standard molting procedures. Take it slow."

"Affirmative."

"Okay, suit separation in three, two, one," Simms said.

Popping then wheezing came through the speakers.

"Systems?" Richards said.

"Stable, sir," Simms said. "Ensign Smith, you can molt now. Don't forget to connect A/V to your wetsuit and turn the system on after you crawl out of ADS."

"Affirmative," Smith said.

"What's ADS?" Kau said.

Simms turned to him. "It stands for Atmospheric Dive Suit, but we call ours a mix of names because it borrows ideas from most of them like the Newtsuit, Exosuit, and the WASP. Ours is lightweight, maneuverable, and specially designed for ease of—"

"Shut it, Simms," Richards said.

"Sorry, Captain." Simms focused on his laptop.

Richards pressed a key and spoke down toward the monitor. "Any sign of Dr. Blake?"

"Negative, sir."

Cyan stood. "I wonder what's keeping Mack."

Mack's voice came through the intercom. "Cyan, meet me at the quarters hall."

"What is it?" she said.

"Now."

Kau faced her with a concerned expression. "Can you check on Maia while you're there? I haven't heard from her in a while."

Cyan walked toward the door then stopped. "Please, let me know if you come across any sign of John."

"Yes, ma'am," Simms said.

Lights came on as Cyan walked down the hall to quarters, but an uneasy darkness there remained thick and unmoving. "Mack? Where are you?"

"In your room," he said.

"What?"

All sleeping quarters had underwater view windows. Mack had his forehead pressed against the glass. But instead of clear, bright blue ocean with fish swimming by, stacked layers of black sea cucumbers blocked all sunlight. Crawling mouth holes puckered and sucked while their tentacles groped for purchase the way they did on Smith's helmet.

Cyan shivered. "Oh my god."

"I may just be the guy who fixes things 'round here, but I think you're right, and these dogs are up to something."

"Is it just this window?"

"Nope. Every one of 'em."

"How do you know?"

"Checked. Can't find Maia either," Mack said.

"Kau asked me to check on her. What am I supposed to tell him?"

Mack pressed his lips to the glass and kissed.

"That's bloody disgusting. Get your shit together. We need to find Maia."

"I think she's out there," he said.

"What?"

"Thought I saw her speargun just over there, before these fuckers came and covered the window."

"That's impossible. They can't move that fast."

"Didn't you say that topside? About their mass exodus down the devil's throat."

"Do you think that's what happened to John?" Cyan said, holding in a sob.

Mack backed away from the glass. "Let's find Maia. Then we'll go after John. She'll be all right. Don't you worry." He led her out by the arm.

Cyan and Mack circled the deck and met at the stern where they found Maia's shoes.

"Looks like she went in for our din-din," Mack said.

"Then where is she?" Cyan scanned the water's surface. "I don't even see the float she uses to bring up her catch."

"Possible she were the one caught this time." He climbed down and stretched his leg out from the last rung of metal stairs that went into the water. After a minute, he pulled in Maia's yellow mask and snorkel. "She couldn't have gone far without these."

"We've got to tell Kau."

When they stepped back into comms, Captain Richards looked up at Mack. "You figure out what all that rattling was? It's happened again twice now."

"Didn't make it to engineering, cap'n sunshine, but I think I know what the problem is."

Cyan walked over to Kau and whispered in his ear.

"What?" Kau pushed away from the desk and stood.

"Calm down, mate," Mack said. "She'll be right."

Cyan rolled her eyes. She wished he'd stop saying that. Especially since she knew he thought the rori had killed her. Murdered by sea cucumbers? No way.

"Smith find any signs of John?" Cyan said.

"No," Richards said. "He's suited up again and is heading to Shelf 9."

"Other than the ones he ran into on the bottom of Shelf 5, has he come across any more of the black sea slugs?" she said.

"Three hundred meters down any hole, everything's black. Is there something we should be concerned about?" Captain Richards glared at her.

"I don't know, exactly," she said. "What's on Shelf 9 that's so damn important?"

"That's classified."

"Then anything I've got to say about the slugs is likewise."

"Where's Maia?" Kau shouted.

He'd never raised his voice before. Mack and Cyan looked at one another with wide eyes.

Smith's voice came through the comms speakers. "Heading into Shelf 9."

They all turned to his video feed. Richards hadn't lied when he said it was black down there. The cave walls absorbed the light beaming from Smith's ADS.

"Can you get a close-up of the rock on the sides?" Cyan said.

"I'm in charge here, Dr. Blake. In fact, all non-authorized personnel, leave the room."

"Piss off, Captain," she said.

Richards reached for his sidearm. "I'm not asking. Taylor?"

Taylor stood up with a pistol aimed at her.

Mack put his hands up. "Oy. Stay calm, mate. We were just leaving." He backed up and pulled Cyan along with him. "Come on Kau. Let's get Maia."

They left comms ass-first and didn't utter a sound or turn around until they passed the corner. Cyan broke their silence. "What the hell, Mack? I wanted to—"

"Get shot?" he said. "They're not going to let any of us see what's down there. It's classified. Don't you get it?"

"He's right," Kau said. "I listened while I was in there, playing dumb so they spoke over my head. The military hid something back in the caverns of Shelf 9. Something dangerous."

"Great," Cyan said.

"Forget about it. Let's get some gear on and head down. We need to find Maia and John and bring them back. Then we can figure out what to do about the diggers." Mack headed for the equipment room.

Kau followed. "You know I'm too big to get into any of that. You two go. I'll get on the lab computers and set up your A/V. You need me here in case the soldiers try something stupid."

"They've already done that, but you're probably right," Cyan said.

"Cy, suit up." Mack had already donned half his gear. "Put the drysuit on. We don't want the...uh, cold to get in."

He loaded their vests onto nitrox tanks and checked the regulators and gauges. The air mixture had to be just right for deeper dives. "I'll carry these up," Mack said. "Grab knives, spearguns, lights, flares, and whatever else you can carry."

"You really need all that?" Kau said.

"I don't want to take any chances." Mack headed for the diving deck.

"Let me make sure A/V's working before you jump in." Kau walked toward the lab.

After putting on his Predator full-face mask, Mack helped Cyan with hers. "Can you hear me?" he said.

Cyan nodded. "Loud and clear."

"Copy that," he said. "Kau?"

A high-pitched squeal, static, and then Kau's voice came through the Predator's speakers. "Audio's solid. Turn each other's cameras on."

Mack pushed the button on the side of Cyan's mask.

"Cy's is working," Kau said.

Cyan adjusted Mack's camera then turned it on.

"Cams are up and recording. The pressure in your suits is good, too. Be careful down there."

They gave each other the thumbs up in front of the cameras for Kau.

"Fill up," Mack said. "Let's float to the hole."

"I'm right behind you."

Mack stepped off the deck and into the water. He submerged less than three meters then popped to the surface. She followed him in, eyes fixed on the bottom as they moved toward the devil's throat.

"You seeing this?" Cyan adjusted her mask.

"Yeah," Mack said.

"Are those all rori?" Kau said. "They look like they're moving as fast as you."

"Reckon that's 'cause they are, mate."

"Doc, what did you do to them?" Kau said.

"Since the Cook Islanders let other countries come and harvest them to near extinction, we genetically altered them to increase filtration. That's it. The breeding rate and motility of these are... It's unprecedented. Are you recording all this, Kau?"

"Yes, Doc. But I've got a bad—"

"Don't say it," Mack said. "We'll go around the platform and look for Maia."

The piles of sea cucumbers decreased the original depth of the ocean floor around RURF by five meters. Incredible.

Mack moved his fins in long, steady kicks with Cyan gliding in his wake.

"I'm not seeing any signs of her," Kau said. "Only the rori. So many..."

"I'm sorry," Cyan said. "We'll look again on our way back."

"You're right. Go. You'll need all the nitrox in your tanks to find Dr. Blake. I can look for her, too. Maia's a good swimmer. Maybe she went further away from the deck then she realized."

"You're right about that," Mack said. "I wouldn't be surprised if she'd swam all the way to the nearest atoll, looking to bring you home a good sup."

Talking between them ceased as if they knew she'd gone, giving her a moment of silence. Cyan pictured Kau in the lab, crying. Mack neared the blue hole's opening and waited for her to catch up. Just the two of them took up most of the circle, its size deceptive compared to what waited below.

"Going in," Mack said. "Lights on, Cy."

He reorganized his spearguns. They each carried two with four extra shafts. Cyan turned on her torch and secured the cord around her wrist. At the entrance to *rēwera o korokoro*, they faced each other, floating upright.

"Ready?" Mack said.

"Let's go." Behind him, the darkness of the rock wall moved.

"Look at me," he said. "Keep your eyes on me as we descend, understand?"

She nodded, grabbed her buoyancy control, and released air in quick bursts from her suit and vest. Sunlight coming through the small opening faded as they drifted down into the devil's throat.

"With what we've got on, we're going to have about ten minutes of nitrox more or less, plus whatever's stored in the tanks on the shelf. We might have to take turns so one of us can watch the other," Mack said.

"What if he's not there, and went down to Shelf 9 like the captain said? If he's been at that depth—"

"Don't think it. Smith's on nine. If John's there, he'll bring him back, make sure he stops and decompresses."

"Oh, yeah," she said. "They'll figure out a way to link up and buddy-breathe."

"That's it," Mack said. "Doc Cy's back in action. Kau, you reading us?"

Nothing but silence came through the speakers. Most dives, no matter how deep, the ocean always made sounds. A cacophony of fish rummaging and nibbling on coral, and popping and crackling came from all around, even movement of the surrounding water created gulping and swooshing noises. In the devil's throat, though, silence made a deafening background. So, she focused on her breath sounds, slowing her respirations by listening to her breathing pattern. The deeper they went, the harder the pressure made it to inhale. Cyan often had to remind herself to draw in a breath.

She and Mack stared at one another, and she knew John's chances by the look in his eyes. Not a bit of evidence marked his way. They'd waited too long.

Static blasted through the darkness and into their headset speakers. Kau panted then stopped. "Doc? Mack?"

"Kau!" Cy said.

"They're not far behind you."

"Who?" Mack said.

"The soldiers. They locked me in the supply closet, but I busted out. Something happened to Smith on Shelf 9. They lost comms with him, then came and found me. Saw that you'd left."

"How many of them?" Mack said.

"All three," Kau said. "And they've got guns. RURF's been overrun by rori. Biting ones. They knocked out the battery and panels. Internet's down. I'm using my laptop on deck to talk with you."

"What?" Cyan shouted into her mask.

"They tore Taylor's leg up pretty bad, but he didn't want to stay."

"You need to get in the boat and head to land, Kau. Get help!" Cyan said.

"I can't leave you though—"

"The hell you can, and will," Mack said. "Go now! We'll find John and shelf up for air and decompression."

"Mack's right," Cyan said. "You're the only who can get away to call for a rescue. What did the captain say they were going to do down here?"

"Protect Shelf 9 at all costs," Kau said.

The audio went out.

"Can you hear me?" Cyan looked at Mack who shook his head no.

"Dammit," she said.

They both looked up, and the opening appeared smaller, as if the devil's mouth might swallow them whole.

Mack gently rolled sea cucumbers back into the water with his boots as they walked up onto Shelf 5. They neither went guts out or attacked him. Mack leaned his spearguns against the cave wall next to a row of ten nitrox tanks then helped Cyan take off her mask.

"Do you think they brought another exosuit with them?" she said.

Mack removed his full-face Predator as well. "Don't think so. One set of huge cases was all I saw. Unless they had one drop-shipped after we went under."

"Kau said the backup generator... But they probably have military satellite phones. Maybe they got a call out before it shut down. Please, god. I hope Kau made it."

"Of course he did. She'll be right yet. You'll see."

"Stop. If you tell me now he likely found Maia snorkeling and picked her up on his way, you'll lose me."

Mack laughed. "I'm not crazy, Cy. Maia was hiding in the boat this whole time, and Kau found her when he threw the cover off."

"I really wish that were true. It would give me more hope..." Cyan looked behind him, up the rocky trail into the cave of Shelf 5. "Come on. Let's find John."

A single layer of sea cukes covered the trail. They parted as she and Mack headed in. "How are they surviving on dry land?" Cyan crouched and pointed her torch down then up the walls. "Where do you think they're going?"

"Hell if I know. These ones look confused."

He was right. Some slithered deeper into the cave, while others wiggled the other way. One plopped onto her shoulder from the ceiling and she screamed. Mack brushed it off and it fell onto another one, then headed up the wall again.

"Maybe being out of the ocean is affecting their behavior," she said.

Mack stopped and shined his light along the cave floor. "Why would John go deeper if what he came to get was all around him?"

"You're right."

They eyed one another, thinking.

"There's no way we can get to Shelf 9," he said.

Shouting and screaming echoed from the entrance. Mack raised his spearguns and rushed toward the calamity. Cyan stood and pointed her torch down the long dark path. "John? I know you're down there."

She'd never come this far into the cave before. Her instincts told her to go deeper still.

A gunshot boomed then rang out. "Mack!" Cyan readied her

spearguns and ran back the way she came.

Three men stood near the water, one lying on the ground in a pool of blood. Her hands shaking, she raised her speargun.

Mack turned around and saw her. "Stop! These dills shot their own man."

"He was dead anyway," Richards said. "We should've left him at the first shelf. Those things followed his trail. We couldn't keep them off him."

"So you killed him?" Cyan said.

"No. We gave him mercy. Your man topside told us you modified these things. They're what killed Taylor," Richards said.

"We need this nitrox," Simms said. He opened up his laptop case and started typing. "Smith's still not replying, sir."

"You can't have it," Mack said. "We're using it to find John. Then we're heading back."

"There is no back," Richards said. "Your platform was on fire when we descended."

Cyan stepped closer. "And you left Kau there? You bastards!"

"Don't believe him, Cy. He got away. We'll find John and then head up." Mack raised one of his spearguns.

"You won't win this fight, *mate*." Richards pointed a handgun at Mack. "You can either help us, and we all get out, or fight us and die here."

Something bobbed to the surface at the water's edge. "I got it!" Simms set his laptop down, went over, and pulled floating pieces of exosuit out onto the rocky ground.

"Is that the one Smith had on?" Cyan said.

Richards nodded.

"Then he must've made it onto Shelf 9," she said.

"Maybe," Richards said. "Not that it matters much now. Lower your weapons."

"All right, be calm," Mack said. "You opened it while he was in it, though? You dag."

"Oh my god." Cyan gasped and slipped forward, squeezing her trigger.

A shot cracked the air. Wet heat splattered Cyan's face. She dropped to her knees. "Mack!" His body fell back with a thud. The bullet left a hole between his eyes. Half of Cyan's spear stuck out of the captain's shoulder. He grabbed the base of his neck and winced. "Simms, get this out!"

"It's barbed, Captain." Simms grabbed a pair of bolt cutters and a small package from his case then placed the blades around the shaft.

"I'd have pulled it myself if it wasn't."

"Okay, then. On my count. Three, two..." He snipped, and the captain howled then swore, spewing saliva from the corners of his lips as Simms dropped the cutter and yanked the metal from Richards's flesh. He tore open the package and injected white into the hole. Richards screamed as the substance foamed. Simms went around and removed the other half of the shaft then filled the exit wound. Then he dropped the syringe, picked up Richards's gun, and went back to his laptop. "There's morphine if you want it."

"Not before I go down," Richards said. He glanced at his shoulder, no longer bleeding, then eyed Cyan. "Polyurethane. I don't think it'll help your friend, though. Sorry. Involuntary finger twitch to being shot with a speargun." Richards dragged Taylor's body to the water's edge and rolled it in with his foot. Hundreds of rori on the cave floor twisted and flopped in after it.

How were these sea cucumbers surviving on land? They also seemed attracted to blood. They'd covered every inch of Mack while Simms worked on Richards. Cukes slithered over one another on top of his corpse, excreting slick, milky froth, a spawning and fertilization practice that occurs underwater. The DNA manipulations she and John had made shouldn't have caused these runaway evolutionary developments, and so fast. Her mind raced, but she remained kneeling, unable to move.

Richards put on the upper half of the exosuit. Sea cucumbers climbed his leg, sucking at the blood that had run down his wetsuit. With a few keystrokes, Simms sealed the helmet on. Richards shook his foot. All the rori on him went guts out, shooting white strings like fireworks across his lower extremities. "Get them off!"

Simms yanked them free, chucking their carcasses at the water. He brought over the bottom half of the suit and secured Richards into it.

"You ready, Captain?"

Richards nodded.

Simms went back to work on his laptop. The suit arm pushed Taylor's bobbing remains aside then descended.

She had a mission to complete too. Cyan scoured the cave entrance, stopping at the nitrox. Her Predator mask and vest sat on the ground nearby.

Simms watched her switch tanks and gear up.

"Where are you going?" he said.

Richards' voice came through the laptop's speakers. "Better be Shelf 9."

"I wasn't talking...never mind," Simms said. "I see you've made it to the opening. What's your status?"

"I can't see anything down here but shit. Like swimming through a long drop with the sea slugs everywhere. Tell Dr. Blake I'll be reporting her for shooting me with a speargun, and for creating these bloody monsters."

"Um, yes, sir."

"Lead the way in, Simms. And make sure she's not watching the footage!"

Cyan stepped over to the rori cocoon that encased Mack and picked up one of his spearguns. "I don't think John set off an alarm on 9. The cukes probably did. I'm heading further in to find him." She pointed at the dark end of the cave with the spear tip. "Try not to bleed while I'm gone. Seems they're drawn to it."

"Thanks." Simms eyed her weapon then glanced down at his guns. "You'd get there faster without all that equipment."

"I'm taking it with, in case you two decide to head out on your own and take everything with you. But, eh, you wouldn't want to give me one of those now, would ya?"

"Don't think so. Besides, I've seen your handiwork, and you're better off with that."

"Can you tell me now, then," she said, "what's down there on Shelf 9?"

"It's classified. But don't worry. There's no chance it's anything to do with your science project run amok, I promise."

"That's bloody reassuring."

Screams blared through Simms's laptop. Richards came on, yelling blather about the rori cracking his helmet glass.

Cyan clicked the torch around her wrist and headed in, carrying her mask in one hand, speargun in the other. She didn't want to be around for the captain's return.

Who knew Shelf 5 went back so far? Fewer sea cucumbers traveled to and fro along the tunnel the further in she went. After about an hour, her body ached, and she sweated buckets in the neoprene, which sloshed in her boots as she hiked deeper still. Something glinted near a rori. A bolt snap from John's buoyancy compensator with a miniature US flag attached. She knew he'd gone into Shelf 5. Cyan put the clip in her pocket and carried on.

The cave narrowed, and the hefty tanks bore down her shoulders. Their steel scraped against the rock walls, shoving her off balance from one side to the other. Cyan unfastened the vest and let everything slide to the ground. Then she dragged the gear, hoping the nylon BC wouldn't snag and tear, harming the inner air bladders.

Gunfire, then shrill screams, bounced off the rock surrounding her. Richards and Simms, she thought. They'd have to wait. Cyan trudged on, and hunched then crawled as the cave walls closed in. When she had to lie prone and pull herself forward, rori inching alongside her, she debated leaving the gear. The torch went out, and

Cyan whimpered then cursed. Cold stone met her punching fists, but she avoided striking sea cucumbers on the ground, getting her sad out.

A distinctive blue glow rippled several meters ahead—an easy distance. The tunnel ended in a short drop to a brilliant pool at the bottom of a dome covered with bioluminescent algae. It would be the most beautiful thing she'd ever seen under any other circumstance.

John's glove floated in the water below.

He'd come this far, and she would too. Cyan stretched and wiggled forward with a firm grip on the gear. Her neck strained to keep her chin and the top of her head from hitting solid rock underneath and above. She inhaled, held her breath, and squeezed out as if the stone bore her.

Icy water stung as she plunged in, gasping for air after bobbing to the surface. The speargun slipped away and sank while she geared up with shaking hands. She turned on the visor light and released air from her BC in bursts, descending into the unknown.

Cyan trembled at the abyss beneath her. No light could penetrate that darkness. Its depth, she hoped, would remain a mystery. Her heart clenched and she forced herself to look away. Light beamed up the wall, revealing a lava tube opening. She spun around and lit up what she could, not finding anything else. The entrance appeared to get smaller as she approached.

Damn. The tanks won't fit.

After securing her mask and hoses, Cyan once more dragged her equipment along as she pulled forward, propelling through the small tube. Much easier floating with almost weightless gear behind her.

The visor light was bright in the smaller space. In the middle of her mask, swirling salt and fresh water made visibility zero. Just above and beneath the halocline, the separate waters were clear. Fresh water, down here? This had to be an ancient tube. It's no wonder John had gone to such lengths. But what led him to it?

She hadn't seen a single rori since the dome pool.

The lava tube narrowed, and the tanks clinked against stone. Exertion quickened her breaths as she pulled her body ahead. Neoprene caught at her chest and scuffed along the bottom. If the space got any tighter, she'd get stuck and have to back out.

Another pull moved her forward and then her upper torso floated in a larger area, possibly a dead volcano vent. Across the way, she saw John staring at her with wide eyes through his mask.

"John!"

Cyan twisted and writhed to be free of the lava tube. She put the BC on, then swam to her husband. His arms floated in front of him. A bare white hand with a missing glove glowed underwater. She pulled hers off and fumbled for his carotid, unable to find a pulse.

"No!" Tears came, then crying, followed by sobbing and choking. "Why, John? Why? We should have left them alone."

She lowered her head then took his hands, pressed her booties against the wall and pulled. His body budged a little. After a few attempts, she stopped. "Damn you, John! I'm not leaving you here. Help me!"

Cyan braced hard, then yanked, freeing John from the lava tube. His mask bumped into hers and his mouth opened. His jaw moved, and she waited for him to speak.

Black rori young crawled out.

Her mask puffed out with a scream, and she pushed him away.

A cloud of black sea cucumbers encroached John. Cyan took off her vest and kicked until she'd re-entered the tube, pulling her gear along as it tugged the seal around her mask. Cold saltwater rushed in just up to her nostrils and sloshed up with her movements. Hustling, she focused, breathing only through her mouth. Searing pain shot through her skull as she snorted seawater through her nose and bumped her head across craggy rocks. Her chin slammed against the bottom, filling her vision with stars, but she kept going and grabbed whatever felt solid, launching forward, using the tips of her toes to propel.

The tube opened up, but it grew difficult to draw in a breath. Tanks and gages behind, as well as a rori horde, she couldn't stop to check them but knew the supply had dwindled.

Nitrox from the tanks sweetened and grew colder as it thinned. Her next breath stopped short. Cyan reached out, clutched a rock and pulled, shooting ahead and kicking hard. Fog coated the interior mask. The seal squeezed, and her head pounded. Air!

She reached the dome, nothing coming through the regulator as she kicked upward, the tanks a dead weight behind her. Hitting the surface, she took in a deep wheeze of air that burned her throat and lungs. Without looking back, she climbed the rock face up into the cave.

Pain bit her knees, elbows, and hands, crawling then walking crouched in shredded neoprene over sharp rocks and jagged stones. The cavern's diameter increased, and Cyan stood and ran. Sea cucumbers massaged her calves as they clung and squirmed over the drysuit. She lost her footing on goo and slid out the tunnel entrance into a wall of rori.

Richards and Simms wrestled, rolling and squashing sea cucumbers as they fought. The exosuit pieces lay near the edge of the water. Cukes mashed as she rolled then crept toward Simms's gun.

A shot fired, and she froze. Richards kicked Simms's body into a mountain of cukes, then he spun with his gun aimed. Rori enveloped him from head to toe. Half of one wriggled from his neck, streaming trails of blood down his chest.

"You did this!" Crimson gurgled from his mouth and down his chin. "You and your husband deserve—"

Cyan squeezed the trigger. *Saving him from misery.*

She pulled herself up and trudged on, ignoring the ocean's salty sting. Its coolness soothed her sore legs. Exosuit parts scraped rock and squished more cukes as she dragged them out. Cyan shed what remained of her dry-suit laden with carcasses. Leaving her diveskin on, she slipped into the torso housing.

The leg component landed on a wrestle of cukes after she'd thrown it, unable to connect the pieces. "Dammit!" She stomped over, then crouched to pick it up. Rori reached out and grabbed her wrist, human flesh visible beneath the slimy black.

Her screams reverberated as Simms pulled closer. Holes and gouges marred his face. Several rori remained latched there, sucking. Cyan gripped and yanked, lugging him from the pile. His other hand held onto the laptop.

"Put it on." Simms moaned and swiped cukes off the keyboard with raw skeletal fingers.

Cyan ran and grabbed the other parts, then suited up.

He sealed the ADS then waved her off.

"Thank you," she said.

Simms typed, and the exosuit came to life and squeaked, pumped air bursts, then moved into the water. Sea cucumbers ebbed and flowed as she swam out of the underwater cave.

Ascending the vent, Cyan exhaled, looked up through cracked class and saw no light.

The devil's mouth had closed.

The End

A PLAGUE OF LOCUSTS
Michael McBride

Army Air Forces NewsReels, Reel 2, 1942

*A **country at** war! The Army Chemical Corps is in double-step to provide the armaments of war an embattled world must have if democracy's to survive. America's vast resources are being harnessed to produce chemical and incendiary munitions for our boys overseas. With construction completed on the Rocky Mountain Arsenal in Denver, chemistry genius joins with the muscle of thousands of patriotic men and women to win for the ways of freedom. Its present-day production of chlorine and mustard gas, lewisite and white phosphorous is but a mere fraction of the job that lies ahead. As cluster bombs and loaded shells roll off the assembly line and begin their journey around the globe, the forces of liberty can rest assured that the Chemical Corps will meet the demands of the war efforts and bring victory to the side of the right. Take that, Hitler!*

1966

Rocky Mountain Arsenal, Commerce City, Colorado

"How did it happen?" Major Jack Randall asked.

"We're still trying to figure that out," Dr. James Thompson said.

The two men were diametric opposites. Where Randall was broad and muscular, Thompson was narrow and soft. They made for an unusual pairing as they strode down the corridor toward the laboratory known as The Warren. The soldiers guarding the door saluted and parted to make way for their commanding officer and chief civilian scientist.

"You'd better figure it out in a hurry."

Chemsuits and gas masks hung from hooks on the wall beside the chemical showers. Randall watched the men inside the sealed lab through the reinforced glass while he donned his protective gear. He entered the outer chamber of the airlock and waited for Thompson to close the door behind them before opening the inner seal.

The entire wall to his right was covered with racks of wire cages. The rabbits housed here were designated for the nerve gas program, which had been established in response to the Army arriving in Germany with its mustard gas and lewisite only to find itself confronted with an arsenal of chemical weapons that made theirs look like novelty itching powders by comparison. The Nazi G-agents were lethal in minuscule concentrations and had the potential to wipe out armies with a single warhead and, worse, entire cities with a barrage of intercontinental ballistic missiles.

Thus, the plants at the RMA had been transitioned to the production of sarin—the deadliest of the G-agents—and the race had commenced to stockpile as much as humanly possible in the shortest amount of time, which necessitated the installation of early detection mechanisms in case of accidental release, a job perfect for these rabbits.

Had any of them still been alive.

Randall opened one of the cage doors, grabbed the lifeless ball of fur, and lifted it from the litter. Its tongue protruded from between its long, hooked teeth. The glimmer of life had faded from its waxen eyes, but its body remained limp.

"This couldn't have happened more than a few hours ago," he said.

"3:56 AM, to be precise," Thompson said. "The men were alerted by the screaming."

"Screaming?"

"That's how they described it. They were at the end of the hall. By the time they arrived, all of the rabbits were dead."

Randall set the animal on the stainless steel examination tray behind him, then reached into the cage. The rubber gloves minimized the sensitivity of his fingers, forcing him to grab handfuls of the litter and sift it through his fingers until he found what he was told would be there. Even then he was surprised to find the locust carcasses.

"How did they get in here?" he asked.

"We believe through the ventilation ducts."

"How in God's name did they get out of their cage in the first place?"

"You wouldn't believe me if I told you. It's one of those things you're just going to have to see for yourself."

"Wasn't someone supposed to be monitoring them?"

"According to the logs, he rounded right on schedule."

Randall manipulated one of the dead insects into the palm of his glove. The African desert locust. *Schistocerca gregaria.* It looked like the grasshoppers in the surrounding plains, only larger and rust-colored, with a black face and red eyes. Its entire body was riddled with holes, as though someone had repeatedly punctured its carapace and abdomen with a pin.

He turned around to qualify his discovery with the doctor, only to find him studying the rabbit on the examination tray so closely that his face shield was within inches of it. Thompson sorted through the animal's fur, revealing fresh pinprick lesions inflicted so close to its time of death that neither bleeding nor attempted healing had occurred.

"The locusts attacked them?" Randall said.

"That's how it appears, although these look more like puncture wounds than bites."

"But that shouldn't have killed them."

"You're right, but, for the life of me, I can't tell you what did."

While Uncle Sam considered the chemical warfare program his priority, he invested heavily in the burgeoning field of biological weaponry. Four square miles of the arsenal had been devoted to growing grain infected with a plant pathogen called wheat stem rust. *Puccinia graministritici,* known as Agent TX, was more than a mere nuisance species. An infection not only decreased the yield of a crop by twenty percent, it increased the risk of contracting mycotoxicosis from ingestion, effectively wiping out entire harvests. This one anticrop agent had the potential to cripple even the mighty Soviet Union and starve its people, ending a theoretical third world war before the first shots were even fired.

Of course, this particular fungus had an added benefit with extraordinary military applications. It could be used to harvest deoxynivalenol, a toxin that could be used to both incapacitate and kill, depending upon the concentration.

Randall supervised both the plant responsible for its purification, storage, and shipment to Beale Air Force Base in California and the laboratory where they tested experimental methods of dispersal. TX couldn't simply be loaded into a bomb and dropped into a field without serving as a declaration of war. There was an entire team devoted to stealthier means of release, chief among them the use of insects as vectors to spread the infection.

The Japanese had successfully tested the use of fleas to spread the plague, but their plan to disperse them by balloon was impractical. Even if the fleas managed to survive the plummet from high altitude, once they were free to roam the streets, the efficacy of the plan was under the direct control of so many mindless creatures. There was no doubt the plague would eventually take root, but as a weapon it lacked the immediacy necessary during times of war, which were won in the here and now, not some number of months into the unknown future. Plus, there was no means of containing the bacterium. Had the Japanese not surrendered when they did and Operation Cherry Blossoms at Night been set into motion, those infected during the planned assault on San Diego could have easily carried the disease right back across the Pacific with them on any of the Naval vessels stationed there. What they needed was both immediacy and containment, which was where Randall's hand-selected team of scientists came in.

It wasn't enough that a wheat stem rust infection would set into motion a series of events that would slowly lead to economic ruin and starvation, it needed to do so in a fast and predictable manner. The African desert locusts were the swarming variety, the kind that descended as a cloud upon a field and left nothing but inedible stalks in their wake. This particular species could be counted upon to lay siege to the targeted fields, but the problem quickly became one of containment. An aggressive swarm could follow the grain belt west and cut a swath across the Ukraine and Eastern Europe, leaving behind worthless acres infected with wheat rust to such an extent that nothing would grow there for years to come, but if their theory was correct, they'd finally found a solution.

Or at least they thought they had.

Randall stood in the center of the entomology lab, surrounded by six-foot-tall glass aquariums swarming with locusts. All except for one, anyway. The glass was cracked and the lid canted upward ever so slightly. It took him a moment to realize that the damage had been inflicted from the inside, where, unlike the other cages, wheat plants grew largely unmolested. The soil, however, was littered with small bones, feathers, and scavenged bird carcasses.

"What the hell happened here?"

"Show him what you showed me," Thompson said.

Like all of the civilian scientists, Stephen Waller wore black-rimmed glasses, a white lab coat, and his ID badge clipped to his breast pocket. He was their resident entomologist, a field Randall suspected he'd chosen because of his physical resemblance. He was tall and slender and moved as though he possessed joints where others didn't.

"If you'll follow me, Sergeant," he said, and led the way around the back of the aquarium to the ladder leaning against it. He gestured to it and Randall ascended until he was just above the level of the lid. It was immediately apparent what had happened.

Randall traced his fingertips across the raised edge of the lid. The bodies of hundreds of locusts were crammed into the seam, one on top of another, so many that they'd used the sheer mass of dead bodies to raise the lid high enough for the remainder to squeeze out.

"Extraordinary," Randall whispered.

"More than that, sir. This level of coordination is beyond anything we've ever seen. Not even honeybees exhibit such extreme hive-mind behavior. These individuals willingly sacrificed themselves so that the others could escape. That's higher-level thinking not traditionally associated with so-called lower orders of life."

Cattail-like spines protruded from the carcasses. They were actually the stalks of a fungus called *Ophiocordyceps unilateralis*, an entomopathogenic species from Thailand that infected ants, causing them to climb a specific plant to a predesignated height, bite onto the underside of a leaf, and cling there until the fungus consumed its body and produced an explosion of spores from its fruiting bodies. The locusts had been suitable vectors for the wheat stem rust bacterium, but the *unilateralis* had only infected one of the twelve groups exposed to it—the one bred for aggressiveness toward avian predators, a flock of which could end their infestation before it began—and even then only a small number had survived to repopulate the swarm.

"We suspect the locusts' behavior served a similar function to that of the 'death grip' of the ants' mandibles, which the fungus utilizes to immobilize its host while it parasitizes it," Thompson said. "Or at least that's our working theory."

"You're telling me the fungus made them cram themselves into a tiny crack until there were enough dead bodies to raise the lid?" Randall said.

"That's how it works, sir," Waller said. "The spores attach to the exoskeleton, burrow through it using a combination of enzymes and mechanical force, and spread throughout the body in their yeast stage. They then infiltrate the insect's brain and assume control of its motor functions."

"A fungus can't think."

"It can in the sense that the ant—or, in this case, the locust—is able to. Its sole biological imperative is the perpetuation of its species, which means that it will do everything within its power to achieve its reproductive potential."

Randall lifted one of the compressed carcasses from the rim. It looked like it had been stomped by a shoe. Several others came away with it, all of them tangled together by a snarl of stalks and some kind of white fuzz.

"What's this furry stuff?"

"Hyphae. They're thin filaments that spread throughout the host's body while the fungus consumes it. They help maintain structural integrity and form a network not unlike our own circulatory or nervous systems."

Randall remembered the holes in the exoskeletons of the locusts he found in the rabbit cages.

"So where are all of these growths on the ones that escaped?"

"*Its rate of proliferation is staggering,*" Thompson said through the speaker, which made his voice sound tinny.

Randall leaned right up against the window to get a better view of the rabbit on the dissection tray inside The Warren's sealed lab. Its front and hind legs had been stretched out and pinned to the black wax. The flesh had been parted straight up its spine, the skin and fur retracted, and the naked musculature exposed. The spinous processes of its vertebrae were elongated by the stalk-like growths protruding from them. The base of its skull had been opened to reveal its brain and cranial nerve bundles.

He pressed the button and spoke into the microphone so his chief scientist could hear him.

"It looks like it's already infiltrated the central nervous system."

"*We theorize that it entered the circulatory system via the superficial capillaries and crossed the blood-brain barrier in the same manner it breaks through the exoskeleton of an insect,*" Thompson said. "*There's a minimal amount of hemorrhaging and midline shift, but the greatest hematological difference appears to be in the total volume of residual blood, which we estimate to be roughly half that of a living specimen.*"

"There was no blood on the substrate."

"*Precisely.*"

"The fungus is feeding on the blood?"

"*More likely incorporating it into its biomass in much the same way other multicellular species of fungi grow from corpses and* accelerate the process of decomposition."

"Then how did they manage to infect the locusts in the first place?"

"Ophiocordyceps unilateralis *is incredibly susceptible to infection from other fungi, which is why it doesn't simply wipe out entire ant species wherever it goes. It's nature's way of keeping its reproduction in check. To protect the fungus-host ecosystem, it engages in what's known as secondary metabolism, a process by which it produces the antibacterial agents necessary to stave off pathogens during the reproductive cycle. That's why none of the other test batches survived. The antibodies they produced caused the wheat stem rust to produce deoxynivalenol in response to the threat, killing the* unilateralis *before it could assume command of the host's motor functions. The locusts that had been bred for their aggressive response to predatory species added an element to the equation in the form of a foreign blood source, a threat against which all three species—fungal and host alike—were forced to work in tandem."*

Thompson used a pair forceps to lift off the crown in the rabbit's skull, which peeled away from the brain with long strands reminiscent of worms. The fungus had already taken root and was in the process of growing through the cranium.

"It's metabolizing the blood," Randall said.

"*That's our working hypothesis*," Thompson said. "*It's consuming some component of the blood to produce the antibodies that allow it to circumvent the immune response and proliferate unchecked within the host's body."*

"So what's the end result?"

"*Any speculation at this point would be premature."*

"I don't want speculation, Doctor. I want answers."

Randall glanced at the rabbit one last time before leaving the lab. He could have sworn there were even more filaments protruding from the muscles to either side of its spine than there'd been when he arrived.

"Are you sure this is what they want?" Corporal Lyle Benjamin asked. "Because there's no going back from this. We've never decommissioned a well of this nature before, largely because such a thing has never existed until now. This is uncharted territory for us. This isn't a well where we've extracted oil and water's going to take its place. We've actively injected massive amounts of chemicals into porous rock where there wasn't space for them to begin with."

Randall looked up at the rigging of the derrick, which towered over them like a five-story spike driven into the earth. The chief engineer was right, of course, but he resented having his orders questioned. The instability was the whole reason they were decommissioning the 12,045-foot deep injection well, which had been commissioned for the disposal of waste chemicals from the weapons program and the commercial interests leasing space on the arsenal.

The original plan had been to allow the chemicals to precipitate in open-air, asphalt-lined holding basins the size of small lakes. Unfortunately, they'd contaminated the groundwater to such an extent that farmers dozens of miles away were losing entire harvests. The backup plan of sealing the waste in drums and dumping it into the ocean had proven too costly, necessitating the alternative of burying it so deep that it couldn't infiltrate the groundwater through the bedrock. The flaw was that the high pressure required to force fluid into a space not designed to accommodate it had triggered a series of earthquakes, a regrettable outcome, to be sure, but nothing catastrophic. At least it wasn't until the cause of the unprecedented seismic activity made the papers.

Honestly, Randall didn't care one way or the other. Production was his concern, not disposal, and he had enough on his plate today that he didn't have the time or the patience to hold the hand of an engineer who'd already received his orders from higher up the chain of command.

"Just get it done," he said.

"It's not as easy as plugging a hole. We have no idea how the concrete casings held up to the corrosive effects of the chemicals. We thought three concentric layers was overkill at the time, but we also thought the waste wouldn't be able to eat through half an inch of asphalt. It's possible that the pipe itself is the only thing holding the well together and once we remove it, the whole damn thing will collapse."

"Then leave the pipe."

"If we do, we risk the pressure building and creating a toxic geyser like Old Faithful."

"Then take it out. What do you want me to say?"

"Here's the thing," Benjamin said. "The bottom seventy feet has no lining whatsoever. We've pumped hundreds of thousands of gallons of toxic chemicals into permeable Precambrian metamorphic rock. Lord only knows what effects they had on it. There could very well be a cavity eroded under half the state and we're about to destabilize the whole works."

Randall heard his name shouted from a distance and turned to see Thompson running across the field toward him. The production plants were little more than silhouettes against the plains behind him. He'd never seen the scientist in the sunlight before, let alone moving at a pace anywhere close to a jog. Something must have happened in the lab. Something of a sensitive nature that couldn't be broadcast across the open airwaves. Time to end this conversation.

"You have your orders, Corporal. Tear the damn thing down."

Benjamin's eyes narrowed and his jaw muscles bulged.

"Yes, sir."

Randall turned his back on the engineer and struck off down the dirt road to meet Thompson. Benjamin immediately started barking orders behind him and the engines of demolition vehicles roared to life.

Thompson stopped a hundred yards away and had to double over to catch his breath. Randall closed the gap and pulled the scientist upright by the back of his lab coat.

"What is it, Doctor?" he asked.

"There are no words to describe it. You have to see it to believe it."

TODAY

Channel 7, News Update

"We have breaking news to report," the newscaster says. *"For those of you who somehow missed it, seismologists are reporting a magnitude 5.3 earthquake that shook the downtown area. The USGS is holding a press conference in Golden right now, where the chief seismologist, Dr. Rana Ratogue, is talking to reporters. Let's hear what she has to say."*

The image on the screen cuts to a woman with jet-black hair and blue eyes. Her name is displayed above the words United States Geological Survey and between the station logo and a rushed graphic with concentric circles at the center of the Colorado map.

"...a swarm of earthquakes that have occurred over the last twenty-four hours along the Front Range, about ten miles northeast of Denver, on the Rocky Mountain Arsenal National Wildlife Refuge. We've tracked more than a dozen in all, most of them nowhere near as strong as the magnitude 5.3 we experienced at 10:58 AM Mountain Time. The thing to note about the sequence is we've had swarm activity in this very same region before, although not since the 1960s..."

TODAY

Rocky Mountain Arsenal National Wildlife Refuge, Commerce City, Colorado

Rana trudges through the hip-deep weeds of one of the nation's largest urban refuges toward the epicenter's GPS coordinates. She's surrounded by willow groves, marshes, and seemingly eternal stretches of grass, and yet she can still see the skyscrapers of downtown Denver from the corner of her eye. The air positively shivers with the roar of planes passing low overhead as they descend into DIA, mere miles to the east. It's strange to think that this sanctuary filled with bison and ferrets, deer and bald eagles, had not so long ago been a toxic swamp unsuitable for habitation. She knew of its history, which was why she was unsurprised to learn that the coordinates corresponded to the location of the deep injection well that had been the source of the quakes that necessitated its closure in the first place.

According to the Environmental Protection Agency, the well had been properly sealed in the eighties and the process of remediation was moving along at an unprecedented rate. In fact, they were debating opening the final remaining closed area to the public a full year before the original Superfund timetable. A new swarm of earthquakes was more than a setback; it potentially compromised all of their hard work by creating fissures through which the chemicals trapped below the bedrock could seep into the groundwater. This wasn't just another earthquake caused by the subterranean disposal of wastewater from fracking, like she dealt with on a daily basis, but a potentially disastrous contamination issue, which was why she and her team were forced to wear CBRN isolation suits matching those of their HAZMAT escort.

Sydney Partridge tromps through the field beside her. The cumbersome suit makes the young seismologist appear even smaller than she is. She carries the digital seismometer in one hand and its instrumentation in the other. Tim Telford had offered to help her, despite being overburdened by his own infrasound sensors, but she'd declined, largely because she knew how the geophysicist felt about her. The Hazardous Materials Response Team had its own equipment, which Rana would be more than happy if they never had any reason to use.

The grass gives way to bare earth, where absolutely nothing is able to grow. She's still contemplating how bad it must have been if this is what progress looks like when she sees the jagged chunks of concrete standing from the earth.

"There it is," she says.

Lightning-bolt crevices riddle the hardpan, none of them more than six inches deep. The hole at the center, however, is a heck of a lot deeper than that.

Rana climbs up onto an arched section of concrete that must have once been part of the containment shell and stares down into darkness that stretches seemingly to the planet's core.

"I'm picking up some strange seismic readings from down there," Sydney says.

"What do you mean?" Rana asks, and crouches behind her so she can better see the monitor on her colleague's laptop.

"That's just it. They're hard to qualify. The seismogram is incredibly sensitive and displays every little vibration. We're talking air traffic and passing cars. In an area like this we're dealing with an absurd amount of interference, but I can tell you that something down there is causing faint, irregular vibrations similar in amplitude to waves on the ocean."

"You think there's still fluid down there?"

"It's possible, but that's definitely not the source of the vibrations."

"I'm picking up sound in the infrasonic range, too," Tim says. "Nothing I'd attribute to tectonic activity, though. More like the resonance of air flowing into an enclosed space, a subtle increase in pressure like you feel in your ears when you change altitude."

"The well must still be patent," Rana says.

"That's a safe assumption."

One of the men from the HAZMAT response team scuffs across the dirt behind Rana. She glances back and reads the nameplate on his isolation suit: Stephens.

"We're picking up high concentrations of volatile organic compounds," he says. "I'm afraid you're stuck with the suits for the duration. And I wouldn't suggest lighting a match. There's enough benzene in the ground to burn for weeks."

He turns and heads back toward where his team is already cordoning off the area.

"How deep is that well?" she calls after him.

"A little over two miles, ma'am."

Rana walks as close to the ragged hole as she dares. It's nearly ten feet wide at the surface, but narrows to thirty inches somewhere below her in the darkness, provided they're right in their assumption that the passage remains open. She kicks a rock over the nothingness and watches it plummet out of sight. It clatters from the walls several times before passing beyond the range of hearing. She stares into the ground for several more seconds before returning to the others.

"It just hit the ground," Sydney says.

"You're certain?"

The seismologist leans back and gestures toward her monitor, where the seismogram reveals a distinct, if small, uptick.

"I'll be right back," Rana says.

"Where are you going?" Tim asks.

"Back to the van. Turns out we're going to need that drone after all."

Rana watches the live feed from the drone as she pilots it downward into the earth. Its range is more than four miles, but it only operates for thirty minutes at a charge, which means she's going to have to throw caution to the wind if she hopes to reach the bottom and have time to explore before starting the return trip to the surface. There are broken sections where the chute narrows to such an extent that she fears she'll clip the rotors, and yet somehow she manages to guide it ever deeper.

The light mounted to the bottom barely limns rounded concrete walls in varying stages of decay. Most segments are cracked and severely eroded, while others are absent and offer glimpses of the underlying strata. All things considered, the well has held up miraculously considering its age and the nature of the chemicals consuming it, like stomach acid eating its way up an esophagus. The fumes make the darkness appear to shimmer at the most distant reaches of the beam's range.

"How much farther?" she asks.

"You're passing negative eleven thousand feet now," Tim says. "You'll reach the end of the reinforced sleeves in about eighty vertical feet."

"Most of the concrete's already gone. It's amazing the entire well didn't collapse years ago."

"The sound of the drone's rotors is affecting the seismic readings," Sydney says. "I've lost our anomaly. Wait...there it is again."

Rana watches the depths of the tunnel, where the downward-facing beam diffuses into the darkness. The residual concrete abruptly gives way to metamorphic rock so heavily eroded that there are shadows too deep for the light to penetrate.

"The drone's too loud," Tim says. "I'm no longer picking up any readings in the infrasound range."

"There's nothing natural about these vibrations," Sydney says. "I can't detect any rhythm or pattern. There has to be something down there causing them."

"You mean like an animal?"

"Nothing could have survived falling two miles," Rana says.

"A burrowing animal could have tunneled—"

"I hate to burst your bubble," Stephens says, "but with the levels of contamination we're detecting up here, I guarantee you there isn't a living being on this planet that could survive down there for very long."

The walls fall away to either side, revealing a massive cavern so large that the drone's light shines upon nothing beyond open air. The original engineers had expected the chemicals to disperse into the porous rock, not completely degrade its physical structure and carve right through it.

"I'm telling you," Sydney says, "there's something down there."

The bottom comes into view. It's pitted like the surface of the moon and riddled with deep fissures caused by the recent quakes. Crystalline formations unlike any Rana's seen before sparkle from their depths, a consequence of the reaction between chemicals used to make weapons of mass destruction and deep strata that had never been exposed to their like before. The results were positively breathtaking.

"They're beautiful," she whispers.

The drone's light abruptly swings, blurring the image of the cavern floor and projecting a shadow reminiscent of a grove of skeletal trees onto the wall. The light abruptly darkens and the drone becomes unresponsive.

"What happened?" Tim asks.

"I don't know," Rana says. "I must have hit something."

"I didn't see anything."

"Neither did I, but I've totally lost communication with the drone."

"The vibrations are growing stronger by the second," Sydney says. "And I'm detecting a pattern, almost like a drumroll."

"Someone fire up the ground-penetrating radar," Rana says. "We need to make sure we didn't compromise the structural integrity of the well. If what we're picking up is the sound of falling rock, this whole area could be about to collapse."

"It's not falling rock." Sydney's voice rises an octave and takes on a note of panic. "I'm telling you, there's something down there."

She turns her monitor so Rana can see it and heads toward the mouth of the well.

"What are you doing?"

"Watch the seismogram and you'll see the difference."

She crouches and shoves a large piece of concrete over the edge. It strikes the wall and rebounds into the chute.

"Give it about forty seconds to hit the ground and—"

The chunk of concrete fires upward from the hole and clatters onto the rubble.

Sydney doesn't even have time to turn around before the shadows scurrying from the earth swarm over her.

1966

Rocky Mountain Arsenal, Commerce City, Colorado

"What in the name of God happened here?" Randall asked. "I saw them with my own eyes. Hell, I even held one. There's no doubt in my mind they were dead."

The rabbits had all moved to the front of their cages and pressed their foreheads against the mesh, their fur sticking out at odd angles. Fungal growths protruded from the bases of their skulls and the lengths of their spines. A fuzz of hyphae covered their eyes, completely obscuring their vision, and yet Randall could feel the weight of their stares upon him.

"We theorize the fungi never actually killed the rabbits," Thompson said, "but rather suppressed their vital functions to such an extent that they were able to override the immune response. They essentially created a state of deep hibernation, the physical characteristics of which match those of a moderate dose of deoxynivalenol."

"You're suggesting they can produce the toxin at will."

"Fungi don't have a 'will' any more than they have a brain to exert it, but it wouldn't be untrue to imply that the two species—*graministritici* and *unilateralis*—have formed something of a mutualistic relationship by which the former produces the toxin in response to a threat to the latter, in this case the white blood cells of the host life form."

"Surely there's a way to manipulate that to work in our favor."

"You mean as an incapacitant?"

"We could win a war without excessive loss of life."

"Hoping for the fungi to pass from the locusts to the enemy is adding the very element of unpredictability we were seeking to avoid. Not to mention the fact that we know nothing about the physiological interactions of the fungal species inside the rabbit, let alone an infinitely more complex organism like man. This could be more than a mere fungal infection that their bodies can ultimately fight off; it could be actively killing them from the inside out. Or maybe any attempt to remove it will cause it to release a lethal dose of toxin."

Thompson plucked one of the growths from the head of the nearest rabbit, which thrashed and hurled itself repeatedly against the wire mesh until its white fur darkened with blood.

"Their rate of growth is beyond anything we've ever seen," he said, and turned it over and over in his gloved hand. "An hour ago those protuberances were barely longer than the fur. Now they're close to three inches. Their life cycle hasn't merely been accelerated;

it's been altered beyond our ability to form a predictive model. If it continues to metabolize the blood—"

"The rabbit will just make more."

"That's not the point. Fungi don't grow indefinitely. Like I said, their sole purpose is to reproduce. Once they do, the host no longer serves a purpose. Biologically speaking, it will have outlived its usefulness. Like the ant that bites onto the leaf, the fungus will eventually consume it."

"Which would effectively make it the most lethal weapon in our arsenal," Randall said.

"But one outside of our control. You've seen what happened to these two simple species of fungus during the act of transmission from the locusts to the rabbits. There's no way to predict how they will respond to the human body. We have much more complicated immune and nervous systems, but we're no less susceptible to the effects of deoxynivalenol. I find it hard to believe the fungi could exert any influence over our actions like they do insects, but in sufficient quantity they could produce deadly levels of toxins."

"Don't you think that's something we should look into?"

"Human testing? That's not a road I'm prepared to go down."

"What do you think it is we do here, Doctor? We're don't cure diseases. We dream up ways of killing as many people as possible and hope to God we don't have to use them. But if—heaven forbid—we're forced to do so, we need to know exactly what to expect, both for our men and our adversaries."

"You see this tiny bulb here?" Thompson said, and held up the fungus for Randall to see. "This fruiting body holds thousands of microscopic spores that it will disperse in an explosive cloud. If they're able to enter the body through superficial capillaries protected by several layers of skin, they'll make short work of the bronchi in our lungs and the mucous membranes in our noses and mouths. We can't control their dispersion like we can chemical weapons. They don't have half-lives like radiological weapons. They can remain dormant for years. They can cross special barriers. We could inadvertently eradicate all life forms on the planet."

The doctor was being melodramatic. Any one of the weapons at their disposal had the potential to wipe out all life on Earth. If they could eliminate the Communist threat without risking a single American life, then they at least needed to explore the possibility. Chances were this idea wouldn't work, anyway. But if it did...

Randall imagined an invisible cloud of spores settling over Moscow.

"We need to try, Doctor."

"No," Thompson said. "What we need to do is proceed with the utmost caution. We could very well have created the means of our own extinction."

The setting sun cast Randall's shadow across the wavering grasses, through which a cool breeze rippled. It was strange not to see the massive derrick lording over the dark horizon, but, truth be told, he was happy to be rid of it. The earthquakes had been getting stronger with each passing year and it was only a matter of time before they ended up doing some serious damage. Granted, Denver wasn't especially close to any major fault lines, but the fact that they'd been able to create seismic activity as though it were was more than a little troubling.

He'd ultimately relented and taken the engineer's concerns to his commanding officer, who'd seen the benefits of maintaining the integrity of the well, if not the means of actively forcing pressurized fluid into it. None of them wanted the public relations nightmare of having thousands of gallons of chemicals erupt from the earth or the entire base collapsing into a toxic pit. The resolution had been to strip everything aboveground, from the generators and electric control house to the manifold and mast, and leave only a simple surface casing and blowout preventer, through which they could bleed the pressure. Eventually, they'd have to make a more permanent decision, but for now it bought them time to determine the best course of action.

Benjamin and his team were still out there, although they were about to lose the last of their light. Randall was just going to have to trust the Engineer Corps to work its magic because he already had more than he could handle on his own plate. With such a promising development in their biowarfare program, the brass cared about little else and expected another update once Thompson had a working theory regarding the fungal organism's life cycle and the exact means by which it triggered what they were calling the "resurrection response," a reaction they believed could be utilized on its own under the right circumstances to penetrate enemy lines inside corpses felled in battle.

Randall should have been more excited, he knew. Such unprecedented success would lead to rapid promotion and commendations galore, but the doctor's trepidation had become contagious. His gut was a seething ball of nerves that he couldn't calm, no matter how hard he tried.

He headed back inside. The fresh air hadn't helped as much as he'd hoped it would. Thompson was still in his lab, trying to keep up with the rapidly proliferating fungi. The growths on the rabbits now looked more like the branches of trees than antlers and covered the entirety of their backs. The fruiting bodies were definitely more pronounced, too. If the chief scientist was right about their biological impetus, then it appeared as though it wouldn't be long before they achieved it.

Thompson glanced up from his microscope and their eyes met through the glass. He looked like he hadn't slept in days.

Randall pressed the button to activate the speaker so the scientist would be able to hear him.

"How are you holding up in there, Doc?"

Thompson shrugged as though the question were of no consequence.

"*The fungi appear to have been made for each other*," he said. "*It's almost as though they fit together like pieces of a puzzle. I've only just discovered that their spores adhere to form an aggregate. The* graministritici *are a fraction of the size of the* unilateralis, *and cluster around it in much the same way metal filings cling to a magnet. Their bond is easily enough broken by adding water but doing so produces a trace amount of an acid I have yet to qualify, one I speculate functions to wipe out white blood cells. I've never seen anything like it. It's almost as though they're metamorphosing into a single organism before my very eyes.*"

"All the brass cares about is whether or not we can control it."

Randall couldn't shake the feeling that the rabbits were watching him. They were still pressed against the wire walls of their cages, their fungal protrusions poking out like porcupine quills.

"*It's too soon to tell*," Thompson said. "*At this point I can't even be sure what the final product of their union will be.*"

"I need to throw them a bone. Give me something to work with."

"*Tell them—*"

The rabbits screamed in unison, a shrill sound that caused the speaker to crackle. Thompson whirled to face the cages. The fruiting bodies exploded as one, releasing a mist of spores that expanded outward like glittering drapes blowing on the wind. They washed over the chief scientist and accumulated against the inside of the window like a dusting of pollen.

Randall cautiously approached and touched the glass. It was warm against his fingertips.

"You okay in there?"

The chief scientist turned around.

Randall staggered backward at the sight of him.

The lenses of Thompson's mask had melted in amoeboid shapes and blood flowed freely from the skin around his eyes. He cried out and dropped to his knees.

A sharp *crack* preceded the formation of fissures that spider-webbed through the window.

Randall sprinted toward the emergency shutdown button. Slapped it. A klaxon blared. The overhead fixtures snapped off and the reserve lighting kicked on, casting a red glare over the entire facility. Airflow through the ductwork ceased. Electromagnetic doors closed and locked with thudding sounds he could hear echoing from the hallways as he donned his protective suit.

A fine mist of spores shivered from the ceiling vents.

He ducked under the chemical shower. Tugged the cord. Frigid water rained down upon him, drenching him inside his suit. He pulled on his mask and watched helplessly as the spores settled to the ground.

The window shattered and glass shards spread across the floor. The same combination of enzymes and mechanical force that had allowed the spores to penetrate the exoskeletons of the insects must have worked every bit as well on the glass and Thompson's gas mask.

There was no sign of movement through the empty frame. Only rows of dead rabbits that stared back at him through hollow, skeletal sockets.

The chemical shower might have saved Randall's life, but by the time he set off the fire alarm and triggered the building-wide sprinkler system, it was too late for the other scientists still in their labs. Spores had circulated through the air ducts and felled them in the midst of their work. Like Thompson, they demonstrated superficial lesions where the spores had worked through the skin and into the circulatory system. While he couldn't detect any appreciable signs of life, he knew better than to take their deaths for granted. If they exhibited the same resurrection response as the rabbits and the fungi subsumed their physical forms, then he was dealing with more than mere infestation. As the chief scientist said, they were potentially dealing with the means of the extinction of their very species.

He knew exactly what his commanding officer would say when he called in what had happened, which was why he wasn't about to do so. At least not yet. This was far beyond their ability to contain, let alone control. If a handful of locusts was enough to begin a cycle deadly enough to kill everyone inside the building, then he could only imagine what could be accomplished with four human beings whose bodies were currently in the early stages of fungal subsummation.

There was only one thing he could think to do, and it would likely derail his career. Maybe even more than that if anyone figured out he'd done so deliberately. As it was, he was taking a sizable risk removing the bodies from the facility, but he couldn't allow the Army to get ahold of them.

He collected all four of the men and wrapped them individually in plastic tarps. The whole lot of rabbits fit into a fifth bundle, which he loaded into the back of a Jeep and drove out to where Benjamin's team had been mere hours earlier. The well was sealed beneath a temporary iron hatch that was easily enough leveraged open to reveal a great black orifice from which chemical fumes rose with such intensity that they made his eyes burn.

Randall recognized the enormity of what he was about to do, but couldn't afford to dwell on it for fear he might talk himself out of it. His plan was wrong on so many levels, and yet the consequences of doing the right thing could prove catastrophic. Thompson had recognized the dangers prior to his death and had planted the seeds of doubt in Randall, who believed in their mission to rid the world of the enemies of freedom and liberty, but not at the expense of all humanity.

The time had come to end this experiment once and for all.

He dragged the wrapped bodies from the Jeep and forced them through the orifice, which was barely wide enough to accommodate their shoulders. Used a metal post from the demolished mast to tamp them deeper, until he was certain they'd fallen into the depths, where the brass would never think to look for them, let alone be able to recover them.

By the time he returned to the main building, dawn was a pink stain on the horizon. With the interior drenched by the fire sprinklers, it was going to take more than a tank of petrol to do what needed to be done. Fortunately, there was a gas line in the lab and thousands of gallons of combustible precursor chemicals, more than enough to turn the entire facility into an inferno that would burn so hot and fast that there would be nothing left of it by the time the fire department arrived.

Randall felt the heat of the blaze on the back of his isolation suit as he walked down the dirt road toward the security gate. He hoped he'd made it look good enough that the powers that be would believe the bodies of the missing men had been incinerated inside. Maybe he should have just dropped a match into the well and blown the whole base to hell, but he still had faith in what they were trying to do, despite the fact that they'd created an abomination of nature in the process. At least he could count on the toxic chemicals two miles down to destroy the evidence of what they'd accomplished.

TODAY

Rocky Mountain Arsenal National Wildlife Refuge, Commerce City, Colorado

The pain is more than Rana can bear. She cries out and registers surprise at the sound of her voice echoing away from her into darkness so complete she can't tell if her eyes are open or closed. She tastes blood on her lips, in her mouth. The intense pressure in her head is worse than any migraine she's ever experienced and it feels as though someone's sitting on her chest, making it difficult for her to breathe. Her arms and legs are sluggish and heavy. It has to be well over a hundred degrees. Her clothes are already soaked with sweat. She realizes where she is with a start and screams once more into the bowels of the earth.

A muffled moan from somewhere nearby. The acoustics make it impossible to pinpoint its origin.

She pushes herself to her hands and knees and crawls in what she hopes is the right direction, sweeping her palms across the uneven ground in front of her. Each inhalation brings with it chemical fumes that burn all the way down her trachea and into her lungs. The intense heat is worst near her left breast, where her suit must have torn during the attack, the memories of which come flooding back to her.

The creatures had come out of the ground with such speed that she hadn't gotten a clear look at any of them. Mere silhouettes bristling with sharp, quill-like protrusions all over their bodies. She remembers Sydney turning around and sprinting toward her as the monsters washed over her. Hitting the ground on her chest and clawing at the packed dirt as she was dragged backward toward the hole. People shouting and running in every direction. Rana had barely managed two strides before she was struck from behind. Her mask cracked a heartbeat before her face slammed into the ground. Then, only darkness.

"Help me!" she screams, her voice reverberating into a space far vaster than the readings had led her to believe.

Silence.

She's about to call out again when she realizes that the creatures that dragged her down here are likely still lurking somewhere nearby.

A faint scratching sound betrays the presence of something moving through the darkness.

Her right hand meets with a soft, somewhat rounded object. She pats it down until she recognizes it as a shoulder. The body is much larger than Sydney's, meaning it belongs either to Tim or a member of the HAZMAT team. She works inward until she finds the helmet. The shield is broken, fully exposing the man's face. She traces it with her gloved hands, but can't feel the contours well enough to identify who it is.

Another scratch, closer this time.

The Tyvek fabric of his suit is torn. She reaches underneath it and feels his chest, but can't tell if he's still breathing. His button-down shirt is warm and wet with what she hopes is sweat. A quick search of the pockets of his jeans produces a wad of bills in a money clip and a set of keys with—

She nearly sobs out loud at the discovery of the mini flashlight on his keychain.

Once she turns it on, whatever's down there with her will know exactly where she is, but if she's to have any chance of getting out of here, she's going to have to be able to see her surroundings.

There are tears streaming down her cheeks when she finally musters the courage to switch on the flashlight.

And immediately wishes she hadn't.

Her screams reverberate seemingly all the way to the center of the Earth.

The old man hobbles past the cordon, stands at the edge of the hole, and leans heavily on his cane. All of his life he's feared this day would eventually come and has spent the intervening years preparing for it. The soldiers under his command have fought in some of the tightest quarters known to man, from the caves of Afghanistan to the apocalyptic cityscapes of Syria. They might not know what was waiting for them at the bottom of the well, but he had no doubt they knew how to kill it.

The blood on the hardpan is congealed into the dirt and there are obvious signs of a struggle near the lip, leaving little doubt as to what happened to the USGS survey team and the HAZMAT crew, whose vehicles still sit in the lot several miles away, a trek the old man had no desire to make at his advanced age. Fortunately, a colonel didn't have to walk if he didn't feel like it, so instead he rode in the expanded mobility tactical cargo truck, which had been specially equipped with a motorized winch and more than two miles of steel cable. His team was already unraveling it so they could attach their harnesses in sequence. They'd spent years preparing for this kind of penetration, if not the unknown that awaited them two miles down. Even the old man couldn't predict what kind of changes might have occurred underground during the last five-plus decades.

He'd been watching the news closely since the first earthquake in the swarm, but it wasn't until after the USGS failed to raise its chief seismologist on her transceiver that he was alerted through formal channels to the rapidly unraveling situation at the site of his greatest failure. While he'd never actually uttered the truth of what transpired here all those years ago, his commanding officers had recognized that something was amiss and kept him on a short leash throughout his career, which served him well since he couldn't bring himself to leave the mess he'd made behind. If ever anything unusual was reported in the vicinity of that well, he'd be damned if he wouldn't be in a position to handle it.

He looks at the pictures of the men and women who'd been dispatched to investigate the cause of the earthquakes one last time before passing the digital tablet along to the rest of his unit. He'd hoped to arrive to find the response teams in perfect health, despite the satellite imagery upon which he could clearly see there wasn't anyone within two miles of the well. If anything has happened to them, their fates will weigh heavily upon his conscience.

"We're burning daylight," he says, and stares down into the darkness.

He thinks about all the things he could have done differently, knowing full well that if he had the opportunity to do it all over again, he wouldn't change a thing. This was how events had always been destined to play out. It was why he'd persevered through the damage his tenure at the arsenal had done to his career and spent the balance of it working his way through the ranks until he was in position to command a team as loyal to him as they were to their country, a team that would follow his orders without hesitation. He'd survived two bouts with cancer, a triple bypass, and the Army's best attempts to force him into retirement, all so he could be here at this precise moment in time.

Colonel Jack Randall raises his face to the sky and feels the heat of the sun on his face. He couldn't have asked for a more perfect day to die.

Rana's cries fade into the unfathomable darkness beyond the range of the tiny light. It's all she can do not to scream again as something moves through her peripheral vision. The walls and ceiling are positively covered with fungal growths reminiscent of briar patches, which can't quite conceal the dark forms scurrying through them. One of the men from the HAZMAT team has been hauled up onto them. The sharp protrusions pass through his protective suit, summoning the rivulets of blood that trickle down the branches and eventually begin to drip to the ground with a soft *plat...plat...plat.*

She sees Sydney from the corner of her eye and rushes to help her. Kneels and rolls her onto her back. Her protective suit has been torn nearly all the way around and the clothes underneath are ripped. Her skin is bloody and raw and covered with pale white fuzz that almost appears to originate from within the wounds themselves. Worst of all are her eyes, which remain open and stare blankly into space. The vessels in her sclera have ruptured, turning the whites to red.

Rana stifles a sob.

Movement to her right. She whirls and shines her flashlight at a man in a suit matching hers. He tries to rise from the ground, only to collapse onto his chest again. Tries once more. When he looks into the light, she catches a glimpse of Tim's face behind the reflection on his mask. His features are awash with blood. He makes a high-pitched keening sound and manages to crawl several feet closer before his arms give out.

"Oh, God," she gasps, and runs to his aid.

The back of his suit is punctured in countless places. She struggles to roll him over. The inside of his mask is freckled with expiratory spatter, through which she can barely see his pallid features, contorted into an expression of sheer terror.

"Please..." he sputters. "Help...me."

His eyes lock onto hers a split-second before the tiny veins burst and they flood with blood.

He screams and his face vanishes behind the expulsion of crimson that strikes his visor from the inside. His chest deflates and his body becomes still.

She shakes him.

"Tim?"

Shakes him hard enough to rattle his teeth, but his body remains limp.

Rana scuttles backward, swings the light in a wide arc. Sees another man from the HAZMAT team, sprawled on his side with his facemask shattered and blood dripping from the corner of his mouth.

The pain in her head intensifies and her stomach clenches. If the heat doesn't kill her, the pressure at this depth eventually will. Assuming the chemical fumes didn't finish her off first. Maybe if she closes her eyes and tries to reserve what little strength she has left, she'll be able to last—

"Oh, no you don't."

Someone grabs her by the back of her suit and jerks her upright. She glances over her shoulder to see Stephens towering over her. While his suit appears largely intact, his left arm hangs at his side and he's bleeding heavily from a laceration along his hairline.

"Get up," he whispers. "Right now."

He offers his hand and pulls her to her feet.

"The others—" she starts to say.

"Listen to me. There's only one way out of here and we'd better find it before they come back."

"Before who—?"

"Shh! Keep your voice down!"

She knows there's no way in hell they're climbing two miles straight up, but if even a small amount of fresh air—

The shadows shift ahead of them. Just beyond the farthest reaches of the flashlight beam.

"This way," Stephens whispers.

"I saw something. Right over..."

Her words trail off as her light limns what looks like another bramble of fungal growth.

Until it moves.

Randall closes his eyes as tightly as he can and tries to imagine himself somewhere else. Anywhere else. Unlike his men, he's unaccustomed to being wedged into such tight confines. He thought he'd be better able to deal with the psychological effects of claustrophobia, from the crippling feeling of suffocation to the complete and utter inability to move.

He risks opening his eyes. Sees the eroded concrete passing mere inches in front of him, spotlighted by the narrow beam from the light mounted on his tactical helmet. And quickly closes them again. He concentrates on the sensation of descent, picturing himself inside an elevator, one moving much too slowly for his tastes, and cradles the specially designed, pneumatic-pressure powered assault rifle against his chest. While less powerful than its traditional counterparts and largely untested in battle, it still has enough force to punch a .45-caliber hole through a car door, should the need arise. More importantly, its discharge won't ignite the combustible chemicals. Each of his men carries one, but only he carries the *coup de gras*, the incendiary grenade he wishes to God he'd used all those years ago.

"*Passing the ten-thousand-foot mark*," Omega says through his in-helmet speaker. Each of his men has assumed a Greek letter based on position rather than rank, with Alpha serving as the tip of the spear and Omega manning the vehicle on the surface. "*Not much farther now.*"

Randall nods to himself. The airflow from the slender tank designed to attach to his thigh has done an amazing job of staving off the worst of the effects of the pressure change, although his forehead still throbs as though the vessels have swollen nearly to the point of aneurysm.

"*I can see the opening underneath me*," Alpha says.

The point man is a good thirty feet below Randall and separated from him by three other men. Two more are harnessed above him, although he can't tilt his head far enough back to see the boots hanging above the crown of his head.

"Slow descent by half," Randall says.

"*Slowing descent by half, sir,*" Omega says.

"Tell me what you see, Alpha."

"*The chemicals have eroded through the rock, creating a vast cavernous space of indeterminate size.*"

"Activate LiDAR."

A faint reddish glow blossoms below Randall as a pulsed laser shoots out of the remote sensing device, which will create a three-dimensional digital elevation model of the cavern. It's just bright enough to see through his closed eyelids.

The cable snags and Omega is forced to retract the line just far enough for the man who became stuck to work himself through the narrowing, before resuming once more.

"*It's roughly circular in shape,*" Alpha says. "*Just over a quarter mile in diameter with a domed roof approximately twenty feet high at its apex.*"

Randall silently curses himself. The scientists had been wrong about the reaction of the chemical waste and metamorphic rock. They'd been wrong about so much...

"*There are formations on the ceiling and floor reminiscent of helictites,*" Alpha says. "*Only they don't appear to be speleothemic in origin.*"

"*What else could they be?*" Beta asks.

"*They appear to be biological.*"

"Fungal," Randall says.

A pause.

"*What aren't you telling us, Colonel?*"

"Just keep your eyes open, Alpha."

The sinking sensation slows, and then ceases altogether. A hint of slack ripples through the cable.

"*I'm on the ground,*" Alpha says. "*It's riddled with fissures, but feels stable enough. Just be careful where you—*"

A sharp intake of breath and a gurgle of fluid.

The cable whips to the side, causing Randall to strike his head against the concrete chute. It jerks the other way and they all drop several feet.

"*What's going on down there?*" Omega asks from the surface.

"*We're fish in a barrel inside this tube, Colonel,*" Gamma says.

"Damn it," Randall says. "Omega, release the brake."

"*Sir?*"

"That's an ord—" The line suddenly goes slack and they

plummet into the depths. Randall presses outward with his upper arms to slow his momentum. Waits as long as he dares. "*Reengage!*"

He abruptly halts right after he passes through the ceiling of the cavern. His headlamp spins wildly as he twirls in his harness.

"*Jesus Christ!*" Beta shouts. "*What the hell happened to—?*"

The cable jerks again. The men below Randall disengage their harnesses and drop into the darkness, where twin beams of light lying on the ground highlight swatches of bare stone and rapidly expanding pools of blood.

Two more headlamps take up position between them. Gamma and Delta stand back-to-back, pivoting to examine their surroundings down the barrels of their rifles.

While all around them, the darkness begins to writhe.

The creature steps from the shadows into Rana's light and she realizes that it's at least partly human. It's skeletal, as though little more than a being of desiccated skin mummified to a framework of bones. Its veins are like serpents trapped beneath translucent tissue, its muscles braided wires. Tatters of clothing remain, befouled by bodily functions and dissolution. Its ribcage stands apart from its breast and its head juts forward on a neck bowed like a vulture's, a consequence of the long protuberances reminiscent of wires growing from its back.

"Jesus Christ," Stephens whispers. "What the hell is that thing?"

The monstrosity lowers its head and cocks it from one side to the other in a predatory manner. Its lips have shrunken from its bared teeth, which have grown long from its receded gums, and its nose has collapsed to the triangular formation of cartilage and bone. The vessels in its forehead throb with the sluggish flow of blood. Where once there were eyes, the sockets are now lined with wispy, filamentous hyphae.

Rana stumbles backward.

It matches her retreat and snaps at the air. Its teeth make an awful clicking sound.

She detects movement in her peripheral vision, but can't bring herself to tear her eyes from the creature advancing toward her on legs that tremble as though unaccustomed to movement.

Again, it strikes at her with its jaws. It's all she can do to keep from screaming, especially when she hears the sound of snapping teeth to her right.

She turns to see Sydney approaching in halting movements, her face covered with a shimmering mask of blood. Her eyelids have peeled all the way back to accommodate the hyphae sprouting from her irises. She bares her teeth and snaps them.

"Run!" Rana yells.

"**Keep going, Omega,**" Randall says, and their descent immediately recommences.

A shout echoes from the cavern below them.

It's not one of his men.

The voice is undeniably female.

Dear God, the people who were attacked on the surface...

They were still alive down here.

Both of the lights below him swivel in the direction from which the sound originated, but reveal nothing beyond the crevice-riddled stone and several oddly shaped stones from which long fungal appendages grow.

"Any sign of Alpha or Beta?" he asks.

"*No, sir,*" Gamma replies.

"*There's an awful lot of blood down here,*" Delta says.

"Focus on the mission," Randall says.

"*It would help if you told us what we were up against.*"

Randall knows his man is right, but the truth of the matter is that he simply doesn't know.

The moment his feet hit the ground, he disconnects from the cable and picks his way over the coils. If he trips, he'll become more of a liability than he already is. His cane is bound to his left leg, effectively immobilizing it. In the process of unstrapping it, he loses his balance and feels himself falling, but Delta grabs him by the back of his suit and rights him. They can all clearly see that he's not physically fit enough for the field op, but he has to know what's down here. Not only is this his fault, it's his responsibility to make sure that whatever managed to survive down here never reaches the surface.

He frees his cane and balances himself with one foot planted to either side of a deep fissure, at the bottom of which residual chemicals continue to eat through the earth.

"Gamma take point," he says. "Epsilon. Zeta. Mark this location and watch our six. Delta, activate sonar. I want to know the second you ping anything else down here."

Randall steps over one of the strange rocks. It's knobby and covered with gray fuzz that almost looks like brittle, broken strands of hair from which the fungus proliferates in spikes. One of the tips brushes against his leg and a cloud of spores billows upward and swirls in his light, tiny golden sparkles like he remembers overtaking Dr. Thompson.

He shines his light down at the source, but it's no longer there. It's now several feet away and looking up at him from a skeletal face only vaguely resembling that of a rabbit, its fur sparse and its skin clinging to its skull. Its hooked teeth are long and yellow and its eyes have sunken into shadows.

"*I'm picking up several distinct signals*," Delta says. "*And they're closing fast.*"

The rabbit rises to its haunches, opens its mouth, and clicks its front teeth against the exposed bone where its lower gums had been.

"Where?" Randall asks.

"*All around us.*"

Rana sprints through the darkness, the beam of the small light swinging in front of her, but hardly illuminating anything. She has to watch her feet to make sure she doesn't trip on the fissures and nearly runs into a fungal growth hanging from the ceiling like a massive spiny stalactite. She's within inches of it when it unfurls its arms from its chest and grabs the sleeve of her suit, knocking her off stride. She tumbles to the ground and the flashlight clatters away from her.

She rolls onto her back as the creature disengages itself from what almost looks like a briar-lined cocoon and drops down beside her feet. She kicks at the stone. Propels herself in reverse.

It scuttles after her in strange, disjointed movements, its head lowered and teeth snapping.

"Get up!" Stephens says, and drags her away from it.

Rana struggles to her feet and turns to run. Too late she sees the creature approaching from the opposite direction. It's on top of Stephens before she can warn him, its clawed fingers gripping his suit while it tears at the seal around his neck with its teeth.

A popping sound, almost like the noise of a silenced pistol, and the air fills with what looks like motes of dust.

She shouts and strikes the creature repeatedly on the side of its head. Over and over. Until it disengages from Stephens. His mask is covered with the dust, which appears to be the only thing holding all of the cracks together. It disintegrates before her eyes and the creature seizes the opportunity to shove its face through the gap.

A spatter of blood strikes Rana's mask, which begins to crack as the dust settles on it.

She brushes it off and dives for her flashlight, narrowly dodging the slashing arm of the creature from the cocoon, which joins its brethren in tearing Stephens's suit to get at the man inside. His cries reverberate deep into the darkness, from the depths of which she detects a faint source of light.

"*It came from somewhere over there*," Gamma says. "*Approximately two o'clock.*"

"Assume defensive formation," Randall says. He peeks at the sonar monitor from the corner of his eye. Scattered dots ring the perimeter of the circular map and slowly converge upon the crosshairs at the center. "There are at least six of them. You get a clear shot, make it count."

A part of him has always known the fungi survived down here, but never in his worst nightmares had he imagined that the rabbits had, too. The way the parasitic fungi had been able to slow the host's metabolism to the point of mimicking death must have allowed them to enter a state of suspended animation, during which time they'd ceased all non-essential functions and absorbed their own physical forms to keep them alive. And if the rabbits could survive, then was it possible that—?

The faint aura of light in the distance coalesces into a single beam. A flashlight. He's certain of it. Coming toward them. From the same direction as the scream.

Rana sprints toward the light, which grows brighter by the second. She trips and falls. Pushes herself up, only to fall again. She screams in frustration and has to slow her pace to combat the treacherous terrain.

They're still behind her. She feels them gaining ground on her. Hears the clicking of their teeth.

An image of Sydney flashes before her eyes, the seismologist's face wet with blood and her eyes... Dear God, her eyes... She'd been dead when Rana found her. And yet that couldn't have been the case. But she'd been so certain...

A gray blur knifes through her swinging beam. Toward her feet. Before she can even look down, it strikes her foot and sends her sprawling. She goes down hard, the impact causing the cracks in her mask to expand even more and allowing the furnace-heat to seep through.

She feels whatever attacked her scurry up onto her back, its teeth tearing through her suit and burrowing into her—

Rana screams when its hooked teeth penetrate her skin. She reaches behind her. Grabs a handful of what feels like spongy weeds. Hurls it to the ground in front of her. Pushes herself upright. Her mind barely registers it as having once been a rabbit as she stomps on its skull until there's nothing left of it.

The spines on the creature's hunched back explode in a cloud that shimmers in her beam, just as she'd seen in the moments before Stephens's death. They're spores, she realizes, and they have the ability to break through what little is left of her face shield.

She ducks her head and runs, but the damage is already done. Her visor makes a cracking sound. She tears off the entire hood and casts it aside before the mask shatters and drops the spores into her suit. The chemical fumes flow like fire into her chest and smolder in her lungs.

The light is so close now that she can make out the silhouette of the man holding it. And beside him, two more figures, whose lights converge upon her. Along with the barrels of their rifles.

"They're right behind me!" she screams.

"Get down!" Gamma shouts.

The woman throws herself to the ground a heartbeat before the entire unit opens fire. Only they aren't all shooting at the same target. Randall detects movement all around them. He glimpses pale, skeletal creatures with wiry fungal growths protruding from their cadaverous forms as his men's lights pass over them. Hears high-pitched screams, like air leaking from so many ruptured valves. The clicking of teeth.

"Get her to the cable!" he yells.

"They're blocking our retreat!" Epsilon shouts.

"What's going on down there?" Omega asks.

A naked figure darts from the darkness, tackles Zeta, and the two tumble across the eroded rock. It all happens in the blink of an eye, but even after so many years Randall recognizes the face of the man he found dead in his lab. The memories of wrapping him in a tarp and dumping him into the well haunt him. He turns his head until the beam mounted to his helmet shines straight into the monster's emaciated face. Stephen Waller, the civilian scientist in charge of the locust-breeding project, stares back at him from the eerily sentient hollows of his missing eyes, his lipless mouth dripping with Zeta's blood.

"I'm sorry," Randall whispers.

A shot from somewhere to his left collapses the side of the entomologist's head and hurls him outside the range of the light.

"There are too many of them!" Delta shouts.

A mutated rabbit clips Randall's heel and he loses his already tenuous balance. The ground rushes to meet him. He lands with a snapping sound he hears as much as feels. One he knows means he won't be getting back up again. His rifle clatters into a crevice beyond his reach.

Epsilon grips him around his chest, underneath his armpits, and attempts to drag him to his feet, but the fractured bones in his hip shift and produce pain beyond anything he's ever imagined. He cries out in a voice filled with more anger than pain as Epsilon slings him over his shoulders.

"Put me down, goddammit!"

His subordinate ignores the order and blindly fires upon the creature blocking their way. The bullets impact squarely with the chest of a man in a HAZMAT suit, but barely serve to slow him down. His white teeth are a stark contrast to the blood flowing from his ruptured eyes. He bares them and gnashes at the air. Collides with Epsilon and sends Randall once more crashing to the ground.

Epsilon jams the barrel of his rifle underneath the man's chin. A burst of compressed gas and the monster's head jerks back. The contents of his skull splatter against the ceiling.

The woman scurries to Randall's side. Her eyes are wide with terror and blood flows freely from lacerations on her cheek. He recognizes Dr. Rana Ratogue from the newscast that alerted him to location of the earthquakes and, later, from the intel provided by the Army when the USGS was unable to reach her.

"Clear a path!" she shouts at Epsilon. "I've got him."

Epsilon bellows and charges into the darkness. Gamma rushes to catch up with him. Their lights converge on a skeletal man, whose deformed face quickly vanishes into an explosion of blood and bone.

"*Someone answer me!*" Omega says. "*What in the name of God is going on down there?*"

"Prepare for emergency extraction," Randall says through teeth gritted in agony.

Rana grabs him by the wrist and drags him after them. Delta clasps his other arm and they cover the uneven ground at a much faster rate. Randall bites his lip to keep from crying out from the pain. It feels like his joint is made of shattered glass, which slices the muscles and tendons with even the slightest bump on the rocky earth.

Another man in a HAZMAT suit emerges from the darkness behind them. Delta fires repeatedly and drives him back into the darkness.

"*There's the cable!*" Epsilon shouts through the speaker.

"*Fire up that winch, Omega!*" Gamma shouts. "*We need to get out of here in a hurry!*"

"They're still coming!" Rana screams.

The creatures are little more than shadows passing through the darkness beyond the reach of their lights, but Randall can tell there are at least three of them, and they're gaining ground in a hurry.

They abruptly stop and he turns to see Gamma holding the cable in one hand and his assault rifle in the other. The hole above him appears even smaller than before.

Randall grabs Rana by the sleeve and pulls her down to him. He unfastens his harness and slips it over his head.

"Take this," he says. "It attaches to the cable that'll take you back to the surface."

"What about you?" she asks.

Randall smiles, but it's not the kind meant for others.

"This is where the road ends for me." He shoves the harness into her chest. "Now go!"

"*Sir?*" Delta says.

"Give me your weapon, soldier. I'll make sure nothing follows you."

"*We can get medical attention topside—*"

"These things have already proved they can climb up that chute. Someone needs to make sure they don't do it again. Now get the hell out of here while you still can!"

Delta offers his weapon and salutes him.

Randall seats it against his shoulder and sights down the darkness.

Rana dons the harness and cinches it around her chest. One of the soldiers pushes her toward the cable dangling from the hole in the dome and clips her to it.

Sydney rushes into the light, her features contorted by what can only be described as rage. The old man with the broken hip shoots her squarely in the chest, lifting her from her feet. She lands on her back and sputters blood. Flips over and pushes herself to her hands and knees. Allows the fluid to drain from her mouth before starting to rise—

A second shot collapses her face inward, like a fist clenching.

Rana sobs and attempts to rush to her friend's side, but the cable hauls her into the air. She can only watch as another soldier attaches himself to the cable below her and the old man and lone remaining able-bodied soldier fend off creatures stolen from her worst nightmares.

A malformed rabbit streaks across the ceiling toward her.

She barely recognizes the danger in time to swat it away, sending it plummeting to the ground. When she looks back up, she catches a glimpse of a humanoid monster scurrying across the earthen dome toward her.

"On the ceiling!" she shouts at the man below her.

He raises his rifle and fires a triple-burst into its spiny back. It loses its grip, but catches her arm as it falls.

Her shoulders and the back of her head meet with the sides of the orifice. The pressure threatens to snap her spine. She beats at the creature's fingers until it lets go and she's able to contort her upper body into the narrow chute.

"Get it off me!" the man below her shouts. The monster must have caught him on the way down, but there's nothing she can do to help him. She can't even lean her head far enough forward to see him.

"*Don't move!*" **Gamma** shouts, and fires straight up between Epsilon's thrashing feet.

Randall hears a steam-whistle scream, followed by the *thump* of the creature hitting the ground behind him. He can't afford to turn around to make sure it's dead, not if he has any hope of holding the monsters at bay. The moment they step into the light he's already shooting, but he can tell they're only testing him now. Learning from their mistakes. His best shots only serve to drive them back into the darkness and he has a finite number of bullets left. For all he knows, his next shot could very well be his last. He needs to give his men the largest possible head start and hope their suits protect them from what's to come.

"Get out of here, Delta!" he shouts. "That's an order!"

"*Yes, sir,*" Delta says, and Randall hears the clicking sound of the harness attaching to the cable. "*Everyone will know what you did here.*"

"I pray to God they don't."

Delta rises from the ground behind him and follows Gamma into the orifice.

A rabbit dashes across Randall's useless leg. He resists taking the shot for fear of wasting the bullet.

"Better make this snappy, Omega," he says. "I'm not going to be able to fend them off very much longer."

A man in a HAZMAT suit appears in his peripheral vision and rushes straight at him. He pivots. Takes a fraction of a second to aim. Catches his attacker in the forehead. Knocks him backward, only to watch him rise to all fours. Everything above his right eyebrow is gone, and yet he still snaps his teeth.

Randall finishes him off with a shot between the eyes.

"How far up are they?" he asks.

"*Nearing a hundred feet, sir,*" Omega says. "*The last of them should be entering the concrete casing.*"

Randall turns and sights down a creature that's now less than twenty feet away. It must have used the distraction to sneak within striking distance. He recognizes its face immediately, as, he's certain, it recognizes his.

Dr. James Thompson creeps closer. The fungus grows from his forehead in a configuration reminiscent of a crown. Rather than white, the hyphae in his hollow sockets are a mold-like shade of blue.

"There are no words to express how sorry I am," Randall says.

Thompson lowers his head, snaps his teeth, and breaks into a sprint.

Randall sights down the center of his old friend's forehead and pulls the trigger, but the firing pin strikes an empty chamber.

Click.

Click-click-click.

"How far?" he asks Omega as Thompson closes in on him.

"*A hundred and fifty feet, sir.*"

"Give it everything you've got, Omega!"

Randall turns the empty rifle around and grabs it by the smoldering barrel. He grits his teeth and stares down the monster hurtling toward him. It lunges and he swings the weapon like a bat. Connects solidly with its head, but barely slows its momentum.

It lands on top of him and sends him skidding across the ground under its weight. He shoves its snapping jaws away from his neck as the fruiting bodies adorning its crown burst with an explosion of spores, so many he can hardly see through his mask.

"How far?"

A crack races diagonally across his face shield. The creature claws at it in an attempt to break it open.

"*Two hundred feet, sir. I can only raise them so fast—*"

"It'll have to do."

Randall unclips the incendiary grenade from his utility belt. Feels for the pin.

Another creature strikes him from the side, knocking it from his grasp. His mask shatters and shards rain onto his face. Talon-like fingertips sink into his cheeks. Through them. Pierce his gums and bone alike, making it impossible to open his mouth to cry out.

He frantically slides his palm across the ground until he finds the grenade. Slips his gloved finger through the pin.

Teeth sink into his biceps and he nearly drops it again.

The fingertips retract from his face, releasing his trapped scream.

He pulls the pin and drops the grenade as the scientist whose warning he failed to heed bites his face and tears—

A blinding light flashes below Rana. The earth lurches, then draws a deep breath, nearly wrenching her harness from its moorings.

She closes her eyes as a column of fire races straight up the shaft, propelling her toward the surface on a superheated current of air. Screams as the flames singe her hair and blister her cheeks. The cries of the men below her are deafening, even over the roar of the blaze.

Her head strikes one wall, then the other.

She tastes blood in her sinuses, feels it trickling down the back of her throat.

Sees darkness.

Then stars.

And, finally, nothing at all.

Omega rushes toward the hole. Picks his way down the rubble-lined slope to the edge of the well, where the cable has eroded a furrow into the concrete and produces a buzzing sound as it channels even deeper. He grabs the first of them by the harness. Drags the limp body onto solid ground and unlatches it from the cable. It's a woman. She's severely burned, but he recognizes Dr. Rana Ratogue from the picture in his file.

Sirens wail in the distance, and beneath them, the thupping sound of the flight-for-life helicopter streaking across the sky.

Smoke billows from the plains to the west, where the ground has collapsed in upon itself, releasing the fire that spreads through the grasslands.

Omega drags Gamma from the hole next. Then Delta. Lines them up beside the seismologist. Their face shields are warped and black with soot, obscuring their features. He tears off their helmets to reveal faces covered with blood. Lowers his ear to Gamma's lips and feels the subtle warmth of his breath. He's still alive. As is Delta, whose eyes move beneath his closed lids.

Rana shows no signs of life, though. He can't feel her breath against his ear, nor can he detect her carotid pulse in the side of her neck. The burns on her cheeks begin to crack and suppurate. He peels back her eyelids in hopes of eliciting a pupillary response, but the vessels burst and a skein of blood floods the sclera.

"Jesus," he whispers.

Rana's other eye opens and she bares her teeth. Sinks them into the soft flesh of the soldier's neck. And drags him, kicking and screaming, down into the well.

The End

PIT OF GHOSTS

Kirsten Cross

Knock knock...

A tapping on the walls. Echoes through the tunnels.

Knock knock...

A place where light is life and darkness is death.

Knock knock...

Welcome to the underground world of the Coblynau, deep underneath the Welsh hills where coal and sometimes even gold was hewn from the rock face by bare-chested men and carted to the surface by blackened, soot-covered ponies. Where a canary could warn of lethal gas pockets with a last, haunting song before it dropped dead to the bottom of its cage. Where men's lives were cheap, and the mine owners regarded dead children as an everyday nuisance. The cost of cave-ins was calculated in money, not lives.

Eventually, the picks and drills fell silent. The mines closed, and the communities died.

Still, if you pushed past the wrought-iron gates, the rusty padlocks and the "DANGER! DO NOT ENTER – MINE UNSTABLE" red and white signs, you could hear the distant sounds of an abandoned world.

The dripping of water.

The sound of creaking timber supports.

And occasionally, in the dead of night, 'Knock, knock...'

Morfa Colliery had a deeply unsettling history. With a series of disasters throughout the 19th century and hundreds of lives lost, it had earned itself the moniker, the *Pit of Ghosts*.

Huh.

Pit of Hell, more like.

The sweat, the tears, the broken hearts and shattered bones—they were all still down there, caked in thick, choking dust. The Earth didn't want these miners here, but She didn't want to give up their bones, either. It was payment. A debt due for allowing men to scavenge black coal out of the dark and silent depths. Tap, tap, tapping away with their pathetic little sticks, blasting great gashes and fractures into the rock with explosives.

Occasionally, the Earth fought back. It could happen at any second. The men knew that with every blow they could be unleashing a wall of death. The Earth was merciless. She took life after life, both underground and in the respiratory ward of the local hospital, where men gasped and choked their last breath, their lungs filled with cancer and black dust.

Then, the Earth started to claim more lives—a higher and higher payment for the black and gold riches men ripped from the darkness. The Pit of Ghosts earned its grisly name time and time again. Four men killed in 1858. A further forty in 1863. Another twenty-nine souls consigned to the ever-dark hell in 1870. Then eighty-nine men killed in the explosion of 1890, despite warnings from the pit workers just days before. The mine wasn't safe, damn it. The men weren't safe. You need to get them out of there, now!

Warnings were ignored. So the men died, the dust choking their lungs, the mountain's intestines crushing their bones. Pockets of lethal gas ignited into roaring infernos that were over in a heartbeat and left nothing but scorched earth behind. The fire back-drafted down the tunnels and spewed up and out of the shafts, venting at the top of the winding pit. The flames enveloped the massive lifting wheel at the top, bringing it crashing down. Below ground, poor quality timbers used to shore up the roof crumbled like stale bread and brought thousands of tons of rocks crashing down on the remaining frail, terrified men. Their lives were snuffed out instantly, although those who found shelter from the rockfalls and pit-gas fire died slowly.

There were even reports that the last few had resorted to eating the flesh of their dead comrades, before finally succumbing to the blackness of Morfa Mine...

"That's bullshit. You made that last bit up, dude."

Alex Davis had paid good money for a ghost tour of the mines his ancestors used to toil in, but shit, cannibalism was taking things a bit far, even if this was the first tour and the guide wanted to ratchet up the atmosphere a notch to impress his boss. He glared at Joshua, the tour guide who had recounted the grisly tale of Morfa Mine. "There's absolutely no proof that anyone went around eating their mates, buddy. I mean, I get scaring a customer is part of the whole 'obbly-woobly' fuckin' ghost tour experience BS, little man, but cannibalism? In *Wales*?" The American snorted.

Joshua Llewellyn-Jones, Jay to his friends, fixed a smile on his face that went no further than the corners of his mouth. *The customer's always right, the customer's always right...* He was acutely aware of the penetrating gaze burning into the back of his neck from Adam Hughes, PR guru for the company that had taken over the old mine and now organized tours for the gullible. The people on this personal tour had paid a pretty hefty premium for the "small group" rate, so it was Jay's job to make sure they got their money's worth. Cannibalism seemed like a good idea at the time, so he fronted the American's challenge.

"I can assure you, sir, it's not. Bones have been recovered from within the mine that had cut marks on them, cut marks that could only have been made as a starving miner hacked off the flesh with a knife...and *ate* it." He grinned, knowing this was total bullshit.

The American's eyes widened. "Really? Well, shit..." Alex whipped out his camera, taking pictures of anything he could find.

Adam Hughes, publicity executive for Grant Holdings, the new owners of the mine, sidled up to Jay and patted him on the shoulder. "Nice save, Josh. And how did you know about the bones?"

Jay looked at Adam. "I didn't. I genuinely made that bit up. Well, let's be honest here, I'm making all of it up, right?"

Adam patted his shoulder again, a strange look on his face not quite disguised by a smile. "Yeah. Whatever you say, fella..."

"Um, guys? We're getting some seriously weird readings up here."

Ahead, in the tunnel, a group of four people clustered around a hand-held device that was currently blinking like a set of mini-traffic lights. Bright green LEDs flashed like fireflies in the gloom.

"Christ. What now?" Ewan Jones muttered under his breath. Six foot three, and with muscles that made him look like a prop forward rugby player, Jones was a blue-eyed, cynical ex-squaddie who was finding the adjustment to civvy life tough. Ghost hunters were pretty low down on his list of "people you should respect the fuck out of," just below Taliban fighters and REME mechanics. The ex-soldier was only on the tour because Adam Hughes didn't go anywhere without his own personal bodyguard. The company had received threats as soon as they'd taken over the mine to run their ghost tours, and people further up the food chain than Alex had decided to take the threats seriously. Ewan never thought he'd end up doing CPP duties to a PR prick on a haunted mine tour, but hey. Here he was. Anything to earn a living, right?

The gaggle up ahead consisted of three men and one woman. Two of the men, David and Ifan, muttered to one another in Welsh. They were local lads who'd ticket-hopped because they were friends of Jay and the tour needed to make up the numbers.

The final couple was Matt and Louise Williams, ghost hunters extraordinaire and kitted out with all the latest sensors, infrared cameras and sound recording equipment, all packed into two bulky camera bags.

Louise flicked a lock of red hair out of her eyes as her fringe flopped forward. She thrust the flashing piece of equipment towards Jay and grinned. "Waddya think of *that*?"

Jay shrugged. "Miss, I have no idea what I'm looking at. My guess would be that the bats have set your little flashy bleepy thing off, if I'm honest."

"Bats?"

"Yeah. Bats. Or, ooh yeah, I didn't think of that."

"What? Didn't think of what? Dude, you're supposed to be our damn guide down here. What are we looking at? Bats or something else?" Matt's voice had a tinge of annoyance threading through.

Jay looked down the tunnel and then back at the ghost hunters. "Well, it *could* be the flock of skeletal canaries that swoop through these tunnels."

Louise looked at Jay. "Canaries."

"Yep."

"Skeletal *canaries?*"

"Yeah, ya know? Small yellow birds. About yay big." He held out his hands palm to palm. "They go cheep-cheep a lot..."

Louise bristled. "I know what canaries are, thanks. What would they be doing down here?"

Jay mentally shifted through his tour notes stored in his brain and picked out the one marked Skeletal Canaries. "Miners used canaries to warn them of pockets of explosive gases in the tunnels. Now, they fly around the mine tunnels, forever warning the unwary of the dangers hidden in the darkness. They fear only fire, they feast on flesh. The legend goes, if you hear their warning cry then your blood will boil and burst from your veins." He added a "Kaboom-splat" hand gesture for emphasis.

"Boiling blood." Louise pursed her lips.

"Yep."

"Feasting on flesh."

"Uh-huh."

"You are *so* full of shit, you know that?" Louise glared at Jay. "We're here to do a *serious* investigation of one of the most haunted places in Wales, and you're feeding us bullshit flying skeletal canaries stories? What do you think we are, fucking amateurs?"

"Easy, Lou. The guy's just doing his job." Matt laid a hand on Louise's arm and shook his head. "Listen, fella, let's keep the tourist ghost stories to a minimum and just focus on the evidence, okay?"

Jay sighed and nodded. "Okay. I won't bother telling you about the Knockers, then."

Matt stopped staring at his bleeping, flashing EMF reader and focused on Jay. "The what?"

"The Knockers. The Coblynau. I guess you don't want to hear about them, right?"

"I would." Alex flashed a friendly smile at Jay. "Don't worry about the Scooby gang over there, buddy. Some of us are here to find out more about this place, and that includes its legends. My great great grand-pappy worked this mine." He paused, and a dark look crossed his face. "Right up to the point that they canned him."

"Why'd they do that?"

"Because he was a union man." Alex straightened up a little. "He fought hard to try and get better conditions for the guys down here. So the company accused him of theft and he got deported to the US. Ended up working in the coal mines in Pennsylvania. Died in a cave-in." Alex paused. "You see? This place is in my heritage, buddy. So you carry on with your stories because us Americans? Yeah, we love all that shit." He slapped Jay on the shoulder and let out a laugh.

"Our great great grand-pops were probably friends, Yank." Ewan flashed a smile. "My ancestors worked this mine, too."

"No way! That's awesome!" Alex grinned back at Ewan. "We're probably related somewhere along the line, right?"

"No doubt." Ewan tried hard not to roll his eyes.

"Well, it seems we *all* have some connection to this place, then. Jay, how about you lead the way in and we'll see if we can find some of these...what did you call them?" Adam paused.

"Coblynau," Jay filled in the gap. "And believe me, sir, you wouldn't want to find them. Unless you're a miner."

Matt interrupted, "You still haven't told us what they are, fella."

Jay stared hard at Matt. "Evil, mate. They're pure evil."

The walk through the tunnels to the next point of interest kept the group busy for ten minutes. The oppressive, claustrophobic atmosphere of the tunnel pressed in on them. The air was so thick and humid that you could almost chew it. Even Ewan, a man who'd spent six months rooting out Taliban insurgents in the caves and tunnels of the Tora Bora mountains, started to feel uncomfortable.

The old timbers creaked as they passed under them. The constant drip-drip-drip of water became a torture that burrowed into the group's consciousness and made the hairs on the backs of their necks stand on end. The darkness was dense. Impenetrable. It was...

Shit. The darkness was moving. Straight towards them. Shit. *SHIT!*

"Um, Jay?" David's voice wavered. "Jay? Is there another group in here? Because—"

His words were cut off mid-sentence as the cloud of bats whooshed and swooped around the group. Matt let out a yell and Louise screamed as the fluttering forms streamed past them. The swarm circled and started chittering. Initially, the sound was barely within the range of human hearing. But then it got louder. Louder. Louder. Everyone covered their ears, trying to block out the sound. They tried to take shelter as the swarm, acting as one, bombarded them. Louise's screams echoed through the tunnel as she was hit time and time again.

Blood flowed down her cheeks as she flailed against her tiny attackers. She fell to the tunnel floor and curled into the fetal position, trying to defend herself against the bats, who poured down and covered her body.

The shriek of an airhorn sent the swarm back into the air and chittering off into the darkness. Ifan stood with the canister in his hand, ready to give the horn a second blast if needed.

"Where'd you find that?" Alex stared at the young Welsh lad.

"Carry one in my pack, see?" Ifan grinned. "Always do. Bloody bats are a nuisance when they start all that. If they can't find an escape route they just circle and circle and circ..."

"Lou!" Matt dropped down next to his wife. She was still fetal.

"Christ... " Ewan turned to Ifan. "Got a medi kit in that pack of yours, fella?"

"Boyo, I'm a potholer. We never go anywhere without a medi kit." Ifan opened his pack and pulled out a green pouch.

"I'm okay. I'm okay." Louise unfurled and sat up. Her face was covered in scratches, none of which were particularly deep, but there were enough to make her look like she'd gone face-first through a car windscreen.

"We need to get you out of here, babes." Matt fussed and started trying to clean the blood off her face and hands with a wipe from Ifan's medi pouch.

"No." Louise shook her head. "There's no way. This place is amazing. I can feel them, Matt. I can *feel* them!"

"What's she on about?" Ewan frowned and handed Matt another antiseptic wipe.

"Lou's psychic," Matt responded, giving Ewan a little smile. "Seriously. She's better than an EMF detector."

Ewan sighed and glanced briefly at Jay. "Oh, great. Now there's two of you giving it the ghoulies and ghosties bullshit."

"It's not fucking bullshit, you hired thug!" Louise flared and balled her fists. "I can hear them calling out for help. Just because you can't, doesn't mean they're not there."

Ewan opened his mouth to give the woman a sharp retort when Adam laid a hand on his arm and hissed in his ear. "Let's not upset the paying guests, shall we, Ewan? I *insist.*"

Ewan moved away from the "distraught, bloodied psychic and her doting husband" tableau. He felt vulnerable. Exposed. This mine was giving him the creeps. For the umpteenth time since his demob from the army six months earlier, he found his hand going to where his sidearm should've been. His fingers patted empty thigh and he balled a fist in frustration. He muttered quietly to himself. "Can't hear a fucking thing."

But he could. They all could. You didn't need to be a psychic to hear the bone-chilling wail that floated down the tunnel.

"The *fuck* was that?" David snapped on his torch and shone it up the tunnel. "Jay, you *sure* there aren't any other parties in here?"

"No. We're the only ones." Jay's torch beam joined David's and the light punched deep into the darkness.

"You did hear that, right?"

"Of course I did." Jay's fingers tightened around his torch and he edged forward. "Hello? Anyone out there? Hello?"

The group followed Jay's slow and steady path along the old tracks. Up ahead they could see that the tunnel opened out into a larger space. The tunnel roof timbers creaked as they passed underneath, and little falls of dirt and dust rained down on them.

"I don't like this." Ewan scowled and turned to Adam. "Sir, this tunnel isn't safe. I suggest we go back to the entrance."

"You're letting your imagination run away with you, Ewan. We wouldn't have opened the mine up to parties if we didn't think it was safe."

A thunderous crack echoed down the tunnel and the rumble of large amounts of earth shifting roared through the mine. The shockwave nearly knocked the group off their feet.

Alex snapped his head around and saw a dust cloud billowing towards them. It moved with terrifying speed. Rocks bounced and rolled in front of the cloud, spinning in the air and crashing back down, sending shards of jagged shale through the air like black daggers.

"Cave in! RUN!" Ewan shoved Alex in the back. Matt, Louise, Jay and Adam were already sprinting towards the open area in front. Screw the bats; they'd rather face a bunch of black flapping mammals than tons of crushing rocks. The group dived into the open space as the last of the collapsed ceiling smashed into the floor where they'd been standing seconds earlier. The rumbling subsided until the only sound they could hear was the occasional pebble clattering down the rockfall.

The fine dust made them all cough and splutter, but, eventually, it subsided. The cavern fell quiet as the last pebble clunked and clinked its way down the wall of boulders and came to rest at Adam's feet. In the heart of the pebble was a glint of metal.

His eyes widened. Gold.

Welsh gold.

He scooped up the stone and stuffed it in his pocket. Once they made it out of this hole in the ground then screw the ghost tours, they'd be firing up the mine again looking for more gold. Gold. His heart skipped a beat.

Fucking *GOLD*.

He barely heard Ewan speak, so focused was he on that hard

lump of shale in his pocket. He refocused back as he heard Ewan say, "Where's the other two?"

"What other two?"

Ewan pointed at Jay. "Your mates, fella. The potholer with the medi pack and the other guy."

Jay felt panic rise in his throat. "David and Ifan. Shit. SHIT. They're on the other side of that." He pointed at the rock-fall. "DAVID! IFAN! Can you hear me? David, Ifan!" Jay scrambled up the rock-fall. There was a tiny gap at the very top. He slipped and slid back down again. "DAVID! IFAN!"

From the other side of the rock-fall came David's voice, "We're okay. You guys alright in there? Is anyone hurt?"

Jay looked around. Apart from being covered from head to foot in dust, the party seemed relatively intact. He returned his focus to the rock-fall. "Yeah, we're okay. Can you get out?"

"There's a lot of debris, but we should be able to get to the entrance. You guys stay there; we'll go and get help." Ifan's voice floated through the hole in the rock-fall. "Don't worry, we'll get you all out, I promise. Just stay put."

"Hurry up, boyo. This roof looks about as solid as a piece of day-old lava bread." Jay studied the ceiling of the chamber. The timbers looked more robust than those in the tunnel, but they were still ancient and crumbling. Another rock-fall like that and the whole lot could come down on top of them.

David yelled through the rock-fall. "We won't be long, Jay. Just hold on, okay? Just hold...what was that?"

Jay could hear the two men on the other side. Just a few feet away from him.

"What IS that?"

"Hello? Is there someone there? Hello...oh JESUS!"

"Christ! What the...get it off me, GET IT OFF ME!"

Then the screaming started.

Jay and Ewan frantically tore at the rock-fall, calling out to the two men on the other side. They didn't answer back. They were too busy screaming and pleading for mercy. Snarling and snuffling noises mixed in with the sobbing and wailing, until gradually the cries sounded bubbly and weaker—and then stopped completely.

Silence filled the chasm. Jay stared at the gap at the top of the rock-fall. Tears streamed down his face. He could only imagine what had happened to his two friends. A shred of denial whispered through his mind—maybe they got away. Yeah. Maybe. They got away, right? They *did* get away from whatever that was.

A small boulder dislodged itself from the rock-fall and bounced to the bottom of the pile, skirting Jay's shoulder and landing at Ewan's feet. Jay glanced down at the big man, who nodded.

"Start digging, fella. Looks like the rocks at the top are loose." Ewan started shifting rocks, glanced over to the rest of the group, and snarled. "A little help here, people? This is our way out."

The group moved towards the rock-fall and started shifting debris. Jay, trying to ignore the stinging tears that still tumbled down his filthy cheeks, was tearing at the rocks, ignoring the yelps and "Hey! Watch it, kid... " comments from the rest of the group beneath him.

He reached through the gap at the top. And then yelled at the top of his lungs.

Something cold, hard and slimy grabbed his wrist and pulled. *Hard.* He could feel his shoulder popping out of its socket. He yelled again. "Something's got me!" He heaved backwards, struggling against the tightening grip. "Help me! Jesus Christ, *help me!*" He felt a massive pair of arms circle his waist and haul him backwards.

Ewan and Jay fell off the rock-fall, tumbling and bouncing down the slope. Ewan let go of Jay and they both looked up to the gap at the top of the heap. "What the *fuck?*" Jay pointed to the gap.

Sticking though was a skeletal hand. The fingers grasped and snatched at the air, waving around, trying to find their quarry. Skin hung from the bones, flapping like bunting fluttering in a breeze. The hand was covered in blood. Fresh blood. Blood that dripped from the dagger-like fingertips and ran down the rock-fall in rivulets. Ifan's blood. David's blood.

And now it wanted more.

It wanted them.

The hand scrabbled at the rocks, making the gap wider. The hand was followed by the bones of a forearm, also covered in tattered ribbons of torn, rotting flesh. The elbow joint wiggled its way through. Then the bones of the upper arm. The whole thing started to pivot and a shoulder joint appeared.

"If whatever that thing is gets its head through, I'm guessing we're all royally fucked." Ewan picked up a rock and leapt up the rock-fall. He let out a snarl and smashed the rock against the hand and arm. There was a screech like nails being dragged down a blackboard from the other side and the arm snatched and grasped at the air like a lobster claw, snapping and trying to rake its puss-covered nails across Ewan's face. He ducked and weaved, hammering the rock again and again against the arm. A bone splintered, and the arm's owner let out a wail, followed by a furious screech. The arm vanished back through the hole.

Ewan knelt, poised with the rock raised over his head, ready to start bashing again if the arm reappeared.

From below, Louise piped up. "Is it gone?"

A chorus of screeches and howls from the other side of the rock-fall echoed through the mine. Other, more distant yelps and shrieks responded.

Ewan glanced down. "Nope. And I think it's got friends." He dropped the rock and slid backwards down the slope. He stood and looked at Jay. "Fella, is there another way out of here?"

Jay opened and shut his mouth a couple of times, gulped, and then nodded. "Uh, yeah. The mine has another entrance point that way." He pointed down one of the tunnels that spurred off the main chamber. "Or...is it that one?" He pointed to another tunnel.

Ewan gritted his teeth. "Jay?"

Jay made a decision. "Nope, definitely this one."

"You're sure?"

"I'm sure."

"You're *sure* sure? Because those motherfuckers are gonna come through that wall pretty damn soon, and honestly? I don't want to be anywhere near this place when that happens." Ewan studied the young man.

"It's this way. I promise you." Jay stabbed a finger at the entrance to the first tunnel. "I know that because last time we were in here we..."

Knock, knock...

Jay stopped mid-sentence. The group stared at the rock-fall.

Knock, knock...

A boulder dislodged and bounced down the slope.

Knock, knock...

Another. And another. And another. The rocks started to shift.

Ewan looked at Jay. "This is the bit where we run, fella." He scooped up a torch from the floor and shoved it into Jay's hand. "As in NOW!"

The rocks clattered downwards. The group didn't wait around to see any more. Jay led the way as they sprinted down the tunnel and deeper into the mine.

Behind the fleeing group, the rock-fall shifted and slowly crumbled. The gap at the top got larger by the minute. Eventually another skeletal arm popped through, snatching at the rocks and shoving them out of the way. The hole grew quickly, and the shining top of a skull appeared. The Coblynau pushed its head through the hole and looked into the chamber. It stared down the tunnel and let out a screech. Venom dribbled from its needle-sharp teeth, running down its chin and dripping onto the rock, where it hissed and frothed. The creature wriggled and writhed its way through the hole, ignoring the rock edges that tore the ribbons of flesh from its bones. Finally, with one last heave, the creature popped out of the hole and rolled down the slope. It landed on all fours, threw its head back, and let out a screech that sent cascades of dust tumbling down from the ceiling. It skittered across the floor and up the wall like a gecko, scuttling along the rock face and onto the ceiling where it sat upside down. It let out a series of chitters and another screech.

That was the signal.

Through the hole poured the Coblynau. They dropped into the chamber, sniffing and screeching, scuttling and snapping at each other.

Eventually, they got organized. The leader, its arm still sporting the splintered arm bone inflicted by Ewan, let out a series of sharp barks. They set off down the tunnel after the group.

"We've got about ten minutes before those things end up on top of us." Ewan skidded to a halt and grabbed Jay by the shoulder. "Ideas?"

"We keep going. The way out is down here."

"Down?" Adam shook his head. "No. We can't go down. That way was blocked after the cave-in of 1890."

Jay stared at the man. "How do you know that?"

Adam looked nervous. "I...um...well, I guess we've all got our connections to this pit of ghosts, haven't we? My great great grandfather was in charge of this section when it blew." He ran his hand through his dirty hair. "I never knew much about it. The family didn't mention it. Ya know." He shrugged. "A lot of people died that day."

"And David Hughes told the blasters where to set the charges." Ewan stood over Adam. "Eighty-nine people dead. Including *my* great great grandfather." He got closer to Adam until their faces almost touched. There was a dark cast in Ewan's eyes. "With his last breath he cursed ten generations of your family, so it's said. The mine will take you all, one by one." Ewan let out a little laugh. "Ironic, isn't it?"

"What?" Adam met Ewan's gaze.

"That I'd be the one protecting your arse."

"Do you believe in curses?" scoffed Adam.

"Do *you*?" Ewan snarled back.

"Guys, as much as I get your whole 'the sins of my fathers' therapy session, we got bigger issues to deal with here, don't ya think?" Alex pointed back towards the way they'd come. He turned to Jay. "Okay, buddy. Me and the two Ghostbusters wanna get the hell outta here. You gonna make that happen?"

Jay nodded. "There's another way through." He stood up. "We need to get moving."

Louise and Matt hauled their bags up and stood next to Alex. "And we're not Ghostbusters, mate," Matt growled. "We're paranormal investigators."

"Yeah, whatever, neckbeard. You want my advice?"

"No!"

"Getting it anyway. Lose the bags. They'll just slow you down."

Louise snapped back at the American. "Lose the bags? Do you have any idea how much this kit is worth?"

"Is it worth your lives?" Ewan strolled to the front of the group, leaving his boss sitting on a rock. "The Yank's right. That stuff will just slow you down. You can always come back for it or, oh, I dunno, sue the tour company for the value of it?" He glanced back at Adam and smirked. "They've got plenty of money burning a hole in their pockets, haven't they, Adam?"

Without thinking, Adam put his hand in his pocket and closed his fingers around the lump of stone. He felt the cold vein of gold running through the shale. Adam smiled in the gloom. *More money than you'll ever have, motherfucker!* He stood up and stared at the ex-soldier. "We'll make sure everyone has their ticket prices reimbursed and a complimentary tour once the mine has been made safe again." He smiled a PR smile. "You have my word on that."

"Safe? From creatures that tear you to pieces? *Safe*?" Louise's voice was shrill. "Are you kidding me?"

Jay interrupted them. "If we want to get out of here alive, then I really suggest we leave the compensation claims until we get to the surface, don't you?" He started walking down a tunnel. Screw waiting around for the rest of them. He wanted out of this pit of ghosts right fucking *now*.

A flapping and chittering stopped him in his tracks. Behind him, a worried Matt peered over his shoulder. "More bats?"

A white, ghostly form flickered out of the darkness, chirruping and tweeting. Behind it, a flurry of fluttering sent swirling vortexes through the dust-filled air.

"I don't think these are bats." Jay's eyes widened in horror as a tiny skeletal bird fluttered in front of him. Empty eye sockets stared back at him as the canary buzzed and darted in front of his face. It opened its beak and let out a trill of notes so loud, so brittle and so penetrating that they were physically painful. Jay instantly felt blood gush from his nose. He yelled, "COVER YOUR EARS!"

The group covered their ears and dropped to the ground, trying to stay as low as possible.

A second later, the flock burst from the darkness and poured onto the crouching group like a swarm of angry bees. They seemed to target Louise, pecking and tangling in her red hair. The shrill chittering and cheeping reached a crescendo. Louise screamed, flailing at the birds and trying to get away from their pin-sharp little beaks. Each peck drew more blood.

Her handbag dropped from her shoulder and fell open. A bottle of perfume rolled out and came to rest next to Ewan's feet. He scooped up the bottle, flicking off the lid with his finger. He reached into his pocket and pulled out a lighter. Positioning the lighter immediately in front of the perfume bottle's nozzle, he pressed down on the spray and ignited the lighter at the same time.

A jet of flame shot out and towards the canaries. Two caught in the first blast, immediately combusted, and crashed backwards into the main flock. The birds began to fall to the floor, flapping and thrashing, screeching all the while. Ewan, still sending out jets of perfumed flames into the flock, stamped on the skeletal birds, grinding their fragile bones into dust underneath his heel.

The rest of the flock circled upwards and, with one last chorus, fluttered back into the darkness.

"Holy fuck." Alex uncovered his ears and slowly stood. "This place is the worst fucking theme park *ever*." He turned to Ewan. "Nice work with the improvised flamethrower there, MacGyver."

In the corner, a battered and bleeding Louise sobbed loudly. "Why do they keep going after *me*? Why?"

"You've got red hair. It's thought to be seriously unlucky in a mine to have red hair," Jay answered matter-of-factly and shrugged. "Perhaps put a hat on?"

"Fuck you!" Louise snapped back. "You're the guide, aren't you supposed to be getting us out of here?"

"Then get up, pull your panties up and let's go." Jay's voice was sharper than he meant it to be, and he held a hand up. "Look, I'm sorry. I'm sorry. I didn't mean that. I'm as scared as you are. The only thing we can do is keep going, okay?"

"The kid's right." Alex stood next to Jay.

"Thanks for the moral support, but I'm twenty-five, *buddy*. Not a kid. Shall we get our arses moving?" Jay turned to Adam. "Oh, by the way, dickhead, once we're out of here, I quit, okay?" Jay flicked the finger at Adam, turned back to the tunnel, and stepped forward.

Just in time, Ewan grabbed his arm and hauled him back from the edge of the huge shaft right in the middle of the track.

"Fuck!" Jay swayed backwards, pivoted and grabbed Ewan around the waist. "Damn this place, whose bright idea was it to open a fucking crappy old mine as an attraction anyway?" He staggered away from the shaft and sat down heavily in the dirt. "Can you see any way around that thing, Ewan?"

Ewan scanned the tunnel with his torch, the beam bouncing off solid rock. The shaft filled the entire floor. It was too wide to jump across. Ewan shook his head. "Nope. It's a choice. Back that way…"

He jabbed a thumb over his shoulder. "...and back into the warm embrace of the Coblynau, or down that." He pointed to the side of the shaft.

Jay scowled at the big man. "How do you know they're Coblynau?"

Ewan paused briefly, and then shrugged. "Process of elimination, fella. You mentioned them earlier. I figured they were scary-evil enough to be what you described, am I right?"

"Honestly, I have no idea. I've never seen one before. Because if I had, you can be damn sure I wouldn't be back here today." Jay peered down into the shaft. "Oh. Goody. It's a rickety, rusty old ladder that looks like it's been there since God was a lad. What the fuck did they mine here? Horror story clichés?"

Matt sighed. "Look, Louise is pretty beaten up. We need more of a plan than just run away all the time."

"You want to tell *them* that you need a time out?" Alex's voice sounded full of fear.

Behind them, the Coblynau edged forward. Every time a light beam from one of the group's torches hit them, they hissed and recoiled. But as soon as the light moved somewhere else, they crept forward again. Some skittered up the walls and onto the tunnel roof, hissing and chittering with every cat-cautious creep.

Now, the group could see the Coblynau in all their gory detail. Their arms and legs were elongated with the flesh hanging off the bones in tatters. Stocky, muscular bodies were crisscrossed with blue veins and covered in alabaster skin that had a strange translucency. It made them look as if they were covered in thin tissue paper. Huge milky eyes stared back at them, filled with hatred.

And pain. Terrible, terrible pain.

Behind the snarling faces, the slashing, hooked fingers and toes that let them hang from the walls of the mine like geckos, and scarred, muscular torsos, were what remained of once-proud, strong men. These creatures, these Coblynau of myth and terrible legend, were the miners who had toiled in a black world beyond the sun, where death waited for them all in a blast of mine gas or a cave-in that would bury them alive. They didn't want to be here. They never wanted to be here. But their fate, and the entrance to the mine, had been sealed in that massive explosion. Now the light was creeping back into their dark tomb. New people were coming. People who would drive them ever deeper into the darkest passages, the deepest shafts, the most forgotten of places.

People who would take their gold.

Pain and sadness fermented over the years. It thickened. It dissolved their humanity until all that was left was fury. A terrible, burning rage that was directed towards anyone connected with those who had left them to their doom.

People like Adam Hughes. People who saw profit in exploitation, who cared about the gold, not the men.

They could smell the gold. They could hear its call. It was right there, sitting in his pocket. And they wanted it *back...*

"They don't like the light." Ewan watched as the Coblynau flinched and hissed, the second the torch beam hit them. Keeping his eyes locked firmly on the swarm, he whispered at Jay. "You got anything in your pack that might keep them busy?"

"What, you mean like a flare?" Jay held up a cardboard tube.

"D'ya know, I genuinely wasn't expecting that." Ewan grinned at the Coblynau, who stared back silently and then let out a chorus of hisses and screeches. Ewan, his eyes still glued on the undead enemy, spoke rapidly. "Okay. I need you to hand me the flare and then get everyone down the shaft. It doesn't look too deep, but be careful of that ladder."

"Yeah, they're way ahead of us on that bit." Jay looked around to see the top of Adam's head disappearing below the edge of the shaft. The creak of rusty iron bolts straining within an inch of snapping drifted into the tunnel as Louise stepped on to the first rung, immediately followed by Matt and Alex.

Jay focused his attention back on Ewan. "What do we do?"

Ewan reached out behind him. "Give me the flare. Then get down the shaft. If I don't follow you, then get running and keep running until you hit daylight."

"What about you? Those things'll kill you!"

"I'll be fine. Go. GO!"

Jay frowned. "You're sure?"

"Don't make me push you down the honking big hole, little man." Ewan shooed Jay towards the shaft with a wave of his hand. "Now, off you fuck, there's a good lad."

He didn't bother to watch Jay scramble down the hole. The Coblynau were creeping ever closer, like a pack of lions hunting a lame wildebeest. They chittered and hissed. A bold one skittered across the ceiling and dropped down in front of Ewan. It reared up on its hind legs, threw its arms wide, and let out a long, wailing shriek.

"Noisy bastard, ain't ya?" Ewan snarled, popped the top off the flare, stepped forward and thrust it straight into the open maw of the Coblynau. "Chew on that, motherfucker!"

He sprang back, rolled, and let himself tip over the lip of the shaft, grabbing at the ladder. He felt a bolt pop. The ladder started to creek ominously. Ewan felt gravity kick in as the flaking metal crumbled in his hands and the ladder detached from the wall. "Bugger..." Another bolt popped, and then another. In quick succession, the century-old iron bolts gave way and, still clutching the ladder, Ewan dropped. He rapidly shimmied down the disintegrating steps, knowing that in a race between him and gravity, the universal force was going to kick his arse pretty hard in three...two...one...

The ladder parted company with the shaft wall and Ewan tumbled down the last few feet. He landed at the bottom in a heap and immediately kicked the rotten ladder away from him. The landing hadn't been too bad. He did a quick pat-down check to make sure no bones were broken. All good. Ewan stood and looked up. The roof of the tunnel suddenly lit up with a bright red glow. The Coblynau let out a chorus of wails as their leader's body burst into flames, ignited by the flare Ewan had shoved unceremoniously into its mouth. Ewan smiled. That should keep them busy for a few minutes at least.

He turned and ran after the group, who were already a few hundred meters down the tunnel. He caught up with them and jogged to the front, where a determined-looking Jay was scanning the route ahead. Ewan was impressed with the lad. He had guts, was resourceful, and pretty damn brave, too.

"How we doing, Jay?" Ewan trotted alongside the lad.

"These tracks should take us to the old south exit point. The slope's facing the right way. The south exit was cut lower into the mountain face, that's why it's lower down than the entry point we came in. It's weird shit, but it was designed so the ponies would be able to walk downhill away from the coal face and out to the processing yard in the valley."

"Mate, I don't care how fucking weird this mine layout is, as long as we get out," Alex's lazy American drawl floated from behind them.

"Yeah, how much further is it, fella? I want to get Lou to a doctor before these scratches get infected."

Matt sounded worried, despite Louise muttering, "I'm fine. Stop fussing," in response.

"A way out would be pretty damn good about now, lad. No pressure, obviously, but it would be pretty fucking amazing if you could actually do your job and get us the hell out of here." Adam's voice joined the chorus.

Jay suddenly stopped and rounded on them. "Look, I'm doing my best, okay? Usually, tours don't factor in zombie flesh-eating miners and fucking skeletal canaries. You see these?" He pointed at the rusting remains of rail tracks embedded into the floor of the tunnel. "We keep following these. They'll take us out. We may get a bit dirty and shit, but if you prefer hanging around until the Knockers come for you and suck your eyeballs out, then be my fucking guests." He huffed a couple of times. The rant had been bubbling inside him for at least an hour now.

"What's that?" Louise held up a hand.

"What's what?" Alex stared at her. "Getting another ping on your ghost-o-meter, lady?"

"No, I hear it, too." Adam looked behind him. "It's a kind of rumble. Shit. Another cave-in?"

"No, that's water." Ewan frowned at Jay. "As in a LOT of water."

The group looked down the tunnel. First to hit them, was the pressure wave, driven hundreds of meters in front of the water and enough to make even the six-foot-four Ewan stagger.

Then, something even more terrifying than the thought of a wall of foaming water smashing into them came into view. First, it was just a white taloned hand, the tips of the finger bones poking through tattered skin and trailing tendons. Then a wrist. Then an arm. Then, shining like alabaster and snarling like a demon, came the face of the first Coblynau. It crept towards the group, hissing and chirruping, cackling and cawing. Behind it, answering its chatter with their own screeches and yelps, came the rest of the swarm. They kept their distance, but it wouldn't be long before they gathered up the courage to rush the group.

"Stop staring at the fuckers and RUN." Ewan spun Matt and Louise around and shoved them hard. "JAY, GET US OUT OF HERE!" Already the roar of the water was getting louder and louder. Mist floated down the tunnel as the advancing tsunami churned and crashed. The group were already running when the foam wall turned the corner and bore down on the Coblynau, who reacted far, far too late. The creatures just about managed to utter a single united screech before the water slammed into them.

You can outrun most things, but you can't outrun water. The group were next. The boiling, thrashing wave smashed into them and lifted them off their feet as if they were made of balsawood. Everyone tried to swim with the flow, but the overwhelming force of the tidal wave was too much.

Matt made a grab for Louise just before she disappeared under the water. He managed to snatch the back of her jacket and the two clung to one another for what seemed like an eternity, as they were swept down the tunnel on the worst fucking slip-and-slide ever.

Everyone bounced and slammed against the sides, trying to keep their faces turned up and grabbing any lungful of air they could.

Alex grabbed Adam and the two of them slammed into a rocky outcrop in the wall. With his free hand, Alex held on to the rock, wedging his fingers into cracks and crevices in a desperate bid to get some purchase. He gritted his teeth and strained as Adam was pulled away from his grip by the water. He let out a grunt of effort as he hauled the drowning man back towards the outcrop and relative safety. Adam, almost spent and half-drowned, coughed up a lungful of putrid mine water from the bottom of his lungs, wrapped an arm around the outcrop, and held on for dear life.

The water was slowing, and the level dropped slightly. There was now a gap of around three feet between the roof of the tunnel and the surface of the water. Debris floated past—broken timbers, the smashed remains of a cart, bodies...

Jay watched as the limp form of a Coblynau floated past him, dead at last. As the tattered body bumped past, it suddenly erupted from the water in a foaming fury and made a lunge for him. Jay kicked at the water and swam as hard as he could, feeling the creature's bony fingers scrape at his back. Jay got sucked beneath the surface briefly, and then felt a hand close around the back of his neck. He struggled and fought against the grip, but it held fast and dragged him back up into a small air pocket.

Jay lashed out, expecting to make contact with rotting skin and a snarling maw. Instead, he came face to face with a bedraggled Ewan, who managed to dodge Jay's fist. "Easy, fella, I got ya."

The body of the Coblynau floated past, face down and with a large length of wood embedded in its neck. Ewan helped Jay to the side of the tunnel and they clung to the rock, watching the body float away. "Nasty little bastard nearly had you, mate." Ewan grinned.

"What the hell are you grinning for?" Jay squeaked. His brain was at the point of no return, yet the ex-soldier seemed to be almost enjoying himself.

"Because it's nearly over, little man. It's nearly over. You'll be fine."

Before Jay could ask the man what he meant, Adam shouted out. "Light! There's light, can you see it? We've made it!"

"Oh my god, he's right." Louise yelped and wriggled free of Matt's grasp. "Come on, the water's dropping, I can feel the bottom." She stumbled and staggered through the water, which was still up to her chest and filled with mine detritus. She pushed away the body of the Coblynau as it drifted past her, recoiling from the touch of rotting skin that flaked away from the body and floated in the water like wet tissue paper.

"I can feel the rails." Alex pushed himself away from the rock outcrop and stumbled, briefly disappearing underneath the surface of the water before reappearing, spluttering and coughing. "Man, that water tastes real nasty!"

He waded forward towards the light. It bounced and flickered, luring them all forward like moths towards a flame. "Hello?" Alex called out. "Help us, please, we're stuck down here!"

The light swayed back and forth in response, as if signaling to them.

"Can you hear me? I'm down here. Help me!" Adam yelled towards the light and shoved his way past Alex, ignoring the robust, "*Asshole...* " curse that followed him.

Jay peered into the light. The whole tunnel was lighting up with a strange green glow. He looked down. The water was phosphorescing, enveloping the whole cavern in a strange, otherworldly luminance. A hushed chittering filled the tunnel, and Jay glanced back. Hanging from the tunnel roof and walls, staying just out of reach of the water, the remaining Coblynau nattered and chattered, all staring towards the light. Jay had watched how they recoiled from light before, so why were they so mesmerized by this source? He watched as they swayed their heads back and forth, never once taking their milky white eyes off the light source, and all the time chittering like demented grasshoppers.

No.

Something wasn't right.

Jay felt the hairs on the back of his neck stand on end, and he shouted out a warning. "Wait!"

Adam ignored him and stumbled on, pushing past Louise and Matt. "I can pay you. See? Get me out of here and you'll be a rich man, that's a promise." He reached into his pocket and pulled out the lump of shale.

Even in the strange green light that filled the tunnel, the glint of gold was unmistakable. Adam held the rock up.

Behind, the chittering and chattering of the Coblynau abruptly stopped. A low hissing started, rising ever louder and louder. Figures skittered across the ceiling, ignoring the rest of the group below, who flinched and ducked as the Coblynau swarmed above them.

Jay started forward and then felt a strong hand on his arm. He looked back at Ewan. The big man had a strange look on his face. "Don't, lad." Ewan shook his head. "This is how it has to be. Don't interfere."

"What?"

"Trust me. This isn't about you." Ewan shook his head again and then simply stared towards the light.

The glow got closer. Out of the darkness, a shadowy figure approached.

Adam spluttered. "Thank god! It's about time you guys got us out of here. What are you, Search and Rescue? Fire Brigade? Did the company send you? They did, didn't they?" He let out a shout of laughter. "Ha! See? I knew they'd come for me." He spun and looked at the group. "Lucky you had me with you, right?"

Alex raised a shaking hand and pointed. "Buddy, I don't call that lucky. And I don't think he's Search and Rescue, either."

Adam turned back to look at his rescuer. He choked back a wail.

Alabaster white skin covered a muscular torso streaked with blue veins and mine dirt. He held aloft the miner's lamp in his powerful arms, swinging it hypnotically from side to side. His trousers were ragged and tattered, ending just below the knee in shreds that fluttered in the breeze. The skin on his face was tissue thin and crisscrossed with scars. Beneath, the skull and jawbones were clearly visible, as if an inner light was illuminating them in silhouette.

He was no rescuer. He was a Coblynau. The king of the Knockers. Lord of the Mine. The Cursed Man...

Adam's expression changed from selfish relief to absolute horror. He stumbled backwards and sat down hard in the sticky mud left by the rapidly receding flood. The lump of shale dropped from his fingers and plopped into the mud. The gold vein running through the rock was undimmed by the filth, and shone brightly.

The swarm of Coblynau, still clinging to the walls and roof of the tunnel, fixed their gaze on the gold.

It was theirs.

It belonged to them.

It belonged to the mine.

None shall take it from them...

The swarm looked to the muscular Coblynau with the lamp, waiting for the signal. He stared past the groveling Adam and straight at Ewan. His mouth opened and a guttural voice rasped out a single word. "Hughes?"

Ewan nodded and smiled. "Payment, Da. As promised four generations ago, and promised for six more."

The Coblynau smiled, his dazzling white teeth shining in the phosphorescent glow. "Welcome home, my boy."

Ewan dropped his head, and the Coblynau king turned his gaze on the group. He took a single step aside, and nodded his head. "Go. This does not concern you. Leave this mine. Do not come back. Never come back."

Jay stared, open-mouthed at the Coblynau, and then turned to Ewan. "You? You knew?"

Ewan nodded. "You think all this was an accident?"

"You!" Adam pointed a shaking finger at Ewan. "You were the one who suggested the ghost tours. I knew it!"

"You know *nothing*." Ewan snarled at the cowering Adam. "Only greed. You saw that gold and you practically pissed your pants. You're the same as your great, great grandfather. Greedy for the riches from the mine, whatever the cost. All you had to do was say you're sorry. But you didn't, did you? You didn't."

"But Ifan! David! They're dead and they had nothing to do with whatever the hell this is all about." Jay couldn't stop himself. The two men had been his friends since junior school. And now they were dead.

"Wrong, Jay. Wrong. Their ancestors were blasters. It was their explosives that brought the roof down. They followed Hughes' orders. Their families are cursed, just as his is." Ewan pointed a finger at Adam.

Jay recoiled.

Ewan's finger had taken on a strange alabaster cast. The skin seemed loose and translucent, blue veins pulsing just below the surface. The tip of his finger peeled back to reveal the distal phalange bone poking through.

Jay looked up. Ewan's eyes were milky white. His skull was visible just below paper-thin white skin. He leaned forward, his teeth bared. "Do as my da says, Jay. It's his turn to rest, and my turn to take his place as King of the Coblynau. And so it will be for generations to come. Now go. Go, and *never* come back."

Ewan stepped away from Jay, threw back his head, and let out an ear-shattering screech. The swarm of Coblynau responded.

Jay had seen enough. He yelled at the others. "Run!"

They didn't need telling twice. Matt and Louise skittered past the King of the Coblynau and on up the tunnel. Alex was a step behind them. Jay shot past the alabaster man, flinching as he ducked underneath the upstretched arm that held the swaying miner's lamp.

Beyond the standing man was a second light source.

Daylight.

Pure. Welcoming. *Safe*.

They ran towards it, their feet slipping and sliding on the muddy ground.

A deep rumble from the depths of the mine indicated that once again, the ground was shifting.

The rumble was joined by a rising chorus of screeching. The Coblynau were singing the song of their people. A song of death. Of pain. Of loss. Of a curse that would blight the lives of families for hundreds of years to come.

An epitaph for men whose only crime was to scour beneath the crust of the earth, searching for black coal and shining gold. Men in the service of masters who cared for nothing except the profits of the men's labors. Masters who drank port and ate quail while their impoverished, starving workers were crushed by cave-ins, slowly choked by black dust, or incinerated in an instant by mine gas.

It was little wonder that the song of the Coblynau was one of mourning and loss, not just anger and hatred.

Jay stumbled through the southern exit just in time. He turned to see the Coblynau, led by the old King and his son Ewan, swarming over the hunched body of Adam Hughes.

Another generation lost to the Pit of Ghosts. Four more souls destined to spend eternity in blackness, driven mad by the curse and the endless drip-drip-drip of water.

The final rock-fall sealed the southern exit behind tons of boulders. It would be years before anyone else ever found their way back into Morfa Mine. At least a generation. And then the cycle would begin again.

The rumbling stopped, and a final shower of small rocks cascaded down the face of the cave-in.

Matt, Louise, Alex and Jay all sat there, staring at the sealed entrance. Louise sobbed quietly while Matt rocked her gently in his arms.

Alex ran a shaking hand through his hair, turned, and promptly vomited the contents of his stomach on the wet grass.

Jay sat looking at the cave-in, tears running unhindered down his cheeks.

The silence was absolute. No birds sang. The universe paused briefly, acknowledging the sacrifice of the Morfa Colliery men.

Then the faintest of sounds could be heard.

Jay strained to listen.

Knock knock...

The End

WHERE THE SUN DOES NOT SHINE
Paul Mannering

"**Okay Lucy, over** you go." The treads of the eight-wheeled robot bit into the grey powder of the lunar dust. Lights and cameras mounted on the front tilted up, staring blindly into the clear, dark sky, before pitching forward and illuminating the crater slope. "Lucy has begun her descent into the crater."

"Christ. Would you look at this fucking mess?" Private Howard asked.

"No, because unlike some assholes, I have a real job to do," Corporal Pierce snapped in reply. Her focus never wavered from monitors that showed her everything LUSE saw through its cameras.

"Howard, have you found any survivors?" Sergeant Block sounded calm over the comms channel.

"Uhh, negative, Sarge. I'm still in the control room with Pierce. This place is fucked up." Howard picked up a twisted metal girder and casually tossed it aside.

"Pierce, how's your grid search?" Block asked.

Pierce sighed in her pressure suit and responded to the voice in her ear. "Lunar Utility Survey and Exploration unit is conducting the first sweep, Sarge. The facility has depressurized in several places. No sign of corpses yet."

"No survivors either?" Block replied.

"Not yet," Pierce said, her hands hovering over the drive controls for the robotic unit.

"We're on our way back to your position," Block advised. "ETA, five minutes."

"Roger that, Sarge." Pierce brought the robot to a halt and swiveled the cameras, scanning her view over the featureless floor of the lunar crater.

"Hey Pierce," Howard said over the comms. "I said, hey Pierce."

"What?" She twisted in her seat, the lightly armored suit she was wearing moving with her.

"I found someone." Howard grinned at her from across the room, his face turning skeletal in the halogen lights on Pierce's helmet.

"Alive?" she asked.

Howard lifted a torn piece of meat and exposed bone that might have once been a human arm. "Possibly."

"Christ." Pierce turned back to her equipment. A shadow moved out of the ring of LUSE's lights. "Whoa," the corporal muttered.

Pierce moved the joystick and panned the camera through a

ninety-degree arc. "Lucy, turn right fifteen degrees." She waited while the robot responded to the voice command. The wheels on LUSE's right side clicked into reverse while the left side rolled forward.

The camera showed a sharp deviation of shadow. Less than ten meters away, a gaping hole in the crater floor came into view.

"Lucy, hold position," Pierce instructed. She checked the other sensors; nothing indicated a meteorite strike or subterranean gas explosion.

Bringing the camera feed up on a second screen, she rolled back the recording to the few seconds when Howard had her attention. The shadow appeared in the bottom right of the screen. A dark shape that vanished into the darker shadow of the crater wall. Pierce took a few stills and went back to the live feed.

"Lucy, move forward to the edge of that hole." The wheeled robot moved forward, navigating over the rocks until it perched against the sudden drop off. Laser measurements said the machine was at the lip of a shaft with a diameter of nearly three meters, and the walls were marked with a spiral pattern like drill marks.

"Sarge, I think I have a drill site," Pierce reported.

"We're outside the door," Block replied. "Howard, open the airlock."

Howard crunched his way to the room's only exit. Pulling on it, Pierce could hear him grunting with strain.

"Mi casa, su casa," he said as three more members of the Black Light Security team entered the room.

Sergeant Block started issuing orders. "Gordy, get a link to the satellite. Korbin, see if you can put a tent up in here."

The troops moved without question. Howard stepped forward, holding up the severed limb like a piece of road kill.

"And what the hell is that?" Block asked him.

"Casualty, Sarge," Howard replied with no trace of guile.

"Where's the rest?"

"Missing, Sarge."

"Well, when you find a piece that can tell us exactly what happened here, you bring it to me. Until then, get that shit out of my face."

Block moved across the room, his armored boots crunching Perspex rubble underfoot. "What have we got, Pierce?"

"Drill site. Lucy's prepping a probe."

"Show me."

Pierce tilted the screen towards Block. He watched as Pierce relayed instructions to the unit. A cylinder popped out into the open space of the shaft, and then as the weak lunar gravity caught hold, it dropped out of view. The cable spooling out behind the probe relayed sensor data back to the LUSE unit.

"How deep is this?" Block asked.

"One twenty meters," Pierce replied.

"Where's the equipment?"

"Sarge?" Pierce asked.

"The drilling rig? A prospector drill makes a hole about ten centimeters across. That's not a prospector shaft."

"No sign of equipment, Sarge."

"What about tracks? Any marks to indicate that any mining operations were ongoing in that area?"

"No, Sarge. Not yet."

"Then why are you in that crater, Pierce?"

"Lucy picked up a beacon signal."

"Where is the beacon?"

"Well, I'm not sure. It should be in this crater, but there's nothing here."

"Except a damn big hole in the ground. If the beacon is in that hole, I want you to find it."

"Sergeant," Wong's voice came over the comms channel.

"Go ahead, Wong."

"I have found what appears to be the remains of multiple base personnel. State of the bodies suggests violent trauma."

"Decom?" Block asked.

"Sergeant, the highest point in this facility is five meters below the lunar surface. The redundancy systems on all airlocks with access to the outside mean that the chances of a decompression event are nine hundred and forty-six thousand to one," Wong said.

"Save the details for your written report, Wong. Tell me what you see."

"Sergeant, I do not believe these people died of exposure to null-atmosphere. It appears they died from trauma and were possibly consumed pre-mortem."

"You're kidding?" Block asked.

Pierce stifled a grin. She could almost see Wong's puzzled expression.

"Sergeant?" Wong asked. "I request permission to patch you in to my helmet cam."

"Pierce, hook one of these monitors into Wong's feed."

The corporal's hands swept across the monitor. The interface sensors in the suit's fingertips interacted with the touch screen surface, translating touch into keystrokes.

"Okay Wong, your feed is on screen," she reported.

They stared in silence as Wong's vision swept over a room painted in blood. Corpses, torn and mutilated beyond recognition, lay in a tangled heap.

"Jesus..." Block muttered.

"Wong, how many are there?" Pierce asked.

"I'm not sure. I could start sorting through them. Counting heads would give an accurate determination. Provided that the number of bodies equals the number of—"

"Get started. If you find any identification on them, put it aside," Block said.

Pierce disconnected the video feed from her screen.

"Weapons check," Block announced. Pierce picked up the EM14 mag rifle from where she'd propped it against the bench. The electromagnetic charge showed a hundred per cent and green. The magazine of projectile slugs was full. Propelled by a relay of electro-magnets, an aerodynamic high caliber slug would leave the end of the barrel at twice the speed of sound. The armor-piercing shot could penetrate plate steel and concrete to a depth of eighteen inches.

Block listened as the team counted off, confirming their weapons were locked and loaded. "Stay frosty, people, this is not your daddy's desert patrol."

"Sergeant, please come to my position on level four, Section H. I have found a survivor," Wong announced over the team comms channel.

"On my way. Pierce, bring the med-kit."

"Sarge, the Lucy unit and the probe?"

"Will be there when we get back," Block snapped. "Move out, Corporal!"

Pierce scowled. She set LUSE to autonomous control and stood up. The soft tug of lunar gravity made her feel like she was bouncing. Pierce scooped up her rifle and the med-kit that sat among crates of emergency supplies next to the console.

"Sometime today, Corporal!" Block barked.

She followed the sergeant into the emergency airlock that secured the room.

"Crazy shit huh, Sarge?" Pierce said to break the silence.

"Bunch of prospectors blow themselves up? That ain't crazy shit. Sending us up here to check for survivors and sabotage. That's some crazy shit."

"Yeah, but think of the overtime."

The airlock cycled through and they stepped into a gently curving corridor marked section F of the mining base.

"Keep your helmet on; there's pressure, but you know the rules," Block ordered.

"Roger," Pierce replied. The lightweight but armored pressure suit kept out the smell. "You know Sarge, with the amount of casualties Wong reported, the air-con in this place must be pushing around a lot of airborne particulates."

"Pa-tick-u-lates?" Block replied.

"Yeah, Sarge. You know the tiny bits—"

"I know what the damn word means, Pierce. Now pay fucking attention. This is an unknown situation."

"Amen, Sarge." Pierce shifted her rifle to a ready position and together they moved down the narrow corridor.

"Shit hit the fan here, too," Block commented as they stepped over torn wall panels and ducked under hanging cables.

"This is mining laser damage," Pierce pointed to a burned streak along the wall.

"What the hell were they doing?" Block frowned through his helmet visor.

"Barbeque party? Maybe it got out of hand?" Pierce flashed a light into a room filled with supply crates. The floor panels had buckled upwards into bulging humps.

"Sarge, what's below us in this section?"

"Ahh...nothing. Just rock. Wong, what's the count so far?" Block asked over the comms.

"Twenty-three individuals, Sergeant. All American Water Corporation prospector personnel from their ID."

"Which means eight unaccounted for."

"Yes, Sergeant," Wong replied.

They reached a door lit by a flashing red strobe warning that the atmospheric pressure beyond was dangerously low.

"Suit check," Block said.

"All green," Pierce replied. Together they twisted the manual handle of the metal door. The air around them hissed out into near vacuum as they pulled it open. Stepping through, Pierce turned back to close the door. "Fuck me!"

Block's rifle snapped to his shoulder. "Report!"

"Dead man. Startled me." Pierce took a breath and prized the frozen hand off the door handle. "Okay...door is sealed," Pierce reported.

"Keep moving," Block said.

Pierce walked with her rifle ready, scanning the damaged walls. In places entire sections had collapsed, spilling moon rock and dirt across the floor.

"We're in section H. How far to you, Wong?" Pierce asked.

"Forty-seven meters," Wong replied. "Follow the trail of destruction around to the right. I will keep an eye out for you."

Pierce swept her view over the torn panels that lined the corridor. "Sarge, what the fuck happened here?"

"Shit went down," Block said ominously. Pierce took it to mean he had no idea either.

"Hold it," Block commanded.

Pierce froze, sweeping her rifle in a surveillance arc across the darkness.

"Movement," Block said in her ear. "Eleven o'clock. Something moved over there."

Pierce moved to the wall, her rifle butt pressed tight against her shoulder. She eased the safety off and waited.

"Korbin, Howard, Gordy, advise your positions," Block said over the squad channel.

"Still at home plate, Sarge," Howard replied.

"I'm here too, Sarge. Working on getting the pressure tent up," Korbin said.

"Gordy?" Block asked. "What's your position?"

Howard came back on line. "She left right after you did, Sarge. You told her to go set up a satellite relay."

"So why isn't she responding?"

"You know what women are like, Sarge. Maybe she's not talking to you?" Howard couldn't keep the chuckle out of his tone.

"Stow that shit, Howard. Can you patch in to her helmet cam? Get eyes on Gordy and report."

"With pleasure, Sarge. Howard out."

"Goddamn amateur hour," Block muttered.

Pierce kept up her scan of the grey dust that had drifted across the corridor.

"Feed's dead," Howard advised.

"Well go and get eyes on her. She might be in trouble," Block said, clearly annoyed that he had to spell out basic support to a squad veteran like Howard. He waved Pierce forward to take point.

She crept forward, ducking under hanging tangles of cable and stepping over buckled plates.

"Wong?" Pierce activated her comms unit. "We're closing on your position."

"One moment, I will meet you in the corridor," Wong replied.

Ten meters along the curving corridor, Wong stood with his rifle ready, the lamp on his helmet casting sparkling beams in the dust and ice flakes floating from the ceiling.

"It's just us, Wong," Block announced.

"Is Gordinski okay?" Wong asked.

"Howard is checking on her." Pierce turned and looked back as far as the bend in the corridor, an uneasy feeling tightening the muscles at the base of her neck. Block marched towards them.

"Where's the survivor?" he demanded.

"First, I would like to show you the casualties. I hope you are not easily nauseated," Wong said and stepped clear of the door.

The room looked worse close up than it had via helmet-cam. The men—no women were deployed on lunar prospecting missions—lay in a neat pile. Along one wall, Wong had placed a line of heads.

"Those are the ones I believe can be matched to a body," he explained.

"Jesus. H. Christ," Block muttered. "Cause of death?"

"Initial examination suggests multiple contusions, lacerations, blunt-force trauma and some decompression injuries."

"They were stabbed?"

"Stabbed, bitten, slashed, crushed and then exposed to null-atmosphere. Most of them were already dead when they were exposed, though."

"Isolation psychosis?" Pierce suggested.

"Isolation psychosis would be a reasonable assumption," Wong replied.

"It's not our job to make that call," Block said. "Where is the survivor?"

"He has sealed himself in a pressurized room. Breaching the seal would kill him."

"He doesn't have a pressure suit?" Pierce frowned. The idea of being anywhere on the moon without a suit made her shiver.

"It does appear that he locked himself in without following normal procedure."

"Can we communicate?" Block asked.

"Yes, Sergeant. There are working communications outside the room."

"Show me."

Wong led them down the corridor. It ended at a sealed door and a shattered door control panel.

"Manual override," Block said without a trace of sarcasm.

Wong went to the shattered panel and pressed its only remaining button. "Mister Salvatore," he said.

"Still here, Sehnor." The voice that crackled through their comms sounded tinny, a side effect of the limited transmission range of the intercom.

"Mister Salvatore. We'd like to find out what happened here and then get you to safety."

Pierce felt the vibration under her boots in the airless corridor. Within a moment the entire section shuddered as if struck by an earthquake. She fell against the wall and steadied herself until the rocking subsided.

"Minhocão!" the voice from behind the door screamed.

"Howard, report!" Block barked into the comms.

"Shit, Sarge! What the hell was that?" Korbin's voice crackled.

"Not sure. Howard, what's your situation?"

"He went to get eyes on Gordy. Couldn't tap into her helmet cam," Korbin replied. "Want me to go and find them?"

"Hold your damned position, Korbin."

"What's Saliva saying?" Block snapped at Wong.

"Salvatore, Sergeant. I'm not sure what it means. He screams that word occasionally."

"Pierce?" Block asked.

"No habla Espanol," Pierce said.

"From what I have heard, I think he is speaking Portuguese," Wong suggested.

"And do you speak Portuguese, Wong?" Block asked.

"Not currently, Sergeant."

"Goddamn amateur hour," Block muttered again. "Hey! You in there! We're going to get you out of there safe and sound, comprende?"

"Please..." Salvatore's voice came through the intercom. "Por favor senhor, me tira de aqui embora."

"Wong, come with me. We'll get a pressure tent and seal off this tunnel. Get some atmosphere in here. Then we can open this door and get him in a suit and ready for evac."

"What do you want me to do, Sarge?" Pierce asked.

"Talk to him. A female voice might calm him down."

Pierce stared in blank surprise at Block until he walked away down the corridor, Wong trailing him.

"Ahh... Hola?" Pierce said to the intercom.

"Sim," came the hesitant reply. "Who are you?"

"Pierce, Corporal Pierce. I'm part of a Black Light Private Security team."

"Black Light Security? Why did the company send you? Why not proper military?"

Are you kidding me? Pierce thought. Lunar territory was a complex jigsaw of corporate land claims. No Earth government or country had a claim to any part of the moon. Landing federal troops on the moon would start a war, or worse—a court action.

"Mister Salvatore? We are proper military. Bought and paid for by the same board of directors who sent you and your colleagues up here."

"Have you killed them all?"

"Killed who, Mister Salvatore?"

"Minhocão," came the hissed reply.

"I don't know what that means, sir."

"They burrow through the ground. The drilling, it brought them to the surface."

"What are you talking about, Mister Salvatore?"

"They will kill you! Just like they killed everyone else!" Salvatore's voice broke into high-pitched giggles. Pierce clicked off the intercom connection and shivered.

Backing down the corridor, she turned to follow Block and

Wong. Her gaze swept over the room where the bodies had been dumped. Wong had tidied up, sorting the remains from the tangled pile they were in and laying them out in orderly rows.

Pierce stopped and stared at the floor. The thick rivers of blood that flowed from the corpses had frozen in the absolute zero of open space.

The bodies should have frozen too; the liquid leaking out of the gaping wounds welding the corpses together like slabs of hamburger in a blast freezer.

Pierce walked into the room, breathing in slow, shallow breaths. Even though she was carrying her own atmosphere, she could imagine the smell and that made her nauseous.

Sinking into a crouch, Pierce picked up a soft and floppy piece of meat. A clear gel-like resin dripped from it. Anti-freeze?

The ground shuddered again. Pierce thrust her hands out to keep herself from plunging face-first into the nearest body.

"Pierce, you okay?" Block came through her comms unit.

"Five by five, Sarge." She straightened up and checked her rifle was clean.

"That one was definitely closer," Block said. "How is our civilian?"

"He's fine. Scared and, well talking crazy. But he seems okay where he is for now."

"Hold your position, we're on—" Block's transmission collapsed into static as the ground shuddered again with renewed violence.

"Sarge?" Pierce reached up and touched the side of her helmet to improve the audio connection. It was an instinctive gesture but a futile one. "Sarge?" The comms link remained quiet.

Pierce left the room, her rifle leading the way as she moved down the corridor. The ceiling had collapsed, filling the passage with drifts of lunar dirt and rock. Pierce pushed the dirt away until she had excavated a narrow crawl space. Her helmet and air tanks scraped against rock as she wriggled through. Her progress ground to a halt when she was barely half way. Pierce scratched at the dirt with her hands and then froze as the ground vibrated around her. The dirt cascaded down, allowing Pierce to crawl out of the narrow gap and sending her rolling down the slope on the other side.

A dark shape with glistening black skin like a whale slid past a ragged hole in the wall. The clear gel scraped off the smooth hide, the drops leaving wet tracks in the fresh dust.

"Sarge!" Pierce yelled into her comms unit. She crawled backwards, away from the thing that continued to pass uninterrupted.

"Pierce? What is your situation?" Block barked in her ear.

"There's something alive over here," Pierce replied.

"Another survivor?"

"Sarge, I think it's some kind of animal. It's alive," she added, feeling the need to clarify the point.

"Hold position. We're en route to you."

Pierce could hear Block running and yelling for Korbin to move with him. She stood, straining to feel any vibration, trying to hear, even though there was no atmosphere to carry a sound. Pierce touched the dripping gel with a heavy gloved finger. It hadn't frozen in the vacuum of space. Just like the goo on the mutilated bodies.

The ruptured wall panel revealed a circular tunnel that sloped sharply downward. Something was in there. Pierce did not imagine things. She observed and analyzed.

No indicators of life had ever been found on the moon. Nothing in the water, nothing in the thick layer of dust and rock on the moon's surface. In the hard vacuum, nothing eroded under the influence of wind or water. Footprints from the first men to set foot on this tiny globe were still out there, unchanged in nearly one hundred years.

Pierce moved her gaze slowly, assessing and cataloguing the signs. The clear gel glistened on the tunnel walls. The shape that passed her had ground through the dry stone at a phenomenal speed and left no waste in its wake.

When the squad had landed, they passed over a field of wreckage. The scattered debris showed the violence of an explosion that had ripped open the utility domes on the surface of the mostly underground facility. Now, this far underground, something had impacted the wall, tearing a hole too large for the emergency response systems to patch. Explosive decompression had done the rest. Sudden exposure to vacuum would not have inflicted the kinds of wounds they saw on the bodies. It also would not have piled the dead up in a single room. The loss of atmosphere meant that the tunnels either reached the surface or had enough volume to suck the air right out of the sealed environment.

Pierce noted the swirling grooves cut into the rock. It looked like rifling on the interior of an antique rifle barrel.

She shivered and turned carefully in the hardsuit. Looking both ways into the bored tunnel.

"Pierce, you gotta copy?" Block's voice crackled through heavy static.

"Go Sarge."

"Korbin and I are closing on your position. Any change in the survivor's condition?"

The ground shuddered again. Pierce fell face forward and scrambled to lift her head as a wall of dust exploded silently out of the tunnel next to the corridor.

"He's secure." Pierce hoped it was true. Pierce rolled onto her back, arms and legs waving like a pale four-limbed beetle.

The floor bulged, and the panels burst out of their frames. A gigantic black worm emerged from the dust. From the ground to the top of the head that rippled with a peristaltic convulsion, the bullet-shaped creature stood over six feet.

Pierce wiped the dust away from her helmet with one gloved hand and stared, fascinated. This thing, exploring the cold vacuum around them, was clearly alive. How it could survive in open space was beyond her understanding.

The featureless head split open in four triangular segments, revealing row upon row of inward pointing teeth. A snake-like tentacle flicked from its mouth like a whip. Four other tentacles lashed from the worm's gullet, striking the ground, the twisted floor panels, and one slapping against Pierce's faceplate. She squirmed backwards, trying to see through the goo-smeared visor. Any sound the worm might make would not travel in vacuum. The only noise Pierce could hear was the panicked rasp of her own breathing.

Raising her rifle, she slammed the safety into the OFF position and fired. The firing mechanism ratcheted a donut-shaped round up from the magazine. The projectile accelerated down the barrel, reaching the speed of sound in a pico-second. One-thousandth of a moment later it left the muzzle of the rifle at Mach-2. The impact on the slug-like body was silent but explosive. The ring shot tore through the alien's flesh, exploded through the back of it, and punched into the ceiling.

The worm thrashed its bulk. Mouth parts slammed shut and then flicked open. Its tentacle tongues flailed wildly. Pierce fired again and again, moving her aiming point to different parts of the worm's head and tearing the thing into large black chunks of steaming meat. After four rounds, the worm collapsed. The moisture rising from its body froze immediately. Only the anti-freeze gel still dripped from the jagged wounds and mouth parts.

Pierce got to her feet, alarms in her suit systems warning that she was hyperventilating. The beams of her personal lights played on the destroyed corridor. Pierce focused on controlling her breathing and waited while Block and Korbin emerged from the darkness.

"What the hell happened, Pierce?" Block asked.

"I ran into something. Something big. Like a worm. But with teeth."

As Block came closer, Pierce could see the frown on his face. "You losing your shit, Pierce?" he asked.

"No, Sergeant." She pointed to the lumps of black flesh glistening under their headlamps.

"What the hell?" Korbin asked.

"Wong," Block said. "You get that net relay set up?"

"Affirmative, Sergeant," came Wong's reply.

"Did you find a reference to that minnow thing?"

"Minhocão," Wong replied. "Yes, Sergeant. It is a reference to a creature of South American legend."

"Some kind of oversized worm?" Block asked.

"Minhocão means Big Earthworm, in Portuguese. Their existence has never been proven. Though there are numerous reports of damage being attributed to their tunneling activities."

"Pierce may have found one."

"That is interesting, Sergeant. I have taken the liberty of bringing your helmet cam feed on screen. If a sample could be taken, it would provoke interest in the scientific community—"

"Yeah, whatever. Wong, it looks like one or more of these worm things might have done for the prospector crew."

"May I have permission to come to your position and assess the specimen?"

"Knock yourself out, Wong. Any word from Howard or Gordy?"

"Negative. However, the activation of the satellite uplink would suggest that Gordinski has completed her assigned task."

"Goddamn, Barbie dolls," Korbin muttered.

Pierce shot him a look, which he ignored. Having an artificial like Wong on the crew took some getting used to. After three months, only his formal mode of speech made him stand out from his human comrades. Pierce didn't get bothered by having a robot with a human face in the team. Korbin was one of those people who didn't like working with artificials.

"Alright, Korbin, Pierce, we'll find out what's happened to Gordy and Howard. Wong can cut himself some worm steaks and then we'll regroup at the primary camp. Got it?"

"Hooh-rah," Korbin and Pierce said immediately.

"Wong, we're moving out. Going to find Gordy and Howard. Get your samples and return to primary site."

"Yes, Sergeant," Wong replied.

"Follow me," Block said and tramped past the splattered carcass.

"We're going around the outside?" Korbin asked.

"Yes, goddamnit," Block snapped. "Gordy and Howard should be at the satellite relay tower, which is part of the surface infrastructure. That means *outside* the complex. If they've moved, or are injured, they'll still be out here somewhere."

Korbin didn't look convinced. He held his rifle ready and followed the sergeant. Pierce took a deep breath and exhaled as Block led them into a stairwell and they headed up towards the surface. She tried not to think about the black sky they would walk under.

Block keyed in the access code to open the interior airlock door. They cycled through the chamber and stepped out onto the soft dust. The satellite relay station was several hundred meters away, a dome with metal fingers pointing to the sky and the familiar dish shapes of signal receivers.

Pierce noticed Korbin's footprints shuddering. Tiny avalanches of particles falling into the impressions filled the grooves of his boot marks.

"Sarge!" she yelled, knowing what the tremors heralded. The ground rippled and the three of them stumbled as a boil of grey sand and rock swelled under Block's feet. He fell backwards, landing hard on the ground. A gigantic, dust-coated, black slug burst from the ground. Mouth parts spreading wide as its tongue-tentacles flailed through the empty space, searching for prey.

Pierce dropped to one knee on the quivering soil and fired at the massive target. Korbin opened fire, a silent blast of projectiles blossoming along the worm's side. Block rolled to his feet and fired. The creature convulsed, sweeping around and knocking Korbin off his feet. Pierce leapt and rolled, the lunar dust behind her exploding with the impact of Korbin's stray shots.

She came up in a firing position, lunar silt blurring her face plate. Pierce fired at the dark mass until Block gave the order to cease fire.

"Fuck me..." he said.

"Korbin?" Pierce wiped the dust off her visor and stood up. "Korbin?" Block moved around the still creature.

"Shit. Korbin's down. Wong? Life-signs check on Korbin. Stat."

"Private Korbin is registering as alive, with significant crush trauma and suppressed respiration."

Block dropped to his knees and scraped at the lunar dust. "Pierce, give me a hand for fuck's sake."

Pierce unclipped a tool from her belt, unfolding it into a wide-mouthed shovel with a handle as long as her arm. Digging their way under the collapsed worm, they uncovered the sleeve of Korbin's suit. She put the shovel aside and dug his arm out by hand. Finding his glove, she squeezed it reassuringly while trying to get a verbal response over the comms channel.

Pierce hesitated in her efforts as the ground shuddered. Snatching up her rifle, she scanned the surroundings for movement.

A geyser of dust erupted from under the dead worm and Korbin's arm jerked out of sight.

"Korbin!" Block yelled. "Hang in there, soldier. We'll get you out. Pierce, help me shift this piece of shit."

With lunar gravity less than 85% of earth, the massive creature was light enough for the two soldiers to roll aside though Pierce felt her muscles scream at the strain.

Where Korbin had fallen a circular shaft had opened up. Pierce recognized it immediately. "Sarge, the prospector shafts, what if they're made by these things?"

"Korbin!" Block was on his hands and knees, broadcasting his comms transmission down into the cold darkness without response.

"Sarge, we should get to the satellite relay. We need to report this."

"Right, yes. Fuck!" Block shuffled backwards and stood up, the grey dust clinging to his suit in a random camouflage pattern. "Wong? Get a comms link established to GC. They need to know what we've found."

Pierce felt the vibration through her boots and saw the fine lunar dust quivering a moment before the ground collapsed under her feet.

Her vision went dark in the cloud of dust. The sensation of falling was familiar, though the reduced gravity made it feel weird. Completely blinded, Pierce crashed against the wall of the worm's shaft. The impact sent her tumbling against another wall and then finally, shaken, disorientated, and tasting blood, she hit the ground.

Lying face down, Pierce groaned and took stock, checking her suit sensors. Nothing broken or torn.

"Sarge?" Pierce said into the open comms channel.

Block groaned and crawled out of a drift of lunar dirt. "Goddamn amateur hour. Wong, you receiving?"

Silence hissed in Pierce's earpiece. Climbing to her feet, she looked up to the faint ring of sunlight visible at the top of the shaft. The worm that had made the hole had vanished.

"Pierce? You alive?" Block asked.

"Hell yeah, Sarge."

"Fuckin' A. Now let's get our asses out of this hole."

"We'd need a line or something, Sarge."

Block stood up and tilted back to stare at the hole high above them. "Well fuck," he announced.

Pierce wondered how the giant worms could have existed in the lunar environment undetected for all this time. The creatures had no eyes and only the probing snake-like tongues. Did they sense vibration, or body heat? There was no sound in a vacuum, and they seemed to cope just fine in the extreme temperature fluctuations of the lunar surface. What did they feed on? Where did they get water?

"Wong! You plastic mother-fucker!" Block was waving his arms and yelling at the distant sky. The off-white suit and helmet of Wong eclipsed the ring of sunlight.

"Sergeant Block, are you injured?"

"No, Wong. Pierce is down here, too. Get a line down to us, we need to get out of here before one of these mother-fuckers come back."

"Please remain calm. I will get you out as soon as possible." Wong vanished from view.

"Where did the worm go?" Pierce asked.

"Who cares?" Block was still watching the sky, waiting for Wong to reappear.

"Korbin probably cares," Pierce replied.

Block turned and she could feel but not see his glare in the shadow of his helmet. "The fuck did you say?"

"Korbin is down here somewhere, sergeant. We need to find him and get him into medical, or recover his body. Without confirmation of death on mission, his family only get half benefits."

"Our mission is to determine what happened to the prospectors on site. They are a company asset. We get paid when we have enough evidence to file a comprehensive report."

"Korbin's family deserve the same evidence." Pierce stood firm.

"We're not going to fuck around down here looking for a dead body. We still haven't got a lock on Gordinski or Howard."

"Wong should be able to find their beacons. If they were in the complex or on the surface. He could have gone straight to them."

Block stared at the dirt floor for a long moment. "Which means they're probably down here. Or in a hole just like it."

"How long do you think Wong will be?" Pierce asked.

"As long as it takes. In the meantime, we hold here."

"These tunnels—" Pierce gestured at the curved walls around them. "Those worms, those minhocão things, they burrow through the rock. They excrete some kind of fluid which doesn't freeze. They must eat the rock; there's no rubble left behind, and they move really fucking fast."

"They also don't react well to being shot," Block replied.

"There's no evidence of these things. Not in a hundred years of lunar exploration. You'd think we would have found something before now. A fossil, a track, a few bones…"

"Maybe they're aliens." Block maintained his surveillance of the tunnel and the shaft above them.

"I don't think so." Pierce had spoken before realizing that Sergeant Block was being sarcastic. "I mean, they're clearly adapted for life in the lunar soil. I think they live deep, maybe in caves where it's warm and there's liquid water. Maybe miles deep in the crust. The water prospectors, the drilling. That might have drawn them up to the surface. If they live in the dark, then they have no use for visual senses. They could respond to vibration or hunt by smell."

"Goddamn, Pierce. You should write that shit down. You're smart as a Wong."

"I'm serious. We don't know shit about these things."

"Sure we do. We know they fucked up an entire corporate water prospecting facility. More importantly, we know that a short burst of EM14 ammunition will fuck them. Is there anything else a corporate marine needs to know?"

"No, Sarge."

"Where the fuck is Wong?"

Pierce put a gloved hand on the wall; a vibration like a deep bass tone was humming through the rock. "Sarge, we have incoming." Pierce readied her rifle and waited for the worm to break through.

Block took a position nearby, looking both ways along the tunnel for a target. "Hold your position," he warned.

"You feel it?"

"Goddamn amateur hour," Block muttered. "Yeah, I feel it."

The vibration increased until dust and small stones fell from the walls and ceiling. Pierce felt like she was in a subway tunnel and a train was coming. She hoped it would pass them by.

The rumbling increased. Pierce's internal organs quivered. Then the intensity dropped away, the rocks stopped tumbling, and the dust settled.

"I guess they aren't going to be sneaking up on us," Block said.

"Can we get the fuck out of here?" Pierce replied.

"Wong?" Block broadcast on all available frequencies. "Wong. Come in, Wong."

"Sarge, I have an idea." Pierce marched off down the tunnel.

"Pierce? Pierce for fuck's sake, where are you going?"

Block followed the corporal down the tunnel, stooping slightly to avoid scraping his helmet on the stone roof.

"I know how we can get out, if we're really, really lucky."

"Would you care to share this knowledge with your squad leader?"

"Sorry Sarge, it's just that Lucy sent a wire beacon down one of the shafts. We thought it was a prospector drill site. What if it was made by one of these worms?"

"Well, that's a sweet ass-umption, Pierce. What if the tunnels don't join up?"

Pierce kept moving, Block almost treading on her heels as they followed the curves and dips of the tunnel. "Conservation of energy. It makes sense that they would link up. Why expend precious energy grinding a new tunnel when you can use an existing one?"

Block mentally shrugged. Corporal Pierce was smarter than your average block-head trooper by several orders of magnitude. Her analytical mind and clear eye for detail had saved their asses more than once. "You get us out of this shithole and I will buy you a beer."

"You sure know how to turn a girl's head, Sarge." Pierce wished she felt as confident as she sounded. They followed the tunnel's curve to the left, Pierce estimated almost fifty degrees to the left. The tunnel dipped again and they skidded down the slope, dragging their gloves in the dust and trying to avoid falling on their asses.

"Ohh shit!" Pierce yelled as she saw the lip of a vertical shaft coming up fast. A worm erupted out of the hole and Pierce scrambled to dig her boots in before she face-planted into the undulating sides of the thing.

The bullet head of the worm split open, the rows of translucent teeth glistening with drool. A cloud of rock dust puffed into the vacuum and Pierce slammed into the creature. It felt like hitting a rock wall under a thin layer of rubber sheet. Squirming backwards, she readied her rifle. Block opened fire from further up the slope, the donut-shaped rounds punching into the head of the worm and sending it into a silent, thrashing frenzy.

Under the concentrated assault, the worm retreated into the shaft. Pierce got to her feet and jumped over the void to the rising tunnel on the other side. With her boots planted on the loose lunar soil, she turned and fired into the hole. The worm vanished, reversing as quickly as it had appeared.

"You okay?!" Block yelled in the comm.

"Roger that," Pierce confirmed. "Five by fucking-five."

"I'm coming over," Block said.

Pierce moved backwards, stomping her boots into the dirt and climbing away from the dark circle. Block leapt across the six-foot gap, only to crack his helmet on the low roof and somersault backwards into the pit.

"Sarge!" Pierce screamed. Charging forward, she dropped to her knees at the edge of the pit.

Block hung a meter below the edge. His arms and legs were splayed out and wedged against the spiral grooves of the wall.

"Sarge?"

"Goddamn amateur hour," Block replied. "Pierce, you will not tell anyone that I fell in a fucking hole. That is an order."

Pierce almost laughed with relief. "Roger that, Sarge. Can you reach my hand?" She lay down, wriggling her legs back and keeping her center of gravity behind the lip of the shaft.

"Grab the end of my rifle." Pierce wrapped the strap around her wrist and lowered the weapon.

Block looked up and took a firm grip on the weapon. "Well, pull me up," he said.

Pierce heaved against the reduced weight of the man in lunar gravity, while he started working his way up the narrow pipe.

In less than a minute, Block reached up and Pierce took his hand in hers.

"Sarge, are you even trying, or am I taking your weight alone?"

"Hey fuck you, lady." Block laughed. He jerked against Pierce's grip and she opened her mouth to tell him to stop fucking around when his eyes met hers.

"Pierce—" Block jerked downward again. Hard enough to be ripped from Pierce's grip.

"Block!" she yelled. The sergeant's gloves scraped against the wall as he struggled to hold his position.

"Pierce, the fucking thing's got my leg."

Pierce swung her rifle around and aimed down the shaft. She couldn't see anything beyond Block's helmet and shoulders.

The ground vibrated and he dropped another half-meter. "Goddamn..." Block muttered. "Pierce. Get the fuck out of here. Find Wong. Find Howard and Gordinski. Gnngghh... Go! Fuck!"

Pierce strained to reach the sergeant's hand. Like a cork popping from a bottle in reverse, he vanished into the darkness.

Her breath screeching in her ears, Pierce rolled away from the edge of the hole. The systems in her suit beeped and flashed the first warning that she was getting low on oxygen. Sobbing in terror, she crawled, pushing her rifle ahead as she went up the sloping tunnel.

"Wong? You copy?" Pierce followed the tunnel through twists and turns, dipping under smooth metallic meteorites buried deep in the regolith and climbing ridges of crystalized basalt lava.

Her suit oxygen alarm was now a steady beat, as rhythmic as her pulse and synched with her ragged breathing.

Sweat dripped into her suit, the smell of her terror growing rank in Pierce's nostrils. She blinked furiously and kept moving.

The LUSE beacon hung in a vertical bend of the tunnel like the pendulum in a dead clock. Pierce grabbed it with both hands, almost crying with relief. She tugged on the wire cable and felt it hold. Hauling herself up, Pierce went hand over hand, letting her boots scrape against the walls as she worked her way up to the distant surface.

The rim of light in the blackness grew larger as she climbed. Pierce told herself the cascade of dust and the shaking was all in her head. The worms were not coming up behind her, digging their way through the broken rock and dust, reaching towards her boots with their tentacle tongues and grinding rows of teeth.

"Pierce? Pierce are you receiving?"

It took a moment to realize she wasn't imagining the voice in her ear. "Wong? I'm here! The Lucy beacon. I'm coming up the line!"

"I am pleased you are safe. I will rendezvous with you in approximately forty-five seconds."

"Okay!" Hand over hand, Pierce pulled herself upwards. The grey rocks tumbled down, bouncing off her helmet, striking her shoulders, and catching on her air tank backpack.

The edge of the pit was in reach, the wire cable sawing into the dust. Pierce reached and tried to pull herself up and out of the hole. The rim crumbled, fine lunar dust and gravel raining down on her.

"Fuck!" Pierce shook her head, clearing the worst of the regolith away from her view. A tentacle coiled around her leg. Clamping down on the dense suit material and tightening against her skin.

"Wong!" Pierce screamed. She wound her arm around the cable and tightened her grip as the worm dragged on her.

The wire dug into her sleeve and she could feel it creaking as the LUSE unit took the strain. After a moment, the tension released as the robotic vehicle slid closer to the edge. Pierce yelped as she dropped a meter deeper.

"Wong! Hurry up!" The LUSE unit moved again and a second tentacle curled around Pierce's leg.

"Pierce! Don't fucking move!"

"Howard?!" Pierce looked up. Two shapes crouched at the edge of the hole. One of them raised a rifle and fired. The shot gouged a furrow in the wall next to Pierce's shoulder. She desperately twisted away, throwing herself against the other wall. Howard fired a second shot. The donut-shaped round hit the worm in its open mouth and blasted out the back of the head.

Wong seized the cable and pulled. Pierce flew upwards as the pressure was released from her legs. Wong grabbed her hand, swinging her out of the ground and landing her gently on her feet.

"It is good to see you again, Corporal Pierce."

"You too, Wong."

Howard was firing into the hole, a steady burst of high energy rounds. "We need to move," Howard announced.

"I am detecting increased seismic activity," Wong replied. "It appears further specimens are closing on our position."

"Oh good," Pierce muttered. "We pull out, back to the lander, now!"

"Roger that," Howard replied.

Waves of dirt rolled across the lunar surface. Plumes of dust and dirt erupted in grey geysers, signaling multiple worms burrowing through the rock and dirt.

"Move!" Pierce yelled. She started running towards the landing pad, four hundred meters away.

A worm breached less than twenty meters from her; Pierce opened fire as she ran, her rifle counting down the shots until it buzzed the out-of-ammo alarm.

"Pierce, your oxygen alarm is sounding." Wong ran beside her, his face set in an expression of concern.

"I can fix that at the lander. Right now, we have to keep

moving!"

A silent explosion behind them rained rock and glass. Pierce kept running, Wong simply turned his head to make a visual assessment.

"Meteor shower," he announced.

"Where's Howard?" Pierce asked

"Close and moving on our trajectory. Satellite data indicates a severe impact event is likely to occur over the next twenty minutes."

"How severe?" Pierce ranged the distance between herself and the lander.

"There is a reason corporate facilities are constructed *under* the lunar surface, Corporal," Wong replied.

"That bad?"

"Only if you are out in the open."

Pierce switched to a squad comms channel. "Howard! Get to the lander! We have incoming meteors!"

"Great, things were getting dull around here. Gordy, got a copy?"

The comms link crackled. A voice spoke and then dissolved into static.

"Wong, Gordinski's alive?" Pierce felt a surge of relief. Howard and Gordy surviving was one for the good guys.

"Howard, you receiving?" Gordinski's voice came through strong and clear.

"Gordy!? Hey! We're receiving you," Pierce chimed in.

"We have multiple inbound objects. The alarms are going off in here. You might want to stroll faster."

"We are moving at maximum speed for the humans, given the conditions and mass they are carrying," Wong replied.

"The lander is prepped for dust-off. Get your asses on board," Gordinski said.

Like every LX-7 model orbit-to-lunar-landing vehicle, the lander was a squat box with only minimal design nods towards its ancestor aircraft. The wings were only there to provide a platform for attitude adjuster rockets. The back of the vehicle opened like a garage door, with a ramp for the on- and offloading of vehicles and personnel.

A worm breached the surface between Pierce and the lander. It dived immediately, the body spinning like a drill as it bored into the dirt. Meteors travelled so fast that they couldn't be seen until they exploded on impact. Craters ranging from a dinner plate to a baseball diamond exploded into being. A rock hit the worm in the back. Chunks of black flesh sprayed in all directions.

"If one of those hits us..." Howard trailed off. He didn't need to say it. Pierce knew that even a small rock would punch through an environment suit or helmet. She would be dead before the exposure to vacuum killed her.

"Where's Block?" Gordinski asked.

"He didn't make it," Pierce replied. Details could wait. There were no guarantees that any of them were going to make it yet.

Wong reached the ramp and headed into the lander. Pierce stopped at the bottom, dropping to one knee as she turned to cover Howard who was still ten meters out.

"Gordinski, I will be closing the ramp in eleven seconds," Wong advised.

"Roger," Gordinski replied.

Pierce reloaded her rifle, firing at anything that moved. She aimed for the rising bubbles of dust, the eruptions where a worm might be about to surface.

Howard sprinted, leaping a fresh crater, and kicking up dust.

"We're on!" Pierce yelled. She dragged Howard by the arm and they ran up the ramp. Wong worked the controls, the ramp sliding up behind them. Once it locked in, the door slid shut and sealed.

"Gordinski, we are onboard and ready for evac."

The lander shuddered and tilted, Pierce grabbed a handle bar and steadied herself as the floor shifted. The drag of gravity intensified as the ship accelerated. Howard slid into a seat, slamming the buckles of the safety harness into position.

Pierce found her own seat. Wong walked easily, adjusting to the changing angles as the ship maneuvered.

The ship's interior rang with the blows of meteor fragments striking the hull and then they were clear.

"We all good back there?" Gordinski asked from the pilot's capsule.

"Five by five," Pierce replied and closed her eyes.

NET NEWS FEED: American Water Corporation is reporting the loss of their primary lunar water prospecting facility after a severe meteor impact event. Due to the catastrophic nature of the event, the underground facility was destroyed with no survivors. American Water, chief of operations, Dylan Mali, said today that the future of lunar prospecting lies with current and future generations of autonomous robotic units, such as the Wong model of service android. Claims that Black Light Security military units were involved in the destruction of the facility were categorically denied by both American Water and in a written statement by Black Light Security.

The End

GUARD DUTY
S.D. Perry

PFC Gaines was a horror nerd. The nerd thing, whatever, half the squad was nuts about video games or guns or football; everybody had their thing. Daniel "Robbie" Robb liked mixed martial arts, himself—Anderson Silva was the GOAT—and he enjoyed a good horror flick every now and again...but Gaines didn't want to talk about Jigsaw or Leatherface, he was a *book* guy, and he'd read every story ever about caves and monsters and military experiments gone wrong, and he wanted to share. He wanted to talk about what was in the chamber behind them, and what it might mean.

Fucking Gaines. It was 0230 and they were nearly a mile into the side of a mountain, alone. The engineers had run a line of lights all along the roof of the main tunnel, but the lights weren't that bright and parts of the tunnel were wide. Heavy shadows gathered to either side of the long slope in front of them, leading up from the crack they'd been set to guard. The few openings to dead-end side tunnels were as black as deep space.

Robbie leaned against the cold stone wall, half-listening to Gaines tell another stupid story, wishing he was down here with anyone else. The squad had been pulled off a base rotation in Afghanistan a week ago, flown to the Al Hajar mountains in Oman to set up camp support for a trio of military scientists, all officers. The brass joined a small group of civilians already working the "dig," a tunnel system uncovered in a spring landslide. The lead Army doc, Captain Pruitt, had locked things down tight. No access to the BFD room that had everyone spazzing out without permission and an escort. The civilians were pissed, but they were working on Federal grant money and couldn't say shit. Sarge said the only reason they weren't already locked out was because they'd agreed to help Captain Pruitt. Although why the Captain thought he'd get anything useful from a couple of academic gray-hairs and a half dozen sloppy grad students, Robbie couldn't figure.

Robbie had initially been happy about getting pulled out of the boiling, deadly desert to babysit scientists in an insurgent-free zone, but this was his first shift watching the Rosetta Room and he fucking hated it. A million tons of rock were balanced over his head and the cold was bone-chilling and Gaines wouldn't shut the fuck up with his creepy shit. Robbie was only letting him talk because the silence of the tunnels was worse. Except for a few bats and bugs right at the jagged opening, the system was totally dead. No moss, no spiders or whatever, nothing. All the guys who'd pulled watches had talked about the unnatural quiet and Robbie had nodded along, but he hadn't really understood. It was like being buried alive.

"... so the narrator and the pilot go down into the ice caves and find all these murals that tell about how these creatures had their own civilization, millions of years before mankind even existed," Gaines said. "And they learn that those monsters they found, that they thought were dead? They're actually *immortal*. And then they start hearing all these sounds coming out of the dark, and that's when they realize they're not alone down there in the tunnels."

"What the fuck?" Robbie snapped. "Are you kidding me? Can you talk about anything else?"

Gaines pushed his glasses up his nose. "I can't *think* about anything else. Have you looked in there?"

He nodded at the crack between them. Three feet across at the middle, and tapering slightly at the top and bottom, it ran all the way up the eight-foot wall at the very end of the tunnel system. It reminded Robbie of a cunt, but not in a good way. Absolute blackness lay on the other side. They were calling it the Rosetta Room because it had a bunch of languages carved on the walls, like that one famous stone.

"Yeah, and?" Robbie asked. "Writing on the walls, a rock in the middle."

"There are drawings, too," Gaines said. "Of *things*, with claws. And it's not just a rock, it's some kind of altar. With an inscription, and when the translation programs are done running—"

"Yeah, they're going to figure it out and then somebody will read the inscription," Robbie said. "You said already. Here's the thing, though—you really think anything's going to happen? Do you actually *believe* in magic occult shit? Really?"

"Actually, I don't," Gaines said. "I mean, I never have before. But dude, if it's all bullshit, why are we down here guarding it? The university team only got here two *weeks* ago. When they saw what they had, they sent an urgent request for extra funding, right? With *pictures*. And within days, we're here to back up Pruitt, who *also* got pulled out of some active shit to take this thing over. Since when does the military give a crap about ancient runes? Somebody high up on the chain doesn't think it's bullshit, at all."

"So? Lot of people believe in angels, doesn't make 'em real. And you're overthinking it, *dude*. Isn't it way more likely that the pictures got flagged because it's some kind of code? Sarge says maybe terrorists have been using it to pass messages, or something."

"I don't think so," Gaines began, but before he could get going, they heard sounds. Voices, but distorted by distance, unintelligible. A woman was talking, her voice rising and falling, an edge of desperation to her tone. The sound swelled through the tunnel, carrying through the barely contained blackness.

Had to be Datlow. One of the gray-hairs, an American archaeologist in her fifties. Total lez, probably, unless she was banging the equally unappealing language prof, the Arab with the nose hair problem.

Robbie and Gaines straightened up and unslung their M4s. Someone spoke, a brisk, male response. Captain Pruitt? Another voice took up, deep and rasping. The Arab professor, Safar. He sounded even more agitated than Datlow.

The voices went back and forth, and there were footsteps, lots of them. Robbie held the M4 across his chest and stared up the tunnel's throat, waiting for the visitors to come into view. The lights along the passage's roof were dull and yellow, illuminating only a narrow trail in the deep darkness. The thin, glowing line stretched all the way to where the tunnel branched, nearly a quarter mile ahead of them. There were a couple of battery lamps at their feet, but they were small and didn't keep the shadows from creeping.

Their helmet radios crackled, even as the first shafts of light swung into the tunnel from the west, tiny sparks floating in front of shadowy walking figures. Five, six people.

"This is Washington," the voice in Robb's ear crackled. "Captain Pruitt and Lieutenant Barr are with me an' Young, and the professors. Uh, Dr. Datlow and Dr. Safar."

"Copy," Robbie said, looking at his watch. 0250. He wasn't sorry that there were more people in the tunnels, but why so many? Why so *late*?

Gaines looked stricken. "They figured it out," he breathed, covering the helmet's mic. "Oh, this is bad, I'm telling you."

"Shut up," Robbie said. The woman was talking again, Robbie picking out a few words as the party approached. "...can't...responsible...wait..."

Captain Pruitt said something Robbie didn't catch. He was in the middle of the group; Robbie could tell by his height and the way he walked, a long stride, shoulders back, head up. The two profs were on either side of him, yammering away. Barr was carrying a laptop case, hurrying to keep up on his short legs. PFCs Washington and Young were on either end, the only ones wearing helmets, their M4s slung. As they got closer, Robbie could see that the captain wore his sidearm, a Sig P320.

The conversation got louder, but not much clearer.

"It *says* what will happen," Safar said. "Please, you have to consider how long ago these things were written! How could they have known about specific wars, or space travel, or genetic engineering?"

"Another Nostradamus," Pruitt said, dismissively. "Science

fiction from the past."

"If you don't believe any of it, then why bother with this?" Datlow asked. "There's so much to digest here, we should study this further. There's no reason to do this now."

"There's no reason not to," Pruitt said. "I said I would listen to you, but you're both talking nonsense. Nothing's going to happen."

"Then why go through with it?" Datlow asked again. She had sharp blue eyes and the thin lips of a maiden aunt. "You read the translation. It says that a man of war will secure the end by his ignorance. How can you just ignore such specificity?"

"Because my orders are to see if there's anything to this, and that's what I'm going to do," Pruitt said. "You're doctors, both of you. Honestly, I'm surprised at this...this *reticence* to debunk a prophecy in the simplest way possible. Your superstitions are not at all compatible with science. I'm not the one demonstrating ignorance here."

The group reached Robbie and Gaines and salutes were exchanged. Washington and Young were antsy, shoulders up, jaws tight. Young was high-strung in general, but Declan Washington was usually as cool as shade. Robbie wondered what they'd heard, walking in.

"In other circumstances I would agree," Datlow said. "But we translated the words in the very *year* the prophecy names, a prophecy thousands of years old. Do you understand how astronomically small the chance of that is?"

"That's assuming we've got all of the numbers correct, and I'm not convinced of that," Pruitt said.

"You've touched the stone," Safar said. "You must have felt it. Its *power.*"

Pruitt looked at him with disdain. "Lieutenant Barr and I are going into the chamber now. Washington, Young, please escort the doctors back to camp."

The relief on the guys' faces was almost comical.

"Yes, sir," Young said, nodding so rapidly that his helmet shifted.

"Doctors?" Washington said, and he gestured at the long ascent.

Lucky fuckers. Robbie didn't like how this was sounding at all, and Gaines was dancing around like he had to pee, his mouth a pinched line.

"Captain, please," Safar said. "Please, it costs nothing to wait another day, to talk about this!"

"This is a US military operation," Pruitt said. "It costs a lot, actually, and we've all got other places to be."

He nodded at Barr, who sidestepped into the chamber. A second later the lieutenant threw the switch that lit up the room, a metal clatter of sound. The tunnel's lights dimmed slightly as the generator took on the additional load. The tunnel seemed to grow wider, like the dark had suddenly gained strength, readying itself to swallow them.

A yellow glow spilled from the crack. The captain turned and slid into the opening after the lieutenant, jacket scuffing against the dry rock.

"Doctors?" Washington repeated.

"We have to go," Datlow said, her voice strangely inflectionless. "Now. We have to go now." She turned and started walking quickly back up the slope. Young hurried to catch up, shooting an anxious look back at Washington.

"We can't let him do this," Safar called after her, and Robbie stepped in front of the crack, ready in case the Arab tried anything. He almost *hoped* that he would, that something would break the incredible tension that had gathered in the tunnel, thicker than the shadows. What was this crazy shit?

Datlow looked back at them, at Safar, and Robbie saw how scared she was, her eyes bright with it.

"They've got guns, Ahmed," she said. "And he's probably right. Undoubtedly. It's—I need to call my daughter."

She turned back toward the exit and broke into a jog, Young at her side.

"Let's go." Washington put his hand on Safar's shoulder, trying to pull him away.

"You have to stop him," Safar said, looking at Washington, then at Gaines and Robbie. His dark gaze was feverish and bleak. His nose hair quivered. "It's the end of the world in there, don't you understand? You can't let him recite the inscription in that room. Please, please stop him before he—"

Washington yanked the babbling professor's arm hard enough to back him up a step. "I said, let's *go*. Don't make me keep asking."

"What is it?" Gaines asked, looking at Safar. "A curse? Another dimension?"

Safar's miserable gaze had fixed on the crack in the wall. He didn't answer.

"Ahmed!" Datlow's shout echoed through the long tunnel. Washington yanked the Arab's arm again and the man stumbled but didn't look away from the crack. He'd started muttering under his breath, reciting a prayer or some shit.

Robbie pointed his rifle at Safar. Whatever else was going on, the Arab had been asked and then ordered to leave. He could get the fuck out of Robbie's face, pronto.

Safar turned abruptly and started after Young and the woman, Washington on his heels, hurrying him along with a few more pushes. Within seconds, Safar started to run, too. The echo of boots on rock filled the corridor as all of them fled for the exit. In spite of the cold, Robbie prickled with sweat. The fuck was going on? Had everyone gone insane?

Gaines turned and looked at Robbie. His voice was a harsh whisper. "We need to get out of here."

"You need to calm the fuck down," Robbie whispered back, darting a look through the crack in the wall. There were five lamps in the big room, spaced out in a rough circle. Shadows pooled between them, the lights casting a yellow pall over the intricate carvings that covered the walls, extending to the domed ceiling fifteen feet overhead. The lieutenant had a laptop propped on the big rock in the middle of the room, Pruitt looking over Barr's shoulder at whatever was on the screen.

"Didn't you hear what they were saying?" Gaines asked. "It's some kind of prophecy about the end of the world. If the captain says whatever the words are, something's going to happen."

"Don't even start."

Gaines pointed up the tunnel. "The experts are fucking *running*, man."

The four had already made it most of the way up the slope, the lights dwindling quickly. Seeing the dimly lit figures recede made Robbie feel really shitty, like he was on a sinking ship watching the last lifeboat sail away. Like he'd cut the line himself.

Pussy. You're scared because of some woo-woo college professors and fucking Gaines*?*

"Robbie!" Lieutenant Barr called from inside the chamber, his voice echoing, sounds overlapping. "Bring one of those lanterns in here!"

Robbie grabbed one of the lamps, shaking his head firmly at Gaines, who looked poised to bolt. He mouthed the word *no* and then turned sideways and sidled into the chamber.

The captain looked up and pointed to the south side of the room. "Put it over there, about five feet from the wall. In front of that big divot."

"Yes, sir." Robbie hurried to comply, trying not to look at any of the drawings Gaines had talked about and failing totally. They weren't obvious within the long lines of glyphs and pictograms etched into the reddish tan stone, but they were there, leaning in at the corners, reaching up through cracks in the steep walls. No two were alike, but none of them made sense—long shapes that were more negative space than actual lines, the bodies defined by limbs that curled like tentacles or ended in hooks. Jagged teeth depicted mouths too big for narrow bodies. Holes had been gouged that might have been eyes, blank and misshapen. The creatures were mostly fluid, like octopi or amoebas, but there were several with insectile legs sticking off. In short, they were disturbing AF.

Robbie put the lamp on the floor in front of the divot—a roughly chiseled depression as big as a backyard pool, surrounded by extending rings of etched symbols. Who the fuck had carved that shit out? What kind of lunatics had carried ladders a mile into a black tunnel to decorate a room? Did they even have ladders back then?

He turned to the captain, who nodded. "Good. No one else comes in. You boys keep us locked up tight. This won't take long, then you can walk out with us."

"Yes, sir," Robbie said, and hurried back to the crack, glancing sidelong at the room's single feature, a rectangular rock about four feet high, three wide, and slanted at the top. Symbols were etched all over it, dots and lines and curves like waves. The captain looked like he was getting ready to make a speech to the big divot, Barr's laptop open on the stone. The lieu was messing with his phone close by, holding it up as if to film.

Robbie squeezed back through the crack, stepping back into the tunnel just in time to see the tiny lights far ahead disappear west.

Gaines leaned in, talking fast. "We should get out of here, man, I've seen this fucking movie and it doesn't turn out good for anybody. Let's just go. We can catch up to the guys and—"

"And what?" Robbie whispered. "Go tell Sarge we got *scared?* Captain says no one else gets in and we're on watch, this is our *job.* We're going to stand here and do our fucking jobs."

"But what if it's true, what if—"

"Seriously, if you don't shut up, I'm going to clock you," Robbie said. "You're as crazy as they are, getting riled up over King Tut's curse or whatever. This *isn't* a fucking movie—"

Barr was talking, and Robbie shut up so he could hear. Gaines cocked his head toward the crack, his eyes too big behind his smudgy glasses.

"...was very specific, but obviously the phonetics are a crap shoot," the lieutenant said. "There are alternates for every sound, these are just ranked by probability."

"What's this part?" Pruitt asked.

"Let's see...ah-nee-suh ay-yah *ook*, c'thy oth sai nah-ee oh *kuh*."

The k sounds were thick, like Barr was clearing his throat. The captain repeated the nonsense several times, smoothing the syllables into words. "Anisaiauk, c'thioth sinaio'k."

They went through the process a couple of times, the captain apparently pointing at words, Barr sounding them out, Pruitt repeating them. The language sounded primitive and weird... And were the shadows in the cave growing? No, of course not. Although, if the generator went out suddenly, Robbie thought he might shit himself.

Gaines was making little groaning, anxious panting noises, like he was about to hurl. Robbie stared straight ahead, getting more and more irritated with Gaines because now *he* had a bad feeling, and it was Gaines' fault, and being annoyed was infinitely better than the deep dread that was sitting in his guts like a rotten meal.

"All right, let's do this," Pruitt said, finally.

"Recording at 0304."

The captain started to speak, his voice clear and calm, powering through the foreign language. Gaines had taken a few steps back from the crack and seemed to be trying not to hyperventilate as the ugly sounds of the ancient words whispered up the dead corridor.

A hoarse cry echoed through the tunnels.

For a second Robbie thought horrible things, but the shout turned into words, *stop, you have to stop!* Safar. Running footsteps filled the tunnel, the man's hysterical cries getting louder, Washington shouting after him to halt or he was going to fire.

Goddamn, the Arab lost his shit! Had he gotten hold of a weapon? Robbie raised his M4, gaze straining at the dark, his heart pounding. The captain's voice was getting louder, too, belting out the words like he'd been born speaking them.

"Sethiu'k'atas, esa naiu'shu t'na'k, aiu hath iutho—"

"Captain Pruitt!" Gaines shouted at the crack, voice high and desperate. "Sirs, we might have a situation, maybe you should stop now!"

The captain raised his voice to shout over Gaines, the words thundering, too loud, like a bullhorn had suddenly come into play. Safar was still coming, still yelling, but his shouts were lost beneath the captain's booming incantation.

Safar ran into the top of the tunnel, a smudge of shadow barreling down the slope, no flashlight but clear enough to make out. Robbie trained for center mass—

—and a beam swept into the tunnel behind the running professor.

Fuck!

"Washington, get back!" Robbie called, but the soldier was gaining on the Arab, had slung his rifle and was going in for a tackle.

"Anaiu thi'k'thi lu esa—" The Captain's words were impossibly louder.

"Stop him!" Safar shrieked, close enough that Robbie could make out the black hole of his open mouth and then Washington dove and they both crashed to the tunnel floor. Safar flailed and kicked, punching wildly.

Robbie ran toward them, their struggle drowned out by the captain's recitation. Gaines ran at Robbie's side, deathly pale, his M4 hugged to his chest.

Washington was on top of Safar, delivering a beat down, spitting curses. Safar had stopped fighting back, only tried to cover his head, shouting weakly, incoherently.

"Hey, hey!" Robbie called, and Washington looked up, panting.

"As ethiu'k ah na! Ak na!" Pruitt screamed the final words almost triumphantly, and then Barr cried out, a shriek of absolute terror—

—and the ground shook and rumbled and shifted, and then Robbie was going sideways, plowing into Gaines who crashed to the tunnel floor. Dust rained down, the motes brilliantly lit by a deep, sickly purple light that suddenly poured into the tunnel from the crack at the bottom.

"Run!" Gaines shrieked, stumbling to his feet and then tearing up the slope. Robbie took off after him.

The captain's Sig fired and something screamed, drowning out the blast of the nine millimeter.

Fuckfuckfuck!

Robbie was running flat out, but that scream got him running faster. It was a massive, guttural bellow that shook his bones and made his guts turn to water, the roar of a bull gator the size of a Cadillac. He outpaced Gaines, but Washington had joined them and was faster, pounding past Robbie, kicking up dust.

Captain Pruitt's shriek of agony was cut off cold, the echo chased by an unearthly trumpeting, like an elephant with a wet bone in its throat. Rocks shattered in an explosion of sound and the tunnel in front of them lit up with alien light.

Washington looked back, his bared teeth and the whites of his eyes glowing purple. Whatever he saw sent him diving sideways, toward the unlit dead-end with the covered cess bucket on the tunnel's east side.

Robbie didn't look back. He ran into the narrow passage after Washington, Gaines piling in behind him. Gaines tripped and crashed to his knees, knocking Robbie off balance.

"Help me!" Safar screamed. Robbie swung his rifle up and stepped around Gaines. He darted a look around the edge of the passage.

Safar was stumbling up the slope, blood pouring from his nose— and behind him, a fast-moving wall of slick gray flesh puckered with circles of thick, translucent hooks, curved like claws. The misshapen wall pulsed, morphing appendages at the edges pulling it up the tunnel.

The silent mass swept over Safar, dropping on him like a heavy wet blanket, and Robbie saw a dozen slits in the monster's back, black and shining, the smallest the size of a man's fist. They opened and closed as the thing clenched itself, and Safar's muffled shriek faded to nothing.

Eyes.

The thing's skin started to bubble like mud and change color, darkening. Robbie pulled his head back inside—but not before an entirely different monstrosity crawled through the smashed rocks at the bottom, something with too many legs. More alien screams and howls poured up from the broken chamber.

"I told you, I fucking *told* you," Gaines said.

"It's what they were saying," Washington gasped. "The end of the world!"

"Shut up," Robbie said, because he couldn't call bullshit. Fucking Christ, what the *fuck*?

Horrible noises swelled from the chamber, thumps and slithers and wet slaps, moving into the wide tunnel. Robbie backed up, Gaines and Washington making room, all of them crammed behind the chemical bucket at the short passage's dead end. The shadows of their narrow shelter were smudged by that sickly purple, the light flickering as things moved in front of it. Something chuckled, a deep, humorless clatter that rose and fell.

The light was blocked out completely as the first thing moved past their hiding hole, a smell like gangrene and blood washing over them. It moved quickly for something so big, blocking the light completely for the space of a breath before it was past. Robbie only got a vague sense of its form, a giant, bubbling slab of meat.

Robbie didn't fire, nor did Washington or Gaines. Maybe, like him, they weren't so sure it was a good idea to attract any attention. A second creature the size of a young bull ran after the first on spiders' legs as thick as tree trunks, set wide in its heavy body. It was headless, its yawning mouth on its back, long needles of pale teeth cross-hatched along the spine. The mouth, if that's what it was, was big enough to chomp a man in half, easy. Three bulbous eye-stalks or antennae stuck up from its stumpy rear, the appendages ducking and swiveling as it skittered past, grit crunching beneath its wide, stick-like feet.

The chuckling monster rolled past behind the spider-thing on a trail of glistening slime, a warty, black slug as big as a walrus with thick, wiry hairs protruding from its back. It smelled like old puke, the odor so bad that Robbie felt spit curdle in the back of his throat. He thought he heard Gaines make a choking noise, but it was hard to tell over the clatter of the monster's undulating chuckle, or the deep bellow that spilled up from the shattered Rosetta Room. Robbie pictured a giant alligator down there, but it was probably way worse.

"They're heading for camp," Washington whispered, his voice crackling in Robbie's helmet.

"No shit," Robbie whispered back. He froze as a fourth monster wriggled past, sliding tendrils of flesh hissing over the rocks at their hideout's entrance. It looked like a rolling knot of eels, hundreds of them. The limbs that snaked into their small tunnel were close enough that Robbie could have taken a single step forward and touched the crepey, murky-green of pocked flesh. It smelled like meat dropped in a fire.

It slithered past them, following the others.

"What do we do?" Gaines asked.

The M4s each held thirty. "Anyone got extra rounds, second mag?" Robbie asked.

Unhappy negatives all around. They were on guard duty where the biggest threat was supposed to be pissy college students.

Ninety rounds between them, and a fifth monster stalked past their hiding place, a membranous mass of bizarre angles that hurt to look at. It reminded Robbie of layers of bat wings, and it crawled like a bat, on bony joints draped with stretched skin. The thing slipped on the mucilaginous slime left by the slug and trumpeted from an unseen orifice, its high bray so loud that Robbie's ears went numb.

"We gotta get out of here," Washington said, as the thing moved past.

"Yeah, how?" Robbie asked. "Join the parade? We wait here; we shoot anything that tries to come in."

"What the fuck are we waiting for?" Washington said.

"For these things to clear out," Robbie said. "We leave when they stop coming through."

"What makes you think they're going to stop?" Gaines said. "We don't even know where they're coming from. There could be hundreds. Thousands."

"Everyone's asleep," Washington said. "They're gonna get slaughtered."

"No way," Robbie said. "We got grenade launchers out there. Sarge'll kick these things asses." Assuming he woke up. Assuming everyone woke up and didn't freak the fuck out.

Assuming these things can die.

"If they fire at the tunnel, it's going to cave in," Gaines said. "We'll be trapped down here in the dark, with them."

"Jesus, will you shut up?" Robbie wished he could see to smack Gaines, but the other men were only blurs in the purple-tinged dark. "What the fuck is wrong with you?"

"Listen!" Gaines whispered.

There was something moving below in the room, something wet but maybe not that big... And there was a hum, a thin, reedy pitch, high, wavering. Distant. What was that? It sounded like... Robbie didn't know.

The primordial gator-thing roared again from down in the room.

The sound was so deep it was a vibration, so loud that the tunnels roared back. As the echoes died, Robbie heard the high sound again. It had thickened, lower sounds joining the swelling noise.

"We have to destroy the altar," Gaines said.

"What? No! Why?" Robbie asked.

"Can't you hear them?" Gaines asked. "They're *all* coming."

Robbie's terror spiked at Gaines' desolate pronouncement. It sounded exactly like a million screaming monsters at the end of a long, empty valley, charging across. He could *see* them, broken lines of lurching, leaping horrors running through a vast dark, running toward a pinpoint of purple light far ahead. *Toward us.*

"The fuck," Washington said, miserably.

"Pruitt opened a door," Gaines said. He sounded breathless. "We don't close it, there's nowhere to run. You think twenty guys with small artillery are gonna stop an army of these things?"

Robbie's whole body clenched. He wanted out, bad, but Gaines wasn't wrong about what good the squad would be against a thousand actual monsters.

What could anybody do? How fucked is everything, if they get out?

"Breaking the rock, that'll close it?" Robbie asked.

"It has to," Gaines said. "The invocation or whatever is written on the altar, right? Safar said it had power. We break it, maybe we end this."

Shit fuck!

The wet whatever-it-was slopped closer to their tunnel. Two, three, bird-things zipped past: dark, winged blurs as big as eagles that trailed long, whipping tails. One of them went high and slammed a light on the tunnel's roof. It hissed like a snake and Robbie saw its long, toothy snout and hooded black eyes, feathers that looked like charcoal cobwebs before it flapped out of sight.

Something screamed from the west, a howl that wound into the tunnels from outside, high and alien and malicious. The bull-spider? The living wall of hooks? Shots fired, scattered bursts of M4s and for an instant he felt hope, but the thing screamed again and was joined by the hellish cries of two others, the trumpeter and a new voice like nails on a chalkboard. They kept screaming, a hellish, feral harmony that was dropping in pitch.

That the rounds aren't stopping.

From the Rosetta Room something grunted, an impossibly deep, animal noise. Beneath it, the sound of the encroaching army grew, screeches and roars rising out of the clamor.

"We gotta do this now," Gaines said.

"Okay," Robbie said.

"You're fucking crazy," Washington said. "You hear what's in that room? It's a fucking dinosaur or something!"

"We can't stay here if there's more coming," Robbie said. "You want to run for the exit with a hundred more of those things behind you?"

"Oh, fuck this shit in the fucking *ass*," Washington said.

"I'm in front," Robbie said. "You're right behind me, watching the west side of the tunnel. Gaines, cover our six. Short bursts, we go fast and stick together. We blast whatever's in the room and break the rock, then we are fucking out of here. That's the plan, okay?"

"Good, okay," Gaines said.

"Motherfuckers," Washington said, and exhaled. "Okay."

Robbie edged toward the entrance, the other two lining up behind him. The wet-sounding thing was close, maybe twenty feet south and low to the ground. Whatever it was crept across the rocks in uneven, moist slaps, like fat fish being whacked on river stones.

Robbie ducked to look. The creature was like a thick, pale flatworm, five feet long, maybe, and two across, but barely a foot thick. More than a dozen stumpy legs stuck out of its weird body and it slapped half of them down and rolled over itself, humping its long, muscular form into an arch, more of its legs slapping down, edging the thing up the shadowy tunnel. Its corpse-skin glowed wet in the purple light.

The crack at the bottom of the slope had become a wide, jagged hole littered with rocks, the eerie light blasting from inside, staining the sane light of the tunnel's roof strip with its otherworldly hue.

The screaming of the running horde grew louder.

Fucking do it, go!

Robbie stepped into the tunnel and pointed the short weapon at the humping flatworm, finger light on the trigger. He fired twice, two bursts of three, catching it as it reared up. The steel-topped copper slugs smacked into the strange flesh, ripping off one of the stumpy legs. The monster spasmed silently as dark ichor splattered from the curling, trembling body, flowing like chocolate syrup over its pale skin.

It flopped over and stopped moving, but there were more things coming, three dark shapes emerging from the glowing hole, loping toward them. They were four-legged and the size of large dogs, but their bodies looked flayed, all sinew and bone and dark muscle, with plates of bone rising from the front shoulders. Their heads were flat like a lizard's, their jaws as wide as their heads, hanging open, revealing teeth like knives. As they charged up the slope, Robbie saw that they had insect eyes, rounded clusters of glistening black orbs high on their earless skulls.

Robbie targeted the closest and strode forward, firing.

The first took three shots to its barrel chest and issued a shriek like somebody stomping on a parrot. Holes opened in its body, but no blood came out, only dust or smoke. It staggered but kept coming, still making that horrible noise.

Robbie fired again, aiming for those wide jaws. The grouping went low, tore into the thing's short, thick neck.

The air around the monster was getting thicker, darker, as smoke or dust poured from the new wounds. Its scream turned into a choking rasp. It stumbled a few steps and then pitched forward, still jetting streams of dark gas.

Washington was firing at the one on the right. Its scream picked up where the others had died. Robbie targeted the third.

He aimed for the hanging jaw, but it jumped. The rounds snapped into the thing's left foreleg near the shoulder and it crashed to the tunnel floor, squawking furiously, thrashing against the rocks as it tried to get up.

Washington's target was down, smoking, the gas flowering like ink in water. Robbie walked quickly ahead and fired another burst at his target's sleek, horrible skull. One of its compound eyes ruptured, dark slime spraying, and its stringy body went limp.

Robbie hurried past the bloody flatworm, breaking into a jog. The longer it took them to get to that altar, the more things that could come out. Washington stayed on his heels, cursing softly in a steady stream. Gaines shuffle-stepped after them, breathing heavily.

They had to go through the fog of the dog-lizards' impossible blood, a choking, noxious smoke that burned Robbie's nose and eyes and put a taste in his mouth like fish oil. They were all gagging before they got through the miasma. Robbie's eyes watered, but he kept them fixed on the glowing hole, closer now. His ears rang from the stutter of the M4s.

Something spilled out of the hole, something big.

It came out in a humped crouch but unfolded itself into the tunnel, another wall of flesh like the thing that had gotten Safar—a thing that stretched its pulsing parts to the tunnel's ceiling and one wall, pulling its unlikely body forward. Thick crescents of talon or tooth stuck out of the gray flesh, hooked like claws. It rippled toward them like some giant manta ray, shapeless blobs of flesh at its edges forming into rough clumps that shot off and grabbed the rocks of the ceiling and the west wall.

Robbie and Washington both opened fire, rounds ripping into the pulsing center of whatever it was. Its scream was the bright pitch of a tea kettle, coming from its back, echoing into the glowing chamber behind it. Black sludge oozed from the holes. The claws spasmed and hooked at the air, and they both fired again.

"Ah, shit!" Gaines fired at something behind them.

The shrieking wall of claws was collapsing, folding forward.

Robbie let off a burst at a handful of the winking eyes on its back as it slouched to the floor, then turned to see one of the "birds" flying at them. Gaines fired again and punched through one of its wings. Bloodless, shredded tatters trailed the thing's erratic path. It hissed like a bucket of water on a roaring fire but didn't slow down.

Robbie fired but missed as the thing arrowed its body and dove at Gaines, still hissing. It slammed into his face, knocking him backwards, wrapping its dark wings around his head. Its tail curled like a scorpion's stinger and needled into Gaines' throat, fast, stinging again and again.

Robbie swung the M4 down and tried to rake the creature off while Gaines flailed. He'd dropped his rifle, both hands pulling at the monster as the tail kept stinging, jabbing.

Robbie jammed the barrel under its lean body, pushed up and fired. The burst knocked the thing off Gaines' face, leaving scraps of web and some sticky, whitish liquid behind, like it had cum on him. The monster's wings fluttered and twitched all over, and it went still.

Gaines clapped his hands to his throat. Robbie could see the skin swelling beneath his fingers, going purple.

"The altar," Gaines gasped, and then he was choking, neck puffing into infected lumps, inflating like a handful of water balloons. Dark threads of poison raced beneath the skin of his face, his eyes turning red and then drifting. The swellings went shiny and then split, blood pouring from the rupturing flesh. Gaines was dead before the first streams of blood hit the tunnel floor.

Washington was firing again.

Robbie scooped up Gaines' M4 and turned. Another of the coiling eel monsters had come out of the chamber and was slithering towards them, limbs curling and flexing. It had to be six feet at its girth, but its tentacles stretched to the ceiling.

They both fired into it and dark fluids splashed, running down its limbs. Soundless, it came faster, coiling toward them like living, swirling smoke, like a bad fucking dream.

"Die, bitch!" Washington screamed, and emptied his mag, rounds stitching through the undulating monster's dancing limbs, shredding them, chunks of greenish flesh hitting the rocks.

The thing stopped, collapsing. The gore smell was gagging, burnt meat and tangy metal. Washington was still trying to fire, finger white on the locked trigger.

"Take it," Robbie said, holding out Gaines' M4, looking back up the tunnel. Weird dead bodies and blood smoke, Gaines and purple shadows. Nothing moved.

The gator monster down in the room let out another guttural cry. Robbie could feel it more than he could hear it, his ears ringing too much for him to discern how close the army was getting. How many shots did he have left? Twelve? Nine?

The lights that ran the roof of the tunnel went out, flickering and then dying. There was only the ugly purple now to light their way, a venomous light that the shadows embraced, plunging the tunnel to near blackness.

"We gotta hurry!" Robbie called, and started running. Cursing, Washington ran after him. They steered around the mass of tentacles, Robbie in the lead, shooting glances back when he could, letting the slope carry him down. They had to get to the rock and have enough rounds to destroy it, that was what mattered. Maybe they could outrun whatever else had gotten out, but they had to close that door.

The purple hole bounced closer in front of them, flickering as dark shapes moved in front of the light source. As they stumbled downward, Robbie saw that the light was coming from the altar itself, the whole thing glowing like a black-light lamp.

A hulking creature tore out of the room and ran for them. It was built like an ape but was scaled with heavy spines running down its broad back, all of it a matte dun color. It let out a liquid shriek, a furious sound, from a head almost like a jackal's, but with a shark's dead black eyes, too big on its narrow, demonic face.

Robbie fired into its scaled chest, Washington coming in a beat later. Where the rounds hit the scales turned dark, but there was no blood and it was fast, *too fast—*

Robbie fell back a step and fired again, aiming for center mass and the thing leapt forward on thick, muscular legs, nearly halving the distance between them, landing on its overlong arms and bounding again, straight at Washington.

Robbie emptied his mag into the monster, but it tackled Washington and bit into the screaming soldier's throat, clawing at the tunnel and at Washington's body with its hands and feet, ripping grooves into the rock and through Washington's side, gutting him as it shook its head. Its teeth tore away the front half of Washington's throat. It raised its head to swallow and then clamped down again.

Washington had dropped Gaines' M4. Robbie didn't let himself think about it, he dropped his own empty rifle and stepped closer to the feeding demon to scoop up the weapon, the last weapon with rounds. He was close enough to the monster to hear the whistle of air through its slit nostrils, smell its musky, bitter scent.

He pointed the barrel at its head and fired into one shining black eye, two rounds slamming into its long skull, exiting in a blast of scales from the back of its head.

The thing collapsed onto Washington, shuddered, and died.

Robbie ran ahead. He could see the glowing altar clearly, see part of the hulking, monstrous gator-creature on the chamber's east side, dark and crouched—and he could see Gaines' door, finally, straight ahead of him. A massive hole had opened up where that big divot had been, where he'd put the lantern only minutes ago. The hole was ten feet across and ten high and utterly black, but the edges of it weren't steady. They flickered and wavered like an old movie out of frame.

The monster roared, and turned toward Robbie just as he reached the broken rocks at the entrance. It had eight legs and a long, muscular body, like a big cat's but heavy through the belly. The top of its head was almost bovine, horned and square, but instead of eyes there were a dozen random, empty-looking holes. Its jaw bulged outward like a hippo's, and its bone-shaking cry revealed pointed, blood-stained teeth. There was no sign of the officers, only a slick of blood on the floor, and shreds of meat hanging from the creature's lipless jaws.

Robbie ran into the room, firing at the monster as it stomped toward him, aiming for its fugly head. It roared again, shaking its giant, screaming face, and Robbie put three rounds into its big mouth.

The thing's roar gurgled and it retreated a few steps, legs moving like a spider's, shifting it quickly. It shook its head, watery dark blood streaming from its terrible mouth.

Howls emerged from the black of the flickering-edged hole, screams and shrieks and sounds he couldn't understand, all of it close, echoing into the glowing room, loud enough now to hear even over his busted ears.

The altar.

Robbie aimed at the glowing purple rock and fired, rounds skipping across the top of the stone, small chips of stone flying.

The altar's glow dimmed slightly. The portal flickered, and for a beat Robbie could see etched rock beneath it, but then it was back again, a yawning doorway to some black world of impossible monsters.

The creature started for him again, bellowing, blood dripping from its huge jaws, breath like carrion on a hot day.

Robbie dodged around the altar, fired again at the monster, getting two more rounds into its mouth. It swung away from him tripping sideways, stuttering another gurgling cry. It would have to be enough. They were coming; Robbie could feel the cold air rushing toward him through the door, smell the waves of stink, feel the ground trembling beneath his feet.

Robbie emptied the rest of the mag across the surface of the glowing stone. The rounds cracked the inscription, splinters of rock spinning off—

—and the stone split in half with a rending crunch that shook the chamber, just as the trigger locked out. Both jagged sides fell to the floor and the purple light died, leaving Robbie in the dark, and he felt a second of pure triumph—

—before he realized that he could still see, by the very dim light coming from the open portal. The open, solid portal, no longer flickering at the edges. The abyss was lit by an alien moon, perhaps; Robbie could see the first shadowy shapes running toward the black chamber, the faintest outlines of the opening ranks. Thankfully, he couldn't hear much of anything anymore.

A man of war will bring about the end by his ignorance. It appeared that destroying the altar had made things permanent.

The first of the monstrosities swept through the door, drooling, covered in matted fur. A giant tentacle curled into the room after it, and a dozen stinging birds followed, diving into the cold black of the dead cavern, stingers whipping behind them.

Fucking Gaines, Robbie thought, hating the dead nerd deeply for the rest of his life, which turned out to be not very long at all.

The End

THE OFFSPRING
J.H. Moncrieff

Russia, 1945

Excruciating pain seared Grigory's limbs, shocking him awake.

Everything hurt. His lungs shrieked agony with each whistling gasp.

Look.

His eyes refused to obey his brain. The lids felt stuck, sealed. Enclosed in impenetrable, unavoidable night, Grigory's pulse quickened until all he could hear was his blood swooshing through his body. Razor wire wound tighter and tighter around his chest with every breath.

Panic.

Not here, not now. There was no time. Though he had no idea where he was, it was obviously a life-or-death situation.

Flexing his fingers, it was as if he had plunged them into flames.

He stifled a scream, biting on his lip so hard he tasted copper.

Perhaps death was preferable.

How did I get here?

The bar. The same one he frequented every Friday night. But something had been different, hadn't it? Yes, something had been different.

Think, Grigory, think.

A man's features forced through the fog encircling his brain. A man with a pleasant smile. A man with deep pockets and the highest tolerance for drink Grigory had ever seen.

A new friend.

The 'keep had recognized the stranger, and spoken to him with respect, and that had been enough for Grigory, especially when the man offered to buy the first round. Grigory, whose salary was stretched to the point of snapping, could only afford a single shot. He demurred, cheeks burning as he explained his predicament in a voice barely above a whisper. He could not accept his new friend's gift, because he would never be able to reciprocate.

The man had laughed, he remembered now, and something about the sharpness of it made his teeth ache. But not then. Then, all he'd cared about was the drinks the 'keep brought to their table. Doubles. When had he last been able to afford such luxury? He thought of Raisa, of their children, waiting for him at home, and drowned his guilt with the smoothness of the vodka.

What had they talked about, he and this stranger, this new friend? He struggled to remember, to pry the reluctant memory from his aching brain. The man had asked the usual questions, inquired after his family, his work. Nothing to raise any alarms.

With each new round, Grigory had mounted a feeble protest, a reminder that he could not reciprocate, even when his meager paycheck arrived.

"Worry not, my friend," the man had said. "I have plenty of money."

No one said such things in Moscow, especially now. No one had money, certainly not anyone Grigory knew. But by then, he was too drunk to care.

"You are awake." A light shone in Grigory's eyes, making him squint. So his eyelids hadn't been sealed after all. It was the darkness, the impenetrable darkness. "I told them you would survive. For a reporter, you are in impressive shape."

Reporter.

Only Raisa knew the truth of what he did for a living. Everyone else, even his parents and their friends, believed the lie. It was safer that way.

He hadn't told this stranger. No matter how smooth, no vodka would ever lead him that far astray.

"I'm not a reporter," Grigory slurred, his mouth slipping as it tried to form the words. "I work at the factory; I told you."

"Oh, comrade, you need not to lie to me. After all, I am a fan of your writings. The way you speak the facts about our government; it is so courageous, so brave."

"Where am I?"

Everywhere the light touched, he saw blinding white, shimmering.

"You are in every journalist's dream, Gregor. You are in the story of a lifetime. Too bad you will never write about it."

Confused though he was, Grigory realized the seriousness of his situation. It was what he'd always feared, what kept Raisa awake at night whenever he'd been late.

You must be more careful, she'd warned, time and time again. *You mustn't drink at the bar anymore. One day they will find you, and you will be killed.*

Typical female hysteria. His wife's feeble attempt to control him, or so he'd believed. Now he desperately wished he'd listened.

"Many others would have perished from exposure by now, but not you. You are too strong. How did you get so strong, Gregor?"

Exposure. In the light's merciless glare, he caught a glimpse of his feet, bare and blue against the white. Then his legs, also bare. The fire, then, that burned his flesh was not of heat but of cold. They had stripped him of his clothes and brought him to this snow cave to die.

Raisa.

"Do not worry about your wife," the man said, reading his mind. "She was not nearly so strong. She died hours ago."

His throat was too frozen to emit the scream.

"And my children?"

The stranger clicked his tongue, shook his head. "You already know the answer to that. You are an intelligent man, a smart reporter. You understand we cannot leave any witnesses, especially witnesses who will one day think they should avenge their mother's terrible death. Oh, she was in such pain, Gregor. A pity to have to destroy one so beautiful, but you hardly left us any choice."

"Then kill me. You have surely brought me here to spill my blood, and you've destroyed everything that matters to me. End it."

"Oh, it will end, but not by my hand." The man stroked his chin and smiled. "Left here much longer, you would freeze to death. However, that would be a waste of your considerable talents."

"Talents? I have no talents." Still struggling to accept the death of his wife and sons, Grigory slumped to the ground, his stiff legs no longer willing to support him.

"On the contrary. Our great leader has been quite impressed with your abilities. It is too bad such a fine mind has wasted it on drivel. Your brain and your physique is what we desire. And thanks to a little something I slipped in your drink, we will have it."

Deep in the darkness, farther than the man's light could ever reach, came the sound of breathing. It was a grunting snuffle, like that of a large animal—perhaps a bear. Resigned to death only a moment before, Grigory's muscles tensed for a fight. "What the hell is that?"

The stranger chuckled. "That, my friend, is your new companion. I am sure she will be very pleased to make your acquaintance. She has been quite lonely, you understand."

As the snuffling grew louder, Grigory pushed himself off the ground, nerves twitching. Whatever this creature was, it wasn't a bear. With every step it took, the walls of the cave shook, making snow spill onto his shoulders.

"I will leave you two alone, Gregor. I trust you will find her affection worth dying for. Your body will be sacrificed for the greatness of our empire and the triumph of our people, and isn't that what you always wanted?"

Left alone with the creature, Grigory's bladder let go, but any smell was lost in the fetid stench emanating from the thing's breath. Towering over him, it was covered in matted greyish hair. Its eyes were a muddy yellow, shining like a cat's.

He turned his face away as it approached, squeezing his eyes shut. The stink of it made him dizzy, and he crouched against the wall of his prison, praying for consciousness to leave him.

The horror as the creature took hold of him in the most personal of ways, touching him as no one but Raisa and the occasional late-night indiscretion had in years, brought new life surging into his veins. Now he understood what the man had meant about putting something in his drink. His erection was massive, swollen and throbbing, larger than it had been since his youth.

As the reeking, slobbering thing threw him to the ground and mounted him, Grigory screamed.

Russia, 1959

They had begun the day in deceptively high spirits, but as night descended, one of them fell silent. Like an infection, Sasha's melancholy spread and festered, until everyone in the group could feel it looming over them.

By unspoken agreement, Aleandra was the one to approach him. He was hunched before their meager fire, staring at an old photograph he clutched in his hands.

"Is that him?" she asked, hoping he wouldn't snap at her or otherwise push her away. She had been dating Sasha for over a year, and in the spring they planned to marry, but his ever-shifting moods worried her. Being around him was like balancing on an ice floe, never really sure when the fragile surface would give way beneath her feet, plunging her into freezing water.

He nodded, passing her the picture, which had curled at the edges.

"He's very handsome," she said, and he was. She knew that the man in the photograph had been Sasha's father, a news reporter who had been openly critical of the government's regime. When Sasha was only nine, he and his family had been brutally attacked by government agents. His mother and brother had died, and Sasha himself had barely survived. He hadn't seen his father since that night, and had always assumed the government had murdered him as well.

Aleandra understood the attack had left scars on Sasha's psyche, wounds that would never heal. While his father had been a drinker, they had been a close family, and though it had been fourteen years since the attack, he still missed his parents and brother every day.

"He was here, Allie. I can feel it."

She shivered. Their isolated camp on *Kholat Syakhl* was creepy enough without fretting about the spirit of her boyfriend's slaughtered father hovering over them. Grigory had been convinced the government was conducting unethical military experiments in the mountains, which was why they'd chosen the desolate place to begin their search for answers.

Aleandra shouldered the responsibility for her friends' wellbeing. While they liked Sasha enough, he was not the sort of man who was easy to be close to. She had been the one to appeal to them for help, and she understood they had agreed for her sake. No matter what happened in the next few days, she had to make sure everyone got off the mountain safely.

"Everything all right?" Oleg asked. She suspected that her adventurous friend was the only one who'd actually *wanted* to go, rather than responding from some sense of obligation.

She stood, dusting bark and other debris from her snow pants. "Yes, everything's fine, but it will be dark soon. We should prepare dinner while there's still light."

"Works for me. I'm starving." At six-foot-seven and well over two hundred pounds, Oleg was always hungry. But his jovial nature was a welcome respite from the gloominess that shadowed their camp, so no one minded feeding him. He clapped Sasha on the shoulder. "How are you feeling, my friend?"

Tucking the photograph inside his jacket, Sasha straightened. "I'm fine; thank you."

It was a lie, and all three of them knew it, but Aleandra was still relieved. Maybe this trip would help Sasha put some of the demons in his past to rest. If so, it was worth the risk.

Forced cheer set the tone for the evening as the six friends tried their best to forget the grim reason for their adventure. As the vodka bottle was passed back and forth, they almost succeeded.

An unearthly howl split the night. Oleg stopped talking, mid-joke, and Aleandra felt a crawling along the back of her neck. She shivered.

"What was that?" Tatiana said.

Mishka grabbed the bottle out of her hand and chugged. "Sounds like wolves."

"That wasn't a wolf. I've heard wolves. That was something else." Elena stared into the distance in a way that made Aleandra nervous. She tugged on her friend's hand, urging her to sit back down.

"What, then? Coyotes? A dog?" Mishka narrowed his eyes as he challenged her.

"That didn't sound like any dog I've ever heard," Oleg said. "I agree with Elena. It's something else."

"Canines are pack animals. If it were a canine, it would have gotten an answer by now." Elena retrieved the bottle from Mishka.

The group fell silent, listening, as Aleandra tried to ignore the sensation that something was creeping up behind them, preparing to pounce. When she couldn't tolerate it any longer, she stood, trying her best to appear casual. "It's been a long day. I think I'm going to turn in. Sasha, will you walk me to my tent?"

Her friends' goodbyes were intertwined with teasing remarks and snickering, as she'd expected, but even though her cheeks flushed, she didn't care. She needed to tell Sasha about her concerns privately, and if the rest of them wanted to think there was something more carnal going on, that was the fault of their own sick minds. Her boyfriend smiled for the first time that day, but as they left the fire, his seriousness returned.

"What is it, Allie? I can tell something's troubling you."

She hesitated, regretting they'd left the warmth and light of the campfire behind. The temperature was dropping rapidly, and for the first time, she was concerned their gear wouldn't be enough to keep them from freezing. "That terrible cry. What do you think it was?"

"Probably a wolf, like Mishka said." He slipped his hand into hers, and she clung to it, his closeness making her feel safe for the moment.

"Elena grew up in the country. She's listened to those creatures howl all her life. If she says it wasn't a wolf, I believe her."

"What else could it be?"

As they reached the tent she shared with Elena, she beckoned him inside. Though the thin nylon was hardly soundproof, she wasn't comfortable discussing her fears outside. She still felt that something was out there, watching.

Listening.

Sasha followed and zipped the flaps shut. He tried to wrap his arms around her, but she insisted on keeping her distance. She needed a clear head; now was not the time for romance.

"I'm sure you've heard the stories about these mountains."

Sasha was quiet for a moment, and she could see him turning her words over in his mind. "Please tell me you're not talking about the creatures."

"There have been so many sightings, Sasha. You heard what they were saying at the tavern. The Mansi are too afraid to come up here after what happened to the Dyatlov group, and they're skilled hunters. Surely, they wouldn't stay away on account of a few wolves."

The fate of the Dyatlov group troubled everyone, and had almost discouraged a couple of their friends—Tatiana and Mishka—from joining them. Earlier that year, a group of nine ski hikers, led by Igor Dyatlov, had ventured into the same mountains, eerily close to where they now camped. When an expected telegram from Igor never arrived, a search-and-rescue team had gone after the hikers. Searchers had found their mutilated bodies scattered around their campsite. One of their tents had been slashed clean through, and many of the hikers had been half-naked, as if they'd had to leave in a hurry.

The government, eager to close the case and put an end to any questions, claimed an avalanche was to blame for the deaths, but Elena's father had been on the search-and-rescue team, and said there were no signs of any avalanche. And then there was the photo.

Igor's camera had been abandoned along with the rest of the

group's belongings. When the film was developed, one photo showed a shadowy figure. A figure that wasn't quite human. It seemed related to the strange message that had been left in the tent:

From now on we know, snowmen do exist.

"You know I don't believe in that. Whoever killed the Dyatlov group was human, just like whoever murdered my family and kidnapped my father was human. There are no such things as yetis."

Aleandra prayed he was right. It would make it a lot easier to sleep that night. "Sasha, I don't think we're alone out here."

"Of course we're not alone." He hugged her close, his voice softening. "There are many creatures in the forest: rabbit, bear, deer..."

She shook her head. "That's not what I mean." And she was sure he knew it too—she'd hardly ask to speak with him about the presence of a few rabbits. Why was he feigning ignorance? Since they'd met, they'd marveled at their ability to read each other's minds, and now he acted like she was speaking a foreign language. "All night, I've had a strong feeling that someone was watching us— *listening* to us. And please don't tell me it's a bunny rabbit."

"I've felt the same," he admitted. "But this place would have anyone's imagination running wild. It's so isolated, so plagued with rumors of mysterious deaths and unnatural beings. What we're feeling is our own nerves, that's all."

Aleandra bit her tongue to keep from arguing. Sasha's explanation was rational and sensible, but she knew what she felt was real. It wasn't her imagination, or her nerves, or anything else.

Something was out there, something sentient.

Something that didn't want them here.

Wake up, Allie. *Wakeup, wakeup, WAKEUP.*

Her eyes flew open and she let out a startled cry when she saw a face looming over hers. A hand clapped over her mouth, stifling her.

"Ssh. Hurry, get up."

Aleandra recognized the voice before she could make out the person's features.

"What are you doing?"

Elena had grasped her arms and was tugging her upright, but Aleandra's legs were still entangled in her sleeping bag. She stumbled, grabbing onto her friend so she wouldn't fall. "Elena, tell me what's happening. What's wrong?"

"No time." She shoved a jacket into Allie's arms. "Come on, come on, we have to leave."

The other woman's terror was contagious. Aleandra followed Elena into the frozen night without asking any more questions. She'd known Ellie since they were girls, and had never seen her so frightened.

A bitter wind clawed at her skin, making her grateful for the jacket. She fastened the hood and neck protector while fighting to keep pace with her friend, who ran through the knee-high snow as if it were weightless. Light from the full moon sparkled on the ice crystals, rendering the scene strangely beautiful.

As she saw Elena was leading her to the forest, she seized her friend's arm. "What about the others? Sasha, Tatiana...we can't leave them."

Elena's face was blank, her voice a monotone. Aleandra, who was studying to be a nurse, recognized the signs of shock. "They're gone."

Sasha! "Gone? What do you mean, gone?"

"Just gone. We have to go, Allie. There's no time."

She turned and continued cutting a path through the snow. Hesitant, Aleandra looked at the camp they were leaving behind. It was silent, still. She glimpsed no movement, heard no signs of life. Tears stung her eyes as the painful truth sunk in—Sasha had left her behind without a word. He'd abandoned her to whatever fate had made him leave the camp.

Elena plunged into the forest without pausing, occasionally tripping over branches and rocks. Retrieving a flashlight from her pocket, Aleandra clicked it on and gasped when her friend whirled on her, looking crazed. Elena's hand closed over the light.

"Turn it off," she hissed. "Do you want to kill us both?"

Before she could answer, a chorus of howls sprung up around them, startling Aleandra so much she nearly cried out. Elena jerked her arm, urging her forward. Her pulse pounding in her ears, Aleandra forced herself to concentrate on avoiding the branches that snagged their skin and clothing, and the hidden obstacles beneath the snow.

She strained her eyes until they ached, struggling to see. The howling continued, the creatures sounding close enough to touch. *Those aren't wolves.* She pushed the thought away.

Elena stopped short, causing Aleandra to bash into her, but her friend didn't react. "There's a cave or something up ahead," she whispered. "We'll be safe there till morning."

Her lungs aching, Aleandra felt even more pressure build in her chest. "What if there are bears?"

She could see the cave now, a shadow against the night sky, its maw looming open as if to swallow them whole.

"Allie, if we stay out here, we are going to die. Do you understand me?"

Elena gripped her shoulders with gloved hands, staring into her eyes. But Aleandra *didn't* understand, not really. She'd followed her friend this far as if in a dream, not sure what was happening or why. Not understanding why Sasha had abandoned her, why the rest of the group had left them. What about Oleg? He was so protective, like an older brother. She'd always felt safe with him, and yet, he had left her, too.

"I—I can't go in there, Ellie," she managed, the blood rushing to her brain so that she could barely hear herself speak.

"Yes, you can. You can, and you will."

Before Elena could drag her the rest of the way, she hastened to explain. "You don't understand. I really can't. I'm—I'm claustrophobic." The shame of her weakness, of not being like the others, made her cringe in spite of the direness of their situation.

"Better claustrophobic than dead. We have no choice."

How could she tell Elena the truth—that the cave was the same one she'd seen in her nightmares?

The pressure on her chest worsened, as if something were squeezing her, allowing only the faintest of breaths. She gasped for air, choking it down in great gulps though its iciness stabbed her throat like needles. "I—I can't breathe."

Elena drove her forward, pulling and shoving and dragging, until they reached the entrance. She poked her head inside and then drew back, her mouth twisted in disgust. "Ugh, it reeks."

A bad smell meant the cave was undoubtedly home to some wild animal—maybe more than one—but Elena wouldn't listen to reason, and Aleandra could hardly catch her breath, let alone argue. Pressing her arm across her nose and mouth, she followed her friend into the stinking darkness.

Taking her light, Elena switched it on. Aleandra winced at the intensity as the light ricocheted back at them, reflected by a million snow crystals. Elena directed the beam towards the roof, and both women followed its path with their eyes, staring at the twinkling sugar walls.

"We can't stay here, Ellie." The tension in her lungs increased as Aleandra tightened her grip on her friend's arm, yanking her backwards. "It's a snow cave."

Elena pulled away, shaking her head. "We have no choice. We have to stay low until morning. When the sun rises, we'll leave."

She ventured farther inside, and Aleandra's panic intensified as the light left her. "B-but it's not natural. Some animal made this. It's not safe."

"Do you see an animal?" Elena shone her light over the glittering surface. "Do you hear one?" Her voice had grown heavy with impatience. "Besides, even if there *is* an animal in here, it's a hell of a lot better than what's out there."

The cave was much larger than it had first appeared. Aleandra felt she'd been staggering after her friend for hours, with no end in sight. Thoughts of the structure collapsing and burying them alive tormented her, keeping her breathing shallow and her legs weak. She'd begged Elena to stop, trying to persuade her they were getting too far from the entrance, but her friend moved on as if possessed. She'd quit responding and wouldn't answer questions about the others—just pushed forward.

Finally, she stopped, holding up her hand so Aleandra wouldn't walk into her again.

"What is—"

"Ssh." Elena held a finger to her lips. "Look."

She peered over the other woman's shoulder. The path split in two, each option packed down and free of obstacles. What snow cave was this large, or had more than one passage? No animal had made this.

As if Elena had read her mind, she cast the light over the path on the left. "There are stairs!"

They moved closer, gawking at an old yet sturdy-looking set of stairs heading into an abyss even more foul-smelling than the one they were in. "I don't like it, Ellie. Let's go."

Elena cocked her head to the side. "Do you hear that?"

She could feel it more than hear it—a low, rumbling growl that vibrated through the earth and her boots, tickling her feet. "Are you crazy? There's an animal down there. We have to get out of here, *now*."

"That's not an animal," Elena said, shrugging her off. "It's a generator, and from the sounds of it, it needs some help."

"Ellie, what are you doing? Ellie, *come back*."

"Do you want to spend the rest of the night blind, Allie?" She held up the flashlight, which had been flickering for the last ten minutes or so—a flicker Aleandra had desperately tried to ignore. "Maybe this place has heat too. I have to try."

In a last attempt to keep her friend from descending, Aleandra seized her jacket. "I don't like this. I don't think we should be here. I'm going after the others. We never should have left them behind."

"I told you, they're gone. There's nothing we can do for them now."

"But—how can they be gone? They wouldn't just leave us. Sasha wouldn't..." Her words caught in her throat as she pictured her fiancé. How despondent he'd been that day, only brightening when she'd kissed him goodnight and held him close to her. At first, she'd been furious with him for abandoning her, but now a horrible thought occurred—what if he hadn't abandoned her, but instead she'd unknowingly abandoned him, following a mad woman into the night? Tatiana had often joked that Elena was crazy, but maybe the jokes weren't jokes after all.

The woman lunged at her, shoving her so hard the air went out of her and she lost her footing on the ice. Aleandra sat down hard, staring up at her friend, whom she no longer recognized. Elena's eyes were wild, her expression that of a spooked horse. "Are you daft? They didn't *leave* us."

"But you said—you said they were gone."

"They're *dead*, Aleandra." Her voice rose, echoing back to them.

"Wha—"

Time stopped, frozen. Aleandra gawked at Elena. The woman's lips were moving, but she couldn't hear. *Sasha.* No, he couldn't be gone. They were going to be married in the spring. It was a trick, a cruel, horrible prank, and any minute, their friends would leap out to surprise them.

Elena crouched in front of her, resting her hands on Aleandra's shoulders. Sighing, she leaned forward until their foreheads touched. Ellie's tears fell on Aleandra's face as she took a shuddering breath. "I heard someone screaming. I—I thought it was Tatiana, but it was Mishka. Something had him, something massive. I couldn't tell what it was. It had a human shape, but it was too big. It was gigantic, Allie. I tried, but I couldn't save the others. They were already...gone."

"But maybe—maybe one is still alive. Oleg, Tatiana, Sasha—they can't all be gone." She couldn't bring herself to say dead. It was impossible. She knew how Elena felt about Mishka; they all did. Obviously seeing her beloved killed had driven her insane, causing her to leave the others behind. "We have to go back for them."

She attempted to get to her feet, but Elena pressed on her shoulders, holding her in place. "No, I saw them. I saw the blood, okay? I saw...what was left."

"Not Sasha."

"Yes, Sasha. You have to accept it, Allie—he's gone. There is nothing more we can do for him or any of them. We have to protect ourselves now. We have to survive."

Survive, without Sasha? It was unthinkable. Her world ended then, in cold, foul-smelling misery, as the truth of Elena's words seeped into her unwilling brain. "I want to go back. I can't just leave him there."

"You don't understand. Those creatures, they—they were *feeding* on them."

A cry escaped her then, a thin wail that sounded more animal than human. Elena got to her feet, bringing Aleandra up with her as if she were a life-sized doll. "Sasha wouldn't want you to die down here. Don't you dare give up. Don't you leave me alone."

Death beckoned in the form of the treacherous stairs, and Aleandra pushed past her, flinging herself towards them. If she could break her neck, she wouldn't feel the agony to come. She'd be spared the emptiness of a life without him, without Tatiana and Oleg and Mishka, her closest friends. Why had she been spared? For a moment, she despised Elena for dragging her out here. She longed for oblivion.

The slickness of the ice under her feet slowed her progress and the other woman easily caught up, catching her by the wrist. "Let me go first. I have the light."

Aleandra pictured shoving her friend off the stairs. Whatever was down there, whatever was the cause of that ghastly stench, would surely kill them. Wouldn't it be kinder to end it now, like this? A broken neck didn't hurt—one snap and it would be over.

"Be careful. They're slippery," Elena whispered, bringing Aleandra's murderous fantasies to an end. Even without her beloved Mishka, her friend clearly wanted to live.

Rather than it growing darker as they descended, the atmosphere lightened, making it easier to see. The bottom of the stairs was awash in green and red lights. "What *is* that?" The unnaturalness of it broke through her apathy and the fear returned. "Can you see anything?"

"It seems to be some kind of machine."

Dread weighted her legs until they were made of lead. The smell was so strong her gorge rose, sending bile to coat her mouth. She choked it down. "*Stop*, Ellie." The Reaper waited for them in the greenish-reddish glow, grinning—she was certain of it. But her warning came out as a strangled croak. Her friend didn't hear.

Elena reached the last step and vanished. Aleandra pressed her gloved hand to the wall of the cave, ignoring the chill that crept through her fingers, stiffening them. Her eyes strained to see shadows in the dim light. She waited to hear the scream.

Instead, her friend's voice floated up to her, sounding breathless and excited. "You have to see this!"

Gritting her teeth, she forced one boot in front of the other, her feet numb. *Clomp-clomp, CLOMP. Clomp-clomp, CLOMP.*

Far from the dour dungeon she'd expected, Aleandra gaped in shock as she stepped on the last stair. The cave opened into some kind of laboratory. One wall was filled with metal panels that were covered with numbered dials and blinking lights in multiple colors.

There was a gurney in the middle of the room—if this could be considered a room—with crisp white sheets and a cart with a tray of medical instruments alongside it. It appeared as sterile as a hospital, but who would need a hospital in such an isolated place? Perhaps it was for skiers who got injured in the mountains.

And yet, the foul smell thickened the air, rendering it poisonous. It spoke of blood and gore, of something unclean.

Over the hum of the machinery, she heard another noise, a sound that didn't fit.

Her skin prickled, and she hurried to close the distance between her and Elena. "Did you hear that?"

Before the last word left her mouth, it happened again—the sound of chain links clinking against each other.

Elena shrugged. "Probably another machine."

But it wasn't. Aleandra recognized the sound from her childhood, when she'd had a St. Bernard dog her parents refused to let in the house. The pup had spent most of its days attached to a post in the backyard. She'd never forgotten the clatter its chain made as it rushed towards her, so happy for human companionship it would have garroted itself if she hadn't gotten to it in time.

Her fingers sunk into Elena's arm. "We have to get out of here. *Now.*"

Somewhere in that room, a creature was chained, and it was moving closer. There was no telling where it was, or how far the chain could reach. Or how strong it was.

Pulse racing, her head whipped in both directions as she searched for the source of the clanking, but everything was amplified in the cave. It could have come from anywhere. Her urgency finally inspired Elena, who willingly left with her at last. They shuffled back the way they'd come, even though the gloom above the stairs brought with it no promise of safety.

A white blur flew at them.

Elena tried to run, but the thing was faster, wrapping itself around her legs and tugging at her with incredible strength.

"No!" Aleandra yanked her friend away, the momentum freeing Elena and sending Aleandra toppling onto the stairs, the other woman in her grasp. Before they could escape, the creature spoke.

"Wait! Don't leave."

Shocked to hear it speak Russian, Aleandra's eyes widened. Although it was hunched over and caked with filth, she recognized it as human. Elena crab-walked backwards until she rested against Aleandra's lap, her breath coming in little shrieking whistles.

Long, scraggly hair the color of iron partly concealed the thing's face, but the creature was undoubtedly a man. His chest was bare and sunken, and he wore a heavy metal collar around his scrawny neck. Every inch of his exposed flesh was scarred or peeling.

"Who are you?" Aleandra asked, her voice stronger than she felt. The smell was at least partially coming from this pitiful thing, who revealed a mouth of blackened and rotted teeth when he answered.

"Gri—Grigory."

The name meant nothing to her at first, but the eyes did. They were the only non-offensive part of him, and she recognized them at once, as she'd been looking into them every day for the past year. Her own welled with tears.

"You're Sasha's father."

He sprang towards her, but the chain went taut and his skin choked against the collar. Elena attempted to clamber over Aleandra and bolt up the stairs, but there wasn't room. However, Aleandra was no longer afraid—at least not of this poor, withered, battered man. No matter how disturbed he had become, he was still Sasha's kin and she could never fear him. She didn't flinch as he grasped her boot, squeezing her toes.

"You know my boy?" His voice broke, and rheumy tears trickled down his cheeks. "But how? He is long dead."

Swallowing her revulsion, Aleandra leaned forward, stretching out her hand. The man clung to it as fiercely as he'd wrapped his arms around Elena's legs. "He survived the government's attempts to murder him. I came here with him to look for you."

"My son is here?" The man wavered, appearing on the verge of collapse, and Aleandra's throat tightened. Though haunted by his father's disappearance, Sasha had never dared to hope Grigory was still alive. And now the joyful reunion would never take place. She couldn't bear to tell him the truth, so she nodded, staring into the eyes that were so like Sasha's.

His grip on her hand tightened, crushing her bones and startling her. "Then get him out of here! You must leave before they return. They always come back."

"Who? Who comes back? Who did this to you, Grigory?"

The dread in his voice was palpable, and the panic returned, chewing on her with sharp teeth, but she owed it to Sasha to find out as much as she could. "What happened to you?"

He pushed back against her hand with surprising power. "*Go.* They will kill you. The only reason you still breathe is they hoped I would do it."

Before she could respond, the air reverberated with a howl that shook the stairs. The thunder of heavy footsteps thudded above. Elena launched herself over Aleandra and scrabbled up the stairs, disappearing into the darkness.

"Go—time is short." Gregory shoved her again, this time by her foot. The edge of the stair above her bit painfully into her lower back.

"What are they?"

"Monsters," he said, giving her boot a final push before retreating. His words echoed back at her. "They are monsters. Abominations against God...and my children."

Reluctantly, Aleandra turned away from him and faced nothingness. The darkness was like a wall, it was so impenetrable. Stretching out tentative fingers, she tested the air like a blind person, ascending the stairs one by one, hoping she had time.

Something grasped her hand.

"Don't yell; it's me," Elena whispered. Positive her friend had abandoned her, Aleandra wanted to weep with relief. "This way."

Feeling the cave's icy wall for guidance, they groped their way down the right-hand tunnel as quietly as they could, timing their footfalls with the creatures' so the crunch of their boots on the ice wouldn't give them away.

Descending into the complete blackness was a new level of terror, one Aleandra wouldn't have been able to survive without the pressure of the creatures at her back. They were close enough now that their breathing was audible, along with a constant stream of grunts and snarls. *They are communicating*, she realized. *They are sentient.*

"It's them," Elena said, her voice breaking. "The ones that murdered Mishka. They will kill us."

"No." Aleandra had new purpose now. She must survive so she could tell the world what had happened to Sasha's father. Her beloved might be gone forever, but she could see that his father lived his remaining days in comfort, rather than this disgusting cave.

"They're playing with us, don't you see? They're massive—they could overtake us instantly if they wanted to. They want us to think we have a chance. It's just a game to them."

Aleandra ignored her friend's warnings and took over the lead, walking them deeper into the cave. Whether man- or animal- made, sooner or later, it must end. And when it did, perhaps there would be another way out. A path to freedom and fresh air. The thought made her quicken her pace, hauling Elena along with her, even though she feared she'd walk straight into a creature any second. Only remembering Sasha's eyes in that ragged face drove her forward.

Two dots of golden light appeared in front of them. They were mere pinpoints, but it didn't matter. The sun had risen, and somehow, the light had found its way in. They'd follow it to salvation.

Elena began to fight her, twisting away and clawing at Aleandra's grip. "No," she moaned. "No—it's them! It's them!"

"Ssh, we're almost there. Just a bit farther—"

At first the warmth was welcome, but then the burning began, intensifying until she yelped. Aleandra flailed at her arm, certain it was on fire.

Her fingers swished through nothingness.

Her arm was gone.

Elena screamed, her cries soon drowned out by a horrific tearing noise. Aleandra, temporarily forgetting about her missing limb in her rush to save her friend, went after her until two pinpoints of golden light made her freeze.

They weren't pinpoints any longer.

They were eyes.

In their glow, she watched a hunched and horrid thing—a creature of nightmares—tear her friend's head off with its teeth.

There is nothing you can do for her now, my love. Back away, as quietly as you can. Don't give them a reason to chase you.

She wanted nothing more than to fall to the ground wailing, but hearing Sasha's voice calmed her. She crept backwards, ignoring the chewing and slurping, forcing the atrocious image of her friend's death from her mind. Steadying her remaining hand against the wall, she relied on Sasha to guide her.

A little bit farther, just a little bit farther. Can you move more quickly? That's my girl. Quiet now.

It took forever until she couldn't hear them any longer, but they could close the distance between them in seconds.

Look in your boot, Allie.

She didn't question his voice in death, just as she'd never had reason to question it in life. Dropping into a crouch, she crossed her left hand over to her right foot, where something had been rubbing against her skin. Forcing her hand into the tiny space between her ankle and the boot, her fingers closed around something hard. She knew what it was without seeing. She remembered how Grigory had held onto her foot, how he'd given it that last shove.

You're almost there. Just one more thing, and you'll be free.

She didn't want to do one more thing. What she wanted was to lie down and go to sleep. Her legs grew more unwilling to carry her, and spots flashed before her eyes, temporarily blinding her. Aleandra knew she was going into shock from the loss of blood and her arm but was powerless to prevent it. If she didn't get medical attention soon, she would die. Perhaps she was dead already, since she was listening to a ghost.

You're still alive. Keep moving.

It was as if she were a puppet on a string, lured by his voice, helpless to fight it. She moved forward, feeling like she was slogging through quicksand. She stumbled more frequently now, and each time, it was more difficult to regain her balance. The temptation to lie down was almost irresistible. After all, who would hire a one-armed nurse? Who would love her now that Sasha was gone?

I'm not gone; I'm right here with you. I'll be with you as long as you need me. Keep moving. Only a few steps more, my love.

She sensed it long before she heard it breathing or smelled its fetid stink. The darkness had changed, becoming her friend instead of her enemy, concealing her from view.

It's all that stands between you and freedom, and it's asleep. Do you hear that?

She heard the rumbling snore, human-like except for its volume. This time she didn't need Sasha to tell her what to do. She removed the sheath from his father's gift, tracking the creature by instinct.

When she was close enough to feel its heat, it opened its golden eyes, giving her a target. Silent as a shadow, Aleandra drew back her remaining arm and stabbed the knife through those eyes, hacking away until the golden light was gone. There was a shuddering thud as the creature fell at her feet. She'd struck so quickly, it hadn't had time to warn the others. Panting, she leaned against the cave, wiping away the sweat that drenched her brow.

You did well, my darling. You see it now, don't you?

This time the light was a faint peach, anemic compared to the gold. She wouldn't be fooled again. New strength filled her legs, and her pace quickened until she was half-running, half-sliding through the tunnel. Then freezing air hit her face and she was outside, free from that stinking darkness and death.

She plunged into the knee-high snow, never stopping, wincing against the unfamiliar light. It was difficult to keep her balance with only one arm, but she managed. Sometimes she listed to the side and paused for a moment to catch her breath, but not too long.

They hunt at night. They won't come after you in the daylight, but you need to get help.

The apricot sun was high above her by the time she reached their campsite. Ignoring the blood that darkened the snow outside the tents, she walked towards the one that mattered most.

No, my darling. You need your kit.

Aleandra reluctantly changed course and headed for her own tent, the only one not smeared and spattered with blood. She had Elena to thank for her survival, and once she got out of there, she would make sure the world knew how heroic her friend had been, how brave.

Forcing her stiff fingers into position, she unsnapped the latch on her medical kit, and one by one, withdrew the necessary supplies. Pulling aside her ruined jacket with her teeth, she packed gauze into the gaping hole where her arm had been and wrapped it, securing the bandage against the opposite shoulder. The exposed nerves were frozen, so she felt little pain—only exhaustion.

Crawling now, she left her clean tent for one awash with gore. No matter. She needed to see him, to touch him, whatever state he was in.

His stomach had been ripped open, a terrible wound, but the worst of it was concealed by his snowsuit. She covered him with a sleeping bag, hiding the rest. His face, his beautiful face, looked just the same. Once she lowered his lids, she could pretend he was sleeping. Lying beside him, she lifted his arm, bringing it around her like a blanket, imagining he held her close. She nestled her head on his shoulder, breathing in his scent, memorizing it, ignoring the sickly-sweet tang of his blood.

"You're not dead," she murmured. "Just sleeping."

Stay with me a little longer, my love. You're safe now.

And that was where they found her, asleep in his arms. The sight of the doomed lovers brought tears to their eyes.

The rescuers screamed when she spoke. They'd thought she was a corpse.

Even in her weakened condition, it took three men to pry Sasha from her arms.

It took even longer for her to explain what had happened to Grigory. In the beginning, they thought she was delirious, hallucinating. But eventually, they believed.

The team that went to retrieve him never returned.

The End

BLACK LUNG
Aaron Sterns

1 – Form Up Point

The commission tower rises like an ancient monolith against the darkening Melbourne skyline. Rooftop floodlights flare against the low smog and for a moment the entire top seems on fire, yellow flames of light steaming upwards. *Herald* journalist Liz Henderson tries to focus on the strangely beautiful image from her relegated observer position, but her mind reels so much with everything she's seen in the last few days she can't concentrate.

If only their goal was the roof. At least that'd be visible to the police snipers' cover fire.

The drug raid's target is instead somewhere within the barricaded nightmare building, close-quartered and claustrophobic. As with the other towers in the almost-lawless western suburbs, Force Command knew the building was controlled by the Death To Society (D2S) gang, an anarchic virus of criminals that'd managed to rise above most of the other gangs in the suburbs—mainly because they'd taken over much of the drug trade with such insane violence it'd scared those they didn't kill into early retirement. Liz had written a story during their early days, so she knew how heinous their methods were: Australia had never seen necklacing before their arrival. The images of rivals burning to death with tires around their necks on the shopping strips of Dandenong and Thomastown still haunted many. The thought of entering the building, even if only after the police tactical teams had cleared the way, sent prickles of sweat across her brow. She hoped the drug squad detectives she'd been embedded with over the past month didn't notice. They gave her some concessions as an outsider, but like all cops they lapped up weakness.

Police Intelligence knew that walls inside had been torn down at will, escape holes hidden behind plaster everywhere throughout. But further intel on the internals was sketchy. The hydroponics labs might be scattered throughout the labyrinth of apartments, having shunted the remaining families into the few empty rooms left, or the gangs could have taken over whole floors to network the banks of plants. Then again, the labs might be so well-hidden the search comes up empty-handed. Command just didn't know. And there's only so long the police head honchos could keep covering up the true impact of whatever it was D2S were now peddling.

The raver glimpses through the tangle of bodies, back hunched

*and convulsing, dreadlocks snapping like snakes, and he turns with
eyes black from embolism, and the bile he's spewing in a great torrent
doesn't stop, it doesn't fucking stop, it's impossible for that much to
be inside a—*

She tears herself from the ominous view, glances over the forces
assembled in the hotel rear parking lot with its shielded line of sight to
the tower across the block. All with their jobs to do. The chosen
protectors of society. The black-clad Special Operations Group
members with their muzzled mouths and steel eyes, checking each
other's kits: "You good Jacko?" "You good Mad Dog?" The uniformed
officers waiting to clean up and secure in their wake like puppies
eager to prove themselves. The forensics team in their plastic ponchos
and booties, scoffing down a last biscuit or two at the coffee trolley.
Detective Austin and the other drug squad members, who she and her
usual *Herald* photographer lapdog Fozz—shifting from foot to foot
now beside her—had sat alongside the last weeks. Or the Deputy
Police Commissioner and the other faceless suits lined against the
back of the co-opted parking lot, all stabbing away on their
smartphones or quietly reviewing political strategy with a shrewd eye
over the whole congregation.

She wishes she has their righteous self-belief, their unshaking
confidence in their place in the world. She'd lost hope long ago,
before all this. The only thing that keeps her going anymore is the
puzzle, the story. She has nothing else in her life.

"Who're the work experience kids, Austin?"

The detective beside Liz jumps as the hardass SOG commander,
a lethal bullet of a man Liz had heard tagged Shepherd, passes with a
snarled grin. "Press tagalongs," Austin says. "PR for the Minister."

"Think he'd learn. Like letting the wolves in the door." He keeps
walking. Liz can't help herself.

"Can't criticize the Brotherhood, hey?"

Shepherd turns back, smile turning hard. "That didn't take
much. Dalton know this is going to be a hatchet job?"

"Not this piece. But someone has to watch the watchmen."

Shepherd's pale eyes look through her. She can almost feel the
impact out the back of her skull.

"Just stay the fuck where you're told. Media blood'll take us
years to live down." Shepherd points a finger at Fozz. "And any
footage of our faces, I'll disappear that camera up your arsehole."

The Victoria Police Special Operations Group were perhaps the
most well-trained, well-skilled tactical response team in the country.
They attended hundreds of incidents a year, everything from terrorism
threats, to sieges, to mass shootings. Within the group they called
themselves the Sons of God, a backronym referencing Matthew 5:9:
"Blessed are the Peacemakers, for they shall be called the Sons of

God." Hell, they'd flown down to Port Arthur to stop the killing spree of Martin Bryant because Tasmania didn't have a force capable of dealing with such an event.

They'd also been involved in a number of well-publicized shootings during the Gangland Wars that brought into question whether they'd become a trigger-happy death squad. Liz had thought most of the shootings were justified, considering the heavily-armed opposition they'd been up against. But they'd nearly been disbanded and it necessitated a full cultural review and more emphasis on non-lethal means of apprehending suspects.

She knows she's being harsh, but if you didn't put a rocket up the narky ones early, they'd find a way to get rid of you.

Detective Austin stands a moment, embarrassed. "Jeez, Hendo. Go easy." He subtly turns his back, so they're no longer part of their unit.

"I think we officially have cooties," Fozz says low and she hides a laugh. He steals a photo of Shepherd's back.

She glances up to see the Deputy Commissioner staring at her across the gap. He nods and Liz feels the fingernail up the spine of being someone's puppet. Her smile sours.

"Quiet." Shepherd's voice slaps the assembled horde into silence. "This is an SOG op. You're all tourists for now. Even the Dicks."

The surrounding officers grin at the stony-faced drug squad detectives. Austin's mouth puckers like a cat's bum.

"Our targets are smart. They've barricaded the other entrances. That way they control in and out. Team A will hit the door, Team B in reserve as cover. Once in and we signal clear—*we* signal clear, none of you—uniforms will move in to hold the stairwells, in case any of the fine residents decide they want to join in."

A chuckle among the group eases some tension. Liz listens with half an ear as she takes notes, but she's more concerned with watching the various teams. Imagining their motivations, which of them would make a good character sketch—maybe the young female forensics officer fiddling with the escaping hair beneath her hood, probably on one of her first jobs; one of the older uniformed guys, a Sergeant by his wings, who stares balefully out at the target building, like this is personal. Fozz takes her lead, snapping the tense resolve on the man's face, backlit against the tower in the distance. It's a good shot, as usual. She also thinks of how to describe the scene: the chill in the air, the sound of dishes from the hotel kitchen, impatient feet softly stamping, the sour ulcer-breath of one of the detectives behind her. The devil is in the details, her first editor said with every story, and Jim back at the desk still expects nothing less. She appreciates the mantra now. Anything to calm her nerves.

"...sometimes wired with IEDs, so we spot anything, we'll send in the robots before Forensics enters and starts bagging and tagging. Wouldn't want to get in the way of your afternoon tea." Another chuckle. The ponchoed-ones grin around biscuit crumbs.

Shepherd turns his attention to Liz and the administrators along the back wall. "And then the rest of you can swan in and take the credit."

A thin smile from Daniel, the Deputy Commissioner. As long as the pawns do their job.

Shepherd's already turning to his men, dismissing everything but the mission ahead, when Liz pipes up.

"Any truth to the rumors of what we'll find?"

The commander's icy stare would shrivel anyone else. "We believe D2S is cultivating its marijuana trade here. It's all in the fact sheet—"

"I've read it. It's riveting. Is this where they're growing Black Lung?"

A blink. "Growing what?"

"I'm sure you're aware the recent overdoses are linked. And they're not from intravenous drug use."

"You don't OD from hash." Shepherd glances at the Deputy Commissioner over her shoulder. "Why the fuck you have to over sensationalize..." He dismisses her, finishes final checks with his team.

But his pause is all she needs. She's just casting out a feeler; now knows she's hooked something.

The rest of the emergency personnel mill uncertainly, having never heard the term. Liz'd only heard it herself whispered by a panicked girl in an ER waiting room—before she'd started convulsing and was whisked away by the triage nurses.

The detectives roll their eyes. "Sorry guys. But I have to know."

"Then ask us."

"I have been." She smiles. "And you haven't told me shit."

Austin takes her aside. "Look, whatever you think you saw, I was there—"

"I know what I saw."

The detective sighs, waves her away.

But did she know? The more she thinks about that night, the more she begins to question her sanity.

Black Lung. An unseen new strain of dope said to offer an almost otherworldly high, the potent hashish potentially linked to an outbreak of lung cancer and psychotic behavior, perhaps due to being contaminated with LSD and other chemicals in production, if the attending doctors she'd paid off were right in their speculation.

Or maybe this was the usual apocalyptic mythologizing that heralded every new drug. Crack was supposed to enslave everyone's children. Speed create a nation of zombies. And yet...there's something that sticks in her gut about this one. An unease she can't shake. *The raver vomiting and vomiting, more liters than the body can hold—*

An unease she thinks she'd seen in the face of Shepherd for an instant, too. Maybe that's the true reason for this whole risky operation. Not just a statement to the community after the explosion of violent crime the last few years—a puff piece on the nightly news about how our lawmakers are *getting tough on criminals*. But shutting down something that has real legs before it sweeps aside everything in its path. And who else would be distributing such a nihilistic substance but a group called D2S?

She was sure she'd seen the drug's effect in person, even taken shaky footage on her phone. But before she could file her impossible story, she'd been hauled in before the Police Minister. Dalton had threatened her paper at first, even claimed *they'd* contrived the name, but she'd been doing this shit long enough to laugh at that. She'd take contempt before rolling over to outside influence. So he offered her an incentive: if she held off inciting fear in the community—they'd dismiss the footage as fabricated anyway—she'd be granted exclusive access to upcoming raids looking to break the back of drug manufacture in the state.

What she hadn't known for sure was whether the raids were linked to Black Lung. Dalton obviously thought if he could keep her from publishing until afterwards, the scourge would already be nipped in the bud. And she'd be just one of many good little tools talking about an already contained problem.

But she's no one's puppet.

And this must be Ground Zero.

She feels Deputy Commissioner Daniel's eyes boring into the back of her head and turns and smiles at him. Did he think she wouldn't do her job? A leopard doesn't change its spots.

The only person with the power to keep her here looks away.

"How to make friends and influence people," Fozz whispers.

"Just fishing with hand grenades. Always good to see what rises to the surface."

"It'll be us if you keep pissing off the soggies."

"As long as the good Shepherd tells me what I need to know."

"We onto something?"

"We're onto something."

2 – Move Off Point

The op goes wrong almost from the first moment.

The two six-man SOG teams slink like black wraiths to the edge of the residential block nearest the tower, evidently the last possible place of cover before they hit the open and the gang's spotters could see them.

"Once they get the go-ahead, there can be no turning back," Collins, one of her detectives, leans in and explains. "All forward movement until the target is neutralized."

Austin grins next to them. "Suck up all you want, Bill. She's still profiling me for the story."

"Why? You don't know jack."

"I'm prettier on camera. Ain't that right, Fozzie?"

Fozz glances at the warts on Austin's bald skull, not knowing what to say. Liz just smiles. Let them vie for attention.

The Team A stack, Shepherd at its head, bunches at the corner, weapons extensions of their bodies. Some of them had the non-lethal beanbag shooters, she knew, but the last resort shotguns at the rear were fully-loaded killers. She watches each man tap the shoulder of the one in front, signifying readiness. No one looks back. They can't afford to take their eyes off the danger ahead.

Shepherd nods at his tap and there's a crackle from the radio behind Liz as he breathes into his throat mic: "*Team Alpha in position at Move-Off Point. Good to go.*" Silence all around among the waiting troops.

"Ready Ready," the Head of Operations, a big grizzled veteran the SOG naturally called God barks back. Hunched over the comms equipment, he pauses a moment, then: "Go Go Go!"

The black shapes disappear into the night. Liz has to crane to watch them on the helmet-mounted camera screens arrayed on one of the command desks. The angle's not great and it's dark, but the infra-red view on the closest screen is even worse: just fuzzy glares of yellow bouncing in grainy darkness.

"This is the most dangerous moment out in the open," Austin explains softly. "But inside they'll have the tactical advantage with their infra-scopes."

Liz nods, watching the Shepherd shape run low and hard, sweeping ahead with his rifle across the small courtyard in front of the tower, the team hoping for little resistance until they hit the door and enter.

"*Readying explosives for door—*"

The observation post can hear the screams even at this distance. Banshee howls of rage coming from deep within the building.

"Fuck is that?" one of the uniformed guys waiting at the mouth of the parking lot says.

The advance unit hit their gun barrel-lights, training them on the front door in a tense converged pattern. They barely have time to slow before the doors bang open and half a dozen figures burst out.

Gasps around her and Liz nearly jumps back herself.

"*Contact! Police! Put your—*"

But the crazed gangbangers run headlong into the line of fire, faces wild and frenzied in the flitting lights, like something from nightmare.

It's insane and Liz can only stare, trying to comprehend, mind racing: most gang members do all they can to save their own skin under threat of arrest, knowing how to play the system so they'll be back on the street after a small stretch of incarceration.

They don't run *toward* the guns.

The screams still sound and there's a snapped transmission— "*Engaging*"—then the distant sound of beanbag pellets. Dull thuds carry on the air. Liz tries to get a better angle on the screens and sees the figures jump and jerk with each painful hit then keep staggering forward. More thuds and finally all bar one drop.

The last attacker, a huge bloated form that fills the doorway, keeps coming on despite the non-lethal rounds, his arm seeming too long, unnaturally elongated—

"*Weapon!*"

The SOG split to one side and the rear-guard officer steps forward.

"*Drop it!*"

A dark barrel raises on one of the screens, but the man doesn't stop and there's a flash then a concussive BOOM through the mic as the officer fires the lethal Bennelli shotgun, and the crazed man's arm blows off—literally blasts off still holding the machete; Liz can make out its spiral through the cordite smoke like a tossed snake.

The man doesn't slow.

"Jesus." Liz doesn't know who says that one. Maybe it's her. She notices Fozz zooming in to catch the encounter and Collins covering the lens.

"*Stay back!*" The barrel centers on the man's head and there's a collective silence around her as everyone watches held-breath. One of the SOG tazers the guy from the side, but the wired barbs don't even register on his huge expanse and he keeps coming, he fills the screen—

A second BOOM. The man's head disappears in a cloud of red and he pitches forward, spasms then stills.

"*Shots fired. Suspect down.*"

"Damn it," someone at the table says softly.

"Roger that Alpha. EMT on standby."

The screen holds on the dead man a second. Bit late for that. "*Suggest the body snatchers.*" Then the unit pushes up the stairs.

"Acknowledged."

Liz can feel Austin and Collins watching her like she's a live grenade. "You know they didn't have a choice—" Collins starts to say.

"I know. I'm not a turncoat." She curses herself. It'd taken her weeks to win the squad over. Shepherd had planted doubt there now.

"I don't even know why I'm here," Fozz grumbles.

The team moves in and down the hallway beneath sporadic fluorescent lights, kicking in doors and clearing room after room, then continuing on. The apartments are all empty, most trashed and filled with detritus. None contain hydroponics banks.

"Where are all the families?" Liz asks. Most new refugees were funneled into the government-owned towers upon entering the country. There should be hundreds of people within.

Austin glances at her. A moment of hesitation. Then he must take pity. "Ground floor's buffer space. Leave it empty, they don't lose anything if they're breached. Everything must be on the upper floors, so the guys'll have to clear each one—" He breaks off, stares at the screen.

A shape sprints ahead down the hallway.

"*Contact! Police, halt!*"

Then there's just chaos as the officers pursue the figure, the world tilting and crashing on screen as the soggies sprint and Liz has to look away. When she glances back, they've captured a thrashing, raving gangbanger, the man's eyes like white bulging circles onscreen.

"*You see the truth! We have you now!*" the guy's ranting, a frothing explosion of spit and bared teeth, and the unimpressed police turn him over and pin him, then strap his wrists with plastic ties.

"*Ground floor clear. One captured.*"

"*You're trapped in here with ME!*"

"Roger, Alpha. Proceed to First Level."

"*There is no First Level. We DOWN. We beneath in the pits. ALL laid out.*"

"Wait, Alpha. What's he saying?"

Shepherd crackles in. "*Suspect's reality-challenged, Chief. Proceeding to stairwell.*"

"*—walking over it right now. So close. You keep going, you keep going—*"

"Shepherd. Eyes on a lower level?"

"*Observed no stairs down.*"

One of the other SOG steps toward the man: "*Someone shut him up—*"

"Alpha. Hold."

Someone: "*What's God saying?*"

"*All, hold*," Shepherd commands. "*Awaiting instruction, Command.*"

"We're coming in." The Head of Operations rips off his mic, signals some of the uniforms to shadow paramedics to the downed residents at the front of the building, another group to accompany him to hold the stairwells. "You—" He points to her two favorite drug squad detectives. "With me."

Austin takes off at a run. Liz and Fozz stand a moment, stunned.

"Shit!" Fozz yelps. "Go!"

Before she can follow him, the Deputy Commissioner grabs her arm.

"Why should I let you?"

"I can play the game, Daniel."

He says nothing. Just keeps giving that hard look.

"I'll make sure I forget to mention the Commissioner. This is your op after all, right? Should help your tilt."

He lets her go.

3 – Re-Organizaton Protocol

It's weird. The incapacitated gangbangers in the courtyard are already rousing when they pass, and, before the paramedics can tend them, are fighting to get free. The uniformed police have to cuff them and end up dragging them away even as the frenzied residents bite at their metal bonds, breaking teeth and tearing their mouths to shreds. Liz tries not to look at the smeared concrete spreading out from the big man's body.

The corridor smells dank and the carpet squelches beneath their feet, as if the whole building's begun to liquefy. Black mold honeycombs the ceilings in some of the rooms. Liz covers her mouth and follows the thick backs of the detectives down the long hallway and around a bend, passing guards training their weapons up at silent stairwells. At the end of the next corridor, the black-clad soggies guard a hogtied and very agitated man. As they get closer, Liz can see his pinprick pupils and she fights a sudden burst of anger. *How anyone can give their life away—*

But she knows why people succumb to drugs. She'd seen firsthand those who choose the easy way out.

"—on the list?" the Head of Operations is asking the drug squad detectives ahead.

Collins nods. "The second in command. 'Roach'. Real name: Pharcel Ibrahim."

"Pharcel?" Shepherd says. "That's sweet."

Roach grins at them. Casts his rolling eyes at the Head of Operations. "And God saw all that he had made, and behold the world turned to black."

The Chief stares at him, at the use of his name. "Hell you say?"

"Where are your soldiers?" Detective Austin steps in. "You going to let us just waltz in here?"

"No, no, they went to meet you. They're out there now, still running." The banger giggles and his eyes become whites as his head lurches back.

"This is a waste of—"

Collins cuts off the nearby SOG officer. "How many of your friends you want to lose? How many residents endangered as we work upwards? Map the building and we'll cut a deal. Reduce our risk; we'll make sure you get an easy ride."

"Ride, ride. We ride the pony. And she smiles just before she falls, but we're too far to catch her—"

Detective Collins gapes at him. Then launches in, grabs the guy by the throat before anyone can stop him. "The fuck, you talking about my daughter?"

"Falling. Always falling. We're all falling." Roach cackles laughter as Collins squeezes.

"Detective." The Head of Ops—Liz really wishes someone would give her a name for him, because she's not calling him God—grabs his man by the back of the neck and forcefully hauls him back. Collins' face is about to blow.

"The fuck you know—"

"He doesn't know anything. He's scattergunning, pushing buttons." The Chief steps in, grabs Roach's hair. Forces him to focus. "Cut the act. Tell us what we want to know. Or you never see the sky again."

"The sky is a lie."

"Chief," Shepherd says. "We're losing time. First thing, they'll burn the lot. If the gardens are on the floors above, we could have a disaster. The whole place'll go up."

"Not above. Not above." Roach's head rolls forward like it's too big for his neck.

"He's stalling. There's nothing below us."

"So sure what you can't see." Roach swings his heavy head up, takes them all in, rolls his vision until focusing past Shepherd's shoulder on Detective Austin. "The man there now. Alone in his room, dying. Waiting to be forgiven. But only angels forgive."

"Shut him up!" God barks and Shepherd snaps open a pocket for a gag.

Austin looks like he's seen a ghost, backs up wiping his mouth. "He's scoped us. They've got intel on us." He looks at the others. "That's not scattergunning. He *knows*."

Roach manages to see past the shoulders. "All connected. Just have to tap in." He grins at Liz, as if seeing the only woman there for the first time. "All have a dog in the fight. All trying to escape the ghosts—" Everyone's looking at her and she can only raise her hands in confusion, not let them see the explosions his words cause in her, then Shepherd grabs the guy's head, brings up the thick material to slam it in his mouth, and Roach focuses on him: "You'll all die here. You'll watch them fall. Just like the boat."

Shepherd freezes and the welling anger stays his hand long enough for Roach to rock slightly to one side—and the whole time he's been working behind his back at his bonds, skinning the ties down over his flesh, degloving his hands to get free, and he shoulder-slams upwards into the police officer, knocking Shepherd off-balance—and then he launches to one side, legs kick out, and there's a BANG and everyone crouches.

The surrounding SOG train their weapons in an instant, but Roach is no longer there. "Anyone shot?" the Head of Ops demands, seeing the blood on the floor, but Shepherd isn't listening. The vent low to the floor is now a gaping hole in the mildewed wall and he creeps toward it.

"Fuck. Trapdoor."

"Are you shitting me?" Collins says.

One of the other SOG moves toward the hole, shines his gunlight down. The rusted rungs of a crude ladder jammed into the narrow shaft are just visible. Cold air escapes, chills Liz to the bone. *How did he know—*

"You smell that?" the SOG officer asks Shepherd.

The Commander nods. "Ammonia. Hydroponics run-off." He hand-signals his men and they don gas masks. "Let's go—"

And then they disappear one by one into the hole, leaving the rest of them in the vacuum of the corridor.

4 – Payday

Without the monitors, they can only listen as the radio barks. "*Pursuing—Stay tight—Jacko, Hutch, cover the flank—Got obs ahead... Jesus, look at that.*" The distant sound of their footsteps, then startled shouts below from whoever they've encountered. "*Police! Freeze!*" The staccato tapping of non-lethal pellets. Then: "*We got Roach.*"

The Head of Ops doesn't interject through all this, just calmly talks off to one side with the Command Post, getting updates on their vision. "You can see *what*? How long are they?"

Shepherd radios in. "*Multiple suspects arrested. Workers. Site secured. Chief, you need to see this.*"

"Roger, Alpha." God grins at his troops. "Ready for presents?"

They wait until admin staff ferry in gas masks, then one by one begin to climb into the hole and the swallowing darkness within.

"The whole tour?" Austin asks her and Fozz. Her face says it all. "Then stay close. And we give you any instructions—run, stand still, don't breathe—you do it." Liz starts to open her mouth— "This time just say yes."

She nods.

She'd never worn a mask and it fogs immediately and she wants to rip it off to clear it, knows that's the last thing she can do. The sound of her breathing echoes in her ears. The world narrows and she focuses on the moving shapes in front of her as they descend the makeshift ladder about twenty feet and then hit the damp floor of the tunnel.

There'd been talk of a myriad of tunnels beneath the CBD for years. Hidden underground passages linking the hospitals, allowing escape from Parliament if needed to the nearby train stations, even networking the police and fire stations in case of attack during the wars. She knew some of these mythical routes were indeed real—had even used the access tunnels beneath the old *Age* building to the local watering holes, a necessity once for journos looking to steal more drinking time.

But this is something else. There'd long been rumors of US WWII troops digging vast tunnels linking strategic parts of Melbourne to their campgrounds at Royal Park in the inner suburb of Parkville, the spidered network said to crisscross the city boasting vast bunkers at various points housing ammunition dumps. D2S must have discovered part of it. And restored a massive section beneath everyone's noses.

Glancing around as they walk, Liz takes in the machine-dug precision of the rectangular subterranean highway, the polished concrete dimly lit with a low-bulb, blastproof fluorescent lighting system. The tunnel is meters wide, accommodating enough for two-lane vehicles if necessary. The figures ahead look dwarfed and insignificant somehow, as if blithely walking into the gullet of some giant primeval creature.

The further the observational party walks, the hotter the air gets and her breath begins to steam. She demonstrates it in wonder for Fozz, but he's not looking at her, instead staring up at the dripping green roof. Ever the germophobe. He sees Liz looking over and taps his mask, gives a thumbs-up: *thank god for this little lifesaver.* She can barely see him through fog.

There's a gasp from one of the drug squad guys and Liz looks back to see the world opening up before them. The roof disappears high above as they enter the mouth of a great room and it's then they discover the true scope of D2S's drug empire. Vast banks of mature marijuana plants line the disused ammo bunkers underground, bathing beneath an immense succession of artificial lights. Fozz goes crazy taking pics and Collins and Austin try to get in shot.

A group of workers in plastic suits and masks have been apprehended by the SOG and now writhe at their feet. Roach and two other bangers lie beside them. Roach cackles through a freshly-applied gag, eyes rolling.

"Not gonna listen to his shit again," Shepherd explains. "You got your payload, Chief."

"My God." The Head of Ops walks a long tray of plants, stares at the unending line hugging the wall down and around the slight bend in the distance. "How can this be possible?"

One of the SOG guys is checking a hand-held air tester. "Clear."

Collins removes his mask and Liz stares at him. "Biggest problems are Red P in meth labs getting in your lungs. Worst risk here is starting a fire and dying really fucking high."

Another of the SOG guys, "Mad Dog" she thinks it is, hangs back watching the way they've come, shotgun down but ready. Liz is close enough to hear Shepherd double back. "Why you antsy?"

"They kept running at us, man. That shit wasn't right. You see their eyes—"

"Stay liquid. All right?" Shepherd raps the man's helmet. Focuses him. "We've seen worse."

Liz shudders to think what that might mean. "But where the fuck are they all?" Mad Dog says low. "There should have been dozens of bangers—"

"Maybe they're all whacked out upstairs. They look in control? We got the drop, all that matters. The boys'll hold the fort."

"Yes, boss."

"I want to see how far this goes. You and Halo hold here."

Mad Dog twitches a nod.

Shepherd passes, sees her watching. "We have a problem?"

It takes her a moment to realize he's talking about the shooting. She shakes her head. She has bigger fish to fry. And she's just found a smoking gun. Let the government try to explain away the effects of criminalizing low-level drugs now. She'd have her justice—

"Good. I won't shoot you both, too."

Austin laughs. But Liz can see a tightness around Shepherd's eyes. He's unsettled by all of this as well—the weird behavior of those possibly affected by the drug, the scale of the operation down here, the difficulty they'd have securing the whole place.

If he's unsettled, where does that leave the rest of them?

The plants are bizarre, but Liz can't quite make out why until she moves closer and realizes that their somehow muted color isn't due to the mask she was wearing. The leaves of the mutated trees are darker than normal, beyond a dark green to almost a black, like they've been burnt, somehow leached of pigment growing down here despite the warm lights arranged every two feet ad infinitum.

They're fascinating, and she wants to reach out and touch the darkened fronds, something about the feathered patterns calling to her. And yet something fundamentally wrong about their entire existence screaming *anathema* at the same time.

"Like a negative image," Fozz says softly, chimping at his viewscreen, doing that "oo" mouth snappers do at a good shot. Maybe that's it. Because the plants are so familiar and yet unlike anything she's ever seen. That anyone's ever seen.

"Black Lung's real, hey?" Austin breathes. "This is some hinky shit. Doing the world a favor when we burn this to hell."

Collins claps his shoulder. "Amen to that. Biggest crop I've ever seen though."

"And it's still going," Shepherd says. He checks the bonds on the cackling Roach and his men. The gangbanger tries to get in one last taunt at them, but everyone ignores him. The suited workers lie beside them, resigned and seething. "You good?" Mad Dog nods. "Stay on the radio."

The SOG unit stalk ahead out the vast ammo room and down the concrete tunnel. Liz follows in their wake with God and the drug squad guys. Fozz spray-and-prays the long line of plants, frowning. "Light's shit. They're gonna bleed out, even with the fast lens."

"You can always use my phone," Collins offers.

Fozz glowers, hit right where a snapper-boy hurts.

The black-clad troops move silently ahead, stepping through the gathering puddles like lithe cats. It's only then Liz looks down and notices the increasing lengths of water beneath their feet. The further they go, the more the walls seem to bead with sweat too, and as she looks at the passing plants she can see droplets of moisture on the leaves now. Then she sees a drop pull a leaf off the nearest black lung plant and fly upwards to the roof—

She staggers, hits her back to the wall. The next drop falls and splashes on the metal of the tray beneath. A trick of the light. She's seeing things.

But as her hand slides on the slime of the wall, it suddenly sticks like a flytrap and for a moment she feels she's being pulled backwards into the concrete and everything shimmers around her as she sinks into the choking bosom of the wall.

She flails, trying to pull free, and then freezes when she sees the girl in the distance. A small figure in white moving ahead of them, flickering in and out of sight at the end of the gunlights' range. An ice chill dances up the back of Liz's neck into her hair. It's like death's fingers gripping her skull.

They're not alone.

What would a little girl be doing down here? She has to be seeing things, has to be imagining it—

The girl stops. Starts to turn. And the burning horror flares up Liz's throat and she knows she can't see her face, can't look into the blackness of her eyes–

She jerks her hand clear of the wall, falls forward to her knees, and the girl in white winks out of sight.

Liz kneels panting, staring ahead. There's nothing there. She drops her head and it's like the bottom of the puddle beneath her is stretching away, becoming depthless. Then her stomach contracts and she convulses and almost vomits.

The raver on hands and knees vomiting a great stream—

No, no, that can't be what's happening—

Fozz notices her fall, comes back to help, ever vigilant. Then the radio crackles, echoing in the narrow confines.

"*...all of them— We can't hold—*"

Shepherd and the SOG team freeze. "Repeat. Interference."

It's one of the uniformed officers at the stairwells. "*Killing everyone. They're fucking ripping them apart...insane—*" There's a scream, a sound like growing thunder, then he cuts out.

"Halo: report."

"*Contact! We got movement upstairs. Shots fired. Oh shit, Commander. They're coming down the shaft.*"

Shepherd doubles back, face stretched like thin paper across his bones. "Numbers. What're we facing?"

"*Oh Jesus. All of them. It's all of them Shep—*"

The whole team's radios short out inexplicably as if short-circuited, small bangs and puffs of smoke whispering from the gaps in the plastic, then the sound of semi-automatic gunfire reverberates through the enclosed space.

"Are they shooting at civilians?" one of the soggies—Jacko, Liz thinks he's called—asks. "What the hell are they doing?"

Shepherd starts to sprint then, and the other SOG flash past. Liz and Fozz can only stare, and even Collins and Austin hesitate, unsure what to do. Instinctively, they start to follow, then the entire SOG unit skids to a halt. A distant rumbling in the distance grows to a deafening roar.

Liz's breath hitches as the police switch as one from their non-lethal guns to the AR15s hugging their backs. Take aim as they start to retreat.

"What is it?" she asks.

"Holy fuck," is all one of them says and she follows his wide-eyed look up the tunnel back towards their entry point. The sight paralyzes her.

A wave of shadows surges toward them, pouring in through the gap above. The tower's residents, in an unending stream of bodies, descending after them. They hit the ground and those who aren't trampled are instantly up and racing on, filling the tunnel.

"What do we do?" someone yells as they retreat.

Shepherd is staring stunned at something in the midst of the crowd. Something dark-clad and doll-like in their midst.

Halo. Now just a broken rag puppet as the crowd tear him apart. A glimpse of crazed faces.

"Just fucking shoot!" the commander yells.

They open up. The noise is deafening, disorienting—and their efforts utterly useless. Suppressing fire is supposed to overwhelm with its blanket of bullets. Any rational being will seek cover.

But there's nothing rational about this.

The swarm of screaming, drug-affected men, women and even children—oh God, there's children among them, falling beneath the stampeding feet even as they try to keep pace with the mob like tiny zealots—keep surging forward despite the SOG mowing down their front lines.

The elite police unit fights as they're trained to do. But they're not soldiers, and they've never faced numbers like this. They're seconds from being overrun.

Liz's heart is in her throat as she turns and sprints back into the undiscovered tunnel. The two detectives and Fozz pound behind her with most of the SOG guys she thinks, but the adrenaline floods her system so quickly she can barely focus on anything except the narrowed sliver of sight before her, the tunnel arcing around and around, then angling down even further into the earth. Then the banks of plants beside her suddenly cut out and twenty feet ahead the tunnel splits in two.

She hesitates and Austin barrels into her. "Left, left, go left!"

He pulls her along by the collar and she stumbles, then finds her footing and she's running again, glancing back for a stolen glimpse. Sees the black-clad Shepherd reloading as he runs, waving her on. Behind him roiling shadows.

Two of the SOG members cut right, not seeing them detour as they fire behind. Shepherd roars but they keep running, disappear. The mass of residents pursue them, but that leaves only two remaining SOG, the two detectives, and her and Fozz. To battle an entire building.

It's insane. Too insane to rationalize and her brain is overwhelmed as she pounds on, unthinking. She almost doesn't register the huge room looming ahead until the roof opens out again and she stumbles into another massive ammo dump vault. There's even old marked boxes lining the walls. But the rest of the floor space is taken by banks of Black Lung plants. Row after row. There must be a hundred mature plants in here, bathing under heatlamps. Condensation drips from the ceiling and drainpipes and she's dizzy just looking at the dark bounty. Her vision swims. Then she remembers her mask, realizes she's dropped it far behind somewhere.

"Blast door," Shepherd is yelling, and Liz rouses and turns, sees him and the detectives and the last SOG officer all grab the heavy steel doors on either side of the entrance. A screech and the old machinery starts to crawl shut.

Liz slams next to Shepherd, wrenches with all her strength. Her arms feel like they're pulling from their sockets.

Then the sound of distant gunfire and strangled screams. The two soggies buying them precious seconds.

"Hurry!" Collins is shouting and Liz almost stumbles at the look of uncharacteristic fear on his face. He has kids, she knows—Jasmine and Jasper—had even met them and his wife one night for dinner. Had glanced in at him, sprawled on their bed, reading stories as they jumped and swung from his bulk like he was their pet tree.

Detective Austin has a cat that shadowed his ankles like a dog. Fozz and Liz had been invited to his apartment once, too. Small but neat and clean, and his current girlfriend looked like a stayer. He'd had trouble finding anyone who could cope with the hours, but she was a paramedic, so her shifts were even worse.

Fozz she's known for years. Is probably her best friend in the world. Her only one left. She'd pushed everyone else away. The look of helplessness on his face now is heart-breaking. It's her fault he's here. He'd been putting off leave for months while she chased this drug thing. He was already burnt out and now he'd die in here.

They all will. No one would see their families, their loved ones, their pets again.

Shepherd must see her mind slipping because he's in her face, that tight skin around his eyes like he's a shouting mannequin: "Close it!"

The rusted doors creak closed, the rusted grating echoing the screams again coming toward them, then the steel slabs give a final groan before abruptly stopping, still leaving a gap of inches. There's no way they can budge either one.

"Son of a—" Jacko, the last of the SOG unit says, still straining to shut out the nightmare tunnel behind them. The cords of muscles on his neck like they're about to pop. But panic and wishful thinking mean nothing now.

"The boxes!" Shepherd points at the stacked crates and starts shoving metal tables aside. The others take his lead. Liz grabs one of the hydroponic trolleys to help and looks right into the leaves of its plant, can see every vein spiraling out from its shaft, every feather of its leaves. She's close enough to inhale its ash scent and even that much contact triggers flashes of light behind her eyes. She sags, hands gripping the table as if stuck.

"The girl... She wants us to..."

"Hey!" Collins is shaking her. "Stay back from that shit." He pulls her away until she's on empty floorspace.

"She was there." Liz looks past his shoulder.

He looks to the back of the room. The carved-out room narrows until converging at the far end in a rock formation. A hole to a cave system perhaps. There's no one there. But for a moment she thought she'd seen—

A flash of shadow across the gap: figures hitting the junction again, pouring back down after them. Screaming fills the tunnel.

Fozz drags a box and, in his panic, trips and upends it. He stares down at the contents peeking through the broken lid. "Ah, you think this is the best thing to use?"

Long thick gleaming brass bullets rest on straw: old M1 carbine. Artillery shells nestle within another. All utterly useless to them, but also entirely unstable and volatile. They have no choice.

The screams get closer like a tidal wave of water. Flashes of darkness as shadows surge in the narrow gap. Fill it. Crazed cries of rage, the gangbangers and co-opted residents fueled by whatever psychotropic effects Black Lung causes in its victims.

The ragtag group shoulder the door. Dig in their toes.

Then too many feet stampede toward them, the noise eclipsing everything. There's a huge crash as the first bodies slam against the blast doors. Everyone skids back across the slick floor.

Liz can't help it. She screams. But so do the others.

5 – Contingency Adjustment

Once, when she'd been a young cadet, she'd been sent to interview a home invasion victim. Nowadays you did most interviews by phone or Skype, most research on the internet, but twenty years ago it was all footslog work. There was no substitute for seeing a person's reactions in the flesh. The man had invited her in, hunched and injured, but as she'd spoken to him, she began to see something animal behind his eyes, a too-intense hanging on her words, an unconscious tongue licking his teeth. She realized she'd been invited alone into the house of someone *wrong*, that despite his victimhood, he saw a moment of advantage. And when she saw him break up a tablet into her coffee, she fled. Despite reporting to police he was an innocent random homeowner, the guy was in fact a drug dealer targeted by greedy clients. She'd rubbed up against something evil and tainted, glimpsed beneath the veil of society to the easy corruption lurking ever-present. A glimpse that became a deluge the more she worked, until her own family was torn apart by it.

A voice calls to her. Distant, incoherent. She stares with unfocused eyes, and then makes out a face near hers: Fozz. Saying something, imploring.

She smiles at him. Wishes they could close the gaping rent in the veil. But perhaps she'd known it would always end like this, undone by her own curiosity. Her own pigheadedness.

Behind him, she can see a figure across the room at the rock pile. *See,* she points. *I was right. It calls to us now.*

The figure turns from peering into the cave tunnel and it's Shepherd, sprinting back toward them as he dodges around the hydroponic trolleys.

"Liz! Damn it, listen to them."

Liz blinks as the commander hits the door beside her, lending his weight. The world swims back into focus. Her anxiety returns like a sledgehammer.

"We...we hit it as a group," Shepherd's saying, pointing to the dark tunnel across the room. "Close off the rocks behind. We'll have a better chance of holding them off."

"Do we even know it goes anywhere?" Collins demands.

"You want me to scout more?" They're all close to hysteria, but Shepherd's able to fight it, slow his breathing. He calms himself, looks at the rest of them. "It goes further. They've been using it. That's enough. These doors aren't going to hold." He glances at Liz. "You still spacing?"

"I'm okay."

He looks at her, fighting words. She braces for his sarcasm, knows it might push her over the edge this time. Her defenses are shot. When he speaks his voice is softer: "Just hang in there. I'll get you all out."

She stares at him. Realizes how responsible he feels for them. He's already lost most of his men. And it'll be all of them if he can't get this plan to work.

"It was a trap. They waited for us to enter." Jacko is quiet, the hardened SOG man close to losing it. "They were foxing."

"We haven't got time to worry about—"

"But why?" Austin cuts Shepherd off. They need this, need a moment to understand what the hell's happening. "Why would anyone cultivate anything this psychotropic and destructive? If that's what's really affecting them. And where did they get the strain in the first place?"

Fozz points at the ocean of plants in the room. "*If* that's what's affecting them? You think it's *not* this shit? An entire building's trying to rip us apart is a coincidence? They're fucking evil. You can smell it." He shudders, tries to huddle into himself.

They all know it. Can feel the Black Lung cuttings in the room like a presence. Something malevolent lying in wait.

"Maybe it wasn't intentional," Shepherd finally says, looking around the room. "This has taken too long to engineer. And D2S's empire is founded on a smooth-running organization, violence included. They still had workers sensible enough to be wearing protective equipment, even while others had gone batshit crazy. So maybe there's something down here that affected everything. Maybe the plants *became* Black Lung somehow down here."

"Could it be a fungal infection or something?" Liz says as she stares up at the waterpipes along the line of the roof. They're strangely darkened. Not rusted but more like...the black mold she'd seen in the rooms upstairs.

"Infected how?" Shepherd asks.

"I don't know. But ergot mold used to infect bread and cause hallucinations and sometimes insanity. They think it's where a lot of our fears of monsters and other realities came from, because those affected would see horrifying visions they couldn't explain." She looks at the two detectives. "You guys hear about anything like that—" Something shifts on the edge of her vision. When she looks back at the pipe, there's nothing, just the honeycombed cobweb. But when she turns away again, she has a sense it's moving. She shuts her eyes.

"They built these buildings in the '60s," Fozz says, staring up at the pipes. "Piled people in and let the whole thing rot. Like they do with everything. It'd be fitting if they caused this."

"I don't give a shit who caused what," Collins says, turning to Shepherd. "They'll know this has gone to hell. How long before

Command sends someone?"

"Who are they going to send? Next call's the army. Maybe they'll just bomb the whole fucking thing."

"Maybe they should," Fozz says.

They stare at him. "All the more reason to get as far away as we can—" Shepherd starts to say.

Then Liz nearly screams as a white eye appears at the gap in the door: one of the residents looking in right at her. The man starts biting the metal, scrabbling at the sharp edge. Bright blood splatters in at them and she shies away. She can't take much more of this.

Jacko braces against the door. "I'll buy you some time. Better be room at the end for me, though."

Shepherd grabs his arm. "I'm not leaving anyone Greg—"

"They'll be through before you get across the room. I'll be behind you, Shep."

An unspoken moment between them, a lifetime of service together. Shepherd nods.

He looks at the rest of them. "We good?" They nod, but Liz can see the fear in their faces, the clenched hands, can feel the apprehension descend like a caul over her and almost take the will from her legs. But there's something that continues to drive her, even now, even as the numbing release of death finally beckons her, a promise to her past perhaps. "Then we move out," Shepherd says, and Liz sets her feet, grits her jaw and prepares to push off the door. "Ready... *Now!*"

They burst away from the blast doors and thread through the maze of tables. Behind them there's a shriek as someone spots the movement and the door's slammed with a huge weight. Liz hears Jacko grunt.

She can't risk looking. Can't do anything but dodge through the field of plants. Each passing flash of black leaf seems to dig into her consciousness, tug at her vision and stretch at awareness like elastic. If smoking this substance has taken over the minds of so many, imagine what it could do for her. Imagine what it could blot out in her life. Her memories, her past. Her whole existence. Wipe it clean. Absolve her.

She stumbles with the weight of temptation and Fozz sees and comes back as he always does. Always doing so much for her. Now risking his life. She can't let him.

She pushes him on. He has to save himself first. She'll be okay. She's right behind.

And as she looks past him to the tunnel, she sees Detective Collins just in front of her colleague, sees the big man slow, fixated upon the passing plants so close to his touch. The policeman stops, reaches out a hand.

"No!" she screams, but it's like she's in slow motion, and he runs a hand down a darkened frond then rips it free and jams it in his mouth.

Fozz slams into him, bounces off the big back like he's hit a wall. The broad shoulders turn, and Collins looks down at him, still chewing, as dark veins spread from his mouth across his cheeks. His eyes have turned black and fathomless.

Collins' skin ripples and shifts as if something within is trying to break free, like he's becoming possessed by something. The image is impossible for her to reconcile, and for a moment she can see *another face* beneath his. A man also but not the same detective she's known over so many weeks. A face twisted with hatred.

Collins grabs Fozz's head with one huge hand, lifts him clear off the ground. Her friend flails, scratching at the immovable flesh, then he swings his precious camera like a weapon. It explodes against Collins' temple, shatters in a rain of jagged plastic and blood. It's like hitting concrete.

Liz smacks into them, tries to hook under the detective's fingers, beating futilely at the thick arm. His black eyes turn to her and it's as if she's looking into nothingness, like she's being sucked into the void within him. Then he dismisses her, turns back to Fozz, and squeezes.

Liz screams at the sound of crunching bone. "Get back!" Shepherd's saying, sighting his gun.

Liz is too enraged to listen, to get out of the way. She gives up trying to pull Fozz clear and spots a metal bar against the wall beside them, part of a broken trolley, and she grabs it, turns back. Collins senses her at the last moment, but she avoids becoming trapped in his eyes and just *swings—*

The bar clips his jaw and he finally staggers, but his grip on Fozz's face is unending and his fingers compress and collapse the skull in on itself. Liz swings again. Harder, all her rage in the strike. The bar slams home, the jar numbing up both arms and she has to let go. The length of metal remains stuck in mid-air.

Stuck into Collins' temple. The detective lurches to one side, steadies himself on a trolley that crashes beneath his weight. Fozz is thrown clear and hits the ground in a broken heap.

"No, please," Liz says, sinking to her knees beside her friend, hauling him up onto her legs. His head swings to her and his face isn't a face anymore. Beside her, Collins kicks a last spasm then stills. The metal bar clatters free. She can barely comprehend the sight of either of them.

Then Shepherd's grabbing her by the back of the collar and dragging her with him. She shrugs free, freaking out, and he screams at her. "Look!" Across the room Austin has stalled, and he's ripping at the Black Lung plants too, shoveling the poisoned leaves into his mouth.

Liz snatches up the length of bloodied metal, sprints after the SOG commander. At the blast doors, Jacko waits until the last possible moment, and then he leaps after them. Almost instantly, the door bangs in a foot behind him, the numbers moments from bursting through. And Austin is already turning to him, sensing the man coming, ready to embrace him.

They can't save him. Can only run for their lives toward the cave opening. Gunfire behind them, Jacko's scream as he's eclipsed.

And then it's only the two of them, their numbers cut in an instant.

Shepherd pushes her forward, covering her at the entrance, and she jumps for the hole. The darkness takes her.

6 – Endgame

-Liz scrambles across razored rocks into the swallowing dark. Her knees scream. The only light comes from Shepherd's gun barrel as he skitters in behind her, crawling backwards and sighting on the circle of light behind them.

She looks back past him and sees a face at the entrance. It's Austin, black-eyed, mouth covered in blood. A huge boom that shakes the fragile roof above, that nearly blows her eardrums, and Shepherd puts a hole in his forehead. The detective keels away.

Shepherd keeps retreating, slithering back on his stomach, as the noise comes and the room beyond begins to boil with shadows. Hands claw at the lip of the tunnel, and then suddenly the gap fills with faces. He opens up and Liz can only crouch and clasp her hands to her ears, silently screaming.

"Keep going!" Shepherd cries at her and Liz moves further crouched into the black, slapping a hand against the wall to feel her way forward. She thinks she can feel footprints in the stretches of mud beneath her own, so she knows the gang have been using the passage, but then her head gashes the roof and she has to crawl as the cave tunnel shrinks. Soon she's on her knees again, yelping as the rock cuts into her kneecaps. The ground becomes slicked with her blood.

Behind, the SOG commander rests on his stomach, methodically picking off targets. The light from the room begins to shut off as the bodies mount in the gap. Still they come. And come.

"Reloading!" he yells through force of habit. But what's she going to do, cover him with the iron bar? He slots the mag home, resumes sniping.

The roof continues to creep down, the walls narrow. She's forced on her own stomach now and the air is so stale, she's having trouble drawing breath.

Panic begins to overwhelm her. She's going to get stuck. No one's used this passage before. It's just going to end and they're not going to be able to back up. She's going to be trapped headfirst in the tight rock. Even if the crazed residents don't squeeze in after them and tear them apart they'll be trapped for hours, for days. Slowly dying from lack of food and water. If they're lucky, more quickly from no air.

She starts to thrash, hitting the sides of the tunnel around her. She can't escape it. There's resistance everywhere. No room. The uncontrollable terror builds deep within and she knows if she opens her mouth the sound will never stop, that she'll use the last of the foul air in here screaming at existence.

"Have to...have to back up," she forces herself to say, but she

AARON STERNS | 228

can barely hear her own rasping voice.

"I'm running out of ammo!" Shepherd cries back. "I'm blowing it."

Liz's mouth snaps shut. "No. Wait!"

She's able to just glance back beneath her arm. Sees Shepherd aim at the roof of the entrance. And fire.

Bullets glance off the rock at first, casting sparks. Shepherd steadies himself. "Please," he breathes out. He squeezes the trigger.

A huge whump and the tunnel collapses in a great gout of dust that sweeps all the way towards her, snuffs out her air as it snuffs out the light.

She couldn't scream even if she tried.

She's going to die like this. After everything she's fought through, all the pain, the loss. It ends like this.

Something breaks in her. And the fear goes. Just washes out of her, sinks down through the earth beneath her.

I'll be with you soon, baby...

The rocks settle, and there's silence. Then: something coming toward her. She opens her eyes. Light flicks past her, shines on down the tunnel ahead.

"Can't...breathe..."

"We're okay," Shepherd is saying. "There's air ahead."

She looks up, focuses. Can't see anything, but there's a hint of cold seeping toward her. Shepherd had risked everything, but this isn't a dead-end tunnel. It leads somewhere.

"Don't go to pieces on me now, Liz." Shepherd's just behind, his voice somehow comforting, part of her.

She clutches the rocks beneath her shredded hands, surprises herself with movement. A strength even now. "Don't you." And then she pulls herself on, dragging her snaking legs deeper into the trench.

After torturous seconds, she begins to see something ahead: a rippling reflection on the roof somewhere above. A pinhole light appears in the distance. As she scrambles on, it grows, beckons her.

"There," Shepherd says. "We're almost there."

She pushes to her limit, the tears coming now hot and endless. Her belief in release growing by the moment until the light opens out to a room ahead. She scrabbles the last few claustrophobic numbing feet and tumbles over the end of the tunnel onto the wet clay floor of the room.

She lies panting, sucking in air, staring up at strange rippling reflections on the roof of the cave. Someone has installed crude electric mine-style lighting in here, offering dim but the most beautiful illumination, and the walls are propped up with timeless timberwork. She doesn't know how deep beneath the city they are, but someone once modified the ancient cave system to their own ends. And it's saved their lives. Even at the moment she was finally prepared to let go of hers.

Shepherd tumbles out after her, nearly rolls over her with his kit of heavy equipment. She barely registers the impact.

They lie a moment in stunned silence, staring upwards, breathing through damaged lungs. Cold air wafts over them.

"I didn't think that would work," he says.

She cries then. Turns her face from him. She'd been so close to release. Why did she always keep fighting? Why can't she just let go?

"Hey. Hey! Liz. Look at me. We're okay. We made it out."

Shepherd's face is dark with mud, with his own blood and sweat. As must hers be. She nods. "I know."

"I need you to keep fighting."

"I know." But her eyes are dead as she looks at him. She wants to scream. How, after every horrific thing he's just seen, can he still think this world is still worth fighting for? But she can see the resolve in his face. He'll fight to the last breath.

And if she's going to survive, she'll have to do the same.

"So...so what do we do now? We're still trapped. They're not going to be able to rescue us, are they?"

Shepherd is looking past her, past the huge concrete open-air tank in the center of the thirty-foot sized cave to a door built in the opposite wall. "There's another way in," he says in wonder. "They joined this with the other tunnels."

"So what we just crawled through..."

"A natural opening. It must have been intended as an escape route in case the bigger exit here collapsed."

"So we could have just walked in here? Jesus!" She only now registers the tank in front of her. "Where is here?"

Shepherd creaks to his feet, walks up to the concrete lip three feet off the ground and peers over. His face shines with rippling light. She joins him.

The concrete lid has been smashed on the top of the reservoir, revealing a great semi-circle of the water within. Liz stares into the inviting depths. The cold like soothing ice on her face. Her throat rattles. She wants nothing more than to dip her hands.

"Don't," Shepherd says. She looks up sharply. "We don't know if this is tainted too. It could be the source."

She senses now the moisture in the air, knows it could be entering them with every breath, corrupting them, taking them over. But maybe a part of her no longer cares.

Shepherd edges around the concrete embankment, not seeing the struggle in her face, hugging the wall until he reaches the heavy door set in the far wall. There's no obvious door handle. "The fuck?" He tries pushing it, searching for a seam, growing increasingly frantic until he breaks fingernails. There's nothing.

He sees her looking at him.

"Give me that bar."

She stares down at her whitened fingers clutching the bloodied length. Her only weapon against the world. She hands it over.

He glances at her uncertainly, takes it. He gently takes her shoulders. "I'm scared too," he says, misreading her. "But we'll find a way."

She nods. Looks away from him. To the water.

He heads back to the door. Starts probing the edges. "I'd heard of you before this, you know," he says, still concerned, still trying to distract her from shutting down. "I mean, you were a fairly vocal critic of the police—when it was warranted," he cuts her off. "But I also read the piece about your daughter, the effect on you. How old was she?"

Her voice distant: "Sixteen." The waters dark, stretching away endlessly.

"I know how scared you must have been. How helpless. I've seen the effects of drugs so many times. It's half our job. And nothing we do seems to matter. But decriminalization isn't the answer."

She doesn't answer.

"That's what you were going to do with this piece, right? Show how out of control everything's become, the excessive, futile force needed to contain it. That the battle's lost. But doesn't this prove to you why we have to fight to stop it? Imagine if we were free to take anything we wanted. Look what it's created. If something like Black Lung hit the streets and no one moved to stop it. It'd destroy everything. That's why we have to get out. Because if they don't bulldoze this place immediately, if they allow even one of these plants to get out, we'll never stop it. And it'll keep spreading like a virus, worse than any drug we've ever seen. And more...and more kids like yours will suffer."

"No...I saw her. I saw Kelly."

"What?" He's trying to jimmy the bar into a gap, but there just isn't one. "God damn it. I'm...there's got to be a way. I only have nine-bangers—" He glances over. "Flash grenades. If I had a frag... I can't let this place stand. We have to stop this."

There's something about the water. Its surface moves in swirling patterns, the soft ripples like some fundamental building block of existence, like a mathematical sequence, like genetic code, like the fronds of a plant.

"I have to go back. I...have to risk the cave. The boxes. If I can dig through the rocks, the nine-bangers could blow the lot, the whole building." He's ranting, eyes too bright. Knowing this is probably suicidal but needing something to do. Anything except waiting here in this crypt to die. "But I'll grab some, bring it back. We can use it here to get out. There'll be another way out— Wait. What are you doing?"

She stands by the edge of the low concrete reservoir. The water beckons. Her hands dip towards the black.

"She's here."

Her hands break the cold surface, descend into the depths. Ice races up her arms, deep into her bones and up through her body. She tries to scream, but the dark flood freezes her from inside.

And she sees everything. A clutch of the gang's leaders dragging their rivals down the reclaimed tunnels to the pit far below of the reservoir built over its underground lake—not realizing it's feeding their whole marijuana enterprise upstairs. Holding their screaming enemies over the water, forcing them to watch their reflections as they slit their throats into the water, then drown them in their own blood. Seeing children who've dared steal from the clan chopped up as fertilizer for the plants, their remaining bones scattered in the waters. Investigating police and judges and their families raped and chopped to pieces down here in the depths.

And the infected water being used in an endless cycle to feed the hydroponic banks. Water tainted with the spirits of the dead, somehow haunting the drug itself.

And the dead want their revenge.

It's not the black mold at all. That's just an effect of the true horror at its core.

Liz sees deep into the shadow world, her face frozen in that silent scream, even as she feels the vengeful spirits within surging up towards her, writhing and twisting over each other in hunger.

She sees something through the masses of limbs and faces. A hand reaching for her, small, clutching not in anger but aching loneliness. Then gone.

Despite the fear wiping her mind, Liz searches through the chaos. And there it is again, and she reaches for it through the spitting howl. Grips the sudden clasp and pulls against the darkness.

Her daughter, face sunken and hollow with all she's seen in death, surges free of the clutching hands. And climbs up her mother's body, stealing one last moment from the darkness.

And that's enough. That was worth fighting for all this time after her daughter's overdose, the death that robbed her of all hope in this life.

"Liz!" Shepherd runs at her, launches to knock her back from the water.

Liz turns to meet him. With arms like iron embraces him as if her daughter, Kelly, draws him into her. He screams into the black, never-ending voids of her eyes.

And with the strength of the dead, she pitches them both into the water.

The End

GINORMOUS HELL SNAKE
Jake Bible

"So...we're going in that?" Shane Reynolds stared at the murky green-brown water of the Amazon tributary. "Going into water with low to zero visibility to find a huge hole where a giant snake might be living? That's the mission?"

"A giant genetically engineered snake that probably doesn't resemble its original DNA at all," Max Reynolds said. "No, wait, a *ginormous* genetically engineered snake. I think if ever the word ginormous should apply, it's right now."

The Reynolds brothers were nine months apart and looked almost identical, both with yellow-blond hair, green eyes, and freckles across their noses. They were classic southern California beach bums all the way. However, there was one easy way to tell the difference: Max was missing his left ear and had scar tissue running from his scalp, down his neck, and onto his shoulder, while Shane was missing his left eye which he covered with an eye patch adorned with a very prominent marijuana leaf.

Both built like linebackers, they stood on the bank of the river in full combat gear, most of which they began to strip off as the reality of their mission hit them.

"Uncle Vinny?" Max called into his com. "Are we sure about this?"

"Get in the water, Max," a gruff voice replied in Max's right ear.

"Wouldn't mind a little more backup," Shane said into his com. "Ginormous snake and all."

"We're busy!" Vincent Thorne replied.

Former commandant of the Navy SEALs BUD/S training, Vincent Thorne was leader of the private special ops team known as Grendel. He was a "by the book" man and not one to mince words or take excuses. Unfortunately for him, his nephews were neither "by the book" nor did they have a problem mincing words despite their years of experience as Navy SEAL snipers.

Thorne blamed all the weed the two brothers smoked.

"How busy?" Max asked. "Like gonna be a few minutes busy or gonna be—"

Intense gunfire erupted over the comm and both brothers winced before shoving their fingers into their ears to adjust their com devices.

"Right. That kind of busy," Max said.

"Carlos? Ingrid? Who do we have on the com who can assure us that these compression suits we're wearing will protect us from this giant snake?"

"Ginormous snake," Max corrected.

"Ginormous snake," Shane echoed.

The gunfire on the com was silenced as a new voice responded. "Uh, well," Team Grendel's lead tech, Carlos, replied, clearing his throat, "we cannot guarantee that the compression suits will be one hundred percent effective against the snake."

"Ginormous snake," Max said.

"Too much, bro," Shane said.

"Sorry," Max replied. "It's just fun to say."

"I hear that," Shane replied. "But, time and place, dude."

"Totally get that. No problem," Max said. "I'll let the word lie and bring it back later. Timing."

"Timing," Shane agreed.

"Do you two want to hear what I have to say or not?" Carlos snapped over the comm.

"Oh, I'm sorry, Carlos, are we inconveniencing you?" Max snapped back. "Is the fact we're about to dive into muddy, microbe-infested water and chase down a twenty-meter snake annoying you?"

"Thirty," Carlos replied.

"Excuse me, what?" Shane asked. "I thought Ballantine said it was twenty?"

"No, Ballantine said it was twenty meters long the *last time* it was spotted," Carlos replied. "He gave the files to Gunnar and Gunnar now believes the snake could be at least thirty meters long."

"That's like ninety feet," Max said. "Sorry, bro, but I have to say it: This is not only a ginormous snake, it's a ginormous hell snake."

"Yeah, I'll go along with that," Shane said. He shook his head. "Better get to it then." He shrugged and looked at his brother. His brother shrugged and looked at the water. Then the two of them stripped their gear off until they were down to the compression suits they wore underneath their BDUs.

The compression suits were wet suits on steroids. Similar in look but with the ability to stabilize the pressure around the wearer. Designed to allow the wearer to handle rapid descent and ascent during ocean dives without risking the bends, the suits were also pretty much bulletproof and knife proof. Maybe on the knife-proof.

Only, the knife-proof aspect was the specification the Reynolds brothers hoped was true. No ginormous hell snake was going to be firing an M4 at them, but the thing would have very large, very sharp teeth. Neither of the brothers enjoyed dealing with creatures that sported very large, very sharp teeth.

Yet, that was their job and while the rest of Team Grendel fought off hyper-adrenalized cannibals in a different part of the jungle, the Reynolds had been assigned the mission of tracking (done), finding (about to be done), and killing (dear God, please) the ginormous hell snake. Short straw was an understatement.

Standing only in their compression suits, the Reynolds each held black items slightly larger than harmonicas, if harmonicas also had a set of goggles attached. Both brothers shivered at the thought of what the items did.

"Mustaches. Ugh," Shane said.

"Please refrain from referring to them as mustaches," Carlos said over the com. "They are highly specialized rebreathers that—"

"Shut up, Carlos," Max responded. "You're not the one that has to put this thing on and let those tendril thingies get all jammed up into your sinuses then down your throat, into your trachea, and all that crap!"

"That was an apt description of what these things do," Shane said.

"I listened during the first briefing," Max said. "Try it."

"I might do that," Shane said with a smirk.

"Here goes absolutely nothing," Max said and he affixed the "mustache" to his upper lip. The item instantly reformed to fit his face. Then tendrils shot out of the device and up Max's nose. Max bent over and put his hands on his knees during the process. There was a good amount of gagging and muffled cursing before he straightened up again. He gave his brother a thumbs-up.

"Screw you," Shane said and copied what Max had done, including the gagging and cursing.

"Testing com," Max said.

"I can hear you," Carlos said.

"Me too?" Shane asked.

"Yep."

"Good. Now get off the com and get us Gunnar," Max snapped. "Done talking with you."

"Whatever," Carlos said, and the com went dead.

"We might have wanted to chat first about the rifles." Shane looked at the two experimental weapons on the ground next to their packs. "He said they could be twitchy."

"I wish we could use our own rifles," Max said, picking up one of the weapons. "This just doesn't replace the feel of having a .300 WinMag in my hands."

"Speak for yourself," Shane said, picking up the other weapon. "My .338 MacMilan beats your WinMag any day."

"Agree to never agree with you ever," Max said. "Mainly because you're stupid."

"Hey, boys," Gunnar Peterson, Chief Science Officer for Grendel, called over the com. "Ready to hunt a snake?"

"Don't," Shane said, pointing at Max.

"I wasn't going to say ginormous hell snake," Max said with a smirk, which was hard to do around the mustache rebreather on his face.

"Goggles." Shane depressed a button on the side of his rebreather. "Oooh, night tech. Nice."

"Yeah, you'll need that," Gunnar replied. "When you get into the water, you'll want to stay close to the river bank. Find a deep hole and dive. Then look for the den opening. This type of snake will burrow into the riverbed to create an underground home to give birth in."

"It stays in the water the whole time?" Max asked as he activated his goggles. "Oooh, yeah, this night tech is great. It's adjusting to the daylight and shadows at the same time. Sweet."

"Titanoboa does not stay in the water the whole time," Gunnar replied. "The entrance tunnel to the den will be submerged, but the main area will be above the waterline."

"Great," Shane said, not convinced it was at all.

"All we have to do is get in there and kill it, right?" Max asked.

"And make sure it's alone," Gunnar replied. "Hopefully, there aren't more."

"Ballantine said the lab only created one," Shane said.

"Yeah, but it's Ballantine and that golf pro-looking dude always lies," Max responded.

"Too true, bro," Shane agreed.

"Just double check," Gunnar said. "Shit! I gotta go, guys. Darren is calling and needs help with something."

The com went silent.

Shane hefted his futuristic-styled rifle. "This had better fry the thing. I mean it. If I get eaten by a freaking titanoboa because the tech doesn't work, I swear to God I'll become a ghost and haunt Carlos for eternity."

"Right there with ya, dude," Max said as he held his rifle close to his chest. "Ready?"

"No."

"Me neither."

The brothers shook their heads, looked at the river one last time, shrugged, then jumped in.

Without the specialized goggles, visibility in the river would have been close to nothing. With the specialized goggles, visibility was slightly better than nothing. Only *slightly* better.

"Think I got something here." Max swam through the murky water towards a deep depression in the submerged part of the riverbank. "Yeah. Hole. Big hole, dude."

"How big?" Shane asked.

"Three, maybe four, meters across," Max said.

"Big snake needs a big hole."

"Dude..."

"I'm on your six," Shane replied. "I'll follow you in."

"Thanks, bro," Max said and kicked his legs hard and fast.

With his rifle at the ready, Max dove through the pitch-black entrance to the hole and kept diving as the hole became a tunnel. If he didn't have the specialized goggles, he wouldn't have been able to see more than a few inches in front of his face, if that.

Max swiveled his head from left to right, increasing his field of view as wide as possible, but all he saw were the walls of the tunnel. No signs of any type of animal life, especially not a giant snake.

"Main coms are out," Shane said. "We're going too deep for a signal. Only peer to peer, bro."

"Roger that," Max said.

"You seeing anything?" Shane asked.

"Nothing but nasty water," Max replied. "You?"

"Your ass."

"Nice."

"It is. Way to keep up on your Pilates regimen."

"Boy's gotta stay fit."

"I hear th—"

"Hold up," Max snapped and stopped swimming. His rifle gripped to his shoulder with one hand, he reached out and steadied himself by grabbing onto a stray tree root that poked from the tunnel wall. "Movement."

Streaks of red filled Max's vision, the goggles' tech extrapolating images from the data they were receiving.

"Snakes!" Max shouted as the images solidified. Four very large serpents were headed straight for them.

Max opened fire, shredding the first snake with laser fire. His eyes went wide at the devastation the experimental rifle brought to the creature. Half the thing's head was sliced off, followed by several feet of the snake's body as its undulations brought its coils into the rifle's line of fire.

Hunks and chunks of snake filled the space between Max and the three others coming straight for him and his brother.

"Move!" Shane shouted. He shoved his brother out of the way as a snake struck.

Instead of grabbing Max by the head, its massive mouth closed on the barrel of Shane's rifle. Bright light illuminated the serpent from the inside and a meter-long gash appeared in the creature's back. Its mouth let go of the rifle as the body went limp and drifted to the bottom of the tunnel.

Max recovered from his brother's manhandling and fired over and over, taking the next snake apart bit by bit.

The fourth snake went straight for Shane but missed on its first strike and ended up decapitated as Shane kicked to the side and fired against the creature's neck.

The Reynolds brothers swept their weapons back and forth, staying put for a good five minutes before Max called, "Clear."

They surveyed the bloody carnage, then glanced at each other.

"You see what I see?" Max asked.

"Huge snakes but not native huge snakes?" Shane asked.

"Yeah. That."

"I see it. They were too big to be anacondas."

"Wrong markings, too."

"You know what anaconda markings look like?"

"Yes?"

"Way to sound sure of yourself."

"I leave my options open."

"Then what are we looking at?"

"Yeah, well...babies?"

"Ginormous hell snake babies?"

"That's my guess."

"Shit."

"Yep. Shit." Shane pointed his rifle forward. "After you, bro."

"Thanks," Max replied. "Time to kill mama."

The first thing Shane noticed when they reached the end of the tunnel and found themselves in a wide pool of muddy river water was that it sure was light underground. The second thing he noticed was that despite what his eyes were seeing, he had a hard time believing a ginormous hell snake had mastered the art of fire.

The Reynolds brothers slowly broke the surface of the subterranean pool and Shane was somewhat relieved to see that the snake had indeed not mastered the art of fire. However, the thirty or so partially naked tribespeople that waited at the shore of the pool, arrows slung and spears at the ready, killed Shane's relief quickly.

"Feel like testing the compression suits against those arrows?" Max asked very quietly.

"Not particularly," Shane replied.

"Then we probably shouldn't test them against the big spears those guys are holding," Max said.

"Sexist. Some of the spear peeps are chicks," Shane said.

"My bad."

"No worries. It's dark and you were focused on the spears."

"That I was, bro. That I was."

The brothers held their positions, as did the tribespeople.

"What's the call?" Max asked.

"Rifles are too specialized," Shane said. "We'll take down three or four, but they'll get a lot of shots off before that."

"Thinking the same thing," Max replied.

"What are they doing here?" Shane asked. "I thought everyone had these people occupied up top. No point in splitting the team to take out hyper-adrenalized cannibals up there if there are a bunch of the bastards down here, too."

"We knew they worshipped the damn snake," Max said. "We just didn't know it was all smoking torches in a snake cave level worship."

One of the tribespeople stepped away from the main group and pointed angrily at the brothers. He shouted in a tongue neither of them understood. Then he ran his finger across his throat. The brothers understood that.

The bowstrings tightened and Shane and Max prepped for the incoming projectiles. Then the leader of the tribespeople held up his hands and began to yell a phrase over and over. The phrase was picked up by the others and turned into a monotonous chant. Bows and spears were lowered then dropped as the tribespeople fell to their knees, supplicating themselves on the shore of the pool.

Shane glanced down at the water around him and noticed the ripples were a lot larger than they should have been if it was only the brothers displacing the surface of the pool.

"Max?" Shane said very quietly.

"Yep," Max replied.

The brothers slowly turned and saw the ginormous hell snake making its way down the surface of a wall behind them, just above the entrance of the tunnel. Then it launched itself at the pool and the brothers.

Last thing Shane saw was a ginormous hell snake mouth coming straight for him.

Max managed to get one shot off before the body of the snake slammed into him, knocking his rifle from his hands and sending him flying across the pool to collide with the cave wall. All breath left his lungs. He gasped as he fell back into the pool and sank beneath the surface. Had it not been for the rebreather, Max would have swallowed half the pool.

One side of his goggles was cracked and the other side was useless. The tech began to spark and sizzle in spite of being submerged. Max yanked the goggles off, careful to disconnect the rebreather beforehand. He pulled a flashlight from his belt and flicked it on, sending a thin stream of light into the murk of the pool.

Silt and mud clouded the disturbed water, but Max was almost sure he saw a huge shape moving a few meters below him.

Without pause, Max dove. He pulled a knife from his belt and swam as hard and fast as he could with both hands occupied. Deeper and deeper he went, his ears popping slightly. He had no idea how a pool of water could be so deep in the middle of the Amazon jungle, but he wasn't exactly about to question the geography. All he cared about was finding his brother.

Then killing one ginormous hell snake.

More movement, but from Max's right. Max rolled his body and got the knife up in time as one of the smaller snakes struck at him. The blade jammed up to its hilt just under the snake's chin. The snake's mouth stayed open, Max's blade sticking up inside its lower jaw.

Max let go of the flashlight, grabbed the top part of the snake's jaw, and slammed it down. It took all of his strength, and a little help from the snake as its natural instinct to bite kicked in, but Max got that mouth closed and the blade pierced through the snake's palate and into its brain.

The snake went limp. Max tried to get his knife loose, but it was a losing endeavor. He let go of the hilt, allowing the snake's corpse to drift down into the darkness.

Minus a weapon and any form of illumination, Max made the only choice he could. He swam deeper. With his arms butterflying out in front of him, his legs kicking hard behind, he propelled himself into the depths of the pool.

The pain was bad, very bad, but it would have been a lot worse if Shane hadn't been wearing the compression suit. The suit was doing its job: keeping the intense pressure being exerted on his body externally from allowing his organs and bones to be crushed internally. Shane wasn't a fan of Carlos, but at that moment he said a silent thank you.

Until he felt a rib give, and then he started cursing the tech's name loudly.

"Dude!" Max's voice rang out over the com. "I'm swimming blind! Keep shouting!"

Shane kept shouting as a second rib cracked.

Shane found he was having difficulty breathing. And it wasn't because of the cracked, and cracking, ribs. The ginormous hell snake had its body wound around Shane and was tightening on his every exhale. It was typical constrictor behavior; something Gunnar had told the team before they set off on their nightmare mission. Another aspect of the snake's base behavior was to clamp onto the head of its meal while it coiled and squeezed.

Shane was lucky that part, at least, hadn't happened.

Then all luck ran out. The top half of Shane's body was suddenly plunged inside the ginormous hell snake's massive mouth. It slammed closed just below Shane's shoulders, the constricting coils tightening severely. Shane screamed. Then, the coils loosened.

Shane didn't have time to sigh with relief, mainly because his ribs were screeching in agony, but also because the only reason the coils were easing up was to make it easier for the snake to swallow him.

And send him down yet another dark, dank, nasty hole he didn't want to be in.

"Dude!" Shane yelled, but only static answered.

Max slapped at his belt and realized he still had a trick up his sleeve. He pulled free two glow sticks, cracked them one-handed, and tossed them out in front. They lit barely a few feet of the murky water, but those few feet were enough.

Max's eyes widened then stung as silt and dirt scratched at his corneas.

There it was. The ginormous hell snake. Dead ahead.

Max glimpsed what might have been a boot, but he couldn't be sure. He hoped he was mistaken, that it was a product of his stinging eyes, because that boot could only be Shane's and it was being swallowed by the snake. Max had no knife, and no rifle, which meant no way of slicing the snake open to retrieve his brother. Max dove hard and fast anyway, kicking with all his strength for the snake.

Being an ex-Navy SEAL, Max improvised.

He reached the snake, grabbed a handful of its lip, and, using the grip as ballast, punched the creature in its right eye, over and over and over.

The snake thrashed in the water. It tried to get away from Max, but he held tight to the thing's lip and continued pummeling the snake's eye until it finally popped and milky blood poured from the crushed orb.

The snake opened its mouth wide and Max snatched his arm away, barely getting it out before the maw snapped shut. The snake swiped at him, opening its mouth again, but Max dove under the coils and swam until he was sure he was clear of its fangs. He stopped, spinning about.

The snake's upper jaw slammed into his midsection like a freight train. Max was shoved through the water until his back hit solid earth. He coughed hard and tasted blood through the rebreather's tendrils. Then the glow sticks' meager light faded, plunging Max into darkness.

The snake slammed him against the earth once more. Something in the rebreather broke. River water started to fill his lungs, choking him.

Definitely broken, then.

Grabbing the snake's top lip, Max flipped himself onto the creature's head. He planted his boots and kicked off from the snake as hard as he could. His body launched upward, Max dug deep for all the strength his arms could muster. He swam and swam, his lungs becoming heavier with each stroke.

Far above, the pool's surface beckoned. Max aimed for the flickering torchlight. He kicked. He paddled. Kicked, then paddled. His body was numb from exertion, but that didn't stop Max. He'd been in worse situations.

When his head broke the surface, his first thought was to hope he didn't catch an arrow to the eye. His second thought was that he should capture a spear from one of the tribespeople. His third thought was...what the hell just slammed into his boots?

Duh. Ginormous hell snake.

Launched into the air, Max's body was ejected from the pool violently. He tumbled over the water and onto the shore, landing in a heap on top of several tribespeople who were still prostrating themselves at the altar of their ginormous hell snake god.

Before the cannibals could regroup, Max rolled off his human landing pad and staggered to his feet, throwing punches at anyone and everyone that came at him. He cracked jaws and broke cheekbones, before he was overwhelmed by the warriors' greater numbers. They pressed him to the ground.

Max grabbed a leg and bit down hard on the bare flesh. Its owner screamed and jumped back, giving Max enough room to reach in and grab a different calf. He pulled, a second person falling as Max kicked wildly, his boots connecting with legs, with arms, heads and groins. He was a flurry of booted fury.

One of the tribespeople screamed. Whatever he'd shouted had an effect; all the tribesmen who'd been pummeling Max suddenly left him alone. They moved away fast.

"That can't be good," Max said around a bloody mouth of cracked teeth.

It wasn't.

The ginormous hell snake was slithering out of the pool and headed straight for Max. The tribespeople shouted and ran, moving further into the cave, leaving Max alone with a nightmare bathed in torchlight.

The snake opened its mouth. This time, without the silt and

murk of the water, Max got a clear look at the monster. Ginormous hell snake barely described the creature. Other than the mega sharks Team Grendel had fought, it was the largest single animal Max had ever seen in his life. It rose up, its body coiling back to strike.

"Well. This is how I go out," Max said aloud.

Max waited for the strike.

Towering over Max, the snake tensed. It began to shake and shiver. Still, no strike.

Then about two meters below its head, the snake's skin burst open in a flash of light. Blood flew everywhere, the stink of singed flesh filling the cave. The snake aimed its head towards the ceiling of the cave, its jaws opening wide, wider, and even wider until Max heard muscle tear.

The light grew brighter and a laser shot from the snake's body, cutting deep into the cave's wall, sending rock falling to the ground. Max scrambled out of the way, getting to his feet then leaping at the last second as the snake shuddered one last time then fell forward onto the shore.

The life was gone from the cold eyes and only torchlight flickered in the orbs as the vertical slits dilated and froze.

"Fuck me," Max whispered as he picked himself up and carefully approached the snake.

The snake's body shook. Max jumped back. Then light erupted from the spine and the flesh parted as a laser sliced through muscle and rib.

Shane clawed his way out of the ginormous hell snake's corpse and rolled out onto the ground. He lay there for a moment, breathing hard then held up a thumb. "Did it," he said. He pulled the rebreather from his face, gagged several times, then held up a second thumb. "I rock."

"Dude, way to go." Max hurried to get his brother clear of the snake's corpse, dragging Shane up onto his feet. "You good?"

"Ow. Ow, ow, ow," Shane said. He pushed his brother away. "Ow."

"What's broken?"

"Everything?" Shane shook his head and pointed to his chest. "Ribs. A lot of ribs."

"That thing ate you," Max responded.

"Too bad for it," Shane said. "No one eats Shane Reynolds without my consent."

"Word to that, bro," Max said, and they high-fived.

Then Shane gasped and lowered his arm. He fell onto the ground, landing on his ass with a thud and another gasp.

"No way I'm swimming back out of here," he said.

Max scanned the walls of the cave and found their exit. "I think I know the way out, but we probably won't be alone when we emerge," he said.

"Just get me away from that," Shane said, nodding at the dead snake. "Like now, bro."

The tribespeople had found more bows and arrows, more spears, and some even had pistols.

"Where'd they get pistols?" Shane asked as Max helped him walk out of the cave mouth and into the filtered sunlight of the jungle.

"It's the 21st century, dude," Max said. "Probably ebay."

One of the tribespeople shouted at Shane and Max. The Reynolds brothers only glared.

Bows were pulled taught, arrows and pistols aimed, spears hefted.

"Whelp. It was fun while it lasted," Max said.

"Was it?" Shane asked.

"I think so," Max replied.

"Cool. Just checking," Shane said.

The brothers opened their mouths to shout at the encroaching cannibals, but whatever last words they were going to say were drowned out by rapid gunfire and the screams of the tribespeople. Max and Shane hit the deck. The adrenalized cannibals fell to the ground, ripped apart by bullets.

Max and Shane waited for the gunfire to end before they risked looking up.

Behind the piles of corpses was Vincent Throne, his M4 smoking and sweeping right to left. "You two good?" Thorne called.

"Uncle Vinny!" Max shouted. He got up and helped Shane to his feet. "Damn! Are we glad to see you!"

"The snake?" Thorne asked, all business.

"Killed it dead," Shane said. "From the inside out because that's how this Reynolds rolls."

"It ate him," Max said.

Thorne paused in his movements and fixed his gaze on Shane. "It ate you?"

"It ate me," Shane confirmed.

"As in it swallowed you?" Thorne asked.

"Well, I didn't enter through its butt," Shane said.

Thorne lowered his weapon. "Why am I not surprised you were eaten by a giant snake?"

"Ginormous hell snake, Uncle Vinny," Max said.

"Yeah, Uncle Vinny," Shane said. "Get it right."

Thorne opened his mouth to respond but only shook his head.

GINORMOUS HELL SNAKE | 245

"Come on," he said at last. "Mission accomplished."

"Except we didn't get any DNA samples," Max said.

"Dude, look at me," Shane said. "I'm a walking DNA sample."

"Oh, right, true," Max said. "Nice."

"Boys!" Thorne snapped. "We have six hours to get out of this jungle and to the coast before the Brazilian army homes in on us. Let's move!" Thorne took off jogging, leaving Max and Shane to stand there.

"He's not going to slow down because of my ribs, is he?" Shane asked.

"Nope," Max said. "You cool?"

"I'll make it," Shane said. "No choice."

"I hear that," Max said. "Ready?"

"Ready," Shane said.

The brothers took off, jogging after their uncle, leaving the piles of cannibal corpses, the pools of congealing blood already coated black with insects, and the memory of a ginormous hell snake, far behind.

The torchlight in the cave dwindled, flickered, sputtered and was gone, plunging the space into pure darkness.

Within that pure darkness, water splashed. The surface of the pool was disturbed. Unseen, a new snake, much larger than the corpse that took up most of the pool's shore, slithered out of the water. It paused briefly as it came in contact with its dead mate. But it was a snake and grief wasn't part of its genetic makeup.

The new ginormous hell snake undulated over the corpse and towards the cave exit, ready for the hunt.

The End

GHOSTS OF HYPERIA
Jessica McHugh

It smells like seawater and Aqua Velva in the underground prop room where Victoria Fell stands over her father's coffin.

She wipes dripping blood from her chin and grits her teeth. This can't be real. Not Harlan's cologne, maybe not even the coffin. Certainly not the fingernails scratching the underside of the lid. But then the casket shudders, the lid lifts, and shriveled brown fingers curl over the edge.

Vic stumbles backward into a rack of moldy gowns and quickly snaps up an algae-slicked stiletto as a weapon, but the things in the dark don't care.

It laughs. It wheezes. And it sounds exactly like Harlan Fell, especially after the hurricane. The breathing alone makes her feel like a child again, before acid reflux and Celiac Disease took hold, and fear was the only thing that swamped her gut with pain. It was the same hushed desperation she heard late at night, when her adoptive father stood outside her room, soundless yet somehow screeching for Victoria to talk to him again.

But she could barely look at him after the storm. She wasn't even certain the man outside the door *was* Harlan Fell. Even after she left for Cornell at sixteen, part of her believed the creature in the house overlooking Fell's Fairy Funland was an impostor.

Until Harlan Fell hung himself two years ago in her childhood bedroom. Until he was embalmed, painted up and displayed in a near-empty mortuary. It was him all along, and he died knowing his only child didn't think he was human.

"I'd never hurt you the way you hurt me," he says. "I love you, Vic. You're why I did all this." The voice is changed now. It slips around pockets of familiarity but loses all trace of her father's melodic drawl. Even when Harlan was at his worst and sounded like Vic's most depraved imaginings of the boogeyman, there's no mistaking this thing for Harlan Fell. It is a hundred wet whispers, a wave of angry ghosts echoing in the utility tunnels underneath the once-legendary theme park.

She covers her ears and pain shoots through her skull. She doesn't know the severity of her injuries, but she must be battered to hell. Such a hurricane struck Calvert Cliffs once before, but this time she left the watchtower at the onset, directing as many employees as she could to the house on the hill. But the wind was like a serpent, purposeful as it whipped and crashed through the crowd of fleeing actors. It tossed the sea as carelessly as the people dressed as fairies and forest animals, and once the bay surmounted the wall, Vic had no choice but to flee herself.

But that was before she realized the utility tunnels were still accessible. Harlan was supposed to have filled them in, out of respect for the people who died there years ago, out of respect for the teenager who almost did.

The scratching in the coffin increases so exponentially that Harlan would need at least eight arms to execute such cacophony. When the lid explodes off the coffin, Vic buries herself deeper in the dresses, grabs another stiletto and brandishes them like hatchets as the corpse's pitted face rises above the edge. Harlan Fell's eyes are pale gray, his skin like bleached driftwood, but there's life in his lips. They're theatrically red, and his teeth glimmer Borax white in the musty room.

"You can end this now, Victoria. One wish, and this can all be over."

She shakes her head so much it nauseates her. She says, "no" until it's just a nonsensical moan.

The corpse chuckles like a brush fire.

"Very well. More fun for us."

With a howl, the cadaver lunges at Vic in the costume rack, but she narrowly avoids his skeletal grasp and whips around with the shoe in her fist. The stiletto heel pierces her father's temple and the twisted things inside, and all at once, Harlan's corpse pops like a balloon spraying hundreds of tiny opalescent crustaceans around the chamber. Vic crushes as many as she can, but the majority avoid the hammering and join like water droplets forming pearly pools in the corners of the costume room.

"Remember this," they hiss from all angles, "we gave you the chance to save them."

Their bodies shimmer with mimetic camouflage and they disappear into the walls and ceiling like white twinkle lights dying all around her.

"I hear her!" someone shouts. "She's down here!"

Vic is still holding the shoes when Tiffany Law jogs into the chamber.

"Are you okay, Ms. Fell? Did you get lost?"

She shakes her head and tosses the heels aside. "I'm fine."

The ice-blond actress screws a bloody tissue into her nostril and sniffs. "You've been down here for ten minutes. Is it safe or not?"

With a huff, she says, "Not," and shoves Tiffany from the prop room. She doesn't get far pushing her down the main corridor, however, before they collide with Rina Bestler, a former competitive figure skater, and Raymond Burke, a beefy but jittery first-time security guard who swings his flashlight beam over the scabby walls.

They ask her what's happening, what the plan is, but Vic keeps her mouth clamped shut as they pass the faded maps of the tunnel's chambers and entrances. The drawings seemed so much bigger when she was a kid. The ladder too, stretching up into the massive watchtower at the center of the theme park built along Calvert Cliffs; it seems like a flimsy plaything now, not a gateway to the horrifying storm that struck Fell's Fairy Funland out of the blue just one hour ago.

Planting her feet, Rina latches onto a rusted warm-up barre and forces Vic to stop. "I need you to tell me exactly where we're going, Ms. Fell. And who the hell were you talking to down there?" She tilts her head as if the correct angle will spill her boss' secrets, but despite the insistence in her rigid stance, her left pinkie finger twitches like a worm on a hook.

It's the first time since they met that Rina Bestler has shown a chink in the lofty and impenetrable air she boasted as a competitive figure skater. She's too young to have experienced Fell's Fairy Funland in its heyday and its revival in the mid-90s, but the cast of the new and improved park often discussed the legendary storm that struck in the winter of 1991. They called it the "Ghost Hurricane" because it appeared out of nowhere, with not a single indicator that a storm would break across a clear blue sky, raise the Chesapeake Bay over the cliffs, and decimate fifty acres of Calvert Cliffs State Park. The Ghost flooded and thrashed the attractions that day, killing nearly a dozen off-season employees.

Rina only heard about it in passing, however. She didn't get along with most of the other actors, partly because of the local celebrity's spectacular fall from grace in an underage drunk driving accident the previous year, but also because spending most of her life in pursuit of Olympic gold left her frightfully inept in most social situations. Add in the fact that many actors would've preferred it if Tiffany Law were cast as Fairy Funland's lead character, Princess Papillon, and Rina tended to keep to herself.

Vic fielded all sorts of complaints about the former figure skater's icy attitude, but when it came down to it, Rina's scandal was exactly the kind of publicity she needed for the grand reopening of her father's once-revered theme park.

"I'll explain everything once we're safe," she says. "But we need to get to the bridge. The water didn't reach the house last time. It's our only chance."

Tiffany wails so theatrically the tissue shoots from her nose. "That's what we came to tell you! The bridge is gone!"

She hopes Tiffany's just being dramatic again. The girl whose mother originated the role of Princess Papillon in 1975 was certain she'd get the part for the grand reopening and was vehemently vocal about her displeasure that the focus of a scandal had stolen her legacy. Whenever Rina winced after a landing or stretched her calves longer than usual, Tiffany offered herself as an understudy, usually with a braggadocious twirl.

But Raymond's expression confirms Tiffany reply. It's not just drama. It's the end of the line... again.

The security guard's voice catches in his throat. Clearing it, he says, "There's no path to the house anymore. The police are on their way, but we lost contact when HQ got submerged, so there's no telling when they'll be able to get to us, especially if we're down here." He takes off his glasses and wipes off dirt with his soaked shirt, which makes matters worse. "If the watchtower goes, we'll be trapped in these tunnels for God only knows how long." He wipes the glasses again and sets them on his nose as he squints at Ms. Fell. "Except you know, don't you? You've been stuck down here before."

"Why are we even discussing this?" Tiffany squeals. "There's no way I'm going back out there. You saw what happened to Chelsea. To Mrs. Popper and her kid. It picked them up; it dangled them in the air—" Her voice disappears into a whimper, and she throws herself against Raymond's chest, which seems to disturb him as much as the omnipresent thunder vibrating the tunnels.

Vic hadn't seen Chelsea, nor Maria and Elias Popper—she'd hoped they were still out there, actually—but she knows precisely what Tiffany means. She was in the watchtower when the Ghost struck in '91. Though she often had birthday parties there as a child, Harlan opened up during the off-season and paid the actors double to let her have the run of the park on Adoption Day.

"To preside over the entire fairy realm," he said, because there was no proving the former orphan wasn't part fairy herself.

Vic despised the reason but enjoyed the solitude. Until the storm began.

She was standing at the eastern window that day, the pane propped open and music entrancing her so completely that her ice cream started melting down her wrist. She was licking it off, her eyes fixed on the Ferris wheel, when the first bouts of lightning struck. She didn't recognize it as lightning at the time, though. The sky brightened temporarily, but it seemed more like clouds clearing than the warning it should've been. The thunder came soon after, disturbingly persistent with jags of non-stop rolling and rumbling that shook the earth. And as the azure sky twinkled above, harsh and violent winds troubled the Chesapeake beyond the cliffside barrier.

Vic watched it rise. Like something out of a sci-fi movie, the churning mass climbed the rocks and broke the border trees. Even when the massive waves crashed through Fairy Funland, it didn't seem real, especially from so high, so far, and so alone in the cloudless sky. She had sounded an alarm and closed the watchtower window, but she could still hear the screams of people tossed from the top of the Ferris wheel and impaled on twisted roller coaster rails. The waves blasted families apart, hurling them like sputtering ragdolls through the air. Some landed on rooftops, dying instantly, while some hit the rising tide and were sucked slowly underwater.

But some stopped in mid-air. As if suspended by invisible nooses, they hung in the sky, bleeding out, pissing themselves over the swamped park. As Vic beheld the catastrophic melee spread out in frothy waves before her, a security guard was snatched up by the wind and dangled just outside the watchtower window. Harlan's voice had charged out of the speakers and ordered everyone underground, but Vic couldn't move. The hanging man was alive. He was praying, reaching out, trying to touch the glass.

Then the wind had taken him. It snapped him out of the sky like a child plucking a wilted blade of grass.

Vic grits her teeth. She smells briny cologne again and tries not to dry heave in Tiffany's face, but the stench is stronger when the actress steps up to Vic, like she's brewing Aqua Velva kombucha in her gut.

"Why didn't you tell us these tunnels were here?" Tiffany demands.

"I didn't know."

"Bullshit. You must've surveyed the land before you overhauled the old park."

"I thought they were filled in," she says. "Harlan said he filled them in."

"But you didn't check?" Raymond asks.

Vic exhales heavily. "Not personally."

Rina's staring at her, looking like she bit into a bad apple. "You said you upgraded the security systems too."

"We did."

"And we're just supposed to believe you?" Tiffany throws her head back with a laugh that echoes through the corridor. "You say you believed your dad when he claimed to fill in the tunnels, but you don't actually think your dad *was* your dad after the first hurricane, do you?"

Rina's face screws up in confusion, so Tiffany looks to Raymond for support, which he hesitantly gives.

"I do remember reading something about that, Ms. Fell. You told the cops your dad was an alien or something."

Vic grunts in frustration. She's a grown ass woman. A Cornell graduate who's worked as lead project manager with Fortune 500 companies. She's run two successful small businesses, not including managing Fairy Funland's massive overhaul. And a twenty-five-year-old actress with bleached eyebrows and scaredy-cat rent-a-cop are making her feel like she's fifteen again: paralyzed with fear and certain she's going to die under this goddamn park.

"You know something?" Tiffany continues, now calling Rina into the circle of scorn. "I don't think this is about protecting us at all. I think this is about you being down here during that storm when you were a kid. I think you're scared, and we're gonna die for it. Well, pardon my French, but fuck that, Ms. Fell."

Tiffany isn't wrong. Vic *is* scared; more than she was an hour ago when she thought the damn tunnels were full of cement. But parts of her still scream out in the voices of the investigators and doctors who convinced her she was crazy. What she witnessed from the watchtower broke something in her, they said, disassociating her mind so far from itself that she invented trauma to suffer underground as well as above. Every harrowing second beneath her father's theme park—the things she saw Harlan do, the demons he worshiped—she'd hallucinated them all, partly to mask her pain and partly to punish the father who failed to protect her.

"This is crazy," Rina blurts at Ms. Fell. "Why aren't you denying any of this shit?"

"Because there's nothing to deny," Vic replies softly. "Whatever you've heard about me, it's probably true... and worse. And you'll see that for yourselves if we stay down here."

With a stifled whimper, Tiffany collapses against a faded cartoon of a pixie beside the watchtower ladder. "Rina's right. This is insane."

"I'm doing the best I can, and frankly I don't care what you think about me right now. Any of you." Peering at the group, Vic lifts her chin. "But I do value your safety, and I'm telling you these tunnels aren't safe. As hospitable as they may seem, there are demons in the woodwork."

Tiffany snorts. "It's stone, honey." Despite her bloody nose and injured thigh, as she rushes to the ladder to call down the rest of the survivors, she looks like the cat that got the cream. They hurry down like starving kittens, thanking God and Tiffany for discovering salvation in the still-accessible tunnels.

The smell rises again, and Vic knows the hyperia are watching her. Though her knees soften at the terror of her earlier decision, she braces herself on the map of the underground chambers and calls for attention from the clammy crowd.

It doesn't come easy. Half of the actors portraying Fairy Funland characters look to Tiffany and a few others look to Raymond as the only remaining security guard. But their gazes eventually sweep to their boss when she says, "I'm the only one who's spent any time down here."

She traces her finger across the faded map and draws several circles in the dust. "There are three access points to the grounds, as well as several chambers that were used for costuming, rehearsal, and breaks, but I'm not sure what condition they're in. As far as I know, they haven't been used since 1991." She glares at Tiffany, who's conveniently tossing her gaze around the corridor. "Raymond and I will investigate the areas ahead to make sure there aren't any leaks or weak spots," she continues.

The security guard flinches but salutes, causing the older man portraying The Sleeping King to raise his tattooed arm.

"I'll come with you," the king says.

"Thank you, Tom. Anyone else?"

Ben, still dressed in his skin-tight time-traveling knight costume, points to the largest chamber on the underground map. "With your permission, Ms. Fell, I'd like to lead everyone here. If it's not filled in either, it stands to reason there might still be supplies."

"Be careful, all of you. Stay together. And should you reach the northern exit," she says, circling what looks like a waffle embedded in a cliff, "turn around immediately."

"Where does it go?" Rina asks.

Tiffany whistles, walks her fingers to the edge of an imaginary cliff, and plummets them into the abyss.

"We're going to check it out, so there's no reason for any of you to take the risk," Vic says. "But for god's sake, speak up if you see something strange."

"Like what? Little alien crabs?" Tiffany snickers and elbows a teenage boy who portrayed a dancing flower.

He doesn't respond. He stares at the floor and continues crying.

As the trio set off to inspect the entryways and the others prepare for the march to the break room situated under the northern quadrant of the park, Vic looks back on the shivering clusters. Nearly three dozen employees stood in the atrium for the mock run that morning. And of the twenty yawning performers and makeup artists, a handful of security guards dressed in padded suits of armor, and a dozen actors playing park guests who lined up with the rising sun at their backs and not nearly enough caffeine in their bloodstreams, only nine remain.

And not one checks to make sure Rina Bestler is following them.

Rina sinks to the floor, alone. Her stomach swells with anxiety as the group heads down the hall. Her fairy princess costume is too tight and she can't catch a breath. With a desperate grunt, she widens a hole in her shredded sleeve and tears along the seam until she can fill her lungs. She isn't supposed to be here. She's supposed to be four hours into her rink time. She's supposed to be bruising the hell out of her ass trying to add another rotation to her double axle. Never mind she was thinking the same thing during morning line-up. And on the drive to the house overlooking the park. And every single goddamn minute since the accident.

Whenever Rina thinks about medals and trophies in dank basement boxes, or how magical it would've been in South Korea under fresh snowfall, a new bloom of self-hatred opens inside her. It's nearly a garden now, reeking and tangled as she fantasizes about Olympic glory while her peers bob facedown in the water.

Her knee is skinned to shiny meat, but she rests her forehead on it, savoring the sticky sting all the way through her body. It might be the last thing she feels, so why not indulge in it?

Covering Rina's toes with her wet slippers, Tiffany extends her hand, and Rina recoils so hard she knocks her head on the wall.

The actress, who said barely a word to her over the last month, drops to a squat and curls her hand around Rina's head. "You okay? I know this can't be easy for you."

Rina didn't let the best skaters in the world touch her when she couldn't remove a warped blade guard, so she shrinks away from Tiffany's touch. Rocking to her feet, she thanks her and starts away, eyes to the floor.

"Would this help?"

When Rina swivels around, the local actress slides a mini bottle of Southern Comfort from her pocket and dangles it in her face. "I found it in the kitchen right there. Plenty more like it too. Must've been Harlan's secret stash."

Rina desperately wants a drink. She had sips of champagne here and there growing up, but in contrast to the rumors flying around the park, she never had more than that before the night of the accident. She never craved it, never thought it was an easy way out. It was all a mistake, exacerbated by the fight she'd had with her parents that night. She told them she wanted to go to college, but they wouldn't even discuss it. Her life was skating and competition. Her life was gold. Her life was theirs.

Sensing her hesitation, Tiffany laughs. "I don't think you're gonna crash any cars down here, honey." She apologizes but doesn't look like she means it. "I'm just saying."

"I wish you hadn't." Rina pushes past Tiffany to the kitchen, but the actress follows close behind.

When Rina opens a random cabinet, Tiffany giggles.

"You really got a nose for it, huh? That's where I found it," she says, twisting off the cap. "Hand me some more, would ya?"

Reaching past a stack of paper towels, Rina discovers an incomplete pyramid of mini liquor bottles.

"We're going to be stuck here a while. Come on. Help me make the best of it."

Rina passes the SoCos to Tiffany and shakes her head. "No

thanks. Being drunk off my ass when we're rescued probably isn't what I need right now."

Tiffany laughs. "You say that like you actually think we're getting out." Spinning on her toe, she dances to a moldering sofa that spews squelchy debris when she flops down. "Don't you know? We're all gonna die down here."

"What makes you think that?"

Tiffany laughs as she twists off another cap and lobs it like a basketball into the scummy sink. "Well," she says after a guzzle, "if this was the first time, I'd say sure, Ms. Fell needs as many of us to survive as possible. She would still be able to salvage her reputation. But there's no coming back from this. She failed on Wall Street, she failed at the family business, and now—" She drinks the rest and hurls the bottle at the sink, narrowly missing. "Dang!" She opens a tiny gin and sniffs cautiously. "Anyway, she doesn't plan on surviving, so why should we?"

"That's a bleak outlook."

Tiffany lifts her eyebrows. "Did you see the same shit I did? All those people? All those *dead* people? And that storm... it... " She drinks the gin and shudders as she swallows. "It was *alive*. It was... fuck, I don't know, some kind of monster." When Rina stares blankly, Tiffany rolls her eyes. "Anyway, don't tell me that *you*, a disgraced Olympian, want me to look on the sunny side. That ain't happening, sister."

Rina wipes sweat from her brow and it stings; she must've cut her scalp. With a wince, she sits beside Tiffany on the crusty couch. "I thought you didn't believe in monsters."

"I said I don't believe *Vic*." Swinging her gaze to Rina, she says, "I absolutely believe in monsters."

"Okay. So what do you think she saw when she was a kid?"

Tiffany shakes her head. "If we're getting into this, you can't make me drink alone."

Rina sighs as she opens her palm and Tiffany slaps on a mini whiskey. Twisting off the cap, she says, "Bottoms up," and takes a sip. She gags and coughs, and Tiffany smacks her on the back.

Leaning back, the actress huffs. "Look, I have no problem admitting I wanted to work here, but it was just because of my mom. I wanted to play the part that made her career. The part that... " She rolls her focus to the ceiling and shakes her head. "I wanted it, okay? But I almost didn't audition at all because of the rumors about Ms. Fell. She went crazy after the Ghost, started telling people her father was an impostor."

Swallowing another mouthful of whiskey, Rina flinches. "Why would she do that?"

"He fell out the northern exit," she says, having too much fun as she jumps her fingers off the imaginary cliff again. "Right into the bay. I guess she thought he was dead or swept out to sea, cuz they didn't find him after. Not until a few days later when some hikers found him on the beach."

"You'd think she'd be happy he was alive. Why would she say he was an impostor?"

Tiffany grabs Rina's shoulders, howling as she shakes her, "Because she's crazy! Why else would she reopen this hellhole?" She shoves Rina a little too hard and the girl tumbles off the lumpy couch with a shriek.

Someone shouts from the main corridor and footfalls echo in crescendo. Ben jogs into the break room, his face flushed with fear when he asks Tiffany, "Everyone okay?" But the fear vanishes, sours to a twitchy pit, when he sees Rina.

She hides the mini bottle behind her back, nodding as she stands and dusts off her gown.

"She's fine," Tiffany says, joining her side. "Though she's much more of a lightweight than I would've thought, especially for someone who carries around little baby boozes." She kicks an empty bottle and winks at Ben.

"Me? You're the one who found them!"

"Well, yeah, after you told me you held onto a bunch during the storm. That *was* pretty impressive. All those people getting killed and you held onto your booze."

"What the hell are you talking about?"

"Look! She's trying to hide one right now!" Tiffany tugs on Rina's arm, exposing the half-consumed bottle, and the skater's face burns in humiliation.

Ben forces an amiable smile. "It's not a big deal. I was coming to check on you anyway and wanted to make sure no one was hurt. And the break room down the way is in pretty good condition if you want to join us, Tiff. Better digs than this. Bunkbeds, cots, the whole nine yards. There's even some bottled water from the 90s."

"Thanks, but I'm gonna stay with Rina a little longer. She needs all the support she can get right now."

Rina's brain boils with baffling rage, but she keeps her head down, her hands clenched, until Ben's footsteps disappear.

"Not that this comes as a surprise to you," Tiffany says as if replying to a conversation taking place in her mind. "She's doing stupid crazy things all the time."

Jumping to her feet, Rina shoves herself in Tiffany's face and backs her against the sink. "What the hell was that about? Why did you lie about me?"

She bats her large blue eyes. "Lie?"

"The bottles! Why did you tell him they were mine?"

Tiffany cocks her head and furrows her brow in puzzlement. "Tell *who*, honey?"

The cut on Rina's scalp aches when her nostrils flare. She backs away, suddenly overcome by nausea. For a moment she thinks she's still in the car after the accident, her swollen head bobbing on her shoulders and dust rising from the busted airbag. Tiffany's image doubles before her, and she stumbles to the side, bracing herself on a wall decorated with a massive cartoon of a smiling sun.

"Help!" Tiffany screams. "We need help!"

Someone shouts from the main corridor, and footfalls echo in crescendo. Ben jogs into the break room, his face flushed with fear when he asks Tiffany, "Everyone okay?" But the fear vanishes again, souring to a twitchy pit just as it did the first time.

"We were just talking and it looked like she was going to pass out," Tiffany says.

Ben helps Rina to the couch, where she flops forward on her lap and hangs her head between her knees. "I don't know what's going on. I'm not drunk. I swear I'm not drunk."

"Of course you're not," Ben says, patting her back. "Where the heck would you find booze around here?"

When Rina lifts her head, Tiffany is crouched in front of her with concern etched into her expression. The bottles and caps she's been tossing haphazardly around the room are mysteriously absent, along with the one Rina was working on.

Rina grips her head and whispers. "What's happening to me? I feel like I'm losing it."

"Hey," Ben says, catching her focus, "we've all been through a lot. You're hurt, you're probably dehydrated. Why don't you join us in the break room, Tiff, and let Rina take some time for herself?"

"Thanks, but I'm gonna stay a little longer. She needs all the support she can get right now."

Ben shrugs and leaves the room, his squelchy footsteps again fading into the distance.

When Tiffany sits beside her, Rina buries her face in her hands. "I don't understand what's going on. Was there never any alcohol?"

"When? During your accident?"

"No! Today! Right now, goddammit!"

"Okay! I'm sorry! Jesus Christ, Rina, I don't know what's going on with you." She grunts. "I hate suggesting this, but maybe we *should* get you to Ms. Fell."

"I thought you said she was trying to kill us."

"What? No!" Tiffany laughs and throws her arm around Rina's shoulders. "No, no. I just think she's not going to *save* us—if it comes to it, I mean. But I'd completely understand if you *do* want to go to her. Hell, maybe I even understand why she chose you over me for the part. You've both been publicly disgraced. You've lost everything." She hums as she stands and looks down on Rina. "Now that I think about it, you probably don't want out of here any more than Vic does. I mean, what do you have to go back to? I know your parents kicked you out."

Rina doesn't answer. She can't. Her gut whirls with such incendiary acid, she feels like it might spurt out in a skull-dissolving geyser if she doesn't lock her jaw.

Tiffany closes their distance with a smirk. "And I know what you want. More than anything in the world, I know you wish you could go back to the way things were—back to the ice, back to the team." She crinkles her nose. "I can help with that, you know."

Rina scoffs, her rage shrinking into laughter. "How? Your mom? The first Princess Papillon? If she couldn't get you the part you wanted, what makes you think she has the sway to help me?"

"My mom's dead."

Rina drops her gaze and mutters an apology.

"She died down here, actually. In the first Ghost. The first Ghost anyone here remembers anyway." She giggles and shrugs when Rina meets her eyes. "At any rate, it's not about sway. People get that wrong all the time. It's not even about who you know. It's about sacrifice, Rina. Are you willing to give whatever it takes to restore order and joy to your life?"

Tiffany's voice is deeper now, silkier, and her lips move with such deft subtlety, she could have a side hustle as a ventriloquist. The voice seems to come from all sides, echoing, dizzying Rina as she whispers, "Make a wish. Anything. Something big, something small. Make a wish."

Holding her swirling stomach, she grunts. "Fine. Get us out of here then."

Tiffany lifts her eyebrows and beckons Rina into the main tunnel. When she places her hand upon the wall, the structure changes, softens, and pores open in the concrete, amalgamating and forming a large dark portal.

Rina approaches the hole cautiously, hand outstretched, and a salty breeze sucks on her fingertips. She pulls back, panting. "Jesus. What is that? Where does it go?"

"You only said 'out.' You should really be specific next time."

"But how—"

Tiffany's smile drops suddenly, and sorrow creases her brow. "*How* isn't important. Rather, *why*. *Why* would you want to leave, Rina? This, like many paths out of here, leads only to a life of loneliness and regret. The path before you will continue to crumble and rot, just as it has since the accident. There's nothing out there for you. No one waiting. No one missing you. You're a brat. You're a drunk."

"That's not true."

"It doesn't matter if it's true. Labeling you is easier than letting you explain, and your gigantic fuck-up makes people like me feel better about *my* failures. That's how America sees you, how they'll always see you."

Rina's heart thumps madly in her breast. Tiffany Law is annoying. She's bitter and sardonic. She can even be vicious if she's backed into a corner, but she's never been so cruel.

"You're not Tiffany."

She snorts. "You sure about that? You don't actually know me very well. Or anyone, really. You don't have any friends, Rina. Or family. Or prospects. This was all you had, wasn't it?"

Rina's hands are cold and trembling, and the apprehensive knot she used to able to ignore on the ice feels like a fist twisting up her guts.

"I can give you what you had and more, Rina Bestler. I can help you find your way back into the spotlight. Whatever you want, it's yours. If you're willing to pay the price."

"What the hell are you?

Tiffany sighs as she saunters into the kitchen. "Harlan called us 'hyperia;' it was better than a lot of the names we've gotten over the centuries. He didn't want to make sacrifices at first either, but he realized soon enough it was in his best interest. In everyone's best interest. But he wasn't strong enough to handle it in the end. It's a balance: sacrifice and success." With a nose-scrunching grin, Tiffany spins to face her. "But you know all about that, don't you? It's why you don't have anyone. You understand what it takes to be great. It takes loss. It takes independence. And the hyperia enjoy rewarding that."

"I don't understand. What did you do to Tiffany?"

"Tiffany couldn't handle the price," she says. "She wanted to be Princess Papillon just like Mommy, and we would've given it to her if she'd been able to deliver."

"Deliver what?"

She hisses through a chuckle. "You, of course. The prized part in exchange for bringing you to us. We made the deal on the day of her audition, while she was walking the beach, just like Harlan did all those years ago." She looks up fondly, lips pursed. "But she obviously didn't have the guts for it. So we let you keep the role and took a different payment." She opens her hands, and thunder shakes the tunnels, dropping debris on Rina's head. "But we still demand a real sacrifice. A human to appease us. Blood in the bay. Do that, and all your wishes will come true."

Rina hardly believes it when the words, "Which human?" leak

out her lips.

A grin consumes Tiffany's milky face and she wheezes in amusement. "Oh, I think you know who won't be missed."

Hatred blooms for new reasons now. From the rotten garden in Rina Bestler's soul, weeds spread like cancer, coiling around her heart until only one unblemished spot remains. It's the part of her that put on skates because she wanted to, the part that pored through college catalogs and dreamed of an entirely different life, the part that was overjoyed beyond belief when Victoria Fell took a chance on her. It's small, but the fact that it's there after all the mandatory rehearsals, competitions, and collisions means it's the strongest part of all.

She says, "No," and Tiffany's face falls dead. It doesn't even twitch before her hand flies to Rina's throat and closes tight. She pushes Rina through the kitchen, but the skater wraps her fingers around a cabinet handle at the last second and rips the door off its rusty hinges. The force jostles both women, and Rina reels around with the door in hand. When she smacks Tiffany in the face, the ice-blonde stumbles backward, babbling, and covers her cheek. There's no blood, though. No bruising. But when Rina drops her hand, the nest of white crustaceans in her skull writhes in screeching fury.

Rina screams, tripping over her feet as she retreats backward, and crashes to the floor. The wounded hyperia drop like sloppy pearls from Tiffany's malformed head, but other areas of her body lose integrity too. Her shoulder slopes, then dissolves into scores of tiny arthropods that skitter down her legs as she clumsily advances. More and more hyperia fall with each step until there's nothing left of Tiffany but her voice. Like mimetic shrimp, they're copying her still as they cluster in corners, flood over cabinets, and from all directions chant, "Make a wish, Rina. Make a wish."

Trying to track them dizzies her so much she has to lie down. Covering her ears, she yells to drown out Tiffany's voice, but it's on the inside now, and it has friends: steel slicing ice... the soft smack of rose petals hitting her boots... a crowd cheering her name... and then silence. Even when she uncovers her ears, she can't hear anything. She screams but can't hear her own voice. She smacks the floor and can't feel it. She's numb. She's broken.

When someone suddenly touches Rina's shoulder, she jerks as if out of a deep sleep. She gasps for air and stares wide-eyed at Vic and Raymond standing over her.

"What happened? Are you okay?" Raymond asks.

Rina shakes her head, her voice a frantic whisper, and Vic crouches in front of her with a mostly empty bottle of stale water, which she downs in one gulp. "I'm sorry. I don't know what's going on."

It feels like a brood of cannibalistic moths are doing battle in Vic Fell's chest, preventing her from speaking in a steady voice, but she's able to muster something comforting enough to coax Rina into lifting her head.

"We're here now," she says, "and we're not going to let anything happen to you." It comes so naturally off Vic's tongue she wonders if one of the rescue crew said it to her the day after the Ghost. "As best you can, tell us what you saw."

"Tiffany—" The misshapen teeming skull flashes into Rina's mind and she shudders. "There were things inside her. Or she was made up of them. They started pouring out of her and then... then she was just gone."

"What sort of things?" Raymond asks.

"I've never seen anything like them. Crabby-spidery things with crazy camouflage. Hyper-something."

"Hyperia," Vic says flatly.

"Wait." Raymond lifts his hands. "What are you saying? These are the same monsters you saw when you were a kid?"

"The word 'monsters' doesn't really do them justice," Vic replies. "Hyperia can imitate anything, and they can give you anything, and they use those powers to convince you to kill people for them. I don't know why. It seems like they're pretty good at it all by themselves. They made me and the rest of the world think I was crazy, but they killed all those people. Everyone in the tunnels, everyone in the park." Vic rolls her gleaming eyes to the ceiling, her chin dimpled in sorrow.

"You mean these hyperia things caused the Ghosts?"

She shakes her head and whispers, "They *are* the Ghosts. I don't know how, but what you saw, Rina, aren't even half of what the hyperia are. There's something in the Chesapeake, something big along the cliffs, and it's been there forever, waiting for desperate people like my father."

Rina's lungs empty in grief. "Like Tiffany. And me." She pushes herself up and glares at Vic Fell. "And you opened a theme park on top of it. You knew they were here, and you had us dancing around like fairies and forest animals!"

"I didn't know they were real!" she screams. "I spent more than half my life believing that I hallucinated everything I saw down here. And even then, believing I invented everything, I couldn't trust that Harlan wasn't those things in disguise. You saw how they mimic people. You can't know. So I left. I put it behind me. I got better. I remade my life."

"But you still came back here. Back to them!"

Raymond steps between and eases them apart. "How about we just calm down and get back to the others. We can talk this out together and find a reasonable solution."

Thunder rolls, ferocious, and shakes the earth, knocking the trio to the ground and raising an ear-splitting alarm from the group in the lounge. They scramble down the corridors, twisting and turning toward the lounge, but despite the persistent howling, there's no one in the passage before the break room. In the break room, either. But blood drips thick from railings and the bunk beds are festooned with sinew, from which glistening hyperia hang like Christmas baubles.

Vic spins out of the room and claps her hand over her mouth, but the vomit comes anyway, spurting between her fingers as she crumples to her knees.

"It's happening again," she mutters as Raymond wipes off her face with a scrap of sleeve. "And there's nothing we can do to stop it. They can take us down whenever they want. Just like that."

"Yes," the voices cry. "Just like that. Just like the two dozen people you watched die thirty-five years ago, Victoria. You had the power to stop it then, and you had the power to stop it this time. But you were selfish, always selfish."

Rina whispers, "Vic..." and the woman peeks around the corner to see lumps of meat and bone sprouting legs and crawling across the floor. They join, grow, and they shift into malformed but seamless amalgamations of her employees. The disproportionate, patchwork bodies shamble toward them, hissing and chanting, "Make a wish! Blood in the Bay!"

Rina scrambles from the room, grabbing Vic by the arm and following Raymond as he races down the main corridor. There are suddenly thousands of hyperia on the walls beside them, a swarm that is sometimes invisible and sometimes a frothy wave, complete with shadows of fish caught up in the tide. The longer the walls resemble the churning bay, the slower Raymond runs. His flesh turns green and he starts wobbling to one side. His knees eventually weaken entirely, and he collapses to the floor in a nauseated daze. When hyperia swarm over his body, Rina and Vic kick and smack them away, but there are too many. They each grab a leg as the creatures begin towing and then rushing his catatonic body to the rusted grate that once opened in the face of Calvert Cliffs. Vic falls when Raymond's shoe pops off in her hands, and Rina hangs on only a few seconds longer, dragged several feet and scraping up her chest.

Jumping to her feet, Vic screams, "Wait!" and the convoy stops inches before smashing Raymond's skull into the grate. "Just don't hurt anyone else and I'll—"

"You'll what, sweetheart?"

The tunnel stinks of cologne again, and Rina scrambles away as the source approaches Vic from behind. The corpse of Harlan Fell hobbles to her side and lays a warm hand atop hers, then lifts it to his moldering lips for a kiss.

She grits her teeth as she finally gazes into his pale eyes. "Why are you doing this to us?"

His brow creases and he caresses her cheek with a chapped hand. "Because there is nothing else. Nowhere to go. Nothing to do. We can't wish ourselves away, or we would've done it by now, and our powers can only be directed outward. So we do our best to remain... entertained... until our rescue arrives. Your family's been quite helpful, thank you." Harlan grabs her chin and pulls her closer with a hiss. "Now, what are you going to do for us?"

Vic pushes away and sucks on her top lip. Looking to Rina, she sighs. "You have to be the one. You have to make the wish. I'll be the sacrifice."

"I can't..."

"I'm okay with it, I promise. It won't be bad. It's just falling."

Raymond stirs when the hyperia begin towing him back to the women, but they aren't returning him—they're getting ready to use him as a battering ram. He shrieks and thrashes, and Vic screams for Rina to make a wish.

"I can't kill someone!"

"They're going to kill us all if you don't!"

Rina shrinks against the wall, her mind a whirlpool of life's biggest and smallest wishes. Which one would make it easier to murder a human being? Would a clean slate or a gold medal really absolve her guilt over killing someone who took a chance on her when no one else would? Even if she wished herself into the perfect life, how could she sleep at night with such an atrocious experience infesting her brain?

Vic grabs Rina's hands and says shakily, "I forgive you, okay? It needs to end. Raymond will back you up about what happened, and you'll go on with your life in a way I never could. Okay? Please, Rina. Make a wish."

The chanting begins again, and the hyperia carrying Raymond begin thrusting him toward the grate. As a ferocious clap of thunder judders the people in the tunnel off their feet, Rina Bestler makes a wish.

"**Hey, are you** with us?"

"Pull her away from the edge, will you?"

"No, don't touch her. Look, she's waking up."

Rina moans as she sits up, shivering and aching from head to toe, with a bevy of people in helmets and orange vests staring at her. Once she realizes they've come to rescue her, she gasps and throws herself into an older man's arms.

"Careful, girlie. You're real close to the edge."

It's an understatement. One sneeze in Rina's sleep might've sent her right over, out the hatch in the cliff face and into the Chesapeake. It's calm now, and the wind has died to a cologne-scented kiss. But the beach is littered with bodies.

Not Vic's though. As Rina stands at the edge, she doesn't see her boss' body, nor does she remember sacrificing Vic Fell to the hyperia—which means her wish came true. Terrified of the guilt, Rina wished to skip forward in time to her rescue, which is precisely where she wakes up. But she also doesn't remember what happened to Raymond until she spots his corpse broken on the shore, his arm hooked inside the grate.

"What happened here, miss?" one of the EMTs asks.

Her heart races. Raymond can't vouch for her story now. They'll think she's just as crazy as the people who found Vic alone after the slaughter in '91.

"Wait, are you Rina Bestler?"

"Holy shit, it is Rina Bestler! The ex-figure skater!"

She wilts to the floor as her rescuers close around her, shouting in her face and raving about the discovery. The noise nauseates her, and her head pounds like a bass drum. Rina Bestler, the former Olympian. Rina Bestler, the sole survivor of the second Ghost Hurricane. Rina Bestler, alone and crazy as hell.

She made the wrong wish. She wasted it, threw it away on fear.

But then the crowd parts, and a familiar face appears between the invasive strangers. Pushing through, Victoria Fell extends her hand to Rina and pulls her free.

"Ms. Fell, you're alive!" one of the rescuers exclaims. "The police need to speak to you immediately."

"Of course," she says. "But first, let me get Rina out of here."

"They need to speak to her, too."

"Later."

"No. *Now*, Ms. Fell."

Vic bats her eyes in shock and wraps her arm around Rina's shoulders. "Well, how about we let the girl decide for herself? What do you say, Rina? Do you wish to be left alone?"

The garden is overrun now, and the strongest part of her withers to dust. Scanning the group of rescuers, she doesn't see salvation anymore. She sees a gold medal. A college degree. And when she turns to behold the source of the hyperia at the bottom of the Chesapeake, a flashing mass larger than the Fairy Funland grounds itself, she sees the beginning of her first friendship.

The End

HE WHO FIGHTS
Sean Ellis

He who fights with monsters might take care lest he thereby become a monster. And if you gaze for long into an abyss, the abyss gazes also into you.—Friedrich Nietzsche, *Beyond Good and Evil*

When viewed through the multiple eighteen-millimeter intensifier tubes of a state of the art GPNVG-18 panoramic night vision device, the stars were so bright it was impossible to see the infinite void surrounding them. Even without artificial enhancement, the altitude and complete absence of any artificial light on this moonless night made for a spectacular visual display, but Major Jeff Hood left his NVGs on. There were things other than stars in the sky tonight, things that were not visible to the naked eye. Somewhere up there, a mile or two closer to the edge of space, men were falling through the sky like wicked angels cast from heaven. Angels who wore infrared strobes which flashed brighter than the surrounding stars and allowed Hood to follow their descent.

"Got them," he said into his lip mic, his voice barely louder than a whisper. "Looks like four... Scratch that, five."

"I see 'em," came the answering voice in his radio earpiece. It belonged to Dale "Mad Dog" Maddox, the sergeant major of Hood's Delta Force troop and Hood's oldest and closest friend.

Mad Dog was a fixture in the Unit, a veritable living legend. No one could remember a time when he hadn't been there, though of course, he hadn't always been the troop sergeant major. Like Hood, he had paid his dues, worked his way up the leadership ladder. The nickname, like most Delta nicknames, was ironic—a play on his name which was completely at odds with his laid-back persona.

Mad Dog was currently positioned on the opposite side of the DZ, which consisted of a ring of IR glowsticks, defining an area about fifty meters in diameter. At its exact center, like the bullseye on a target, a flashing IR strobe, similar to those worn by the incoming jumpers, served as a beacon to guide them in. The area within the circle was relatively level and had been cleared of large rocks and other hazards, giving the men a reasonably good chance of landing without serious injury, but there were no guarantees when it came to jumping out of a perfectly good airplane. The inherent risks were even greater with a HALO jump.

"Five," Mad Dog confirmed. "Who the hell are these jokers, anyway?"

It was a rhetorical question, and one that both men had been pondering since receiving the order to stand down from their original mission and await these new arrivals.

Hood wasn't sure why they had opted for a high-altitude, low-opening insertion. HALO was typically reserved for stealth missions behind enemy lines, and while this valley nestled in the Spin Ghar mountains near the Af-Pak border wasn't exactly friendly territory, the terrain was far more hostile than the small bands of Taliban and Islamic State fighters hiding out in the mountain caves, especially at night. Actually, he wasn't even sure why they were jumping in at all, or what they hoped to accomplish. He didn't even know for certain who *they* were. The only thing he was pretty sure of was that he wouldn't like the answers to any of his questions.

This was his mission—his party—and these guys were crashing it. Worse, they were crashers with an official sanction.

His original orders were to conduct a deep reconnaissance of the border region, mapping all the various routes through the mountains, identifying potential caches and refuge locations. They weren't far from the infamous Tora Bora cave complex where Osama bin Laden had hidden out in the weeks following the 9/11 attacks, and while the initial reports about the caverns had been wildly overstated, Hood and his team had already discovered several previously undocumented caves, suggesting that the mountains still hid plenty of secrets. Two nights earlier, they had observed a small group—six armed men and two *burqa*-clad figures that might or might not have been women—moving along one of the trails from the east—from the direction of Pakistan.

Without knowing for certain whether they were smugglers or enemy fighters, Hood had elected to follow them from a distance, gathering more intel about their movements, taking photographs and even getting close enough to determine that, despite their traditional Pakistani *shalwar kameez* outfits and *pakul* hats they were speaking Arabic.

That wasn't unusual. IS fighters were recruited from every corner of the Islamic world—from Chechnya to West Africa, and all points in between. In fact, Hood took it as evidence of their affiliation, and so when transmitting data back to the JOC via satellite uplink, he had also requested permission to interdict. While Hood waited for a reply, the group of suspected enemy fighters entered one of the caves and had not yet emerged, so Hood's team had set up an observation post nearby, ready to pounce as soon as the insurgents came out. Hood just hoped he would get the go-ahead before that happened.

Instead, he had been told to stand down and await the arrival of a specialized—and highly secretive—operations team.

The unexpected response had left him gobsmacked. He could tolerate a certain degree of micromanagement from higher up—that was part of being a soldier. But he and his team weren't ordinary ground-pounders. They were the Unit. The goddamned Delta Force, the best of the best. They *were* the specialized team that dropped in out of the blue and took over, not the other way around.

The flashing of the IR strobes seemed to grow more frantic as the jumpers zeroed in on the DZ like guided missiles, but then, just a few seconds before the inevitable impact, Hood heard a series of faint but distinctive reports as the jumpers pulled their chutes, stalling their meteoric descent a mere two hundred feet above the ground. Hood could see the square ram-air chutes, five dark silhouettes against a field of stars, orbiting the circumference of the drop zone, and after a few more seconds, he could make out the human shapes hanging beneath them. One of them broke formation and corkscrewed down to the strobe marker on the ground, raising his legs and flaring his chute at the last possible second for what Hood had to grudgingly admit was probably the best set down he'd ever seen.

The jumper quickly hauled in his chute, jamming it into a stuff sack as he cleared the drop zone, making a beeline for Hood's position.

"Looks like we're open for business," he muttered into his mic. "Who's our lucky first customer?"

The man held a rifle—an FN SCAR-H if Hood was not mistaken—at a casual low ready, but while his chest rig sported a holstered pistol, and at least half a dozen mag and grenade pouches, he wore no helmet, and did not appear to be wearing body armor; just black coveralls with matching gloves and balaclava. His eyes were hidden, but not by a set of NVGs.

Mad Dog's voice crackled in his ear. "Is that fucker wearing shades? At night?"

The newcomer was indeed wearing what looked like a pair of Oakley wraparound sunglasses. As he got within a few feet of Hood, he reached up with his left hand and peeled off the balaclava to reveal a square-jawed, unshaven visage that reminded Hood a little of Russell Crowe's character from the movie Gladiator. The man replaced his shades and then, impossibly given the constraints of their respective eyewear, seemed to look the Delta troop commander right in the eye.

"Major Hood?" The man's voice was a flat baritone, and low, almost a growl.

"That's right," Hood replied, feeling more than a little defensive. "And you are?"

"In a hurry." The man glanced over his shoulder just as a second jumper touched down, then returned his attention to Hood. "Lead the way."

Nonplussed, Hood just stared at the other man. Behind him, the second jumper was hastening away from the drop zone as the next man in line spiraled in for a landing. "Don't you want to wait for the rest of your team?"

"They'll catch up."

Hood's patience was nearing its limit. "Look, I was ordered to give you my full cooperation, but it's five klicks to the OP, and it's not like there's a paved trail and helpful interactive signs along the way. I've got men out here, too, and I'm not going to put them at risk by letting you and your people blunder all over the place and draw fire. I'll get you there—all of you—but you're going to have to do this my way."

The square-jawed man regarded him with an utterly blank expression for several seconds. "Major Hood, you *were* ordered to give me your full cooperation, and that means no questions asked. I don't have time to lay it all out for you, and even if I did, you aren't cleared for most of it."

"Bullshit. My clearance—"

"Doesn't cover this." The man paused a beat. "But if it will get you moving, I will tell you this much. My team is utilizing a very advanced battlefield integration system that is way beyond next gen. So, while you're leading me to the observation point, I'll be marking the trail for them. They will literally be able to follow in my footsteps. Nobody is going to be blundering."

Hood's ire did not cool, but it did change focus a little. If these guys were sporting "beyond next gen" tech, then their authority came from someplace even higher up than he had first suspected. "Those aren't sunglasses you're wearing, are they?"

"No."

Before Hood could respond, another voice joined the conversation. "Jeez, Jack. Cut the guy some slack. We're all on the same side." It was the second jumper, and the voice was low and husky but definitely feminine.

The inadvertent disclosure of the first man's name paled into insignificance alongside that second revelation. *A woman?*

There were only a handful of military and paramilitary organizations that required their people to be HALO trained, and none of them—at least to the best of Hood's knowledge—employed female operators. It was of course possible that the woman was an Agency spook, trained on an ad hoc basis for this single operation, but as Hood watched her approach, he dismissed that explanation. The woman—a petite but well-proportioned figure hidden beneath coveralls, balaclava, and the same brand of sunglasses as her partner—exuded the kind of confidence that could only come with real experience downrange.

She took a position at Jack's left elbow, let her SCAR hang from its sling, and stuck out one gloved hand. "Major Hood. I'm Delilah. Sorry to drop in on you like this, but like you, we've got our orders."

Hood accepted the unexpected handclasp. Behind them, another jumper had touched down. Even from twenty meters away, Hood could see that the man was a giant—almost seven feet tall, and built like a mountain. He wore the same kit as the others, but unlike them was armed with an M240B machine gun, though he carried the twenty-eight-pound weapon with the same ease as the others did their battle rifles.

Hood nodded toward the imposing figure that was now lumbering toward them. "If you're Delilah, then he must be Samson?"

"Bonus points for getting the Biblical reference," she said, "But Delilah is my given name. I also answer to 'Lila,' or you can use my callsign, 'Bride.'"

"Bride. Like Uma in *Kill Bill?*" Hood liked the association and decided to go with it.

He could almost sense her smiling behind her mask. "Not exactly, but that would be a better story."

"He doesn't need to hear it," Jack said, flatly. "We're not here to make new besties. His job is to get us to the objective. Nothing more."

Mad Dog's voice sounded in Hood's ear. "What a dick."

"You're not the first to say it," remarked Bride, glancing toward the distant spot where Mad Dog was posted.

Apprehension surged through Hood. Had she overheard the transmission? That shouldn't have been possible. Their MBITR radios were encrypted, and not even the JOC had the cipher key for their internal comms.

"Are they monitoring our freq?" Mad Dog asked, echoing Hood's thoughts.

"Yes, we are," Jack replied, irritably. "Now, can we please get moving?"

Son of a bitch, thought Hood.

"We might as well wait for Sharky and Vlad," Bride countered.

Hood however had enough. "Fine. Let's go." Without waiting for a reply, and not really caring whether Jack and his crew kept up, he turned and started up the narrow goat trail leading out of the valley. He had only gone a few steps when he saw Mad Dog hurrying along the hillside on an intercept course. When the latter realized he had Hood's attention, he raised a finger to his lips and then lowered it a little, drawing it across his throat in a cutting gesture. Hood got the message and thumbed off his MBITR. A few seconds later, the sergeant major fell into step beside him.

"Jeff, I think I know who these guys are," he said in a low whisper.

"Yeah?" prompted Hood.

"You ever hear of the Monster Squad?"

"Wasn't that the name of a cheesy movie from the Eighties?"

"Yeah, but it's also the name of a deep, deep, deep black special operations team."

Hood glanced over, trying to see if the other man was serious. With the NVGs covering half his face, it was hard to tell. "Something's getting deep all right," Hood muttered.

"RUMINT says they're not part of any chain of command," Mad Dog went on. "I'm not sure who they answer to, but they're the guys who get called in when shit gets really real."

"Dale, no offense, but you sound like a fucking fan boy. Monster Squad? It sounds like a bad GI Joe rip-off." He paused a beat. "Why have I never heard about this?"

"Probably because of that gold oak leaf on your uniform. Even in the Unit, there are some things we don't talk about in front of the brass."

"You're shitting me, right?"

"The callsigns are what gave them away. They're all based on famous movie monsters."

Hood glanced over again. At the edge of his field of view, he could see Jack trailing at a discreet ten-meter interval, and ten meters behind him, Bride was on the move. "I don't follow you."

"The Bride...of Frankenstein. Vlad... Dracula. Sharky... I'm not sure about that one. Maybe the Creature from the Black Lagoon."

"And Jack?"

From somewhere behind them a low howl split the air.

Hood froze and immediately brought his weapon up. Wolf attacks were a very real problem in the Spin Ghar region, but as the sound died away, Hood heard Jack snarl, "Knock it off, Sharky."

"What the hell?" Hood muttered, turning slowly to look back. All five of the jumpers—*the Monster Squad*, Hood thought acidly—were on the ground and moving up the trail single file behind Mad Dog and himself. Hood stalked back to join Jack. His right hand squeezed the grip of his HK416, his empty left hand had unconsciously curled into a fist. "What the fuck was that?" he growled.

Jack stared back at him, his face an unreadable mask behind his sunglasses, but Bride hurried forward to interpose herself between the two men. She had removed her balaclava as well, revealing blonde hair pulled back in a tight braid. She was good-looking, albeit in a generic sort of way, but there was something like a streak of dirt on her forehead, right above the bridge of her nose, and after staring at it for a moment, Hood realized it was a scar. "I've got this, Jack. Major, walk with me. I'll try to explain."

She took his elbow and guided him away from the other man. "Sorry about that, Major."

"It's just Jeff."

She nodded. "Jeff. Jack's not really a people person, but his bark is usually worse than his bite. Sometimes when we take over for another spec ops team, it can get ugly. Lots of chest thumping. Obviously, I can't tell you everything, but I think you're entitled to at least know some of it."

Hood was keenly aware of her hand on his arm. If she had been a man, the uninvited physical contact would have prompted Hood to put her on the ground and wrap her up in a submission hold. But she wasn't a man, and that, he realized was the whole point. She was playing him.

He stopped and pulled free. "What the hell was that howl all about?" he hissed, trying to dredge up a little of his earlier ire. "I thought you people were professionals. We're not back on the block here."

"Sharky can be a bit of a clown, but trust me, he would never do anything to jeopardize the mission. We did a full aerial sweep on the way down. Believe me, we're the only living things in a ten-mile radius. And your friend is right. We are the Monster Squad, and yes, our callsigns are all famous movie monsters... I know, it sounds a little corny. It wasn't my idea."

The comment set Hood's mental alarm ringing. He stopped and faced her. "Wait, you heard that? That didn't go out over the net."

"Like Jack said, we've got some pretty advanced tech." She tapped the side of her dark glasses. "Not much gets past us. We're all linked to a VARE—virtual augmented reality environment—so what one of us sees or hears, all of us do. It gives us an edge when things get hairy. Sorry about eavesdropping."

Hood scowled. "So I guess that means your friend Sharky can hear me telling him to quit screwing around and grow the hell up."

"I was just trying to answer your question, hoss." A tall powerfully built man stepped up to join them. He had pushed his balaclava up like a stocking cap. Though it was hard to tell for certain in the green-tinted display of the night vision device, Hood thought the man looked like a Pacific islander, maybe Samoan. The man's sardonic grin revealed teeth that had been filed to points. Sharky, no doubt. "Jack is the Wolfman."

"Wolfman Jack." Hood rolled his eyes behind his NVGs and turned to the dour leader of the Monster Squad. "Is that supposed to be funny?"

Sean Ellis | 272

"I'm sure somebody must have thought so," Wolfman replied.

As her remaining teammates came forward to join the huddle, Bride went on, "The big guy here is Imhotep."

"AKA The Mummy," supplied Mad Dog, coming up beside Hood.

The towering man with the 240B, his face still hidden behind his balaclava, inclined his head slightly but said nothing.

"It fits since he's actually Egyptian by birth," Bride went on. "His family came to the States when he was just a kid, so he's as American as you or me. He's our heavy weapons guy. Doesn't say much, though."

She gestured to the remaining masked figure. "Vlad on the other hand is Russian. And yes, his real name is Vladimir."

"Pleased to meet you," the man said, his voice thick with a Slavic accent. Unlike Jack, Bride and Sharky, his FN SCAR was the SSR variant, outfitted with a long barrel and an even longer sound-and-flash suppressor.

"He's former Spetsnaz. A sniper. Sharky's our demo guy. Wolfman's the field leader, and I'm his 2IC."

"So which one of you is going to tell me why my team has been benched? And why you're here?"

This time, Bride wasn't so quick to answer. She passed the question to Wolfman with a glance.

"We deal with situations that are beyond the capabilities of even special operations units like Delta and Seal Team Six."

"Beyond our capabilities?" Hood shook his head. "Bullshit."

"Boys," Bride murmured. "Let's not turn this into a dick measuring contest."

"Don't get me wrong, Hood. You're good at what you do. I've seen your folder. But at the end of the day, you're a guy with a gun, trained to fight other guys with guns."

"And you aren't? Then who do you fight? Monsters?"

Wolfman's silence was answer enough. After a few seconds, he said, "One of the men you photographed is Saleh al-Hindawi."

The name meant nothing to Hood, but he withheld comment.

"Saleh al-Hindawi is a known associate of Dr. Rihab Ammash. Her stepson, actually."

That name was vaguely familiar, and as Wolfman went on, Hood's recall increased. "Ammash is a former Iraqi WMD expert—you might know her by her nickname, Doctor Tox. She was one of the highest-ranking females in Saddam Hussein's regime. We arrested her after we took Baghdad and held her for more than six years without trial. A few years ago, she was released for political reasons and disappeared, but rumor has it she and Saleh have gone over to the Islamic State, no doubt looking to settle an old score with us.

Further analysis of the photographs gives a seventy-three percent probability that one of the two women in the group is Ammash."

"They were both wearing *burqas*," Mad Dog countered. "How do you do further analysis on that?"

"That's classified."

"So Doctor Tox is the 'monster' you're hunting? We had her once and let her go. What's changed?"

"She ain't out here in the ass end of nowhere because she wants to get away from it all," said Sharky.

"Our intel says she's working on something new," said Wolfman. "Something very bad. We're here to end the threat. Permanently."

Hood shook his head. "That doesn't explain why you're here. Or why we're on the bench. We've hunted high-value targets like her before. And we've done our share of looking for imaginary WMDs. We could have handled this, too."

Wolfman exchanged a look with Bride. She shrugged. "He's not going to just let this go. You might as well tell him."

Wolfman sighed. "One of Ammash's lines of research dealt with teratogenic compounds."

"Teratogenic?" said Hood. "I don't know what that means, but it sounds bad."

"It's the scientific name for any compound known to cause serious birth deformities," Bride supplied. "The word is derived from the Greek word *teratos,* which means—"

"Monsters," Sharky supplied, grinning fiercely.

"Doctor Tox isn't interested in causing birth defects," Wolfman said. "She's after something that can literally transform people into monsters."

Sharky finished. "And now you know the real reason they call us 'the Monster Squad.'"

As they trekked back to the observation post in silence, Hood considered what Wolfman had told him. It sounded completely implausible... No, worse than implausible. It was the plot of a bad science fiction story. An elite spec-ops team with a corny name, hunting a fugitive Iraqi scientist intent on developing some kind of Jekyll-and-Hyde serum that would transform a healthy individual into an unstoppable rage beast.

And yet, somebody a lot higher up the food chain was taking it all very seriously. And as curious as he was to know if any of it was true, Hood was starting to feel less like he'd been cut out of the mission, and more like he'd been let off the hook. But his curiosity was nonetheless aroused sufficiently that he decided to bypass the OP and head directly to the cave entrance. He radioed the team mates he'd left keeping watch to inform them of his decision. "Rollie, Bender. You guys awake?"

The voice of Ron "Rollie" Menzies, the troop's master breacher, crackled in his ear a moment later. "Barely, bossman. This is about as exciting as watching paint dry."

"Boring green paint," added Jeremy "Bender" Graves. "Please tell me our honored guests brought some Red Bull."

From somewhere behind him, Sharky let out a short laugh. Evidently, the Monster Squad was still listening in on their radio traffic.

"Negative on the go-juice," Hood answered. "So I take it all is quiet on the objective?"

"Roger that, bossman."

"All right. Stand by. We're gonna walk our new friends down to the entrance."

"Aw, we don't get to meet 'em?" Rollie asked, affecting hurt.

Bender added, "What's the matter, boss. We embarrass you or something?"

For some reason, the light-hearted banter rubbed Hood wrong, but he fought the impulse to respond abrasively, and instead simply repeated, "Stand by," before switching off his radio again.

They passed within a hundred meters of the OP. Hood didn't look up to the hillside where his men were stationed, but he could feel their eyes on him. This close to the cave entrance Hood chose his steps carefully, moving slowly to avoid alerting the enemy fighters inside. He also kept his rifle at the high ready, pointing at the cave entrance. His finger rested beside the trigger guard, his left hand poised to activate the PEQ-2 laser-aiming device secured to the HK's upper rail. With the Monster Squad's fancy integrated battlefield monitoring system, it was probably an unnecessary precaution, but Hood wasn't going to let his guard down. The technology was unfamiliar to him, and therefore, not to be trusted.

As they got within about twenty meters, Hood felt a hand on his shoulder—Wolfman, signaling him to stop. He complied, but did not lower his weapon as the five-person element continued forward without him. They were all business now, balaclavas lowered, every square inch of skin covered. They looked more like ninja warriors—or maybe comic book superheroes—than soldiers. Hood guessed there was more to their coveralls than just insulation and camouflage; probably some kind of lightweight bulletproof miracle material.

The cave entrance itself was unremarkable, a half-buried scallop at the base of a steep cliff face. But for the fact that more than half a dozen people had disappeared into it, Hood would not have believed that it was anything more than a sheltered niche in the hillside. As the Monster Squad drew close, they broke formation, spreading out to form a defensive line. One of them—Bride judging by physical size and weapon choice—advanced to within a few feet, taking a position that forced Hood to shift his aimpoint to avoid flagging her. She didn't linger there, but instead took something from her chest rig and, with an underhand toss, lobbed it into the cave.

Hood started at the abruptness of the move. He didn't know what she had just thrown in, but whatever it was, it would bring on some kind of reaction.

"Relax, Major," came the whispered voice of Vlad from a few feet away. "Is reconnaissance drone. Very small. Very quiet. Nothing to worry about."

Hood caught his breath.

"A little warning next time," muttered Mad Dog.

Wolfman turned and hiked back to stand in front of him. "No next time, Major. You've done your job. You and your men should clear out."

"I thought we might stick around. Just in case you need backup."

"We won't." He turned and started for the cave entrance without another word. He did not linger outside this time but continued inside, with the rest of the Monster Squad following. Bride brought up the rear, and just before she went inside, she looked back toward Hood and raised the barrel of her rifle in what he thought must have been a salute. Then she was gone, too.

Hood stared into the empty recess for what seemed like several minutes. Finally, he turned to Mad Dog. "Come on. Let's go." He started back up the trail to the OP, and as he moved, he keyed his mic again. "Rollie, Bender. Pick up your shit. We're moving out."

"Finally," replied Bender. "A change of scenery."

"We're buggin' out?" Mad Dog sounded disappointed. "I wanted to see how all this shakes out."

"Hoping to see some real monsters? Or just want to see the Monster Squad in action?"

"Both? Come on, aren't you even a little bit curious?"

Hood was curious, but he didn't want to admit it to his friend. "Frankly, I'm sick of all this GI Joe bullshit. And monsters? There are real monsters in the world, but they're as human as you and me."

Hood was as eager to put some distance between his team and the cave as he was to resume their original mission, and the further away they got, the less curious he felt. The last two days had been a colossal waste of their time and resources. Worse, he hated the fact that higher-ups had dicked his team around. Someone would get an earful when they got back to HQ.

But even his ire began to fade as he focused his attention on basic soldier skills—stealthy movement across uneven terrain and three-hundred-sixty-degree situational awareness. The night was so quiet that he jumped a little at the sound of someone breaking squelch on the comms. A moment later, he heard a strange voice in his earpiece.

"Major Hood, please respond." The strangeness wasn't limited to unfamiliarity. The voice was male, but the cadence and intonation had an artificial quality that immediately marked it as computer-generated speech, probably generated from text entry. The use of his rank was similarly odd. Unit operators weren't sticklers about following regular commo protocols, especially on the internal channel, but one thing they never did was mention rank.

He keyed his mic and spoke in a low whisper. "Who the hell is this?" He actually had a pretty good idea who it was—not the identity of the individual, but definitely the person's affiliation. "You're with them, right? The Monster Squad?"

"You may call me 'Phantom.'"

Phantom, Hood thought, resisting the impulse to spit the word out. *Naturally.* "You need to stay off our comms. If you have traffic for me, send it through the JOC. No, actually, don't. There's a chain of command. If you need something from us, talk to my boss, and he can pass it down."

"Major Hood, please listen carefully. You have been temporarily reassigned to my command. You may confirm that if you like, but the situation is critical and time is short, so please listen to what I have to say before you do so." The flat, automated voice held none of the urgency the words were meant to convey. "First, I need you to instruct your men to switch off their radios. This conversation is for you and I alone."

Hood glanced back at the others, all of whom were staring back at him intently, ready to follow his lead. He wanted to refuse, to demand confirmation before doing anything for this disembodied interloper who had hijacked their signal, and now seemed intent on hijacking their mission as well, but he knew that Phantom, whoever the hell he was, probably *did* have the clout to requisition them. He sighed and gave a throat-cutting gesture, signaling them to turn off their MBITRs. When they had complied, he depressed the push-to-talk again. "All right, Phantom, they're off. What do you need from me now?"

"Major, I need you and your team to return to your original location immediately. When you get there, I want you to collapse the cave entrance with explosives. It needs to be sealed. Permanently."

"What, is clean-up duty beneath the dignity of your precious Monster Squad?"

"Major, they're all dead."

The pronouncement was delivered with such utter dispassion that Hood thought perhaps he had misheard.

Now he understood why Phantom had requested a private conversation.

He turned his back to the others, covering his mouth and lowered his voice even more. "Dead? Are you sure?"

There was a long pause, and he imagined Phantom as a masked figure, hunched over a keyboard, typing furiously. "I lost contact with them approximately thirty minutes ago. There can be no other explanation except total mission failure, with no survivors."

"They're underground. Maybe something is blocking the signal."

Another pause, then, "Our communications system doesn't rely on FM radio waves, Major. And this isn't a discussion. I'm ordering you to seal that cave. Nothing more. Do you understand?"

Hood was still struggling to process Phantom's revelation. How could the man be so sure of the Monster Squad's fate? More to the point, why was he so willing to just write them off? "If there's even a chance that they're still alive—"

"There isn't. I know this must sound cold-blooded to you. Those people were my friends. Now, do you understand your orders?"

Fuck this guy, he thought. He turned back to the others and waved to Mad Dog, signaling him to switch on his MBITR. He didn't know if Phantom would be able to detect that Mad Dog was back on the air, nor did he care that he was violating what was probably a direct order from his new superior. *Let 'em court martial me.*

Aloud, he said, "Monster Squad down, no survivors..."

From the corner of his eye, he saw Mad Dog start visibly, but he pressed on. "Recovery of remains impossible. We are to proceed to the cave entrance and seal it with explosives. No, I don't understand any of it, but I copy."

"You may now contact your chain of command to confirm your status," Phantom replied. If Mad Dog's eavesdropping had been detected, no indication was given. "I will continue monitoring this frequency. Signal me when you have completed the mission. Phantom, out."

Hood switched off his radio and went to join Mad Dog.

"Holy shit," whispered the sergeant major. "All dead?"

"That's what he says. I'm not sure how he knows, but he seems pretty certain."

"And we're supposed to blow the cave entrance? Bury them inside?"

Hood nodded. "So much for 'Leave no man behind.'"

"That's pretty fucked up," Mad Dog said. He shook his head. "I don't buy it. No way did those camel-fuckers get the drop on them.

Not with the tech they were using."

"Tech can fail. Maybe they walked past an iron deposit, something that fritzed their fancy augmented reality system. And don't forget who they were going after. Maybe Doctor Tox cooked up some kind of nerve agent. Or perfected her monster juice. That's probably why Phantom wants to seal the cave. And why he doesn't want us to attempt to recover the bodies."

Mad Dog considered this and then swore softly. "Damn."

"Yeah."

"So, what do we do?"

"You say that like we have a choice." Hood sighed. "I'll verify with the JOC, but I already know what they're going to say."

"Jeff, we can't just leave them in there. You don't even know for certain that they're dead. If they're alive and we blow the entrance, then we're the ones that killed them."

"It's not our call, Dale."

"Isn't it?"

Hood frowned. He knew exactly what his friend meant with that statement. Internal loyalty was one of the key drivers of success in the special operations community, and implicit in that was the knowledge that, no matter what happened, your brothers would move heaven and earth to bring you home. The Monster Squad might not have been part of the Unit, but they were still family.

Mad Dog was right. If there was a chance that even one of them was still alive, then collapsing the cave entrance wasn't an option. And if they were all dead, then they deserved to have their remains returned to their loved ones.

"All right," he said. "Let's dig out the pro-masks. I guess we're going in."

Although they had all spent endless hours training for operations in CBRN—Chemical, Biological, Radiological, and Nuclear—environments, none of Hood's team had ever had cause to don their gas masks in a real-world combat scenario. Hood hated wearing his protective mask. It was hot and constricting—a regular face sauna. Breathing in one was a chore. It severely limited peripheral vision, and using them with NVGs was very nearly an exercise in futility. But the possibility of what might be waiting for them inside the cave was reason enough to stifle such complaints.

The more he thought about it, the more certain he was that the Monster Squad had fallen victim to a chemical attack. Not only did it seem the likeliest explanation for how a handful of poorly equipped insurgents could have overwhelmed a better-armed, better-trained force of spec ops shooters, it also provided a plausible reason for

Phantom's refusal to even consider recovering the bodies. The remains were probably contaminated with whatever nerve agent Doctor Tox had cooked up, and too hot to justify risking more lives. Hood understood that kind of caution; in Phantom's place, he might have given the same order.

Even now, as they moved beyond the mouth of the cave, getting their first look at what lay beyond the scallop-shaped opening they had been staring at for the past two days, Hood questioned his decision. The masks would only provide protection against inhalation agents, and even then, they were not one hundred percent reliable. Since there had been little chance of encountering CBRN threats, they hadn't bothered to bring along their MOPP suits, so if the toxic agent could penetrate clothing and skin, they were fucked. But that was a chance they were all willing to take. He hadn't ordered his men into the cave; they had all volunteered.

Before going in, Rollie had broken out their M256A1 Chemical Agent Detector Kit and deployed a sampler-detector to check for the presence of airborne nerve agents. After observing the test papers for several minutes, he'd raised one gloved thumb, and their journey into the underworld began.

The subterranean darkness was absolute. The cool rock gave off no infrared radiation, and with a complete absence of ambient light for the NVGs to amplify, they were forced to switch on the built-in IR emitters. Though invisible to the unaided eye, the little lights blazed like tiny suns in the NVGs' display, lighting the way ahead, albeit in sickly green monochrome.

A narrow opening at the back of the larger recess led into a passage just wide enough for them to move single file, with Rollie taking point, followed by Mad Dog and Hood, with Bender bringing up the six. Hood would have preferred to take the lead, but Mad Dog had vetoed that idea, as was his prerogative. Ultimately, it didn't matter, because after about fifty meters, the winding passage broadened to allow them to walk two abreast.

The new passage, which sloped downward gradually, was too straight and uniform to be the work of natural forces. Hood recalled stories of the CIA spending millions to dig tunnels in the mountains for Mujahedeen fighters to use as a staging area for their insurgent war against the Soviet Union, and wondered if that explained the origin of this tunnel. If so, perhaps there was more to it than simply a remote mountain refuge for weary extremists.

They moved ahead slowly, silently, scanning for trip wires and pressure plates, searching for any trace of human activity. It took five minutes to traverse a distance of less than a hundred meters. That was where they encountered a four-way junction.

Hood peered down each of the passages, looking for any sign, any hint to indicate which direction the others had gone, but the passages were virtually identical. He turned to Mad Dog, shrugging—a gesture that asked, *What's your gut tell you?*

Mad Dog gave each of the adjoining tunnels a long hard look, then shook his head. He leaned in close to Hood as if to whisper something, then drew back, probably realizing that it would be all but impossible with the mask on.

Hood switched on his MBITR—he'd left it off until they were inside, just in case Phantom was somehow able to monitor them using the radios—and tried to transmit a whispered message, but after a few seconds with no response, Mad Dog shook his head again. Even though they were only a few steps apart, the signal wasn't getting through. Something in the cave was interfering with the radio.

Hood swore quietly into his mask, frustrated. They would have to rely on hand signals to communicate. He pointed to the right passage, then to Bender, signaling him to post and provide rear security, but even as he was doing so, Mad Dog removed his helmet, along with the NVGs mounted to it, then ripped off his pro-mask.

"Shit!" Hood whispered, raising his hands in a frantic but tardy protest.

Mad Dog's face was sheened with perspiration. His naked eyes were spots of bright green staring blindly into the darkness, but he was grinning.

"What the hell, Dale?" Hood rasped in a stage whisper.

Mad Dog ignored him for a moment, turning away to face each of the passages in turn, alternately sniffing the air and listening with a hand cupped to his ear. When he was done, he turned back to Hood, leaning in close.

"Trust me on this," Mad Dog whispered, his voice now easily heard. "We need to use all our senses in here."

"It's not safe," Hood said, fighting the urge to shout it. "Put your mask back on."

"If I get a whiff of anything hinky, I'll mask up right away. And if I start doing the kicking chicken, you can always stick me."

In addition to pro-masks, each man carried a nerve agent antidote kit, with two autoinjectors containing atropine and pralidoxime chloride. The two drugs, used in concert, had proven effective against most nerve agents, but as with everything else in military operations, there were no guarantees.

But Mad Dog was also correct about the need to use all their senses in this benighted environment. He gave a resigned sigh. "All right, but at least wear your fucking headgear."

Mad Dog stuffed his mask back into its carrier, then donned his helmet again though he left his GPNVG-18s tilted up, away from his face. Hood watched as he sniffed the air again.

Well?"

"It reeks," Mad Dog said, and then, noting Hood's immediate response, added, "Like rotting vegetables or sewage. A hint of sulfur. But it's tolerable."

Hood glanced back over at Rollie, gesturing for him to perform another test, just to be sure.

"There's something else, too, but it's kind of faint. A sweet smell. Pine maybe? Yeah, it smells like a pine-scented candle in a shithouse."

"You hear anything?"

Mad Dog cocked his ear toward the tunnels again then shook his head. "Just you guys breathing. You sound like fucking Darth Vader."

Hood laughed despite himself and was about to tell the other men to take their masks off, but Mad Dog wasn't finished. "There's some kind of luminescent lichen on the floor. Big patches of it. I didn't notice it with the NVGs on. It's faint, but now that my eyes are adjusting, I can see it pretty well..." He knelt suddenly, lowering his face until it was just above the cave floor and then began crawling forward, into the center passage. After a moment, he glanced back and was grinning again. "Footprints. They definitely went this way."

Hood looked over at Rollie again. "Anything?"

The other man shook his head.

"All right, Bender, take off your mask. You and Mad Dog will be our bloodhounds."

"More like canaries in a coal mine," Bender said, but nevertheless eagerly removed his mask. "Not that I'm complaining." He took a deep breath, and then his face wrinkled in disgust. "Ugh, maybe I am. It really reeks."

"Canaries or bloodhounds, take your pick. Rollie and I will keep masks on so that we can treat you if we run into something. You let us know the second you start feeling weird, okay?"

"Roger that."

"Take a minute or two to let your eyes adjust."

Mad Dog was back on his feet and looking around. "Wild," he said. "It's almost bright enough to see where I'm going."

He took a step forward, but Hood clapped a hand down on his shoulder, restraining him. "Rollie's gonna take point. We're relying on visuals first, and our NVGs still give us an advantage."

Rollie nodded and, with the sample-detector registering nothing, started down the center passage, moving with painstaking slowness. Mad Dog was right behind him, weapon at the high ready and aimed at a point just to Rollie's right. Hood directed Bender to go next and fell into step behind him, bringing up the rear. Hood's view of what lay ahead was mostly obstructed by the other men, but he watched them all intently—especially Mad Dog and Bender—for any signs of trouble.

Mad Dog, in true bloodhound fashion, stayed low to the ground, bent over to get a better look at the stone floor of the cave, and presumably, the patches of lichen that preserved the footprints of whomever had passed this way before them. Every few seconds, he would raise his head and sniff the air, but then resume following the trail.

Then, without any warning, Mad Dog whirled to his right, training his rifle on the wall beside him. The abruptness of the move immediately put Hood on an alert footing, and he too shifted his aimpoint to the same spot, triggering his PEQ-2 as he did. The normally invisible laser stabbed through the air like the shaft of a spear to splash against the wall of the tunnel, lighting up the surrounding stone like a spotlight, illuminating... Nothing. The wall was completely bare.

Mad Dog seemed to have realized it as well. He shifted the rifle right, then left, then brought it up in a slow arc, but seeing nothing, lowered the weapon again.

"What?" Hood whispered. "What did you see?'

"There was something there. Moving."

Hood probed the surrounding area with his laser but saw nothing out of the ordinary. "I don't see anything."

Mad Dog's rifle shifted again as he searched, but then he shook his head. "I don't know where it went. Might have been a bug or something. You didn't see it?"

Hood hadn't seen anything and hadn't seen any insects since entering the cave. That didn't mean there wasn't something there, but it seemed unlikely. "You jumping at shadows now, brother?"

"What the hell do you know?" Mad Dog shot back, sounding uncharacteristically irritable. "With all that crap you're wearing, no wonder you can't see anything."

"All right, simmer—"

Beside him, Bender stiffened and swung his weapon around toward a spot on the opposite wall. Hood reacted as before, transfixing the wall with his targeting laser, but once again there was nothing there.

"You saw, it right?" Mad Dog asked.

"I don't know what I saw," Bender said. "But there was definitely something there. Just for a second. It was moving, then it just disappeared."

"Like it melted into the wall or something."

Bender seized on Mad Dog's suggestion. "Yeah."

Rollie glanced back, looking at both men and then at Hood. He shook his head slowly, the silent message easily understood. Hood shared the other man's concern. Hallucinations might be indicative of some kind of toxic exposure. "Maybe you guys should mask up."

Mad Dog turned toward the sound of his voice, his expression slightly manic. "Not a chance. There's something here. Something you can't see with NVGs."

Hood debated making it an order but decided that would be overreacting. Mad Dog was probably just having a rare case of nerves. Even seasoned operators weren't immune to the kind of primitive reptile brain response that could happen deep underground. "All right, Dale. It's cool. Just make sure you have PID before you pull that trigger."

"Always." Mad Dog seemed somewhat mollified by the concession, and as they continued forward, there were no further sightings of the ephemeral "bugs," but Mad Dog and Bender remained hyper-alert, their heads not merely on a swivel but practically spinning.

A few minutes later, Mad Dog paused to sniff the air again. In the NVGs, Hood could clearly see the look of alarm on the other man's face. Mad Dog raised a fist—the signal to "freeze"— and then waved in Hood's general direction, beckoning him forward.

Hood approached cautiously, rolling heel to toe to avoid even the slap of boot soles on stone, and leaned in close. Mad Dog seemed to sense his presence in the darkness. "Caught a whiff of burnt propellant."

Hood knew what that meant. "A firefight?"

"I think so. It's faint, but I think we're getting close to where it happened."

Where what happened? Hood wondered. What he said aloud was, "Good job. Let's hold up here for a few, look and listen." He conveyed the message to Rollie with a hand signal, then moved up to whisper it in Bender's ear.

For three full minutes they remained still as statues—Hood and Rollie watching the darkness with their NVGs, Mad Dog and Bender listening for any sounds that might indicate an enemy lying in wait— but they neither saw nor heard anything at all. Satisfied that there was no immediate threat, Hood gave the signal to begin inching forward.

After moving a mere ten meters, he spotted something glinting on the ground, a shiny surface reflecting the invisible light back at him. Another three steps revealed more gleams, a scattering of metallic objects that shone like pinpoints of sunlight on a wind-tossed sea.

Rollie eased closer to the large patch and knelt down to pick something up. Hood could easily distinguish the object pinched between the other man's gloved thumb and forefinger—a brass shell casing.

Mad Dog's nose had not deceived. There had been shooting here, a lot of it judging by the amount of brass that littered the floor of the passage. Hood kept advancing until he reached Rollie's position. The brass was a 7.62-millimeter round, which meant it could have come from an insurgent's Kalashnikov or from any of the FN SCAR battle rifles carried by the Monster Squad, but given the sheer quantity in that one spot, Hood guessed they had come from Imhotep's 240B machine gun.

Hood scanned the surrounding area, spotting more spent shells scattered along the passage continuing forward. Hundreds of rounds had been fired, and it was difficult to imagine that any enemy force could have withstood such an intense barrage.

Conspicuously absent were any indications that the enemy had returned fire. There were no bullet holes or graze marks on the walls of the passage, and no glistening pools of blood drying on the ground. He should have been gratified by the absence of the latter, but Phantom's insistence that the Monster Squad had been killed made it seem only ominous.

"Everyone hold up here," Hood said. He had to speak louder than a whisper in order to project his voice from the mask, and was sorely tempted to remove it, but with this first sign of combat and the knowledge that something terrible had subsequently happened, he knew it was even more important to take precautions.

Careful to avoid stepping on any of the brass, he resumed moving forward, his rifle at the high ready. A few more steps brought him within sight of a rightward bend in the passage. The left wall had been savaged by bullets and the floor beneath was covered with chips of stone and twisted bits of copper and steel—fragments from dozens of M80A1 penetrator rounds. He moved cautiously, inching around the bend, and then froze in his tracks as his light revealed a black puddle on the rubble-strewn floor, and in it, an outstretched hand.

The appendage was barely recognizable. The flesh had been shredded, presumably by bullets, and two fingers were missing entirely, torn away to reveal ragged tissue and splintered bone.

Another cautious step revealed the arm, likewise savaged by the relentless fusillade. The limb protruded from a ragged garment that definitely wasn't one of the Monster Squad's coveralls.

One more step brought the rest of the body into full view.

It looked as if the man had been turned inside out. The clothing, saturated with blood, lay in shreds around ragged chunks of flesh and bone fragments. Hood did not doubt that this had been one of the IS fighters, but short of a DNA test, there wasn't enough left of the man to make any kind of positive identification. The wall beyond was stained with splatter patterns, but not enough to account for the level of damage done to the body.

They kept shooting after he was down, Hood realized. He could understand taking a confirmation shot to make sure a downed enemy was really dead—not strictly legal under the laws of war, but easily justified—but this level of savagery was inexplicable.

There was another body, similarly destroyed, right behind the first, and as Hood took another careful step toward it, he saw two more just a little further down the passage.

None of them held weapons, which Hood found a little unusual. It was unlikely that any of the enemy weapons would have survived the full-on cyclic assault, and he couldn't imagine Wolfman taking the time to have his team collect non-functional weapons, but then again, he couldn't imagine any elite operations team doing what he now beheld. Never mind the carnage, it was poor fire discipline. You might blow through a few mags in response to an ambush, but you didn't waste ammunition turning already dead enemies into hamburger. But the Monster Squad had apparently done exactly that, and then taken the enemy weapons and any remaining ammunition with them.

Hood looked past the bodies and could distinctly make out a trail of dark spots—bloody footprints—leading further into the passage. The Monster Squad had walked through the blood of the fallen enemy and continued on their way, heading toward whatever it was that had killed them. The passage widened and then diverged at a Y-intersection, but strangely, the bloody footprints went both directions.

Hood backed out of the passage and signaled for the others to join him. He noted that Mad Dog and Bender began moving before Rollie could pass on the silent command, and easily avoided stepping on any of the brass as they came forward. Evidently, the lichen was providing more than enough light for them to see by.

As the three men approached, Hood warned them about the bodies. "Four EKIA in here. It's pretty messy, so watch where you step."

"What killed them?" asked Mad Dog, no longer whispering.

Hood looked back at his friend. Mad Dog was looking at the bodies, the green dots that were his eyes darting this way and that as he surveyed them. There was real, unguarded anxiety in his expression. "Don't you mean who?"

"You think bullets did this?" Mad Dog spoke rapidly, sounding faintly breathless. To anyone else, his apprehension would probably have seemed appropriate under the circumstances, but Hood had seen his friend stay cool under far more intense conditions.

"I know it. They shot the shit out of them."

Mad Dog shook his head. "There's something else in here with us. Something inhuman."

"He's right," said Bender. "I think whatever it was got to them." He pointed down at the bodies. "Turned them into..."

He shook his head, unable to articulate what he was thinking, but Mad Dog picked up the thread. "Monsters," he said, nodding. "That's what happened. That bitch figured out how to do it, how to turn people into actual monsters. She used it on her friends and set them loose in here."

Hood frowned behind his mask but gave the bodies another look. There wasn't enough left of the insurgent fighters to confirm whether they had undergone some kind of physical transformation, but the hypothesis accounted for the seemingly excessive use of firepower. It also provided an explanation for why there were no weapons near the bodies and no indication of return fire.

But monsters? Hood thought. It didn't seem possible.

"Four," Rollie said. "We saw eight hostiles come in here. If they were all turned, then there could be four more."

"At least four," Mad Dog said. "For all we know, Doctor Tox has herself a regular monster factory in here."

"At least we know they can be killed," Bender said.

"Yeah," Mad Dog replied. "With a shit ton of rounds. The Monster Squad burned through their ammo fighting these four. One of the others must have gotten them."

"All of them?" countered Bender.

"If they were black on ammo," said Rollie, "they should have gotten the hell out."

"Maybe they couldn't. Maybe those things—"

"At ease," snapped Hood, silencing the discussion. "Enough. We don't know what happened here. We don't know that there are monsters running around in here, so knock it off with bogeyman stories."

He thought the rebuke would end the discussion, but after just a few seconds, Rollie said, "If you're right, then it wasn't gas that killed them. We can take the masks off."

"We don't know—" was all Hood managed to say before Rollie had his helmet and pro-mask off and was inhaling the unfiltered air.

"Ugh, you're right. That's putrid."

"It's worse here," Mad Dog agreed, "but only because of them." He jerked a thumb at the remains on the cavern floor.

Rollie blinked several times and squinted into the darkness. "You don't think those things can smell us, do you?"

"I wouldn't rule anything out. Stay on your toes. Once your eyes adjust, you'll see better without the NVGs." Mad Dog turned to face Hood, seemingly looking him straight in the eye as if to prove his point.

Hood resisted the urge to grind his teeth in frustration, and returned his best poker face, easily done with the night vision device still covering his eyes. Mad Dog, in assuming the role of expert on the as-yet unproven metamorph-monster theory, had effectively usurped Hood's place as leader. And yet, Hood couldn't offer any evidence to the contrary.

"Good call," he said, trying to sound confident despite feeling anything but. He switched his NVGs off and swiveled them up, away from his eyes.

An image of the passage, of his teammates and the four dead bodies, hung in the air before him, the shades of green inverting like a photographic negative before fading into nothingness. Darkness enfolded him, swirling around him like a vapor that he could almost feel insinuating into his clothing. Faint bursts of color, like dim fireflies, hovered in front of him, winking out whenever he tried to look directly at them. The lights were just phosphenes, bursts of electrical energy in his optic nerves, which were probably a little overheated from hours of staring into the NVGs' display. He took comfort from the fact that Mad Dog and Bender had been able to quickly adjust to the low-light conditions.

He found the buckle for his helmet, removed it and tucked it under one arm so he could take the mask off. The smell of death and decay hit him hard. He flinched, fighting a gag reflex, and wiped his face with his sleeve. He blinked, straining to catch a glimpse of the phosphorescent lichen. "How long—"

"Shit!" Mad Dog yelled. "Contact left!"

Like all Delta shooters, Hood's relentless training under stressful conditions had imbued him with near super-human reflexes. In less time than it took to blink, he was moving, shouldering his weapon, swiveling to face the passage to the left, searching for whatever threat Mad Dog had identified. But enfolded as he was in near-absolute darkness, there was little else he could do.

Then that darkness was shattered with fire and thunder.

The noise of multiple reports in the close confines of the passage was truly deafening; an aural assault that nearly drove Hood to his knees. Muzzle flashes scorched the air, leaving streaks across Hood's retinas, but the strobing flashes also revealed something else.

There was someone… Something… With them in the darkness.

Something monstrous.

It was a vaguely human shape but dark, like a living shadow. Hood couldn't make out any distinctive features, only its hulking size. He shifted his aimpoint, flipped the fire selector to full auto, and added his voice to the chorus of violence.

The creature writhed under the assault, flinching with each impact, but then it sprang forward, leaping several meters in a single bound. Hood tracked it, shifting the muzzle of his weapon away as the thing disappeared behind one of his men.

"No!" Hood shouted, screaming to be heard over the din. "Ceasefire! Ceasefire! Ceasefire!"

His warning was unnecessary. The others had seen what he had seen, probably even better than he, and had already stopped firing to avoid hitting their teammate. Even as Hood shouted, the guns fell silent and the darkness returned.

Through the ringing in his ears, Hood heard a wet popping sound and a truncated scream.

"No!" he rasped, fumbling to find his NVGs, only then realizing that, in the chaos, he had dropped his helmet. Before he could locate it, the firing resumed, and in the first yellow flash, Hood saw the creature again, a dark hulking mass, hunched over an unmoving body, but as the first of several bullets struck it, it reared back, howling, and then bolted back down the passage, dragging its kill along.

Shaking off the horror of what he had just witnessed, Hood brought his weapon up again. When the magazine was empty, he let the rifle fall on its sling and drew one of his pistols—a Caspian Arms M1911 .45—from his chest holster. But even as he was aiming it into the tunnel, the creature disappeared from view. The firing stopped again and he was plunged once more into darkness.

In the momentary silence that followed, Hood re-holstered the .45 and quickly exchanged the empty magazine in his rifle for a full one. The well-rehearsed procedure was almost automatic, and he had no difficulty executing it in total darkness. If anything, it gave him something to focus on aside from the horror of what had just happened.

He also knew that, despite its wounds, the creature wasn't dead.

With his right hand still holding the HK's pistol grip, ready to fire one-handed if necessary, he knelt and with his left, began groping for his helmet and the precious night vision device mounted to it. That was when a scream broke the surreal quiet. "Fuck!"

Hood thought it was Mad Dog, but it was hard to tell; the voice sounded muffled and distant. The curse repeated a moment later. "Fuck. Did you fucking see that?"

"What the fuck was it?" came another voice, softer but still a shout. Rollie, maybe? Which meant....

"It fucking took Bender," said the louder first voice—definitely Mad Dog—the statement confirming what Hood already suspected regarding the identity of the creature's victim. Fucking ripped him in half."

"What the fuck was it?" Rollie repeated.

Both men sounded frantic, almost hysterical. Hood certainly felt that way. They were battle-hardened veterans, and had witnessed their share of gruesome tragedy, but nothing in their training or experience had prepared them for something like this.

Hood at last found his helmet. He quickly settled it on his head, swung the NVGs into place, and switched them on. It took a moment for the device to initialize, but when it did, Hood saw immediately that Bender was no longer with them. Where he had stood a moment before, there was now only a dark smear, streaking away into the left passage.

Movement from his right distracted him. He glanced over without turning his head and saw Mad Dog starting forward, weapon at the ready.

"Dale. Wait."

Mad Dog stopped but did not look away from the passage. "We have to go after it. Kill it."

"We have to be smart about this. We don't even know what we're really dealing with."

"I do. I saw it. It's..." Mad Dog hesitated, groping for the right word. "It looks like a... A demon. Or some kind of lizard-man. It was scaly. Like a crocodile. Doctor Tox must have found a way to stimulate latent reptile genes in human DNA."

It seemed to Hood like an oddly specific bit of supposition on Mad Dog's part. Hood did not recall anything remotely reptilian about the monstrosity. Of course, his eyes had still been adjusting to the darkness, but his impression of the creature had been very different. He glanced back to the remains of the jihadists but saw nothing that suggested they had been anything but human when they had died.

"It won't be easy to kill," said Rollie. "It didn't look like our rounds were doing anything to it."

"We hurt it," Mad Dog insisted. "But you're right. With those scales, it's going to be tough. Aim for the eyes."

"No," Hood said, flatly. "We're not going to do that. We're going to head out of here and blow the entrance. Seal this place up. Just like we should have done in the first place."

Mad Dog stood stock still for a moment then slowly turned. He recoiled a little when he saw Hood, as if not recognizing him, but then his eyes narrowed to accusing slits. "That thing killed Bender. It has to die."

"And it will. But I'm not going to lose any more—"

"Go on then," Mad Dog snapped. "I'll do it myself." He spun around and started down the passage, following the blood trail.

"Dale!" Hood shouted. "Get back here."

Mad Dog did not answer, did not stop.

"Dale!" Hood suddenly felt unsteady, nauseated. It might have just been the adrenaline letdown or the realization that one of his mates was dead and they were probably all going to die, but the single thought that railroaded through the fog in his brain was far more terrifying.

I've lost control.

He glanced over at Rollie, looking for support, but the other man was already starting down the passage after Mad Dog.

I've lost control. Failed.

A Delta troop wasn't rigidly bound to military discipline like other units, but a few things remained sacrosanct, and following orders from a commanding officer was one of them. Mad Dog, as the troop sergeant major, knew that—lived it, embodied it. More than that, he was Hood's closest friend.

And now he was... What? A rogue operator? A walking suicide?

I don't know what to do, Hood thought. Without a team to follow his lead, he was nothing.

But some part of him fought back against the despair. *No. They're still my responsibility, even if they won't follow orders.*

Snugging the stock of his rifle into the pit of his shoulder, he hurried to join the others. "Wait..." His voice caught, coming out as a whimper. He cleared his throat, drew in a deep breath of the foul air, and tried again. "Hold up. We'll do this—"

As if startled by his voice, Rollie whirled, his rifle pointing right at Hood's head. Hood immediately let go of his weapon and raised his hands in a display of non-aggression. To his dismay, Rollie's eyes remained wide, almost terrified, with no hint of recognition. "It's one of them!" Rollie shouted.

Mad Dog was suddenly at Rollie's side, his rifle likewise trained on Hood.

Hood reached higher. "Guys, it's me!"

The plea seemed to break the spell of confusion. The two men did not immediately lower their weapons, but they did not fire either. After a few tense seconds, Mad Dog said, "Jeff? Jesus, buddy. You looked just like one of them."

Hood was momentarily dumbfounded.

"Like a freaking bug-eyed-monster," added Rollie.

"Right?" confirmed Mad Dog. "You should lose the NVGs. You'll see better without them. And those things... I think they've got some kind of natural camouflage. Like chameleons."

"Thanks for the tip," Hood muttered, lowering his hands, but keeping his goggles on. Mad Dog's assertion, while spoken with authority, had no basis in fact. The man had removed his NVGs long before their encounter with the creature. More importantly though, if the other man was right about the creatures' vulnerabilities, then they would need every advantage.

Mad Dog didn't wait to see if Hood would take his advice but turned and resumed moving forward. Rollie followed, covering the right flank, and Hood took a position behind him and to the left. As they advanced, the first two men had several false starts, whirling to confront something glimpsed at the edge of their vision, only to discover nothing there. Hood wasn't sure what to make of their reaction—either the men were glimpsing something that he couldn't see with NVGs, something that could burrow under the invisible lichen faster than they could follow, or they were hallucinating.

Even as he contemplated the latter, he glimpsed something in his peripheral vision. It was more a premonition than an actual observation, and when he flicked his gaze to the side to check the edge of the panoramic display, he saw nothing.

Just nerves, he thought. *It's getting to me.*

A few steps ahead, Mad Dog's hand went up, signaling them all to freeze. Hood did so without question, going statue still, but nevertheless searching the darkness ahead. Just beyond where Mad Dog stood, the passage opened up into a larger chamber. The blood streaks continued forward another few paces and then ended beneath a crumpled, vaguely human form.

Bender.

Hood gradually became aware of another shape just beyond the twisted corpse. At first, he wasn't sure what he was seeing, but as he turned his focus to it, it grew more distinct, as if emerging from a fog. For a fleeting instant, he thought he could see the man it had been, but as he continued to stare, he saw only the monster it had become.

The creature appeared to be sitting with its back to the passage wall. Its entire body was covered in rough mottled scales that shimmered through color changes like someone flipping channels on a TV set. The scales rose to form horny ridges that ran from shoulder to wrist. The hands, which rested on the cavern floor to either side of the creatures long, gangly legs, ended in talons, tipped with hooked claws. The hairless head looked vaguely human at first glance, but then after even a moment's scrutiny, it became something else—the slavering, proto-canine visage of a demon. The hellbeast was slumped over, as if sleeping.

Hood blinked in disbelief, desperate for some other explanation, and yet unable to deny what his eyes were seeing. Ahead of him, Mad Dog was signaling for a concentrated assault on his three-count. Hood nodded in acknowledgement, and readied his weapon.

Mad Dog raised his fist and extended one finger.

One.

Hood slowly, quietly, shifted the fire selector from safe to semi-auto.

Two.

The creature's head came up suddenly, its eyes flashing open to look directly at Hood, and then it was moving.

Hood didn't wait for Mad Dog to give the order. He tracked the moving target, while simultaneously activating the PEQ-2 and repeatedly squeezing the HK's trigger. His first shot cracked against the wall behind the creature. He had no idea whether his second found the target because in the instant between trigger pulls, the air was filled with muzzle flashes and smoke and noise. The creature stumbled, its momentum carrying it forward in a haphazard tumble, even as the intensity of the barrage increased. Hood used the targeting laser to correct his aim, placing the green spot on the beast's exposed cranium, and kept pulling the trigger until the scaly head came apart in bloody chunks.

He slipped his finger off the trigger, but Mad Dog and Bender continued firing without letup, savaging the corpse, which continued to writhe, either in death throes or from the relentless hammering of incoming rounds. The blood spray and smoke coalesced around the body like mist, rendered green in the NVG display. Hood was about to shout for a ceasefire, but then he saw something moving in that surreal fog, and instead emptied his magazine into it.

He reloaded immediately, but before he could resume firing, Mad Dog raised a hand to signal the end of the assault. The mist gradually settled revealing the aftermath. Hood immediately noticed that the corpse appeared to be mostly intact, albeit somewhat misshapen, save for the head which had completely disintegrated. The rest of the body had gone pale as if all the chameleon pigments had oozed out of the scales, but numerous dark spots, like bruises, showed where bullets had punched through the tough hide.

Curious despite himself, and keeping his HK trained on the shape, he advanced toward it, moving into the cavernous chamber. Mad Dog shook his raised hand, hissing a warning that was barely audible to Hood's tortured ears, but Hood ignored him and continued toward the body.

Two steps into the chamber, he spied movement from the corner of his eye, and immediately swung around to meet it. As before, there was nothing there... Or if there was, it had moved faster than his eye could follow, but his attention was immediately drawn to something that had been hidden from view at the mouth of the passage. Lying on the cavern floor was a pair of sunglasses.

He knelt to retrieve them, and stared at them for a moment, trying to recall where he had seen them before. It came to him in a rush of understanding. He pivoted back toward the corpse of the hellbeast, seeing it anew. There was hardly anything recognizable about it, and yet he immediately grasped the truth. The beast had not been one of the insurgent fighters in Doctor Tox's retinue.

"It was one of them," he said. "Monster Squad."

Mad Dog's right eye twitched, but then he strode forward and knelt beside the fresh kill. "I'll be damned. You're right. I think it was the big one... Imhotep."

Rollie spat a curse. "So we just fragged one of our own guys?"

"It wasn't human anymore," declared Mad Dog. "We did him a favor. Whatever shit Doctor Tox cooked up, it looks like it works fast. We have to find her and end this."

Hood was only half-listening. He was still trying to come to terms with the fact that they had just killed a fellow operator, and Mad Dog's rationale provided little comfort. What if it had happened to one of them? If Rollie or Mad Dog began to turn would he be able to pull the trigger on his brothers?

How did this happen?

On an impulse, he swung the NVGs up and then, working by feel alone, slipped the sunglasses over his eyes. For a few seconds, nothing happened, but then, like the recipient of some Biblical miracle, he could see again.

The view before his eyes was not the green-tinted reconstituted video image provided by NVGs, but a crystal clear, full color vision of the cavern, lit up as if by sunlight. He could distinguish the gray-brown rock, and the startlingly bright scarlet of freshly spilled blood. He could even see the luminescent lichen, glowing a faint but distinctive hue of lime green. It covered most of the floor, except where it had been disturbed by foot traffic, and crept partway up the walls.

"What the hell?" he muttered.

"Who is this? Identify yourself," said a familiar albeit artificial voice.

"Phantom?"

Mad Dog turned toward him, a look of alarm on his face. "Who are you talking to?"

Hood held up a hand to forestall his friend and listened to the computer-generated voice that was not merely in his ears but reverberating through his skull. "Major Hood. What are you doing? Why did you disregard my orders?"

Hood considered how best to reply and decided that there were more important things to do than justify his decision to enter the cave. "What the hell happened here? Enough lies. What's really going on?"

"Major, listen to me very carefully. You and your men are in extreme danger. You need to get out of there right now. Before it's too late."

"Tell me what's going on. What happened to your team? You said they were all dead, but that's not true, is it?" He glanced over at the motionless form of the lizard-creature that had once been Imhotep. "They changed into... I don't know what. But you knew, didn't you?"

The pause was longer than expected, and despite the complete lack of emotion in the artificial voice, Hood sensed a weary resignation. "Major Hood, I will explain everything to you, but you and your men must leave the cave at once."

"What about the others? Did they change, too?"

Mad Dog advanced a step toward him, his weapon coming up. "Who are you talking to?" he growled.

Hood shook his hand again. "It's Phantom. He's going to tell me what's really going on here."

The last was said as much to Phantom as to Mad Dog, but the latter simply echoed the word, "Phantom," as if hearing it for the first time.

Phantom spoke again. "Major Hood, you must listen to me. Your eyes are deceiving you."

"What do you mean?"

"There is something dangerous in the cave, but it's not what you think. I don't have time to explain everything—"

"Try."

There was another long pause. Mad Dog was now standing right in front of him, eyes darting back and forth as he scrutinized Hood, searching perhaps for some hint of a reptilian metamorphosis in progress. Hood tried to ignore him.

"The change is not physical," Phantom said.

Hood was beginning to wonder if Phantom was stalling, intentionally wasting his time. But why? Was the man behind the disembodied computer-generated voice secretly in league with Doctor Tox?

"It looks pretty physical to me," Hood said, staring at the bullet-riddled corpse.

"Shortly after they entered the cave, the team began to experience changes in their mental status. Increasing paranoia. Hallucinations. Minor at first, but quickly escalating in intensity."

Hallucinations? Hood thought that sounded like the kind of thing an enemy might say. Perhaps Phantom was gaslighting him, trying to get him to question his own sanity. "How did she do it?"

"She?"

"Doctor Tox. How did she expose them? What's her delivery system?"

Another pause. "Doctor Tox is dead. When the squad entered the cave, only four hostiles were present, and all of them were in the final stage of critical exposure."

"You mean they had changed?"

"There is no physical change. Their minds were gone. They killed and consumed their comrades—including Doctor Tox—and were roaming the caverns like wolves."

No physical change. Why did Phantom keep stressing that, when it was so obvious that his own people had been transformed by the teratogenic compound?

Phantom was still speaking. "Your teammate is already showing signs of critical exposure."

Hood jerked his gaze to Mad Dog, surprised. "You can see him?"

Mad Dog, realizing that he was the topic of the seemingly one-sided conversation, bristled. "Stop talking to him."

Phantom's voice was already vibrating through Hood's skull. "I can see everything you can see, and far more. It may be too late for him. It may be too late for all of you, but the longer you stay in that cave, the less likely it is that any of you will survive."

"I said stop talking!" Mad Dog shouted, showering Hood with flecks of spittle, shaking his rifle emphatically.

Already showing signs... Was it true? How else could he explain the profound change in his friend's demeanor?

But why had Mad Dog been affected and not Rollie or himself?

Hood raised his hands. "Dale, it's okay. He's gone. I'm not talking to him anymore. But we need to go now."

"Go? We have to finish the mission. We have to find the bitch that did this."

"She's already dead. The monsters killed her. And they're all dead now."

Mad Dog's eyes darted back and forth for a moment, then settled on Hood again, narrowing into accusing slits. "You're lying. You're trying to protect her." He shifted the rifle toward Hood's face. "You're one of them."

Hood instinctively recoiled from the gaping hole of the weapon's muzzle, knowing with absolute certainty that his friend was going to kill him. He could see Mad Dog's finger sliding into the trigger guard. "Dale, wait!"

There was a flurry of motion behind Mad Dog, followed by a sickening thud of impact—the butt of Rollie's rifle striking the back of Mad Dog's helmeted head. Hood threw himself flat an instant before the weapon discharged, the bullet sizzling through the air where his head had been a moment before, drilling harmlessly into the wall. Mad Dog didn't fire a second time, but instead toppled forward like a felled tree.

Rollie stood over him, wearing a fierce expression and gripping the stock and heat shield of his own rifle. "Damn," he whispered. "He was gonna kill you, bossman. I think he was starting to change."

Hood nodded dully, staring at Mad Dog's unconscious form, searching for any signs of an incipient transformation.

No physical change, Phantom had said. *Increasing paranoia. Hallucinations.*

But why was it only affecting Mad Dog?

The answer hit him like a slap. "Rollie, put your mask back on."

The other man stared back at him in alarm. "No way, boss. I can't breathe in that thing."

"Breathing is what's going to turn us... To get us killed." Hood paused to remove his helmet and, with some reluctance, the sunglasses, temporarily suspending his link to Phantom and plunging him once more into total darkness. "There's something in the air in here that's doing this to him. To all of us. It affected Mad Dog first because he took his mask off first, but it's going to hit us, too."

"I'm fine."

"The lichen," Hood went on, ignoring the rebuttal. He took his mask out of its carrier pouch. "That's got to be it. It's releasing spores... Or maybe a gas. Even if it's not affecting us yet, it will if we aren't protected."

He brought the mask to his face and pulled the straps over his head, snugging it into place. Wearing it brought on an immediate surge of anxiety. He couldn't seem to draw a breath. The mask was suffocating him. He had to fight the urge to tear it off and fling it away into the darkness.

After a few seconds, he managed to get some air into his lungs, but the panic did not relent and wouldn't, he knew, until he could see again. He spread the flexible arms of the glasses as wide as he could and slipped them on over the clear lenses of the mask. When his ability to see the cavern around him returned, he was relieved to discover Rollie likewise donning his protective mask. "Phantom, are you still there?"

"Major Hood. You need to get out of there. Now."

"We're wearing pro-masks," Hood said. "That will buy us some time."

"Those won't protect you from what's coming."

"What are you talking about?"

Something changed in Hood's view of the cavern. In addition to their immediate surroundings, he saw ethereal shapes like lines drawn with smoke, only instead of floating in the air they were inside the walls—or more accurately, beyond them. Phantom was showing him a three-dimensional virtual representation of the entire cavern system, literally giving him the ability to see through solid rock. A segmented line consisting of bright red arrows appeared on the floor and continued into the passages to reveal a convoluted escape route.

"Please hurry, Major." Phantom said.

"Why?"

Something new appeared in the ghost image, or rather four somethings, moving with slow determination down other passages in the smoke-like maze. Although they too looked like ghosts, Hood knew they were actually monsters—the surviving members of the Monster Squad.

"You said they were dead," Hood accused.

"To all intents and purposes, they are. And if you don't move now, you will be too."

"You're just going to leave them here? Like this?"

"There's nothing you or I can do for them. If you don't leave right now, you will be killed. The team may have removed their glasses and severed my link to them, but they are still wearing their battlesuits, which utilize adaptive camouflage and bullet resistant metamaterials. You won't be able to kill them."

Hood gestured at the headless corpse of Imhotep. "Tell that to him."

Phantom did not respond.

Hood looked up again, noting the position of the four spectral figures closing on his location. More information was appearing before his eyes—the course, distance and estimated time of arrival for each. The nearest was less than fifty meters—fifteen seconds—away, and moving faster.

"They're coming," he shouted.

Rollie jerked his rifle up but then started turning uncertainly. Hood mentally kicked himself for forgetting that the other man could not see what he did, and pointed toward the passage from which the target would emerge. "There! Five seconds to contact."

It was more like three.

The ghost image resolved into flesh and blood—it was Bride.

And yet, it wasn't.

Despite Phantom's repeated insistence that there had been no physical transformation, the thing that emerged from the passage was more beast than woman.

Bride's careful braid had come unraveled, unleashing a tangle of snakes that writhed about a face that was no longer even remotely pretty, but deathly pale, like that of a reanimated corpse. The rest of her body was covered in scaly chameleon skin that rippled through random color changes. Her eyes bulged from their sockets, the irises surrounded by whites that glowed with an unnatural green light. Those eyes found Hood and Rollie. Her lips peeled back to bare her teeth in a feral grimace, and then she started forward again.

Hood quickly brought his weapon up, but as he placed the front sight on her, he understood that the monster he was seeing was not real. Whether it was that realization, or the filtered air blunting the hallucinatory properties present in the environment, the illusion of a beast fell away like a veil, revealing the woman—

Delilah!

—that she really was. There was still madness in her eyes, but also a fear so primal that it made Hood's heart ache.

She doesn't know what she's doing.

He lowered his rifle and extended a hand to her, hoping that she would understand. He thought he saw a glimmer of recognition in her eyes....

And then her face dissolved into a froth of red as Rollie opened up on full auto.

Hood retched into his mask as the nearly headless corpse fell back. Rollie moved toward her, firing the whole time. He unloaded the entire magazine into her, and then reloaded and kept shooting. Hood raised a hand, desperate to end the carnage, but Rollie did not stop shooting until there was nothing left of Bride's head.

Hood sank to his knees, struggling to catch his breath. "Why—?" was all he managed to say.

Through ringing ears, he heard Rollie shouting, "Is that all of them?"

He raised his head and, fighting a wave of vertigo, looked around until he found three more ghost images—two moving through the maze of passages to his right, and one closing fast from their rear. He pointed weakly to the passage behind them. Rollie quickly reloaded, then turned and aimed his weapon down the tunnel, but after a few seconds, he glanced over at Hood. "Bossman, are you gonna help out here, or what?"

Hood struggled to find his voice. "Rollie, we can't do this."

"The fuck we can't," Rollie snarled. "Kill or be killed, boss, and 'be killed' is not a fucking option. So suck it up and help me exterminate these things."

Hood's head was swimming. He knew Rollie was right... Knew that if they did not kill the Monster Squad, they would never leave the cave system.

They killed and consumed their comrades...

But he couldn't bring himself to think of them as the enemy. They were American soldiers. Brothers in arms. And they were sick. Under the influence of a mind-altering substance. Maybe if he and Rollie could lure them out of the cave... Get them into the fresh air... Get them medical attention.

The ghost image was approaching fast. Twenty-five meters. Twenty.

Hood tried to speak, tried to articulate his plan, but the words refused to come.

The ghost materialized, a slender figure that could only be Vlad, the Russian-born sniper. Unlike Bride and Imhotep however, Vlad had left his balaclava on, hiding his face from view. Hood barely had time to register this fact before Rollie opened fire.

Vlad went down under the hailstorm, writhing and curling like a worm on a fishhook. His arms came up, covering his head, and he let out a wail that was audible even over the roar of Rollie's HK, a wail that was not silenced by the relentless assault. As he lay there, thrashing and squirming, large dark spots began to appear on the fabric of Vlad's coverall garment and matching balaclava. The bullets were wreaking havoc on the adaptive camouflage. But Vlad was still alive. The rounds weren't getting through the metamaterial.

Rollie's gun abruptly went silent. Hood saw him button out the magazine, letting it fall to the ground in his haste to reload, but he wasn't fast enough. In the instant that the punishing attack ceased, Vlad uncurled from his fetal ball and bounded up, springing at Rollie.

Hood shook off his paralysis and opened fire, aiming at Vlad's chest. The rounds drove him back, eliciting another howl of pain, but this time he did not go down. Instead, he hunched over like a sailor leaning into the wind and started inching forward again.

Hood's magazine ran out, but Rollie was already firing again, taking up the slack long enough for Hood to change it. The concentration of fire on Vlad's chest had turned his upper torso completely black, but now blood was oozing through the fabric. Bullet resistant or not, the unceasing ferocity of the assault was finally taking a toll on the Russian. He managed another halting step, then his agonized howl went silent and he crumpled to the ground, unmoving. Hood immediately let go of his trigger. Rollie kept firing until the magazine ran out.

The air in the cave was thick with smoke, but through it Hood could see two more spectral figures moving beyond the walls— Wolfman and Sharky, running side by side, closing in for the kill.

Hood felt sick to his stomach. There was no turning back now, no hope of any outcome better than the death of two more brothers in arms.

But was that even possible? Taking out Vlad had required a sustained assault from both him and Rollie, and dozens of rounds— maybe even hundreds.

Hood choked down his bile and changed out the half-empty magazine in his rifle for a full one. Running out of ammunition wasn't going to be a problem; he had four more full mags. The real concern was that the weapon wasn't designed for sustained fire at full auto. He could feel the heat radiating from the barrel and upper receiver. The more rounds he put through the rifle, the more likely it was to jam or even blow up in his face.

But there was no time to wait for the rifle to cool down, and no alternative but to meet the approaching threat with overwhelming force. He pointed to the indicated passage. "There! Two of them. Twenty seconds!"

He counted down by fives, and then when he got to five, he shouted, "Get ready!"

Sharky was first to emerge, his filed teeth bared in a feral grimace. He had removed his balaclava, which meant a lucky headshot might be enough to end the threat—end his life—but luck was not on their side.

Rollie and Hood fired simultaneously, but the first round only grazed Sharky, creasing his scalp. He immediately ducked under the rest of the rounds, doubling over as if to run on all fours. Both men tried to track him, but Rollie's weapon burped once and then went silent.

Jammed.

Some of Hood's bullets hammered into Sharky's exposed back, sending him skidding into a fetal curl.

A new sound joined the din, the lower boom-boom-boom of Rollie's secondary weapon, but he wasn't shooting at Sharky. Hood flicked his eyes in the direction of the muzzle flash and glimpsed Wolfman's snarling face in the entrance to the passage. The impacts sent the Monster Squad field leader sprawling forward but seemed only to piss him off. With one arm thrown up as if to ward off the attack, he pushed off the wall and leapt at Rollie.

Hood swung his HK around to meet this new threat. He managed to squeeze off four rounds before the trigger went slack, the magazine exhausted, but the combination of his fire and Rollie's was sufficient to halt Wolfman's advance, if only momentarily.

Then Wolfman did something unexpected. Instead of renewing his attack, he veered toward the still-dazed Sharky, grabbed hold of his coveralls, and commenced dragging him back into the mouth of the passage.

Astonished, Hood let off the trigger. Rollie however, kept firing, hammering bullets into the retreating figures until they melted into the darkness of the passage. As soon as they were out of direct view, they transformed once more into ghost images, huddled in the smoke-like passage.

Hood just stared at them. What had he just witnessed? Compassion? Intelligence? Loyalty? Certainly not the behavior of mindless rage-beasts.

"What are they waiting for?" snarled Rollie. He holstered his pistol and then hurriedly tried to clear the jam in his primary weapon. After prying the crooked round free, he released the bolt and started forward. "Cover me!"

"Rollie, wait!"

But Rollie either didn't hear or chose not to listen. With his smoking rifle at the high ready, he advanced toward the passage.

In the darkness beyond, the two spectral figures stirred, clearly sensing Rollie's approach. Hood could see them moving, shifting position in preparation for a two-pronged attack, crouching like lions getting ready to pounce. Rollie might succeed in killing one of them, but the other would be on him before he could switch targets.

"Rollie! Get back here!" Hood shouted. "It's an ambush."

That got Rollie's attention. He hesitated a moment, and then took a step back, lowered his weapon, and took something from a pouch on his chest rig—a green sphere about the size of a baseball.

"Rollie, don't—"

With a deft twist Rollie popped loose the steel safety band and then yanked out the retaining pin, letting the spring-loaded spoon fly free.

"Frag out!" he shouted as he lobbed the grenade into the passage.

Hood forgot about everything else. All that mattered now was getting as far away from the blast as he could. But as he turned to head down the passage from which Vlad had come, he saw Mad Dog lying directly in his path. Barely slowing, he reached down and grabbed the shoulder strap of Mad Dog's chest rig, and then started dragging him along. Rollie appeared an instant later, grabbed the other strap. They made it into the passage and another five meters or so before the world turned upside down.

The cavern walls protected them from the spray of molten shrapnel but did little to soften the effects of the overpressure wave. If anything, the close confines seemed to channel the explosive force like the barrel of a gun. Hood was knocked flat, and went skidding forward across the lichen covered cave floor.

Then, everything went black.

He knew he had not lost consciousness. Despite the protection afforded by his clothing and pro-mask, he could feel the flash of heat as the shockwave rolled over and through him. Something heavy struck his back. His body armor blunted the impact, but the object, presumably a chunk of the ceiling, stayed where it had landed. Smaller rocks struck him, and for a few seconds, he feared the entire cavern would collapse.

But then, stillness returned.

He reached up slowly, gingerly, to see if the glasses were still on his head. They were not, and he could only surmise that they had been knocked loose during his fall. He probed the rubble around him for a few seconds but was unable to locate them, so he instead flipped the NVGs down and activated them. After a second or two, the green displays lit up, but revealed little. The air around him was opaque with smoke and dust.

He raised his head cautiously and peered into the swirling dust cloud. He was, in that moment, grateful to have the pro-mask; without it he would probably not have been able to breathe at all.

Something stirred a few paces to his left. "Rollie? Still with me, brother?"

The shape moved again and then Rollie sat up abruptly, his pistol in hand. "Did it work? Are they dead?"

"I don't know," he answered truthfully. He searched the rubble around him until he found the glasses, or rather what was left of them. Casting the pieces aside, he got to his feet and quickly checked the rest of his equipment, and then readied his weapon, just in case. Only then did he realize that someone was missing.

"Where's Mad Dog? Do you see him?"

Rollie bounded up, his pistol ready, and turned a slow circle. "He was right here a second—"

Something erupted out of the darkness just beyond him. With Rollie in the way, all Hood could see was a flurry of motion as Rollie struggled with a barely glimpsed assailant. Rollie's pistol boomed, then boomed again, the rounds sparking impotently against stone.

"Jesus!" Hood took an involuntary step back even as he braced his weapon and took aim. The targeting laser stabbed out into the darkness, zigzagging crazily in the air as Hood tried to zero in on the creature, but there was no way to shoot the monster without shooting Rollie.

Letting the rifle fall on its sling, Hood drew his .45 and rushed forward to join the melee, but before he could cross the distance, Rollie abruptly staggered backward and collapsed in Hood's path. His hands were clamped around his neck, under the jawline of his pro-mask, but could not stem the cascade of blood pulsing out of the ragged wound in his throat.

Hood only glimpsed this from the corner of his eye. His attention was wholly focused on the monster crouching just beyond. He lined up the front sight on the creature's exposed head and started to pull the trigger. As if sensing his intention, the monster raised its gore-streaked face to him and snarled.

It wasn't Wolfman.

It wasn't Sharky.

Hood staggered back. "Dale?"

Mad Dog snarled again and then, moving faster than a cat, snaked out one hand to seize Rollie's left leg. Without taking his bulging eyes off Hood, he began backing away, dragging Rollie with him.

Hood gripped the pistol tightly in both hands, willing himself steady, and lined up the shot.

Do it, he told himself. *You have to.*
Kill or be killed.
Put him down like a...
Like a mad dog.
His arm quivered. He couldn't seem to find the strength to break the trigger. After a few seconds, he abandoned the struggle, lowered the pistol.

"Dale," he said again, desperately hoping that the name might break through the fog in his friend's brain. "It's me. Jeff. Dale. Let me help."

Growling, Mad Dog kept retreating with his prize, shrinking into the shadows. Rollie's hands had fallen away from his neck, arms outflung and flapping as he was dragged along. The pulse of blood from his ruptured throat had become a constant dribble; his life already drained away. A long, wet streak trailed after his body.

"Dale!"

But Mad Dog had disappeared from view. Rollie's head and shoulders remained visible a few seconds longer, then he too was gone, swallowed up by the darkness.

Hood staggered sideways, falling against the wall of the passage, and then slid down to seated position with his back against hard stone, weeping into his mask.

He knew what he had to do. What he should have already done.

Kill Mad Dog.

Kill Dale.

If he pushed through his doubt, executed his best friend, he would have to live with that betrayal for the rest of his life. If he didn't...

He had just squandered his best chance to end it quickly, mercifully. To put Dale out of his misery. Next time, he would be the prey. If he faltered, he would die, just like Rollie and Bender had died. Torn apart. Eaten.

Dale certainly wouldn't hesitate.

"Just do it, soldier," he rasped into his mask. "Don't think. Do it. He's not Dale. Not anymore. He's a monst—"

He broke off, choked with emotion.

A monster.

If only I could see you the way you see me, he thought.

And then he realized that he could.

He set his weapons on the ground beside him. He switched off his NVGs, embracing the darkness once more, and removed his helmet, placing it with the guns. Then he removed the protective mask, savoring the feeling of cool air on his face.

He took a breath through his mouth, which helped him tolerate the rancid odor. After a minute or two of trying to breathe normally, the smell didn't seem so bad.

After a few more minutes, he could distinguish the faint glow of luminescence all around him. Soon he would be able to see just fine. Better than fine. He would be able to see the subterranean environment as well as the creature that would soon be coming for him.

When it did, he would see only the beast.

The End

CONTRIBUTOR BIOGRAPHIES

JAKE BIBLE is the author of 55+ novels, including the bestselling Roak: Galactic Bounty Hunter series of space crime novels, the bestselling Z-Burbia series set in Asheville, NC, the bestselling *Salvage Merc One*, and the MEGA series for Severed Press. He is also the author of the YA zombie novel, *Little Dead Man*, the Bram Stoker Award nominated Teen horror novel, *Intentional Haunting*, the middle grade ScareScapes series, and the Reign of Four series for Permuted Press. As well as *Stone Cold Bastards* and the Black Box, Inc novels for Bell Bridge Books. Jake hosts and produces a semi-weekly podcast, Writing In Suburbia, where he gives his take on being a full-time professional writer while also living a suburban life as a father and husband. Find Jake at jakebible.com. Join him on Twitter @jakebible and on Facebook.

KIRSTEN CROSS is a Scandi-Cockney hybrid with an aversion to liquorice and a passionate love of motorbikes. She's a laid-back horror and Sci-Fi writer who, because of a dubious internet search history that includes ballistic profiling of semi-automatic weapons and whether shooting pheasants with a longbow is still 'technically' illegal in the UK, lives in perpetual fear of arrest. Occasionally, to try and avoid being classified as 'shady as all heck' by British Intelligence, she shouts "I'M JUST WRITING STORIES!" at the computer. When not blowing things up, documenting alien invasions or otherwise engaging in literary shenanigans, she writes web content for a living. She now lives in splendid isolation in glorious Devon with a biker husband and a lot of wildlife, some of which makes really weird noises at three in the morning. When not writing, she surfs, and is also an MIA Hall of Famer for her contribution to the advancement of women's martial arts.

SEAN ELLIS is a survival writer and action-adventure novelist. He has authored and co-authored more than two dozen action-adventure novels, including the Nick Kismet adventures, the Jack Sigler/Chess Team series with Jeremy Robinson, and the Jade Ihara adventures with David Wood. He served with the Army National Guard in Afghanistan, and has a Bachelor of Science degree in Natural Resources Policy from Oregon State University. Sean is also a member of the International Thriller Writers organization. He currently resides in Arizona, where he divides his time between writing, adventure sports, and trying to figure out how to save the world.

JONATHAN MABERRY is a New York Times bestselling author, 5-time Bram Stoker Award-winner, and comic book writer. His vampire apocalypse book series, V-WARS, is in production as a Netflix original series, starring Ian Somerhalder (LOST, VAMPIRE DIARIES) and will debut in early 2019. He writes in multiple genres including suspense, thriller, horror, science fiction, fantasy, and action; and he writes for adults, teens and middle grade. His works include the Joe Ledger thrillers, the Rot & Ruin series, the Dead of Night series, *Glimpse*, *The Wolfman*, *X-Files Origins: Devil's Advocate*, *Mars One*, and many others. Several of his works are in development for film and TV. He is the editor of high-profile anthologies including *The X-Files*, *Aliens: Bug Hunt*, *Out of Tune*, *New Scary Stories to Tell in the Dark*, *Baker Street Irregulars*, *Nights of the Living Dead*, and others. His comics include *Black Panther: Doom War*, *The Punisher: Naked Kills* and *Bad Blood*. He lives in Del Mar, California. Find him online at www.jonathanmaberry.com

PAUL MANNERING is an award-winning writer living in Wellington, New Zealand, where he lives with his wife Damaris and their two cats. Author of: The Tankbread/Deadland series (published by Permuted Press), *Engines of Empathy* and *Pisces of Fate* (published by IFWG), *Hell's Teeth*, *EAT*, *The Trench*, and *Hard Corps* (published by Severed Press), numerous short stories and podcast audio dramas (produced at BrokenSea Audio).

RENA MASON is the Bram Stoker Award® winning author of *The Evolutionist* and *East End Girls*, as well as a 2014 Stage 32 / The Blood List Presents: The Search for New Blood Screenwriting Contest Finalist. A longtime fan of horror, sci-fi, science, history, historical fiction, mysteries, and thrillers, she began writing to mash up those genres in stories revolving around everyday life. She is a member of the Horror Writers Association, Mystery Writers of America, International Thriller Writers, and The International Screenwriters' Association. For more information about this author, check out her website: www.RenaMason.Ink.

MICHAEL MCBRIDE was born in Colorado and still resides in the shadow of the Rocky Mountains. He hates the snow but loves the Avalanche. He works with medical radiation, yet somehow managed to produce five children, none of whom, miraculously, have tails, third eyes, or other random mutations. He writes fiction that runs the gamut from thriller (*Burial Ground*, *Vector Borne*) to horror/science fiction (*Subhuman*, *Forsaken*)...and loves every minute of it. He's a national bestseller and two-time winner of the DarkFuse Readers' Choice Award. You can visit him at author.michaelmcbride.net.

JESSICA MCHUGH is a novelist and internationally produced playwright running amok in the fields of horror, sci-fi, young adult, and wherever else her peculiar mind leads. She's had twenty-three books published in ten years, including her bizarro romp, *The Green Kangaroos*, her Post Mortem Press bestseller, *Rabbits in the Garden*, and her YA series, *The Darla Decker Diaries*. More information on her published and forthcoming fiction can be found at JessicaMcHughBooks.com.

J.H. MONCRIEFF'S work has been described by reviewers as early Gillian Flynn with a little Ray Bradbury and Stephen King thrown in for good measure. She won Harlequin's search for "the next Gillian Flynn" in 2016. *Monsters in Our Wake*, her deep-sea thriller with Severed Press, hit the Amazon Horror bestsellers list, beating King's re-released *It* to the top spot. When not writing, she loves exploring the world's most haunted places, advocating for animal rights, and summoning her inner ninja in muay thai class.

JAMES A. MOORE is the bestselling and award-winning author of over forty novels, thrillers, dark fantasy and horror alike, including the critically acclaimed *Fireworks*, *Under The Overtree*, *Blood Red*, the Serenity Falls trilogy (featuring his recurring anti-hero, Jonathan Crowley) and his most recent novels, The Tides of War series (*The Last Sacrifice, Fallen Gods* and the forthcoming *Gate of the Dead*) and *Avengers: Infinity*. In addition to writing multiple short stories, he has also edited, with Christopher Golden and Tim Lebbon, the *British Invasion* anthology for Cemetery Dance Publications.
The author cut his teeth in the industry writing for Marvel Comics and authoring over twenty role-playing supplements for White Wolf Games, including *Berlin by Night*, *Land of 1,000,000 Dreams* and *The Get of Fenris* tribe book for *Vampire: The Masquerade and Werewolf: The Apocalypse*, among others. He also penned the White Wolf novels *Vampire: House of Secrets* and *Werewolf: Hellstorm*.
Moore's first short story collection, *Slices*, sold out before ever seeing print. His most recent novels include *Predator: Hunters and Hunted* and the forthcoming *Gates of the Dead* (Book Three in the Tides of War series) Along with Christopher Golden and Jonathan Maberry he is co-host of the Three Guys With Beards podcast. More information about the author can be found at his website:

S.D. PERRY has worked in shared universes for most of her career, including Aliens, Star Trek, Resident Evil, and Tomb Raider. She lives with her family in Portland, Oregon, and writes original horror in her spare time.

AARON STERNS is the co-writer of *Wolf Creek 2* (Best Screenplay, Madrid International Fantastic Film Festival), as well as author of the Australian Shadows Award-winning prequel novel *Wolf Creek: Origin*. Sterns is the author of various Aurealis Award-nominated and *Year's Best Fantasy & Horror* recommended short stories, including 'The Third Rail' (which appeared in the seminal, World Fantasy Award-winning *Dreaming Down-Under*) and the dark werewolf-bouncer world of 'Watchmen' (the basis for his upcoming visceral and ultraviolent novel *Blood*). He is a former lecture in Gothic & Subversive Fiction, editor of the *Journal of the Australian Horror Writers*, and Ph.D. student in postmodern horror. He also served as a script-editor on Greg McLean's *Rogue* and appeared in a little cameo as Bazza's Mate in *Wolf Creek*. Sterns is currently working on another novel as well as numerous screenplays, including a film version of *Blood*, and dark thriller *Daughter of the Vines* – described as *The Wicker Man* in the Adelaide Hills. He lives in Melbourne, Australia. Official website: www.aaronsterns.com
www.facebook.com/aaronsternsauthortwitter: @AaronSterns

MORE FANTASTIC FICTION FROM GRYPHONWOOD/ADRENALINE PRESS

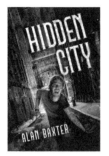

Hidden City by Alan Baxter

When the city suffers, everyone suffers.

Steven Hines listened to the city and the city spoke. Cleveport told him she was sick. With his unnatural connection to her, that meant Hines was sick too. But when his friend, Detective Abby Jones, comes to him for help investigating a series of deaths with no discernible cause, Hines can't say no. Then strange fungal growths begin to appear in the streets, affecting anyone who gets too close, turning them into violent lunatics. As the mayhem escalates and officials start to seal Cleveport off from the rest of the world, Hines knows the trouble has only just begun.

The Amulet by William Meikle

It was supposed to be an easy case. Fast money, and a way to kill some time-something Derek Adams, a down-on-his-luck Glasgow private investigator, has way too much of. Recover a stolen family heirloom, and try to keep the relationship with his very beautiful-and very married-client, strictly professional. Easy. But the Johnson Amulet is no mere trinket...and Derek isn't the only person trying to find the priceless relic. Before long he's up to his armpits in bodies, femme fatales... and tentacles. The stars have aligned... An ancient evil has awakened.To save the day, Derek must take some dark pathways, and not everyone is going to make it back out into the light.

Still Water by Justin R. Macumber

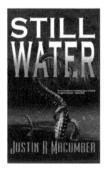

Coal is the hard, black heart of the mountain town of Stillwater, West Virginia, but far beneath it lies something much darker, an evil beyond time, waiting to rise and bathe the world in blood and fire once more. When unwitting miners dig into its tomb, only Kyle - Stillwater's prodigal son - and paranormal investigator Maya stand between humanity and Hell. Time is short and evil runs deep in... STILL WATER

Primordial by David Wood and Alan Baxter

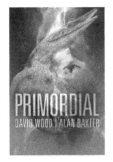

Sometimes, the legends are true.

When eccentric billionaire, Ellis Holloway, hires renegade marine biologist, Sam Aston, to investigate the legend of a monster in a remote Finnish lake, Aston envisions an easy paycheck and a chance to clear his gambling debts. But he gets much more. There is something terrible living beneath the dark waters of Lake Kaarme and it is hungry. As the death toll mounts, Aston faces superstitious locals, a power-hungry police chief, and a benefactor's descent into madness as he races to find the legendary beast of the lake.

Thunder Wells by Terry W. Ervin II

No one ever said surviving an alien invasion would be easy.

Jack Fairbanks made it through the initial wave of attacks, but now the Mawks have seeded the Earth with dozers and crawlers, tracking beasts that crave human flesh and are bent on hunting the remnants of humankind to extinction.

Pennies for the Ferryman by Jim Bernheimer

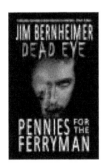

My name is Mike Ross. I'm a Ferryman. I help people with ghost problems, or ghosts with people problems. Funny thing, no one ever helps me with my problems. Civil War ghosts bent on killing me, Skinwalkers who just want my body, and a vindictive spirit linked both to my bloodline and my destiny... It turns out the dead still hold a good deal of influence over the world, and they don't want to give it up. I'm in way over my head.

The Shroud of Heaven by Sean Ellis

On the bloody battlefields of Iraq, one man's quest to find God will unleash Hell. For more than a decade, Nick Kismet has traveled the world protecting priceless relics and cultural heritage sites from looters, while searching for answers to the mystery that has haunted him since the first Gulf War—a mystery that has defined his life. Now, a new war has brought him back to the bloody battlefield where his search began.

CPSIA information can be obtained
at www.ICGtesting.com
Printed in the USA
LVHW040016010319
609156LV00003B/197